U-Boat Scourge

*The Naval Odyssey of
Professor James Brand*

J. Eugene Porter

U-Boat Scourge:
The Naval Odyssey of Professor James Brand

© J. Eugene Porter, 2018

All rights reserved. No part of this publication may be reproduced, distributed, or transmitted in any form or by any means, including photocopying, recording, or other electronic or mechanical methods, without the prior written permission of the author, except in the case of brief quotations embodied in critical reviews and certain other noncommercial uses permitted by copyright law.
For permission requests, email the author at:

porterjeugene@gmail.com

First Edition

This is a work of fiction. All the characters, names, incidents, organizations, and dialogue in this novel are either the products of the author's imagination or are used fictionally.

ISBN: 978-1719593786

Design: Vivian Freeman Chaffin
Yellow Rose Typesetting

Cover Image: Everett Collection / *Shutterstock*

Printed in the United States of America

Dedicated to

Kenneth E. Porter
USMC 1938-1941

*and the Marine Detachment
aboard the USS Chicago CA-29*

Author's Note

This book is a work of fiction but is based on the real events of World War II. It is a story of the underappreciated side of the war which involved science, engineering and the experimentation of new ways to wage war. It looks at this subject from the viewpoint of a young scientist and his team who fight with ideas as well as with weapons. It also deals with the challenges that new ideas encounter when confronted with years of complacency, inefficiency and tradition. The Second World War made the careers of many men, but it also ended the careers of others, not just through the carnage of battle but by the harsh realization that some men were not capable of dealing with new types of warfare.

This novel begins with the events leading up to December 7, 1941, and ends in March 1942 when America was facing its darkest days of defeat in the Philippines and the challenge of stopping the Japanese advance towards Australia. It focuses attention on the U-boat war waged with great ferocity along the Atlantic coast of the United States. Caught totally unprepared by the evolutionary nature of the German submarine attacks, the United States Navy stumbled to halt the destruction of the Allied merchant fleet just miles off its coastline. Starting in early January 1942, the United States and its Allies lost hundreds of ships, some of them within sight of land and only managed to sink three U-boats. This tragic event has been chronicled in many great non-fiction works in the past twenty years, and most of them point to the inability of United States commanders to identify and then deal with the threat posed by this German scourge. It would take most of 1942 to push the German submariners away from their "second happy time" along the American East and Gulf Coasts. These efforts were slow to become a reality as documented by many sources including the seminal work by Rear Adm. Samuel Eliot Morison in his *History of the Naval Operations of World War Two*, as well as the many later studies conducted on both sides of the Atlantic.

This story is just that, a story. It is set in a time of terrible events, which changed the world and changed the people who witnessed it. The fictional characters are not designed to emulate real persons from this era, but as you will see, they interact with the real leaders in government, military, science and production to achieve a better understanding of the issues and problems faced in those dark days. The conversations and actions taken by the real persons are based upon various writings by the participants themselves and by how history now views many of these individuals. Time has changed the image of some of these people; some for better and some for worse, but it does not change how they managed the war, led their people and in some cases, how the leaders of two great nations provided leadership to the world.

The book is divided by date, with each section beginning with the daily information about what was happening in the war. My hope is this device will provide additional context for the events unfolding in the book and will help the reader better understand the scope and immensity of the war effort. This daily information comes from two sources:

- *The United States Naval Chronology, World War II*, published on March 17, 1955, by the Naval History Division of the Office of the Chief of Naval Operations.

- *Chronology: 1941-1945*, published on February 21, 1958, by Chronology Section of the Historical Division of the Office of the Chief of Military History, United States Army.

Prologue

A letter dated August 2, 1939, signed by Albert Einstein was given to Alexander Sachs who arranged a meeting with the addressee on October 11. Things in the world were changing rapidly. Much of the world was now at war with Germany after they had invaded Poland on September 1. Sachs knew these tectonic shifts in world affairs would cause a great upheaval and the contents of the letter needed to be seen by clear-eyed realists without other distractions. The meeting Sachs had was with President Franklin Delano Roosevelt, and the letter discussed something called an atomic bomb.

In part the letter stated,

> *In the course of the last four months it has been made probable—through the work of Joliot in France as well as Fermi and Szilárd in America—that it may become possible to set up a nuclear chain reaction in a large mass of uranium, by which vast amounts of power and large quantities of new radium-like elements would be generated. Now it appears almost certain that this could be achieved in the immediate future.*
>
> *This new phenomenon would also lead to the construction of bombs, and it is conceivable—though much less certain—that extremely powerful bombs of a new type may thus be constructed.*

J. EUGENE PORTER

> *A single bomb of this type, carried by boat and exploded in a port, might very well destroy the whole port together with some of the surrounding territory. However, such bombs might very well prove to be too heavy for transportation by air.*

It also specifically warned about Germany:

> *I understand that Germany has actually stopped the sale of uranium from the Czechoslovakian mines which she has taken over. That she should have taken such early action might perhaps be understood on the ground that the son of the German Under-Secretary of State, von Weizsäcker, is attached to the Kaiser-Wilhelm-Institute in Berlin where some of the American work on uranium is now being repeated.*

President Roosevelt's reaction was positive and gave the scientists the approval to expand their research. He summed up the conversation, "Alex, what you are after is to see that the Nazis don't blow us up."

This famous letter and FDR's reply are enshrined in history as the beginning of the atomic age and development of the atomic bomb as created through the Manhattan project.

Einstein sent other letters to FDR on the project and often communicated outside of normal channels with him. One such informal letter was sent to the president on January 6, 1942, and involved an unusual request for presidential intervention with a young naval recruit.

The letter read in part,

> *I realize that you are being asked to make many decisions on matters that are too terrible to ponder and which affect the lives of millions. This request involves only one person, a young man who in the estimation of many of America's top scientists is in jeopardy of being lost to the bureaucracies of the government. He is a child prodigy, and I became aware of him some four years ago, along with a few other graduate students in physics, mathematics, chemistry and engineering. What made him unique was that he was a graduate student in these disciplines and he was a mere fourteen years old. I met him again, last year*

when my old friend and colleague Dr. Enrico Fermi had him accompany a large group of post-doctoral students to meet our staff at Princeton. I was amazed at his general brilliance, the speed of thought and the ability to think in all disciplines at the same time.

I have been informed by Dr. Fermi that this young man who had a research fellowship at Columbia University, disappeared from his post on December 10. Dr. Fermi has recently found out that he has joined the U.S. Navy and is currently undergoing basic training. Mr. President, this young man is too valuable to the nation, to science and to the future, to have him become a deck hand on a ship or perhaps even a cook. I am sure that he is hiding his name and his intelligence to fit in with his comrades. It is good that the young want to serve their country, but I believe along with many of the top scientists in the nation, that the war will be won not only by bravery but by intellect, science, mathematics, physics and engineering prowess. If you could consider this matter and find a way to have him serve his country in uniform and by using his intellectual gifts, then our future will be much brighter.

His name was James Edward Brand, and he was originally from Flagstaff, Arizona.

PART 1

1

8 December 1941
Columbia University
New York City

- United States declares war on Japan.
- Japanese aircraft in widely scattered operations bomb Guam, Wake, Hong Kong, Singapore, and the Philippine Islands.
- Extensive damage is inflicted on United States Army aircraft at Clark Field, Luzon, Philippine Islands.
- Japan interns United States Marines and nationals at Shanghai and Tientsin, China.

The distinguished looking man gazed out the window at the campus below him. Students walked to class or to meetings, and all seemed to be normal. But things had changed for the university, the students and the entire country. The date is December 8, 1941, and in about four hours, President Franklin D. Roosevelt would go to Capitol Hill and ask for a declaration of war against the Empire of Japan. He held the thought of the president writing out his speech and preparing the country for the death and destruction that would surely come. Finally, he looked back into the conference room and viewed the four men sitting at the table looking at him. Three of them were middle-aged or older, but one was very young, and he knew this young man was being tormented by the thought of going to war.

Dr. Enrico Fermi left Italy in 1938 with his Jewish wife to receive his Nobel Prize in Physics for his work on a statistical formulation. His theory described the distribution of particles in systems of many identical particles that obeyed what was known as the exclusion principle. It was related to the Bose-Einstein statistic model and is now known as Fermi-Dirac statistics that help describe fermions and bosons. The young scientist sitting in front of him was one of the very few people in the world that could grasp the consequences of this work and use it to build newer and more expansive mathematical models of the concept. Dr. Fermi finally stepped away from the window and began to speak.

"Gentlemen, each of you knows the significance of our work at Columbia and the importance of your personal contributions to the projects on which you have been working. It appears that with a war being waged throughout the world, the scientific community will be called upon to aid in the war effort. I have placed a series of calls to my colleagues around the country, and with the continued support of Dr. Bush as the Head of the Office of Scientific Research and Development, I am confident all our projects will continue to be funded and provided with additional support. I would ask that you prepare a short synopsis of your activities as well as people who are critical to these efforts so that I may be able to guarantee their contribution to your project. Please get these to me within the next few days. As you can imagine, there is chaos in all circles of government which will take some time to sort out, so please, let us be the first to have our plans ready for submission."

Dr. Fermi then went to his desk, sat down in the rigid wooden-back chair he favored and began reading a file. The assembled scientists all knew the meeting was over and it was time to leave. As they started toward the door, Fermi spoke once more.

U-BOAT SCOURGE

"James, please stay for a moment. I want to ask you something."

James Brand, Ph.D., turned and walked back to the desk of his mentor and intellectual focus for the past two years. James had turned eighteen in late November and had been working with Dr. Fermi and his team since late 1939 as he pursued his doctorate degree. He had received his Master's in Mathematics at the California Institute of Technology at the ripe old age of fifteen and had jumped at the chance to work with Fermi and his team on applications of Fermi's theories. Fermi had taken an immediate shine to the young genius. James reminded the older man of himself as a teenage prodigy. He knew full well the genius factor often burned brightest in the youngest years, then slowly faded. Einstein had done his greatest work in his early twenties. Fermi had most of his breakthrough ideas when he was under thirty. The problem with being a young genius is that the mind is in overdrive, but the emotions are still those of a teenager. Fermi feared James would not know how to handle the changes going on in himself and the world around him.

"James, I want to take a few minutes to discuss your future role and how you will cope with all of the stress that will be placed upon you."

James felt very uncomfortable with this conversation. He had successfully suppressed most of his emotions for years, looking upon the childish urges of others as just that, childish behavior in which he did not need to engage. "Professor, I am not sure what you are saying?"

Fermi leaned forward in his chair and peered into the eyes of his young protégé before softly saying, "James, you are very young and very bright. The war is now starting for America, and you may be asking yourself, if not now, but soon, what should I be doing to help my country? You are a physically strong and intellectually gifted young man and your country will need you." Fermi pulled back into his chair and decided to take another approach to the subject.

"James, what I am saying is how do you feel about what happened at the naval base in Hawaii?"

James thought for a moment in silence, which Fermi understood, although the long pause usually unnerved most everyone else. James preferred a scientific approach to all his activities and conversation was just one more activity. He was always slow to respond to questions and often overly direct in responses or when asking questions. Political niceties were not necessary in James' world. Finally, after what seemed to be a minute or more, James looked directly at the Nobel Prize winner saying, "Professor, what happened yesterday was a great tragedy for this country. You have told me and others about the terrible things going on in your homeland and in Germany, but we have never discussed Japan. I guess we are going to have to fight the Japanese, then defeat the Germans and Italians. I fear we will be at war with all of them in a few days. The suffering will be great. Is that what you wanted to hear?"

Fermi almost smiled because the answer he received is what he expected from the Doctor of Physics, but it did not come from the red-blooded young man who must be conflicted as to what to do next.

"James, that was a well thought out answer but what I wanted to know, is what do you want to do about the war? I need you to stay here with me and help in our research. There will be other projects that need your special talents as well. I have talked to Connaught at Harvard as well as the people at Bell Labs and they want to borrow you as soon as possible. So, again, what do you want to do to help your country?"

James again looked away from Professor Fermi and considered a different part of his life, that of being a young man. He always wanted to be just one of the guys, but since his earliest days, he had spent most of his time with much older people instructing him or leading him into new aspects of mathematics, science, and engineering. His father, who worked at the Lowell Observatory in his hometown of Flagstaff, Arizona, had been on the team that discovered Pluto.

James had worked side by side with not only his father but with the lead astronomer, Clyde Turnball. They had talked mostly about orbital mechanics and the movement of stars. Normal boyhood things went by the wayside after his father fell to his death in January 1933 while making repairs to the roof of the family home. He had to work more to help support his mother who was a teacher at the Arizona State Teachers College. So, James did not fully comprehend what being a normal young man really meant. He felt anger at what happened at Pearl Harbor, but was more intellectually involved in the technical aspects of what had happened, such as what ordinance was used, where the planes came from and the countermeasure in place by the fleet. Instead of rage, he felt more curiosity. Instead of running to the colors, he wanted to know more about the weapons used.

James finally looked at Fermi and spoke. "Professor, I'm not too sure how I should be thinking about this incident. I know it means a full-scale war and that means many men will join the army and navy and fight somewhere distant from our shores. As to what it means to me, I would think that I should join the military and offer my skills to the country."

Fermi had anticipated this line of reasoning from James and he was swift in his rebuttal.

"James, you can best serve your country by maintaining your position here at Columbia. There are millions of young men out there who are trying to join up to serve, but there are only a few people who possess your capabilities. I'll be speaking to Dr. Bush to make sure you're safe from any conscription, and you'll find many things to work on which will contribute far more than becoming just another soldier or sailor."

James thought for a moment, then looking straight at the Professor, agreed to his line of reasoning. "Professor, you make perfect sense, and if you don't mind, I'll go back to my office and finish the tables I've been working on which tie to your models.'

"Good decision, James. Keep me informed on your progress. I look forward to our next conversation."

James returned to his small room, which did not overlook the walkways but looked directly next to another reddish-brown brick building. He pulled out his binder with notes, then his favorite slide rule, and began entering new calculations which would prove more of Fermi's work. Only later in the day, did the young man inside him begin to stir and throw gasoline on the small embers of doubt that had followed him for the last twenty-four hours.

James spent a sleepless night on the eighth worrying about his life at the University. He would be safe, while others would be in harm's way. He was not a very outgoing person, but he longed to have comrades like he had seen in some of the movies about the British and their ongoing life-and-death struggle with the Nazis. He wondered if he was man enough to even put on a uniform, and if he did, could he fight? He had used his father's old World War I Springfield rifle to shoot deer, but that was all about eating, not about killing. Would killing a man be different? He wondered about his life on the home front doing research and going to meetings with men twice his age, while everyone who looked at him would think him a coward.

Within two more days, the young man's emotions eclipsed the musings of the scientist, pushing them into a corner of his mind, where they only meekly protested. James now developed a plan to become a regular young man who answered his country's call.

2

11 December 1941
New York City

- Germany and Italy declare war on the United States.
- United States declares war on Germany and Italy.
- Marines on Wake Island repulse Japanese landing attempt and sink two enemy destroyers.
- Japanese naval vessels sunk at Wake Island:
  - Destroyer **Hayate** by marine shore batteries.
  - Destroyer **Kisaragi** by marine aircraft.

On December 7 the world changed, and James was like most Americans, shaken by the unexpected attack on Pearl Harbor. He had seen the world changing, and his close association with Dr. Fermi had already colored his world view with the horrors of Hitler and Mussolini and knew full well that America would be pulled into the war. His greatest concern on the day after the attack on Pearl Harbor was that he would miss out on the war and be stuck in some research institution for the entirety of the action. As a young boy, he had heard stories of his father's adventures on a destroyer in the First World War, and he wanted to have similar experiences. But he knew if he tried to enlist with his credentials of being the youngest professor of physics in the country, he would be immediately sent to some research lab and left there for the duration. So, he devised a plan to become a normal eighteen year old who wanted to serve his country.

His first decision was to wait until December 11 to sign up. This gave him time to create a credible story about his life, one that would not expose his identity as a scientist. He knew if he told the people at the enlistment center that he was a college graduate, he would not be taken seriously unless he could prove it, which of course he could. By doing this, though, he would be stopped from entering the navy as a regular recruit. So, he devised a plan to join the navy as an enlisted man, so he could serve on a fighting ship. He would have to be very careful in taking his tests and interviews and not show off his brilliance.

James decided to build a new story for himself. He would have to use his real social security number and date of birth, but he could change his background by leaving out a lot of the details of his education. The biggest roadblock in his view was his quiet and introspective nature which did not fit the profile of a normal eighteen year old. He would have to grapple with himself to appear more aggressive in both speech and attitude which was a difficult internal struggle. He knew the key to securing an immediate appointment was his radio license which he had earned in 1935. The navy needed radio operators, and the skill was deemed critical to the war effort.

He walked over to the Broadway enlistment center which had been besieged for the first few days with crowds of men trying to enlist. He figured if he waited a few days the crowds would ease. There were still some twenty men ahead of him, but he was finally able to get in front of the petty officer doing the initial screening.

"Yes, you want to enlist," the petty officer exclaimed in a tired voice.

"Yes sir, I want to sign up for duty on a destroyer, sir," James said in a strong and resolute voice.

The petty officer looked up at him and asked how old he was even though he could see the young man was tall and strongly built.

"Sir, I turned eighteen last month, and I have graduated from high school."

"What is your name," the petty officer asked looking at the young man in front of him.

"James Brand, sir, and I was born in Arizona, sir."

"Mr. Brand, you do not call me sir, I am a petty officer. You do not salute me or call me sir, is that straight with you?"

"Yes sir, I mean Petty Officer or should I call you something else." James was a bit flustered now and stumbled over his words.

"You can call me Chief. Do you have any special skills or education that would make the navy want you on one of its ships?"

"Yes sir, I mean, Chief. I have a radio license and can send and receive Morse at sixty-five words per minute." James beamed as he took out a piece of formal looking paper with the license information.

The chief examined the paper and verified it was an official FCC document. He then smiled and looked up at the young man.

"Now, Mr. Brand, you came to the right place. The navy needs good radio operators, and if you are as quick as you say, we can get you processed today. Is that what you want?" The chief looked at the young man with a new sense of interest and wondered what other specialties he had. The head of recruiting in Washington sent a telegram to all recruiting locations to be on the lookout for anyone with radio skills or other technical training. These men were to be flagged and their details sent to navy headquarters for immediate selection and qualification. The navy knew it took months to train a mediocre radio/telegraphist and any previous experience was given top priority.

The chief had James sign some papers and then had a seaman first class take him upstairs to interview with the lieutenant charged with finding the especially talented people for which the navy was looking. The seaman had James sit outside an office with two other young men, both about four to five years older than James, who were talking about their experiences in ship building at the Brooklyn Navy Yard. Both, it seemed, had experience in large steam turbine engines that were also very important to the navy. James sat and listened but did not offer anything of importance to the conversation. He had learned from his mother and his mentor at Cal Tech, Iggy, to listen more and talk less, which allowed him to better analyze situations. After a wait of about twenty minutes, he was ushered into the office of Lieutenant Holmes, a reservist who was at least forty-five years old and had been recalled to duty for the duration. He had several rows of ribbons which showed he had seen service during WWI. From the looks of it, he was a technical man.

Lieutenant Holmes looked up from his desk and motioned for James to take a seat. The lieutenant asked for his license, the type of radio he had, how he maintained it, and wondered about his speed in taking and sending messages. Finally, he asked the question that James knew was coming.

"So, Mr. Brand, with your experiences and technical knowledge, why do you want to join up now? You could easily sit out the war in some radio company or get a government job that wouldn't put you in harm's way. Why do you want to join the navy?"

James was ready with his response knowing it had to sound spontaneous and somewhat like a regular eighteen year old would say.

"Sir, I don't like the way the Japs attacked our country, and I know that my radio knowledge would help the navy. I want to see action, and if my radio background helps me get on a fighting ship faster, then I am ready to ship out today."

The lieutenant smiled and said he would expedite the young man's enlistment, schedule for the regular intelligence and physical exams, and get him a quick test on his radio proficiency if possible. If this went as planned and James was not telling big stories about his background, he could guarantee that James would be headed to basic training within a week. James beamed at the news and asked, "When do we get started?"

Lieutenant Holmes barked an order to the seaman sitting at a desk nearby and told him to take James down to get a physical. "Put him first in line and stay with him. If there are no problems, bring him back here and then we can get him tested."

James and the young seaman walked out of the room and into a new life, one that was quite different from anything the young Mr. Brand had ever known.

3

12 January 1942
Washington, D.C.

- Authorized enlisted strength of the navy is increased to 500,000.
- Bataan, Luzon, Philippines--Japanese exert strong pressure against II Corps, particularly on the western end of the line, while taking positions for concerted assault. 51st Division (Philippine Army) is hard hit and gives ground, some of which is regained after reserves are committed.

Adm. Ernest J. King had been appointed commander in chief of the U.S. Fleet (COMINCH) on December 20. The president had charged him with getting the navy going again after the debacle at Pearl Harbor and the subsequent poor showing by fleet elements of the Asiatic Fleet and the growing menace posed by Hitler's submarines in the Atlantic. The U-boats of the German Kriegsmarine had started their Operation Drumbeat along the Eastern Seaboard, and ship losses were growing with little in the way of solutions. Adding to his woes was the lack of ships of all classes, the lack of trained crews and what he sensed as a lack of leadership at all levels of the service.

President Roosevelt had known King for many years, and this connection would be invaluable to King and the navy throughout the war years. FDR had chosen King for the top leadership position, and within another month he would combine Admiral Stark's job as Chief of Naval Operations with that of the commander in chief of the U.S. Fleet. King had asked that these jobs be combined so all decisions would be in the hands of one man, and knowing Stark was now stained with the Pearl Harbor fiasco, things were moving the way King wanted.

He had inherited some of Stark's staff but believed in putting his own people in key positions. Only a few senior officers were with him through the war years, and one of them was Rear Adm. Russel Willson whom he chose as his chief of staff and as his deputy chief of staff he picked Rear Adm. R. S. Edwards. The other person who would have a huge impact on the navy was Vice Chief of Naval Operations, Vice Admiral Fredrick J. Horne, who would be the face of the navy before Congress and who would deal with the huge challenge of logistics and procurement that were not in the temperament of Admiral King.

Added to this group of high-powered people was the head of the War Plans Division OP-12, Rear Adm. Kelly Turner, who would make his mark later in the war as the leader of amphibious operations in the Pacific. Kelly had the unenviable task of developing the plans tied to the overarching strategy being established by the president, the British military, and of course his boss, Admiral King. He would establish the basic formula for the war in the Pacific as well as the logistic life blood for the war in Europe.

King had been at the White House meeting with President Roosevelt and Chief of Staff of the Army Gen. George Marshall. The meeting was an update for the president on the war situation, especially the situation in the Philippines and the planning for movement of troops and material for the expected European front. The president was open to most discussions and liked hearing the views of his two top leaders, but when he decided it was final, both military chiefs accepted this as part of the constitutional process of civilian leadership. Right after the meeting was over and the two military leaders were leaving, FDR asked for a minute of King's time to discuss one more subject. This was common practice, and Marshall was not concerned about anything going on without him. Often, it was the general that was called back for another round of questions, so this was normal for the way FDR operated.

"Admiral, I want you to look at this letter and see what you can do about it," FDR said to King as he took the letter and quickly read it. He knew full well the power that the name Einstein had in the government, particularly with the president and his scientific council headed by Dr. Vannevar Bush. He realized some of the new gadgets and technologies they were working on would help win the war and especially help the navy. King returned the letter asking, "Sir, I can find out if we have this young man and pull him out of training if that is what you want."

FDR, smiled as he picked up his cigarette, "Ernest, I think that would be a good idea, but I also believe this young prodigy would be an asset to the navy, rather than locked up in some college lab doing things for Bush and his colleagues. Perhaps, you could loan him out from time to time, but it may be a good idea to have your own resident wizard under your command. This young man did the patriotic thing, and he should be rewarded for it, but let's keep him in the navy."

"Sir," King stated, "I can find him and have him report for duty on my staff in the research division. If he is a recruit as this letter states, we can make him a reserve officer immediately based upon his completion of college and graduate school. I will let you know when we have him and keep you posted on what we do with him."

"That will be fine, Admiral, and keep me apprised of how he works out so I can tell Professor Einstein that we have saved this young man from the clutches of galley duty." FDR always capped his comments with what he thought was a humorous comment and King knowing his predilection for humor, smiled and asked if there was anything else. "Yes, here is the FBI file on the young genius which makes for very interesting reading. He has been cleared for top secret research, and this may help you in your dealings with him."

The president handed off the file and with a wave of the hand and a shake of the head, King knew he had been dismissed. He stood at attention and said, "Thank you, Mr. President. I will report back when I have some information." King turned and exited the office as the president looked at the pile of correspondence burying his desk.

Admiral King left the White House in his staff car accompanied by two aides and a marine driver. As the car pulled out of the driveway, he pulled out the FBI file and began to read.

Confidential Report—James Edward Brand, Ph.D.
Date of Birth: November 12, 1923, Flagstaff, Arizona
Marital Status: Single

Summary of Findings: The subject of this report is a citizen of the United States in good standing and with a strong sense of loyalty, duty, and patriotism. He is very young to be so highly educated, but appears to be much more mature than most young people. His early family life was astonishing based on his access to the top scientific minds in astronomy and at a very young age participated in the discovery of the planet Pluto. His parents were both college graduates, father deceased, and he excelled early on in all academic endeavors. All the individuals interviewed were unanimous in their praise for his moral character, scientific prowess, and ability to process large and complex information.

Education:
  Bachelor of Science, Arizona State Teachers College, 1936
  Masters of Science in Mathematics, California Institute of Technology, 1938
  Doctorate in Applied Physics, Columbia University, 1941

Language Skills: Proficient in German, French, Italian, Spanish and Japanese

Conclusions: Mr. Brand is well qualified for all areas of scientific research and has no known vices and is therefore recommended for top security clearances for government projects.

U-BOAT SCOURGE

King stopped reading after the summary and scanned the next few pages with the names of interviewees, including several top scientists, the presidents of MIT and Harvard, as well as Dr. Fermi. A full page was dedicated to Brand's publications and various patents in the areas of electrical research, communications, and aeronautical engineering. King smiled as he closed the file and thought about the president helping the navy get a top man like James Brand. But first, he had to find him and then put him to work.

When King got back to the Navy Yard, he called his chief of staff, Rear Adm. Russel Willson, and reviewed the previous meeting. He gave Willson a list of various action items needed for the report requested by the president and General Marshall. He was about to dismiss Willson when he recalled information in the letter and a note written on his action pad which he carried to all meetings with the commander in chief.

"Russel, the president has requested that we find a young sailor, who in his exuberance to fight the Japs, joined up last month. We need to pull him from training and bring him back to Washington."

Admiral Willson, looked perplexed and asked his boss, "So somebody's kid decided the navy was too rough and wants a free ticket out of the service? This kid must have a close connection with the president to have that much pull."

King smiled at his top aide. "Nothing could be further from the truth. Seems the president is looking after the navy for once. This kid is a prodigy of some kind, and Einstein personally contacted the president about him. Our young recruit wants to fight and not spend the war in some research facility doing God only knows what. Our young recruit is only eighteen and has three college degrees including a doctorate degree in physics from Columbia. The man in the White House wants us to get him here and use him as we see necessary. Now, I like the idea of a young man so eager to fight, but knowing full well that once we understood his real background, he would be locked up in some government research facility. He must have lied about his background and credentials so we should talk to JAG about it, but I don't see a problem. Go find out where he is, then get someone to get him out of whatever he is doing, get him commissioned, and back here."

Admiral Willson took the piece of paper with the name on it and walked out of the office. He knew King very well and did not need further direction or small talk. King had a reputation for fast decisions and little time for idle chatter. He expected his people to do the same.

Willson went back to his desk and asked his aide, Lieutenant Morse, to get with the Bureau of Personnel, BUPERS, locate this sailor and report back to him immediately. The aide, knowing his boss had just come from the chief's office knew not to ask questions. Morse went to his desk outside the office of the chief of staff and looked up the phone number for BUPERS, Vice Admiral Randal Jacobs. He wanted to talk to Jacob's aide, an old friend of his from Annapolis, Frank Timmons, to see if he could find the person in question.

He dialed the number and luckily, his friend Frank picked up.

"Lieutenant Timmons, may I be of assistance?"

Morse quickly commented, "Sounds like you're still a plebe, Frank. Are you late for a date or a meal like usual?"

Timmons laughed and said, "Morse, you were never a good midshipman. No wonder they have you stealing things for an admiral instead of getting sick on a ship. What can I do for the aide to the chief of staff?"

"Well," Morse said quickly, "can you get some information on a recruit named James Brand? Seems that Admiral King wants him bad."

"Whatever the admiral wishes, it will be our happy mission in BUPERS to comply," Timmons commented with a level of false solemnity. "I'm sure this person is on the top of everyone's list of who is important today in the U.S. Navy." Timmons did a fake yawn to help his old friend get a belly laugh.

"Timmons, you're a crazy man, thanks for the kind thoughts and I'm sure the head of the navy will rest assured that all is well in the fleet today because of your zeal in doing his bidding. But, to be honest, old friend, I think there is a major push on this case, and I'm to report immediately back to my boss. So can you get some fire going with all those clerks to find a personnel jacket on this guy and let me know where he is, what he is, and how soon we can get him here?"

"Sounds serious and if it's that important, let me get off this call and start the wheels of bureaucracy moving. What is your extension?" Timmons now sounded like the efficient officer he was.

"I am at 6-8-4 and if I am not here, ask for Chief Riley who is the keeper of the admiral's calendar and all around top dog around here." Morse sounded relieved knowing things would move fast but then asked, "How long might this search take?"

Timmons was apologetic, "God only knows. Records are all over the place, and if this guy is new since Pearl Harbor, I don't know how long it will take. Lots of people with lots of records floating around and not one has been centralized. Do you know what he is doing?"

Morse looked at his note from the admiral and said, "Looks like he is a new seaman recruit so I guess that would probably be San Diego or some other of the new training centers. But Timmons," Morse said earnestly, "make some calls and see if you can jog someone's memory on this fast. I don't want to tell Admiral King that we don't know where this guy is. Okay?"

Timmons, sensing the tension in the voice of his old classmate said, "Understood. I will get some people calling all of the recruit depots and get back to you as soon as I get on his trail."

"Thanks, Timmons. I appreciate the help. When I get command of my new destroyer, I will see if I can get you for my exec."

Morse started to laugh at the vision of a distraught Timmons playing second fiddle to him but before the picture in his mind got clearer. Timmons responded by saying, "Being a member of BUPERS, it will be my pleasure to make sure your first command is a slow-moving oiler or perhaps a tug, and I will be on the destroyer as you pass out the gas to my ship. Remember what they said at the academy, never piss off the guys in personnel."

4

19 January 1942
Navy Recruit Training Depot
San Diego, California

- British North Borneo is surrendered to the Japanese at Sandakan.
- General Auchinleck issues operations instructions to commander, British Troops in Egypt (BTE) and commander, Eighth Army, restating that objective in Libya is Tripoli and outlining plan for defensive stand in the event the Libyan offensive cannot be continued.

The day was getting off to a cool almost cold start. Up since 4:30 A.M., James and the rest of the recruits, called scum by their petty officer instructor, felt comfortable as he enjoyed the warmth of the San Diego area compared to New York City or for that matter, Flagstaff. The squad had run for a good hour, and many of the recruits were having a difficult time breathing. When Chief Dugard called a halt to the ragtag group, many simply collapsed to the ground. This was not a good thing to do with Dugard who was on his normal war path. He yelled at most of them and singled out his favorite target for punishment, Recruit Pine.

"You, Pine, who told you to hit the deck? What gives you the right to be tired? Who do you think you are, some damn admiral?" With no reply, Dugard attacked with his foot, kicking the young eighteen year old who was all of five-foot-four and weighing maybe 120 pounds when he volunteered, but now weighed at most 105 pounds. He had done this before, putting Pine in the depot hospital for two days. Because of this and numerous other bruises and contusions, the young recruit was not healing at all. Dugard was a malevolent sadist who enjoyed picking on the young recruits in his charge.

"Mr. Cline," he called to his assistant, Petty Officer Second Class James T. Cline, "do you see this little boy on the ground? Do you feel sorry for him? See if he can get up on his two feet!"

Cline went over to the recruit who was spitting blood from his mouth and frothy saliva as well.

"Pine, get your lazy ass off the ground, or the chief will kick you all the way to Tokyo. Do you hear me, Pine, get up!"

Pine was in great pain and could not even reply to Cline. Dugard came back and kicked him again and waited for a reaction. When he didn't get one, he did it again. Pine writhed in pain and began a low moaning that everyone could hear.

James could not take it anymore and yelled at Dugard. "Stop it, you are going to kill him!"

Dugard turned quickly and strutted toward the tall recruit he knew was not a push over, but that didn't stop Dugard. "What did you say, you piece of shit?" He swung and hit James in the gut and made him double over. "What a pansy you are," he yelled and then began another swing at James' head.

James knew that he had lost his cool and now his temper, but could not restrain himself. His mentor at Cal Tech, Dr. Isuro Tomaguchi, had taught him how to defend himself and to control his emotions which were part of the teachings of the martial art known as karate. Izzy, as Dr. Tomaguchi called himself, had taken a very young teenager, who was large but not too well coordinated, and had educated him on not only the martial arts of his native Okinawa but the language and philosophy of Japan. James had found great peace in meditation and tried not to use force, but used words to disarm his opponent. Izzy had taught him to use force as a last resort to reason, but when forced, he must fight to win. Now he was faced with no option but to use his skills.

This sadist had been attacking people and especially Recruit Pine since they began training the week of Christmas. Dugard was often hungover, and on those days Cline did the drills and seemed to be at least human in his approach to the recruits. But Dugard was a low life. Barely staying in the navy for the past sixteen years by keeping his head down and doing as little as possible. He had spent time on large ships only, preferring life on a battleship to any land-side duty station, but he had been in a lot of trouble and had been demoted on many occasions. So, the Navy Recruit Depot training was acceptable compared to getting on a small ship where he would have to do some actual work.

Now Dugard had some real power over people who could not complain or strike back. He enjoyed this ability to hit people, watching them cower in fear. No one would hit a petty officer for any reason, and he held a lot of stuff over the head of his assistant Cline who would not make complaints against him. He hoped some low life would take a punch at him so he could make a mess out of their face and then get them court-martialed. He hoped one of the smaller recruits would take a swing at him because then it would be easy with little chance of injury to himself. He had been in many brawls in bars and whorehouses during his sea duties, and knew how to fight dirty. But he had never encountered anyone like Recruit Brand.

The swing that Dugard tried to land was parried as simply as one would bat a fly and was followed by a quick chop to Dugard's prominent Adam's apple. He fell to the ground clutching his throat but quickly recovered.

"Lucky punch you shit head. Now you are going to die!" Dugard lunged for James who with lightning speed cut out the chief's legs causing him to sprawl to the ground. At this point, Cline tried to intervene, knowing he had to support his horrible leader, but only because Dugard held his future in the palm of his hands. Cline tried to grab Recruit

Brand from behind, but James sensed his presence, swung around, leveled a fast jab to his solar plexus then one to his shoulder, dislocating it. Cline went down hard, yelling in pain. Dugard got up and charged the recruit. Again, James avoided the force of the man's fist, grabbed the arm it was attached to and twisted until it broke. Then with his leg, James smashed into the petty officer's groin and finally crashed his body to the ground knocking the air out of his lungs. Dugard lost consciousness. At that point, another petty officer and at least two officers charged the scene. James quietly stepped back into formation and helped young Pine to his feet, knowing his naval career was probably over.

But Brand was lucky. One of the officers witnessing the one-sided conflict was Lt. (jg) Hiram Feldman, a navy doctor trying to find out what Dugard was doing to his recruits. He did not believe the reports he received every time a recruit entered the hospital. As the new doctor on the floor, he got all the recruit cases and none of the officer and regular navy personnel who had less serious problems. Feldman knew that no other petty officer had as many serious injuries among recruits as Dugard. He also logged smaller cases from this sadistic trainer, which were four times any other person on the base. No one ever brought charges, but an epidemic of falling in the shower caused the doctor to question this particular unit. He had witnessed the same thing in New York City as an intern doing rounds in the police jail on Ryker's Island. He knew which jailer was a sadist or a homosexual or both, and had found out he needed a lot of evidence to make the authorities take notice.

Today, Feldman had taken the early morning sick call, then decided to check out what Dugard was doing to his recruits. Using his best medical methodology, he had recorded several minor events, and had been trying to develop the entire picture so he could take it to the chief medical officer and then to the base commander. But he needed proof, and now he had it. He had witnessed the brutality of Dugard's runs, which were double what other petty officers did every day, and saw him kick the young recruit on the ground. He was close enough to know the young, tall recruit yelled at Dugard to stop and saw the petty officer turn his wrath on him. He had seen the first hit Dugard landed and wondered why that punch had not knocked the recruit to the ground or at least staggered him. The recruit seemed to stand into the hit, then brace for another attack when he decided to defend himself with the most complex fighting moves the young doctor had ever seen.

Dr. Feldman was the last officer to arrive at the scene, and several petty officers had surrounded the young recruit who had waylaid their compatriot, but the recruit did not take a defensive stand. A superior officer yelled over to the petty officers to march the recruit over to the brig and await further orders. The recruit saluted the officer and marched off with two petty officers who gave him a big lead. The doctor went to the aide of the recruit first, then to Dugard and Cline. Both required stitches and the setting of bones. Both yelled in agony as another officer asked what had happened. The recruits said nothing, fearful of the consequences. The remaining petty officers also said nothing, knowing full well their fellow instructor was a sadist who caused huge problems for everyone.

The young doctor quickly spoke, "I saw the whole thing, and everything will be in my report on Dugard and what has transpired to this point. The recruit acted in self-defense, and these two deserved everything they got."

A second officer, also a lieutenant junior grade, shook his head in an affirmative manner, knowing Dugard was a problem, but knew under navy rules known as "Rocks and Shoals," not every action of self-defense was legal or appropriate. He had only seen the petty officer go down not what transpired prior, so he had only part of the story.

As the ambulance crew put the petty officers and the injured recruit in the van, Dr. Feldman knew he had a difficult case to prove and needed a lot of help which he would not get on the base. He was a new reserve officer, and as such, did not understand the importance of command and discipline. He remembered his experience at the city jail in New York and the problems he had making that case. He hoped he could find someone willing to come to the aid of the young recruit.

Dr. Feldman did not have to wait long for the assistance he was looking for, and when it arrived, it amazed everyone on the base.

5

22 January 1942
North Island Naval Aviation Base
San Diego, California

- Luzon, Philippines--Japanese reinforcements land in Subic Bay area, Philippines
- Allied forces evacuate Lae and Salamaua, New Guinea.

Admiral James J. Bridges had spent some sixteen hours in a Coronado flying boat which departed Pearl Harbor yesterday, or so the calendar said. He felt like he had been in a plane for two days with the constant drumming of the engines and the buffeting of the air on the long passage to California. He had spent the past two weeks at Pearl on assignment for Secretary of the Navy Frank Knox to further evaluate the reasons for the losses sustained on December 7. The Secretary had been dispatched within three days of the disaster at Pearl by President Roosevelt, and his initial report was damning of not only navy leadership but also the army who handled air defenses for the island.

Upon his return, Knox met with the new chief of the United States

Fleet, Admiral King, who had replaced Admiral Stark, now designated chief of Naval Operations. After the meeting, he decided to send a seasoned investigator to Pearl to determine if there were additional grounds for prosecution of all individuals who were associated with the disaster. Admiral King recommended Admiral Bridges for this thankless task.

Bridges had graduated from Annapolis with the class of 1909 and had served meritoriously in WWI and had received the Navy Cross for actions with a German U-boat which resulted in serious injuries to the young lieutenant commander. These injuries ended any hope for a sea career because of muscle and leg damage sustained in the attack on the U-boat. Nevertheless, the navy saw a model officer in the young hero who also possessed a brilliant mind and an uncanny ability to remember the most obscure details. He was encouraged in 1918 by the young Assistant Secretary of the Navy Franklin Roosevelt, to attend law school on the navy's dime, which he did, knowing a sea career was no long possible. He graduated second in his class at Columbia Law and began his climb to the top legal job in the navy, flag rank, and leader of the Judge Advocate General organization of the U.S. Navy. He retired in 1939 but like other flag officers, was held in reserve. When he received a call from Admiral Stark in early 1941 to assist in the challenges with the Lend-Lease program and the U.S. Atlantic Neutrality Zone, he jumped at the chance to serve again.

When war broke out, Admiral Bridges was seconded to Admiral Stark's staff to consider all the legal issues arising with the war and then was sent to Pearl Harbor to begin the investigation of the leadership, and any other such matters that he deemed should be examined. His briefcase was full of interview notes and his young aide, Lt. Paul Haslett, had boxes of papers, reports, and depositions to sort through to make the report not only coherent but factual.

After a long shower, Admiral Bridges put on his uniform, which had just returned from the base cleaners. He was looking forward to a nice dinner and sleeping in a real bed for at least twelve hours when his aide knocked on his door.

"Come," said the admiral, knowing no one else on the base would dare interrupt his time after he left orders with the base commander what his wishes were. No one ever tried to cross a JAG admiral for fear of ruining a career.

"Admiral, sorry to interrupt you, but I received a signal from Admiral King that requires your immediate attention." Haslett waited for permission to talk, and the admiral gave him a come-on signal with his hand.

"Sir, the signal says that you are to meet with a Commander Jameson who should arrive in San Diego at 1200 hours. He will provide you with your orders. It comes from the chief of staff and requests your immediate attention. That is all it says, but it is listed Top Secret."

The admiral took the flimsy as they were called and read it knowing his young aide never added or deleted the facts. "Humph, what is all this about and this secret stuff? I wonder what King is up to these days. Okay, Haslett, when the commander gets here, show him in and stand by. Until then, see if you can get me a steak, eggs, and some decent bread. Get one for yourself and join me so we can talk about our report."

"Aye, aye sir." The lieutenant left as quietly as he had entered. The admiral smiled at the efficiency of his aide who had joined him only three months ago. The aide was a top lawyer at one of the biggest New York City law firms, making more in a month than a rear admiral made in a year. The young man had stayed in the Naval Reserve from his Harvard undergraduate days, and this made him a trusted aide who could handle some of the issues the admiral was investigating.

At 1230 hours, a marine orderly, assigned by the base commander to support the visiting admiral, knocked on the door and was greeted with a "Come" by the booming voice on the other side of the door. The corporal entered, came to attention and stated a Commander Jameson and a marine lieutenant were reporting to the admiral as ordered. The admiral waved his hand, and the corporal did a smart about face and held the door open while a navy commander and marine first lieutenant came in and snapped to attention.

The commander said in a strong voice, "Commander Jameson and Lieutenant Flannigan reporting as ordered." He then opened a briefcase, pulled out a brown regulation envelope, and handed it to the admiral.

Admiral Bridges looked at the envelope, murmuring to himself, "I wonder where they want me to go next?" He pulled out a single page and immediately saw the name of King at the bottom and the name of Roosevelt in the body of the letter. His interest quickly increased when he read the letter in its entirety. Looking to the commander, he asked, "Commander, do you know the contents of this letter?"

"Yes sir, I am familiar with the details and the individual that is the focus of these orders."

"Commander," the admiral said, as he passed the letter to his aide, "am I to believe Admiral King wants me to go over to the Recruit Training Base and pull a seaman recruit out of training and ensure that you and the lieutenant get him back to D.C.? Am I reading this right?"

"Sir, you are correct. We need to get this young man out of recruit training immediately and get him safely to Washington. I know it is a strange set of orders, but I can promise the young man in question is vital to the war effort."

The admiral's aide handed the paper back to Admiral Bridges, then with a silent okay from the admiral asked, "What is so special about this person? Is he the son of a top political donor or something?"

"No sir. If it were that simple, the president would not direct the commander in chief of the U.S. Fleet to ask you to do this. The young man in question is only eighteen but holds a Doctorate in Applied Physics, owns at least a dozen patents in the new field of electronics and is considered by the president's science advisor to be the smartest person in the United States. He joined the navy to serve his country. He evidently did not want to be locked away in a science lab for the duration, which is exactly what would have happened."

The admiral, now intrigued, leaned forward for more information. "So, you know this young man?"

"Yes sir, I met him a few years ago at Princeton where he was touring the advanced physics lab that Professor Einstein runs. He was only fourteen at the time and had finished a Master's degree in Mathematics. Einstein was taken with him as was every other person he met, not only for his brilliance but his lack of bravado evidenced by his small-town boy persona. He spoke fluent German with Professor Einstein, and I understand he speaks very good Italian with Dr. Fermi who he studied with at Columbia."

The aide asked, "Who is this Dr. Fermi?"

The admiral smiled at his young aide and stated, "I met Fermi a year or so ago when he left Italy for the US. I think he is a Nobel Prize winner. Is that correct, Commander?"

"Yes sir, Fermi is one of the leading scientists in theoretical physics. I have worked with him on and off for the past year before my recall into the service."

"So, Commander," eyeing an academy ring, "You were an Academy man and then left the service?"

"Yes sir, I was the class of '21, and the billets were getting small, so I was encouraged to pursue advanced education but stay in the reserves, where I've served for the past twelve years. I have a Ph.D. in Mathematics and serve on staff with the science advisory team reporting to the vice chief of staff."

"Well, this is all good and wonderful, but why do I need to be the one to pull this guy out of recruit training? Why all the fuss, just order the base to transfer this young man to D.C." The admiral knew this was more complex than cutting a set of orders. People would ask lots of questions and if this kid was so valuable, special care was needed.

"Sir, Admiral King considered that but wanted to make sure Seaman Recruit Brand was removed promptly and securely taken to Washington. That is why I am here as well as Lieutenant Flannigan."

"I was wondering why you had a marine with you. Why all of the security for this operation?"

The commander spoke with great authority, "Sir, it was deemed appropriate to ensure the movement of Brand with a higher level of security than would be given a normal individual. As I have said, we do not know how long this will take, and we want to make sure he is safe. As I understand it, Admiral King has plans for this young man. Those plans have not been revealed to me, but I was told by Director of War Plans Admiral Turner to be ready to assist him in any way and on any project, that may come up involving the scientific aspects of the war effort."

"All right," said the admiral. "I guess I have my orders and you have yours, and we do our duty, whatever that may be. So, what do you propose?"

"Sir," Commander Jameson said, "I have three marine non-coms along with the lieutenant and two staff cars. I recommend we depart as soon as possible for the Recruit Training Station, then head directly to the commanding officer's office, get our man, and get out as soon as possible. I have a set of orders in my possession transferring him to Naval Barracks, Washington, D.C., in my care."

"Commander, you have most of the bases covered so let's get on with this mission, and spring a kid from the clutches of navy training, which, I have a feeling, he might not appreciate."

Admiral Bridges, in full winter blue uniform with gold braid shining in the midday sun, and his aide step toward the first car driven by a gunnery sergeant, who looks like he was the original marine. As the admiral approaches, the sergeant jumps to attention and snaps to a parade ground salute the commandant would be proud of. The admiral returns the salute and gets in the car. The aide rushes around to the other side as does Lieutenant Flannigan. The second car was driven by a staff sergeant and accompanied by a corporal. Each of these non-coms have at least twelve years in the corps with the gunnery sergeant showing a sleeve full of hash marks indicating over twenty-eight years of service and a chest full of ribbons or as he describes, "been-there badges."

As the cars start on the drive, Admiral Bridges inquires, "Lieutenant, why is your hand bandaged? And it appears you have a slight limp?"

Flannigan turns in his seat. "Sir, it appears I should have ducked before things started going bad."

The admiral chuckled but the smile quickly leaves his face as he notes the scars on the lieutenant's face. "Sounds more serious than that. What happened?"

Flannigan, knowing he couldn't get away with any more flippant comments, said as matter of fact as possible, "Sir, I was at Cavite when the bombs began to fall. Got hit with shrapnel and doused by burning gasoline."

Bridges is intrigued because he knows the situation in the Philippines and that few people escaped. "How did you get out?"

"Sir, I was attached to Admiral Hart's staff, serving as a messenger between various locations of the Asiatic Fleet. Two other officers were the pouch carriers for various information between the Philippines and other U.S. outposts including Shanghai, Singapore, and Hawaii. I had been with the Fourth Regiment. When they were pulled to the Philippines in November my duties were supposed to be over and I was reassigned to a rifle platoon. Things did not work out well."

The intrigue increased and the admiral asked, "When and how did you get out of the islands?"

"Well, sir, after I was injured and patched up the admiral ordered most of the ships dispersed from Manila Bay. We had lost a submarine in the bombing and most of our PBYs were either shot up or headed south for their health. Admiral Hart, concerned I would be unable to do my regular duties as a marine, arranged for me to go to Batavia, the planned HQ for the Asiatic Fleet. I got on one of the last ships and left Manila on December 14. In Batavia, I continued my courier duties, but the admiral saw I was still unable to walk well and ordered me to Australia then home to the U.S., carrying dispatches and Admiral Hart's situation assessments on the Japanese attack and the immediate aftermath. I have been on temporary duty at the hospital here until last night when I was assigned to the commander."

"Well," Admiral Bridges said to his aide, "seems we have another point of reference for our project." The lieutenant did not reply but looked straight ahead as they drove toward the recruit station.

The office of the commander of the Recruit Training Base, San Diego, was a flurry of activity with sailors walking around with piles of files and other papers looking for someplace to put them. All the file cabinets were full as were most of the boxes stacked against the walls in every nook and cranny in the building. Since early 1941 the base had doubled in size with new buildings and new offices but never enough room for the influx of recruits and training staff. Building the navy would take time and time requires paperwork in triplicate.

The commander of the base was a navy captain named Bailey, who had been appointed only three months before. He was a regular who had been in navy supply and liked the routine duties. The recruit training job was right up his alley. He had the input of new recruits, he had boxes to put them in, and he had a way to ship them out. All very nice and neat but it required dealing with lots of people and constant interruptions. But, the navy had given him the fourth stripe last year, and after twenty-four years in the navy, this would be his crowning achievement. *Do a good job here,* he thought, *and maybe I might make the admirals list in a few years.*

As he thought of the possibility, his senior yeoman entered unannounced. Coming to attention he said, "Sorry sir, but there is an admiral at the front gate heading this way. I was given the heads up by the marine guard who said the admiral's name was Bridges."

The captain, knowing protocol, immediately told the yeoman to alert his entire training staff and to find his executive officer, Commander Blevins. He got up, adjusted his tie, made sure he was completely up to uniform regulations, and pushed the files on his desk into a drawer.

Outside the office in a small waiting room sat Lt. (jg) Dr. Hiram Feldman. He had been waiting to see the executive officer for an hour, and knew he was being put on the cooler because he was causing problems. He had shown his information on the Dugard case to his commanding officer who wanted none of the blowback from it. He told Feldman to take it up with the training officer, a reserve lieutenant commander, who had the same reaction of touching a hot rock with a bare hand. He told Feldman to take his concerns to the executive officer who controlled base discipline matters. Feldman had taken the time to make two copies of everything in case one got lost in the shuffle of bureaucratic inertia. Now he waited for a meeting that seemed to never come.

The sudden commotion of people trying to move boxes around and clean up the place, piqued Feldman's curiosity. He found out when he heard in a bellowing voice, "Attention on deck, flag officer arriving."

Feldman, like everyone else in the area, jumped to attention as a marine gunnery sergeant turned and stood at attention as an admiral entered the office followed by an aide, a full commander, and a marine lieutenant.

The commanding officer walked out his door and saluted. "Sir, I am Captain Bailey, base commander. How can I be of service to the admiral and his staff?"

The admiral noted the mess and chaos seemed to be duplicated throughout the navy as it struggled to grow. "Captain, I need a moment of your time."

"Yes sir." Captain Bailey responded. "If the admiral would follow me into my office, I would be most happy to be of assistance to you and your staff."

"Thank you, Captain, and if you do not mind, I will ask that my aide, Lieutenant Haslett, and Commander Jameson to join us."

"No sir, not at all. Would the admiral care for coffee?"

"Yes, Captain, that would be fine." This was part of the price for being an admiral, everybody asking you to drink coffee all day long. No wonder his stomach was a mess.

Noting the invitation to the captain's office did not include him, Flannigan made his way to chairs outside the office and sat next to a lieutenant junior grade with Medical Corps emblems on his lapels.

The doctor immediately struck up a conversation with the marine with the bandages on his hand and lacerations on his face.

"Hello, my name is Hiram Feldman, and I'm one of the doctors on the base."

Flannigan turned to the doctor who was probably six or so years older. "Hello, the name is Flannigan."

The doctor, being curious about the admiral and the mission they were on, did not at first ask about them but more about the patient he saw in front of him. "Looks like you've been burned and received some serious lacerations to the face. How long ago did this occur because I noted some suppuration on your bandages?"

Flannigan looked down at his hand and sourly said, "Damn, looks like I'm leaking again. You would think after a month it would stop."

Feldman looked at the bandage, asking to look closer. The young marine lieutenant held out his hand, knowing the leakage needed to stop so he could get back to being a real marine. Feldman pushed on the wrapped hand, and got a silent reaction from Flannigan. However, the shudder indicated other problems going on in the hand or arm, which worried the doctor.

"What was the cause of your injury?" the doctor asked as he surveyed Flannigan's arm beneath the now upturned sleeve.

The lieutenant, knowing he should not lie to a doctor who could be helpful said in a very low voice, "The bombing on December 10 at Cavite in the Philippines."

Feldman looked at the marine with amazement and questioned in a guarded voice, "How the hell did you get away from there? No one has any news on what's happening over there." The desperate battle of Bataan was underway with some seventy-five thousand Americans and Philippine troops surrounded on the peninsula of Bataan and the Island of Corregidor. There was no hope of reinforcements. Food and ammunition were in short supply with men on half rations since early January.

The lieutenant said he could not tell the good doctor, but he was serving as a courier to Admiral Hart and was ordered out. That was all he could say. "Okay, Lieutenant, I will not ask any more questions, but I do think you should come to the hospital as soon as you can and let me look at the arm and see if I can find out what the problem is." He then rolled down the sleeve of the marine's tunic and asked the other question on his mind, "So, Flannigan, what are you doing here with the admiral? Or is that a secret also?" The doctor looked at the marine with a slightly skewed face showing a broad smile.

"Well," Flannigan began, "it is not a big secret that I know of so I can tell you we are here to pull a recruit and send him to Washington. I'm here to escort him back to D.C."

Feldman, seeing an opening continued, "Does this recruit have a name? Perhaps I know him and could be of assistance to the mission." Again, he smiled.

Flannigan smiled back. "Sure thing, his name is Brand, James Edward."

"Who? Did you say Brand?"

"Yes, Brand, do you know him?" Now Flannigan was getting very interested in the young doctor.

The doctor got to his feet pulling the lieutenant up at the same time. And in a conspirator-like tone said, "Brand is why I am here. I came to see the executive officer before it's too late."

Flannigan, quizzed the doctor, "Too late for what? What is going on?"

U-BOAT SCOURGE

"See this? I've been keeping a file on what has been going on around here for three months, and your boy is about to be court-martialed. I think he's in bad physical shape because the guards at the brig won't let me see him."

Flannigan pulled the doctor down to the chair and asked, "What did he do and what is the situation now?"

"Well, it all starts with a bastard named Dugard who has harmed lots of recruits, but everyone turns a blind eye to this bully. Let me show you what I know and how Brand became involved."

For the next five minutes, the good doctor went through the entire story leading up to the altercation with Dugard and Brand; how he was now up on charges the doctor knew were false and aimed at getting rid of Brand and keeping Dugard.

After a few minutes of looking at the files, Flannigan noted the time frames and medical reports the doctor had kept on more than a dozen recruits physically abused by Dugard but who's were always reported as accidents. Flannigan said, "Okay, here is what we do. I'm going to get the commander out of his meeting. I want you to show him the files and tell the story. I'm sure he will then get to the admiral on this. Hold onto these. I will be right back."

Flannigan went to the office door now guarded by his marine gunnery sergeant and whispered to the sergeant that he needed to speak to the commander immediately about Brand. The sergeant knocked on the door. The lieutenant walked in and excused the interruption, but he needed to speak to the commander on an issue requiring his prompt action. "Very well," said the commander, "with your leave admiral, captain, I will see what is so urgent." The admiral had been informing the captain about his mission, the need to find the recruit named Brand, and that he needed all the files and reports on him as well. The captain had sent for his chief yeoman and asked for the information knowing it would take a while.

Commander Jameson walked out, questioning the interruption. Flannigan said, "I know where Brand is and you are not going to like it. This place is a can of worms. Come over here and meet Dr. Feldman. He can explain the situation."

Feldman was already standing at attention when the commander walked over to him and said, "You say you know Brand and he is in some kind of trouble?"

"Yes sir, perhaps you could request an office so we can speak in private sir." Flannigan nodded agreement, so Jameson went over to one of the petty officers, asking if there was an office he could use. The sailor immediately walked them to an office down the hall. Flannigan nodded to Gunnery Sergeant Jones and pointed to where they were headed, knowing the old sergeant could locate them if they were needed by the admiral.

Upon entering the office, Commander Jameson asked for an explanation. Flannigan responded, "You are not going to like this, sir, but our boy Brand is in the brig on charges of assaulting a superior officer."

"What?" Jameson said, "I know this kid, he would never do this unless he were greatly provoked so what is the situation?"

Flannigan again pointed at the doctor and told the commander, "Sit down and let the good doctor go through his file and analysis of what is really taking place around here."

Some five minutes later, the commander said, "Okay, this is a mess and if you had not intervened, doctor, a great injustice would have occurred. Worse than that, we would have lost a very important resource."

Feldman said, "Excuse me, sir, I don't understand when you say losing a resource."

"Doctor," Jameson said, "you will be filled in later, but for right now I need to have a chat with the admiral and then we are going to find Brand."

Commander Jameson walked back into the office with the file and had the other two wait outside. "Admiral, we have a situation that needs your urgent attention."

Admiral Bridges, looking a bit perturbed, asked if this could wait and gave the commander a stern gaze, "Sir, this has an impact on your latest mission, and we need to resolve it immediately."

The admiral now concerned by the commander's unrelenting voice and sensing that something was brewing, asked the captain if he could be so kind as to be let alone with the commander for a few minutes and then they would resume their talk. "Certainly, sir," the captain answered.

"Jameson, what the hell is so important?"

"Sir, we found Brand, but there are a lot of problems around here turning our mission into a major incident."

The admiral's legal mind churned as he asked the commander for his report. "Sir, Brand is in the brig for a serious offense but one in which is purely self-defense from a thug petty officer. I have both a report of long standing issues regarding the petty officer and an eyewitness to the altercation. Let me show you this file."

Some ten minutes later, the admiral's aide walked out of the office and escorted Flannigan and Feldman into the room. Another five minutes went by. Base Commander Bailey and his executive officer, Blevins, were now outside waiting for the admiral. Again, the door opened. Haslett, the admiral's aide, asked the base commander and his executive officer to come inside.

The admiral sat behind Captain Bailey's desk inspecting a file. The captain and his executive officer came to attention in front of the desk and waited. They noticed that the marine lieutenant and young base doctor were standing next to the admiral's aide and Commander Jameson.

"Gentlemen, at ease." Admiral Bridges bellowed. There was no doubt about the commanding officer in charge.

"It appears, Captain, that I found my man, Seaman Recruit Brand." Questioning the executive officer, the admiral asked, "Are you familiar with that name, Commander Blevins?"

"Yes sir," the commander responded.

The admiral continued, "And where is he now?"

"Sir," Blevins responded, "Seaman Recruit Brand is in the Brig waiting for a court-martial for assaulting a petty officer."

"Yes, Commander Blevins, I found that out. Captain Bailey, why didn't you know this information?" The admiral gave the captain a stare that went straight to the heart and turned around inside the now fearful captain like a knife.

The captain glanced at his executive officer before answering the admiral, "Sir, I have not been informed about this man or any pending charges."

"So, Commander Blevins, you have not informed the base commander of an assault on a superior officer, nor have you provided said base commanding officer a set of formal charges? Would you say that you have been derelict in your duties?"

Blevins, now visibly concerned about the inquiry, did not know how to respond but said, "Sir, we have not formalized the charges, so the captain would be unaware of them, sir."

Admiral Bridges continued, "How long ago was this offense against the petty officer?"

"Sir, it was three days ago," answered Blevins.

The admiral looked down again at the file that Dr. Feldman had prepared and asked, "Commander Blevins, have you or any other officer provided counsel to the accused? Have you physically met with him?"

"No sir," came the reply.

The admiral stood, looked at Captain Bailey, then Commander Blevins before speaking. "Commander, you will escort Commander Jameson, Lieutenant Flannigan, and the doctor over to the brig where Commander Jameson will talk to Seaman Recruit Brand, and the doctor will examine him for any physical issues. You will then come back to this office and report on his condition. At that time we will begin our discussion of the abuse of recruits by Petty Officer Dugard and any others that may be involved; plus we will discuss who knew about this and did nothing. Flannigan, take two of your marines with you and make sure all is secure."

Flannigan, walked out of the office, informed Gunnery Sergeant Jones of the situation, asking him and Corporal Pride to accompany him and Commander Jameson, explaining Staff Sergeant Laird was to stay and support the admiral as required. The sergeant stepped outside, brought in the two marines, and gave them their orders as the officers moved from the building to the waiting staff cars.

Within a few minutes, they were on the other side of the base and parked in front of the brig. Both vehicles emptied. The corporal opened the door of the brig and yelled to anyone within two miles, "Ten-hut, officer on deck."

In walked Commander Blevins with Commander Jameson immediately behind with the doctor and Lieutenant Flannigan bringing up the rear of the column. Two marines jumped to attention and faced the door while a weary looking sergeant slowly rose and faced the officers. He knew the executive officer, Commander Blevins, well but who were these newcomers? Sgt. Howard Wright was known across the base as a sadist who loved to kick around his prisoners. Rumors were rampant that he often sexually abused the youngest and smallest of the recruits who landed in the brig, but no charges were ever filed out of pure fear of life and limb.

Sergeant Wright slowly said, "Commander Blevins, sir, how may I be of help to you today?"

Commander Jameson replied first, "I understand you are holding a recruit named Brand, is that correct?"

"Yes sir, he is being held on assault charges on a superior officer, and he is a nasty piece of work if I may say, fought and kicked our men badly. He's a troublemaker from what I heard from Petty Officer Dugard."

"Sergeant," Jameson said, "please take us to him. And that means now."

Wright looked to Blevins for cover but none came, motioned to the brig corporal to bring the keys and stepped down the hallway toward the cells.

When the door opened, they saw Brand sprawled on the floor with blood running down his head and his eyes swollen shut.

"Doctor," Jameson yelled, "get in here. Flannigan, call for an ambulance."

Wright opened his mouth to protest, but the look in the eyes of the new commander silenced him. As Flannigan picked up the phone he motioned to Gunnery Sergeant Jones, saying, "Sergeant, do a little asking around the brig as to what is going on and quickly if you can. I will back you up on any promises you might make." Jones, winked knowing exactly what the young lieutenant wanted.

Dr. Feldman was attending to Brand when Commander Jameson turned to Blevins and asked, "Were you aware of this man's condition?"

"No sir," came the answer, followed by a pause. "Hmmm...I have not been over to see him, just waiting to get more details on the case."

Jameson turned to Dr. Feldman, "What is the situation?"

Feldman quickly responded in his best medical voice, "Looks like broken ribs, a broken right arm below the elbow, damage to both eyes, and possible internal injuries that will require x-rays and perhaps exploratory surgery."

Flannigan returned and told the doctor the ambulance should arrive in a few minutes. Feldman then told the commander, "Sir, I recommend we take him directly to the District Naval Hospital in San Diego on Coronado Island. They are much better equipped to make the diagnosis and have the expertise we need."

Commander Jameson agreed and told Blevins to inform the drivers of the ambulance.

A few minutes later they placed Brand on a stretcher as gently as possible, loading him into the vehicle along with Dr. Feldman and Corporal Pride to ride along as a guard.

Following the ambulance's departure, Sergeant Jones approached Flannigan. "I have some information that may shed light on the situation." Flannigan, still angry at what he has seen and heard, waves Jones on.

"Seems," Jones began, "that Dugard and Wright are old ass-kicking buddies who go way back. Wright found out about our boy dropping Dugard on the parade ground and decided to get even. Two of the brig marines handcuffed Brand while Wright beat him up against the bars of the cell with no way to defend himself. The private will testify to this, and the corporal will go along because they hate the son-of-a-bitch. They also said they had seen many more of these beatings since being stationed here. Both have been hit by Wright for not going along with his stories."

Flannigan, thinking aloud said, "I thought there was more to the story. If those two marines will testify and make a statement, we can clean up several lines of inquiry. But, Sergeant, who else knew of this and how did it get covered up for so long?"

Sergeant Jones, knew he was on thin ice. "Sir, I think Commander Blevins knew, but I think that the good Sergeant Wright had something on him going way back. Not sure of anything particular but it smells funny to me."

"Sergeant, marine gunnery sergeants are known for ingenuity and the ability to do the impossible, and you have just provided us a way of getting our boy out of here and in one piece hopefully."

"Glad to be of assistance to any China marine, sir." Jones smiled and walked to the door shielding the two eyewitnesses from the hated brig sergeant.

Flannigan walked up to Commander Jameson who was asking more questions of Blevins and asked if he could have a moment of the commander's time. "Sir, something has come up and if the commander will allow me a few moments?"

Jameson was looking for an excuse to hit the smug base XO and walked down the hall with Flannigan. "Sir, I have the details you were looking for, and I think Blevins is complicit, but I don't have any proof." He quickly recounted Gunnery Sergeant Jones' report and suspicions.

"Okay, let's do a few things first. I will call the admiral, tell him we are on our way, and give him a quick report on Brand. Next, I'll tell Blevins that Sergeant Wright is to be held under house arrest and confined to barracks until we can investigate. Have Sergeant Jones get those two marines out of here and hole them up somewhere on base until we can get some reinforcements. We'll keep Blevins occupied."

"Commander Blevins," Jameson said in his commanding voice. "You are to place Sergeant Wright under immediate house arrest and confined to barracks pending an investigation. You will accompany us back to the base commander's office for further discussion."

Shock washed over Blevins as he whispers to a marine lieutenant from base security who had arrived with the ambulance to place Wright under arrest. The lieutenant turned to two of his security detail, and they approached Wright who immediately yelled at Blevins, "Goddamn pansies, the son of a bitch had it coming, you know what will happen, Commander!" He continued yelling as they took him away.

Returning to the base commander's office, Commander Jameson entered with Flannigan. Jameson had called Admiral Bridges, from the brig to let him know of Brand's condition. In turn, the admiral called the commanding officer of the naval hospital to alert him the ambulance was on the way and the young man was to be treated like a senior officer. In other words, the best doctors, best nurses, a private suite, and the senior physician was to personally inform him about Brand's condition. Assured of at least some good news out of this mess, he anxiously awaited the arrival of his officers.

Jameson spoke first. "Admiral, what happened to Brand is more than criminal, it was inhumane. The entire navy should be shocked by this situation. I believe Lieutenant Flannigan has more information on the situation."

Flannigan began his report with the information Sergeant Jones had pulled out of the two marines who were now happy to detail a long list of other injustices, beatings, and perhaps more. He also revealed that Blevins knew what was going on but that some form of blackmail was involved. He went on a few more seconds when the admiral put up his hand.

"I've heard enough," the admiral said and picked up the phone next to him. The call was immediately answered by the senior yeoman in the outer office.

"Yeoman Carter, sir, how can I be of help?"

"Yeoman, connect me to the senior JAG officer of the Twelfth Naval District. I think his name is Lee."

"Yes sir," the yeoman said, "Please hold the line."

In a few minutes, the phone rang on the desk with the yeoman saying, "Sir, I have Commander Lee on the line, I will connect you."

"Admiral Bridges, this is Commander Lee. How may I be of service?"

"Lee, I need you and at least two of your investigators to get over to the office of the commanding officer of the Recruit Depot and take charge of a hell of a mess."

"Sir, may I have more information on the need for an investigation?" Lee asked bravely.

"No, Commander, you don't need to know more until you show up here. Bring your two best gumshoes and make it fast."

"Aye, aye, Admiral, I will be there in fifteen minutes tops."

The phone went dead which did not surprise Admiral Bridges, for he had known Lee as a top investigator on his staff in D.C. when he was the JAG admiral.

"Listen, men." The admiral surveyed the room.

"First, Flannigan, you wait here with your sergeants because we need your insights on the situation. Commander Jameson, you head down to the hospital and keep me informed of how the young man is doing. Tell that young Dr. Feldman he did a good job and tell him to stay with Brand. I will cut orders to ensure he is on this case until relieved by me."

"Haslett, get on the phone and tell the aviation boys I will not be flying out tomorrow. I want to stay here and make sure this mess is cleared up and Brand is going to recover. I do not want to be the one to tell Admiral King how screwed up this thing is until we get all the facts."

Everyone snapped to attention. "Aye, aye, Admiral."

Admiral Bridges liked this impromptu team but hated the situation. This is the kind of thing that is very bad for public relations and even worse for morale. There have always been sadistic SOBs in the service, but it was the job of the officer cadre to find out who they were and get them out of the service.

After having a few words with Flannigan, Jameson left for the hospital in one of the staff cars. When he arrived, he located Dr. Feldman who gave him good news and bad news. "The bad news first," the commander told Feldman.

"Well, sir, in descending order of importance, Brand is in surgery with the top surgeon, formerly of Johns Hopkins Medical School. They are searching for bleeding, perhaps in the spleen area. We are not sure. We have pumped him with blood, but his blood pressure is still dropping so there may be a bleeder. We should know soon. He has three broken ribs that will mend, but it will be painful for some time. His lower arm below the elbow joint was broken in two places, but it was an easy job to set, and he should have no major problems. The good news is that his eyes are just bruised heavily, and it appears he will not have any sight issues. His nose was broken which we reset. He has enough bruises and cuts to kill a normal person, but he is in remarkable physical shape which allowed him to endure this torture. I had a photographer's mate take photos of his injuries where he was handcuffed and tied by his feet. This is one of the worse cases of abuse I have ever seen as a physician."

"Doctor, you have done a wonderful job, and I want to thank you for everything. The Admiral has ordered you to stay with Brand and your commanding officer knows of these orders so do not worry about anything but Brand."

"Thank you, sir," Feldman said. "I would like to stay with him and make sure everything is in good order before he leaves the hospital. He will need to be handled with care for some time based of course on what Dr. Lansky finds out during surgery."

Jameson, again said, "Thank you, Doc, for all you have done. If not for your diligence in investigating Dugard, we may have lost our young man."

"No problem, sir. I meant to ask you and Lieutenant Flannigan, what is so special about this young recruit that has an Admiral and a team of officers here in the first place?"

Commander Jameson smiled and stated calmly, "Well, Doc, perhaps you'll find out soon, but for right now be assured you are doing your part for the war effort. In other words, you do not have the need to know."

Feldman looked at the commander with his slightly askew smile that he used to such great effect. "Rest assured, your young Mr. Brand will be well taken care of, and I do hope to find out what is going on."

Commander Jameson said, "That may come sooner than you think, Doc. And you might like the answer to those questions."

Jameson excused himself to call the admiral and report the status of Brand. He made a second call to Washington to notify his boss of the situation and to advise him to stand by to help, in case Admiral Bridges had trouble cleaning up the mess caused by the altercation, beatings, and cover-ups at the base.

Commander Lee and two investigators reported as promised to Admiral Bridges. Bridges was glad to have someone on the case that he personally knew and trusted. "Commander, you are very prompt, and I do appreciate it."

Lee said, "Sir, it is a pleasure to meet you again. I would like to introduce to you Agents Rains and Johnston."

Bridges nodded at each man and said, "Glad to have you gentlemen on board and it is good to have you on this case, Commander."

Lee beamed at the accolade and the way Bridges welcomed him. "Sir, what can we do for the Admiral?"

Bridges introduced his aide, Haslett, to the JAG team and moved

U-BOAT SCOURGE

on with a quick admonition. "Gentlemen, I am about to dump a mess in your laps that is a stain on the navy and which could be a public relations nightmare. Furthermore, there are serious national security issues that I can only divulge to you in a limited way without getting approval from Admiral King personally." This, of course, was a hedge to ensure the investigation would tread lightly on anything related to Brand and his purported importance to the navy. "Is this understood?"

"Yes sir," came the chorus from the investigators and Commander Lee.

"Good," said the admiral. He asked them to be seated and continued, "Let me begin this story with the facts, and then I will give you the background." The admiral had rehearsed what he would and would not tell the JAG officer and his team so he could make sure the focus of the investigation would not touch Brand and his identity.

Some fifteen minutes later, Bridges finished by showing them the file and list of witnesses Lieutenant Haslett had prepared, plus a timeline of the event. Haslett, as a good attorney, had packaged the evidence and witnesses in such a way as to lead to a quick conviction of the two assailants, Wright and Dugard, and provided enough background to get at the cover-up and the reasons behind it. He knew this would end the career of Blevins, and it would impact other officers on the base, but this kind of savagery could not be allowed to happen in the U.S. Navy.

"Gentlemen," Bridges intoned, "do you have any questions for me or my aide?"

Lee, knowing how to handle a possible difficult question, asked, "Sir, the information contained in the file and the brief provides us with a large amount of the information we will need to conduct a thorough investigation. The list of witnesses who will provide testimony as to the facts of the case is also invaluable. One question, Admiral, how did you find out about this in the first place? Were you on some sort of inspection trip or is there something else we need to know?"

Bridges had anticipated the question because if Lee did not ask it, he would not be a good JAG officer. "Commander, I was requested by higher authorities to locate an individual on this base and to ensure his safe arrival in Washington. That is all I can tell you of my assignment, but while here I was made aware of this situation by an officer in this command. Subsequent investigation by members of my staff provided enough proof to make this a formal inquiry. I would be derelict in my duty to do otherwise. Do you have other questions on this matter, Commander?" Bridges looked straight at Commander Lee with the same look that Lee had gotten when he reported to Bridges many years before, which made him shudder then and it did the same now.

"No sir, I do not need to inquire further into your mission. I will proceed to our investigation without any further information from you or your staff."

"Thank you, Commander, but if you run into anything that you need clarified or supported, please get in touch with Lieutenant Haslett."

"With your permission, sir, we will take these files and begin our investigation. Oh, sir, there is one more thing. Where do we find this Recruit Brand?"

Admiral Bridges, knowing this would be coming said, "He is at the Naval District Hospital under the care of the same Dr. Feldman who brought this mess to your attention. I will arrange Mr. Haslett to set up an appointment with them both once Brand is stabilized."

Lee nodded to Haslett, stood at attention along with the two plainclothes investigators, and did an about face and left the office.

Haslett looked at the admiral and said, "What next, sir?"

"Mr. Haslett, we are about to give the good doctor and young Mr. Brand acting lessons."

Haslett smiled in appreciation of the admiral's legal mind and ability to control any situation.

6

24 January 1942
San Diego Naval Hospital

- Battle of Balikpapan--Japanese Borneo invasion convoy undergoes night torpedo attack off Balikpapan, Borneo, by destroyer division under the command of Comdr. P. H. Talbot composed of the USS **Parrott**, USS **Pope**, USS **John D. Ford**, and the USS **Paul Jones;** four enemy transports and a patrol craft are sunk.

Brand awoke two hours after his surgery and was groggy but felt no pain because of the anesthetic. He looked around the room to see a young doctor looking at him with a silly smile on his face.

"Well, well, well," Feldman smiling said. "Glad to have you back with the living."

Brand asked in a very groggy voice, "Where am I and who are you?"

"Mr. Brand, I am Dr. Hiram Feldman of the U.S. Naval Medical Corps and you are in the Navy Hospital in San Diego. You just had surgery to fix a few blood vessels that burst when you were beaten by a very nasty marine jailer. Should I go on?"

"Sure, can I have some water first?"

"Yes." The doctor handed Brand a cup of water and held his head off the pillow so he could slowly sip.

"Can I call you James?" Dr. Feldman asked.

"Sure thing, sir. Thanks for the water and the help. I feel like I have been run over by a truck or something."

"James, you were beaten by a sadistic bastard who now faces charges for what he did, as does Dugard who you so gloriously knocked on his ass on the parade ground."

"Oh, yes, I forgot about that. Did you see it or something?" James had very blurry vision out of one eye and a patch on the other, so he was unsure of exactly what he was seeing.

Feldman nodded his head in the affirmative. "Yes, I did, and I was glad to be there to report what I saw. Certain people were going to steamroll you into a long jail term for what you did in self-defense, but luckily, I did see it myself. I had been following Dugard around for a month after I had so many sick call issues coming from his recruit class. I knew something was afoot, but needed to get proof."

"Tell me, Doc, what else is wrong with me?"

"Well, from top to bottom here is the list." The doctor picked up a chart and began reading. Feldman told Brand all the minor and major issues he faced with emphasis on his surgery that proved only minor bleeding occurred and there was no major internal damage. He also told him that he would be in pain for some time due to three broken ribs plus a broken arm which he began to feel for the first time.

"All in all, you are a mess, but you will heal up just fine. You should be ambulatory in a week or less, but you are going to feel those ribs for a month or more. The broken arm will be in a cast for four weeks, but should be just fine. All of the X-rays looked good, and you should recover full function within six weeks." The doctor finished his report by looking at his chart then asked Brand if he was up for a visitor.

Brand asked, "Who knows I am here? I don't know anybody."

The doctor walked toward the door and smiled again, saying, "Seems a lot of people know you, Dr. Brand, and have been looking for you for some time."

"Shit," said Brand on hearing his academic title being used for the first time in nearly two months.

Feldman opened the door. Brand saw the doctor speaking to a tall marine sergeant on the other side of the door, then a navy commander entered the room.

"James, how are you feeling?" Commander Jameson inquired with a big smile. "You had a lot of people looking for you and some of them are pretty unhappy with you."

"Sir, do I know you?" Brand asked still groggy, suffering from information overload and a few too many pain relievers.

"We met at Princeton during Professor Einstein's symposium on theoretical physics. You were quite the star for asking so many questions of the great man." Commander Jameson turned to Dr. Feldman who was stunned to hear the name, Einstein. "Yes, Doc, everyone started to call young Dr. Brand, the great inquisitor after his meeting with Einstein. By the way James, the Professor has asked me to tell you hello and looks forward to more questions from you."

Feldman had been informed that Brand was no ordinary seamen recruit and was a prodigy with advanced degrees, but he did not know the levels at which Brand played. He was stunned but said nothing, watching the interaction between Jameson and the recruit.

Brand looked harder at the commander and then it dawned on him. "Dr. Jameson, sir, I had no idea you were in the navy. It's great to see you again but why are people looking for me?" Jameson looked at Feldman who had started for the door to give the two some privacy, but Jameson told him to stay.

"James, you have a special set of talents and skills too valuable to the nation to have you spend your time as a seaman in the navy. I'm gratified that you wanted to serve your country and wanted to stay hidden, but you can serve your country in so many more important ways by using your God-given talents in science to help the war effort."

James looked up and shook his head yes, but said, "I want to serve my country, but I don't want to be locked up in some university lab working on a couple of projects for a few years while everyone else is out doing the dirty business of war. I just wanted to be like everyone else."

Jameson expected this line of reasoning because he knew that under all the brilliance lurked a very young man still in his teenage years with dreams like every other warm-blooded American boy.

Jameson did not want him to stew on this any longer and said, "James, we have searched for you not to put you in a laboratory somewhere but to put you in the uniform of a navy officer and have you serve your country doing the big things that will win this war. I cannot go much further on this right now, but Admiral King wants to put together a staff of the best minds in America which will help build a new navy to win the war. You are already in the navy, but we want you to serve where you can best assist the nation. I cannot promise you more than this but I can foresee great things for you, and I assure you, you can help win this war sooner by using your knowledge, skills, and abilities than being a seaman on a ship somewhere."

James looked up, smiled and said, "Sir, when can I get started?"

7

27 January 1942
San Diego Naval Hospital

- Submarine **Seawolf** delivers ammunition to Corregidor and evacuates navy and army pilots.

Commander Lee and his investigators had interviewed all the witnesses except for Brand. The previous day, Lee interviewed Lieutenant Flannigan and most importantly, Dr. Feldman. His interview with the doctor had taken three hours as he reviewed all the documentation Feldman had accumulated on Dugard and went over the logs of the sick bays for injuries that Dugard probably inflicted. All the information was sound and would enable a quick case with maximum penalty. He had not heard from Admiral Bridges since the first day nor had he contacted him to discuss his progress. He knew the admiral did not want any special treatment or perhaps did not want to add undue influence on this case which Lee agreed was an affront to the United States Navy. He was still concerned about the admiral's comments on why he was in San Diego.

Lee had found out that Bridges had been recalled to duty before Pearl Harbor, and was doing special assignments for the secretary of the navy and for Admiral King. He was told the admiral had just returned from a few weeks in Pearl Harbor and was informed by his sources that he was talking to people from Nimitz down to commanders of individual warships and aircraft squadrons. Evidently, Lee figured, he was looking for additional reasons for the Japanese sneak attack and the navy's lack of preparation and active defense. This was a topic Commander Lee wanted to avoid.

Lee was cleared to interview Seaman Recruit Brand and informed of the seaman's room number. When he got to the Naval Hospital and entered Brand's floor he found himself amid the treatment area for senior officers instead of that used by normal enlisted men. As he came down the hallway filled with the sanitized smell common to all hospitals, he spied a marine posted at a doorway. As he got closer the marine sergeant snapped to attention. "Sir, may I be of assistance to the commander?"

Lee replied, "Is this the room of Seaman Recruit James E. Brand, Sergeant?"

"Yes sir, may I ask if the commander has an appointment?"

Lee was struck by the comment and said, "Sergeant, my name is Commander Jerome Lee. I have an appointment to interview Seaman Recruit Brand at 1100 hours. Please admit me, now."

"Sir, I need to verify your appointment with my commanding officer, if you would wait here for a moment, sir, I will be right back."

Before Lee could comment, Sergeant Laird turned and walked into the room and secured the door behind him.

Inside the room were Admiral Bridges, Dr. Feldman, Commander Jameson, Lieutenant Haslett, and a new face, Rear Adm. Kelly Turner, director of U.S. Navy War Plans. Turner had been questioning Brand about mathematical models to speed the loading of ships bound for the war. This was especially important because of the heavy losses currently occurring on America's eastern seaboard as German submarines were slaughtering unescorted merchant ships daily. Brand was briefed on current strategy and provided with several lengthy documents on anti-submarine practices.

Turner was on his way to meet with Admiral Nimitz on war plans being developed for the serious challenges in the Pacific and how best to use the limited offensive capabilities of the remaining fleet. Turner was about to ask Brand's opinion when the marine sergeant walked in.

U-BOAT SCOURGE

He turned and asked in his normal brusque manner, "Sergeant, I told you to secure the room and allow no one in except my aide. Do you have a problem with that?"

Sergeant Laird, knowing Turner as the hard-ass captain on one of his previous shipboard assignments, came to attention. "Sorry, sir, Admiral Bridges informed me a JAG officer was due to interview Mr. Brand. He is outside and not very happy about not being allowed in."

Turner was about to speak, but Bridges cut him off. Turner's senior by four years at the academy and date of rank, Bridges said, "Kelly, this is the problem I have to get fixed, but I can get you more time with Mr. Brand. Can you hold off for a few minutes? Then I promise you can continue with your inquiries as to Mr. Brand's ability to be of assistance to War Plans?"

"Sorry, Admiral, it was just getting interesting. This young man's ability to grasp key elements of a problem and provide specific solutions based on reality isn't the normal crap I'm fed in Washington. Do you want me to leave while the JAG commander does his questioning?"

Bridges pondered for a moment and said, "Admiral, I think it would be a boost to your career to have you see how navy justice works." He smiled widely as did Turner who quickly got the message.

"Sergeant, show Commander Lee in."

"Aye, aye sir." Laird pulled the door open and walked outside, announcing to the angry commander, "Sir, you may go in now."

Commander Lee was about to tell off the sergeant as he crossed the threshold, but then he saw a sea of navy gold braid in the form of two rear admirals. Bridges he knew, but he had no idea who the other one was. Lee snapped to attention and looked right over the head of Admiral Turner who stood by the bed. "Sir, the commander begs the Admiral's pardon for interrupting your meeting. I shall retire, sir, and reschedule my interview with Seaman Brand."

For a moment, Lee was not only stunned but somewhat frightened at having two admirals in a room with several other officers around the bed of an injured seaman recruit. His mind raced and wondered, *What the hell is going on here? Did I miss something or what?*

Never shy about giving orders, Turner barked out, "At ease, Commander. I was just in the middle of a top-secret conversation with Mr.

55

Brand when you walked in." He scooped up two files with red tape, each marked TOP SECRET in large letters.

Bridges, stifling the need to laugh at the uncomfortable commander who must be about to pass out or worse, spoke up. "Admiral Turner was interviewing Mr. Brand on issues that are not part of your investigation, but I do recall you were going to be here at 1100 hours, so I apologize to you Admiral for this interruption." The gruff head of war plans, nodded his head in agreement. Bridges, turned to the JAG officer saying, "Commander, it would be best if you perhaps ask Mr. Brand a few of your questions so Admiral Turner could get on with his briefing. I would request you make your questions brief and to the point. Is that all right with you, Commander Lee?"

Lee was now in a box. He was not happy asking a witness questions in front of a bevy of officers, including two admirals. But, he knew he needed to move on this for he feared that whoever Brand was, he would not be available again.

"Sir, I have only a few questions to ask Seaman Recruit Brand about his treatment at the hands of the brig sergeant and the petty officer in charge of his training."

Admiral Bridges looked at his watch and said, "By all means, proceed. And by the way, Mr. Brand is no longer a seaman recruit. As of yesterday, he is Ensign Brand of the Naval Reserve."

"Thank you, sir." Lee's mind now began screaming two things, *What's going on here and who is this young man? Why would a rear admiral be reviewing top secret documents with a one-day old ensign and why does everybody want to get me out of here?*

Lee began by telling Brand who he was and why he was there. He also informed Brand there were no charges against him, but that he was a material witness in an ongoing legal investigation and to answer the questions truthfully and fully. Brand shook the hand of the commander with his left hand because of the cast on his right arm and hand and agreed to the instructions. The doctor had provided a complete list of Brand's injuries and Lee was surprised how he acted despite the evident pain. The kid looked like hell and he felt sorry for even putting him to all these questions, but with admirals looking on he did it by the book.

Lee took Brand through the timeline of the case and asked what he remembered, especially the beating in the brig. He asked about the attack from Petty Officer Dugard and his subsequent defense of himself. He wanted to know additional details about the other incidents he witnessed while in training. Lee wanted to start another line of questioning about his self-defense when Admiral Bridges interrupted.

"Commander, do you have enough information from Mr. Brand to support your indictment and prosecution?"

"Sir, I believe we have a solid case against both defendants. I just want to ask Brand a few more questions."

Lee was trying to continue when Admiral Bridges walked over to stand next to Admiral Turner.

"Lee, if you have enough information from all of the other witnesses and the outstanding documentation by Dr. Feldman, I think you should begin your prosecution. Mr. Brand needs his rest, and Admiral Turner has got to get on a plane to Pearl, but he needs to finish his conversation with Mr. Brand."

The last comment was a definite signal to Lee that the case was closed concerning Brand and additional questions would not be appreciated.

Lee stood by the bed, picked up his folder, and said, "Admiral, I will keep your aide informed about the case and its resolution." He snapped to attention. "Thank you for your answers, Mr. Brand. I hope to meet you again in the future under much better circumstances."

The commander snapped to attention once more, did a smart turn, and marched out of the hospital room. He was followed by the admiral's aide.

Once they were outside, Lieutenant Haslett said softly, "Commander Lee, may I have a moment of your time."

"Certainly," came the reply from Lee.

"The admiral would like a word with you in a few minutes. Sir, if you would wait in this room," pointing across the hall, "the admiral will be with you shortly."

Commander Lee sat down but wasn't too sure about what had occurred. Two admirals, some scientist commander, and a dangerous looking marine lieutenant had been in the hospital room of what had been an ordinary seaman recruit who was now an ensign. Top secret files had been spread around. Admiral Turner whom he knew only by reputation was evidently briefing a young kid who didn't look old enough to be out of high school. None of this made any sense. Now, the former head JAG admiral, the personal hatchet man for Admiral King, wanted to speak to him.

After what seemed like an eternity, Admiral Bridges entered the room. Lee jumped to attention, but the admiral said "At ease and sit down, Lee. I wanted to have a chat with you about what you just saw and explain a few things although I cannot discuss everything. Will you listen to me for a moment without asking any questions?"

Lee was taken aback by the friendly manner of the admiral's voice and the almost fatherly way he had voiced those words.

"Of course, Admiral," Lee said as he studied the older man's face in a new light.

"Lee, I asked you in there about having enough information in which to convict those two SOBs as well as anyone involved in the cover-up."

"Yes sir. I believe I have sufficient information to put both Dugard and Wright in Portsmouth for at least forty years to life."

"Good, Commander. Now do you have enough information without using the testimony of Mr. Brand or of even bringing his name up in the trial?" The admiral now stared into Lee's face with a steely look of power.

Lee thought for a moment and decided to go with his gut instinct by saying, "Sir, I have enough information to get both men convicted for ten to twenty years if I do not use any references to the Brand incident. Without his inclusion in the case, the defense could whittle away at some of the testimony, but I think we would get a conviction."

"Lee, I am not telling you how to run your case. If it is of great significance, you may use the Brand situation, but Brand will not stand in testimony before any court proceeding. As you ponder that information, I want to suggest you use the Brand information in a pre-trial meeting with each of the accused counsels and offer them a deal. Twenty years

U-BOAT SCOURGE

minimum with no chance of parole and a dishonorable discharge. If they balk, tell them because of the nature of the crimes, the current national situation, and the good of the naval service, you will go for life without parole and you will win it. I think the other side will work very hard to convince their clients it's a no-win situation and this is their best deal."

Lee thought for a minute, and asked, "Sir, I take it that Mr. Brand is not who I assume he is and his situation requires a high degree of secrecy?"

Bridges thought for a moment. Finally, his face turned hard. "Commander Lee, I am about to impart knowledge that is more than top secret. Any discussion or mention of this information to anyone without the express knowledge of the commander in chief of the U.S. Fleet, the chief of naval operations and the secretary of the navy could be considered an act of treason. Do you understand this and do you wish me to continue?"

Lee now was in over his head and had never been faced with knowledge so high to cause the word treason to be used in any conversation. Lee sat ramrod straight and said, "Yes sir, I understand. I would never compromise the security of the nation or bring disgrace to the United States Navy."

Bridges continued to stare at the commander, then backed away. "Commander, I know you as being a man of his word. So here is what you need to know, then you will forget what you heard."

"Mr. Brand joined the navy in December as an act of great patriotism, demonstrating his love for country and willingness to put his life on the line if necessary. He did not disclose his entire record or abilities to the recruiting station so he could slip into the navy and away from his civilian career. Mr. Brand is considered by many to be the smartest person in the world and at the age of eighteen already possesses three college degrees including a Ph.D. in physics, holds over a dozen patents in technologies that will be very important to winning this war, and has one of the greatest mathematical minds in the world. He sees answers to the most complex problems before most people could even begin writing the problem down. He is fluent in five or six languages including German and Japanese. And, most importantly, he is now a possession of the

U.S. Navy for the duration. I was told by Admiral King two days ago that Brand will be used to the utmost to beat the enemy."

"Lee, I cannot tell you more because even I don't have the need to know. Admiral Turner just left and wants Brand assigned to his War Plans Division exclusively. The admiral told me as he left, young Brand gave him a dozen suggestions on how to fix bottlenecks in supply, reconfigure submarine escort duties, and how to improve range finding for naval gunfire. He was astounded at Brand's ability to quickly grasp a situation and examine it by using both logic and science. I have known Turner since he was a plebe and I have never seen him so impressed with anyone."

"So, Commander, speaking for the navy, we do not want Brand's name out in the public domain, nor do we want him in any public testimony. If you cannot get a conviction on these two or any others without Brand's help, then we will find other ways to remove these people for the good of the service."

Lee's eyes must have increased in size when he heard the last comment, and as he looked into the admiral's eyes, knew what he had just heard was a real option.

"Sir, I can assure you that we will gain convictions of Dugard and Wright and any others without using Brand's name, testimony or appearance in any court. I also assure you again of my complete loyalty to the navy and the country and will abide by your wishes of secrecy."

The admiral rose slowly. "I knew it all along, Commander, that you would find a way to rid our navy of these bastards, and at the same time keep the secret of Mr. Brand. Keep Mr. Haslett informed of your progress. If you have any setbacks, let me know personally. Is that clear, Commander?"

"Aye, aye sir," the commander said, quickly standing at attention.

"Good seeing you again, Lee. I hope I don't have to see you again on this issue."

Lee said nothing as the admiral left. As the door shut, Lee sat down on the chair and began tearing up his notes. No one would ever hear of a seaman recruit named Brand.

8

3 February 1942
San Diego Naval Hospital

- Submarine **Trout** delivers ammunition to Corregidor and removes gold, silver, securities and mail.
- Japanese bomb Surabaya, Java, Netherlands East Indies.

"So, how is our patient this morning?" Dr. Feldman with his ever-quizzical grin began. "Are we ready to leave this white palace?"

Brand looked up and enthusiastically said, "Yes sir! Can I get into some regular clothes and out of these pajamas or whatever you call this thing?"

Feldman let out a short laugh and replied, "Yes, but we must get you some new uniforms. Flannigan went out yesterday with a shopping list from the commander and is supposed to be returning today with all of the uniforms a young ensign should have plus some suitable luggage."

"As I recall," the newly minted ensign said, "I must pay for my clothes so I'll need to get some of my money. By the way, how about my navy pay?"

The doctor smiled again, "Well, I'm not much on naval protocol, but I started getting paid about forty-five days after I was called up. We had a few classes on navy procedures and who gets saluted and when, then they sent me here. I am thankful I had some money with me from my prewar life or it would be a matter of borrowing from others, which reminds me, I'm owed some money from at least two colleagues."

"Doc, I saw a lot of recruits get in trouble on the first day of training because they had no money. They fell in debt to some bad people very quickly. I had a small stash with me that I hid in my locker. I don't think it was found. I believe the good Sergeant Laird got my locker articles and amazingly everything was still there."

"How much did you have stashed?" Feldman asked.

"I think I had $300 with me and it all showed up," Brand replied.

"That's a tidy sum for a recruit, but again, you were no normal recruit," Feldman retorted.

Brand looked at the man who saved his life and said, "If you need something, anything, Doc, just let me know."

Dr. Feldman smiled. "Brand, unless you can end this war today, you don't owe me a thing. Getting you out of that brig and on your feet, is all the thanks I need. Also, it is my job, and I think I do it quite well."

Just as Brand was going to reply, the door opened and in came Lieutenant Flannigan followed by Sergeant Laird who was carrying a set of large boxes. Flannigan also carried a square canvas duffel bag with a handle on it just like those toted by officers on the train that brought Brand to San Diego. They were much nicer than the big green duffel bags the navy issued, but they were not nice leather suitcases like the ones he had back in New York City.

"The ensign is up I see and ready to do some work for once," said the marine officer. "I have brought you gifts from the navy stores in town. Laird, put the boxes on the end of the bed so we can bedazzle Mr. Brand."

Laird did as asked and smiled approvingly of Brand who he now knew was a very special young man and one in which a lot of people, including him, had worked hard to save.

"Thank you, Martin, I appreciate you helping out the lieutenant," Brand said in his usual non-navy way.

"My pleasure, Mr. Brand, anytime you need something, you let me know." Laird backed up and stood by the door.

"Well," the doctor said, "let's open all of this stuff and get Brand outfitted as an officer and maybe even a gentleman. Sergeant Laird, please stay because we may need your help in getting him up and dressed. I don't want him to fall and hurt himself again and spending more time making eyes at Lieutenant Commander Watkins."

Everyone in the room but Brand chuckled, although he smiled sheepishly at the joke. Nurse Watkins was the chief floor nurse and was about as tough as any battleship. She didn't take kind to fools, especially young fools. She had been upset about a recruit being put on her officer floor and had a chance to complain only once to the chief medical officer before she understood the importance of the young man. Admiral Bridges had taken her aside on his first visit and kindly informed her the young man would soon be an officer and was a national security asset of the first order. Nothing was to be discussed outside of the hospital floor about the patient. Those providing his care were to be in their top form. For a full week, the admiral dropped by with his aide. A few days later a second admiral appeared and spent quite a long time with the now young ensign.

Before he left for Washington, Admiral Bridges came by the hospital. He spoke with Nurse Watkins and all the nursing staff who had cared for Brand and expressed his personal appreciation. He told them he was going to see the chief medical officer of the navy to personally commend their performance.

Since her first meeting with the admiral, she and her staff of nurses could not be more helpful, and Watkins personally took charge of most of the daytime duties, including giving the young ensign baths. His condition would not allow him to move for several days so she would come in, strip him of his pajamas, and slowly wash the young man like an infant. She would talk to him like he was her own son. No doctor, including Feldman, would cross her in her duties.

Flannigan had been the first person to rib Brand about his special relationship and soon the entire team, including the non-coms, were asking how he was doing and how was his girlfriend, Eunice Watkins.

Brand could take a joke well, but it was getting a bit weary so he was grateful to soon be leaving the hospital.

The first order of business was to get Brand out of bed and standing on his own. He had done this each day for the past week, and now with the surgical sutures removed he was ready for regular clothes. Feldman helped him stand with Flannigan close by to steady him, but Brand got on his feet with no major problem. Everyone could see the young man grimace with each step, mostly because of the taped ribs, which would take a long time to heal. The doc had him walk around the room with everyone waiting in apprehension of his falling, but he did fine. After a minute of standing, Dr. Feldman asked, "So how are you feeling? Any shortness of breath or lightheadedness?"

Brand said, "No, Doc, it's all good. It still hurts to take a big breath, but all the equipment is in order."

Flannigan could not help himself and asked, "Shall we call in Nurse Watkins to check out all of your equipment?"

Everyone including Brand laughed, but then Brand stopped and commented, "Damn, it hurts to laugh, but one day, Lieutenant Flannigan, sir, I will get you for that."

More good humor ensued and this time Feldman noticed more evidence of pain as Brand laughed. He moved closer, holding Brand by his good arm.

"Let's get on with the dressing of our young knight of the seven seas so we can get him out of here."

It took a while but, Ensign James E. Brand was now looking like a young ensign in the U.S. Navy. They had put on his hat and showed him how to adjust it when Commander Jameson walked in.

Everyone, including Brand, jumped to attention, and Jameson quickly said, "At ease and carry on. So, this is what a new ensign looks like? How do you think you look, James?"

"Well, sir, except for getting this cast through the sleeve, it looks very fine indeed."

"Doc, when can we move Brand? I would like to get him back to Washington as soon as possible."

The doctor, now in his true element, looked at the commander then at Brand, saying slowly, "Commander, he is still in a lot of pain from the ribs. His last sutures will be removed tomorrow, his eyes have healed well, but the bruising will take at least another week or so to go away. He is still shaky on his feet, but otherwise he appears to be in good spirits."

The commander gave his familiar "give me more" sign with his hand.

The doctor continued, "I would prefer to keep him here for another week, but after tomorrow he should be out of all danger. His injuries will take time to heal, but I think in about two or three more days he should be good to travel."

The commander was hoping for less time and Rear Adm. Russel Willson, chief of staff to Admiral King, wanted Brand out of San Diego and working on a myriad of projects essential to the war effort. Admiral Turner had sent a report on his meeting with Brand to Admiral King stating in part, "This young man is even more than you had suggested. Incredibly insightful, not afraid to confront anyone to secure more information and has the uncanny ability to do the highest level of math in his head. He provided me with three suggestions on combat loading ships that would increase the speed of loading as well as how a ship should be configured for seaworthiness that took him a few minutes instead of a few days. I would like him assigned to the Plans Division as soon as possible. And he did all of this while in great pain after having been terribly beaten."

King thought Turner to be one of his top officers; a man possessed of keen mind, not as good as his of course, but one of the top thinkers in the navy. If Turner thought this highly of the young man and wanted him for his command, then King knew, he had a very valuable addition to the navy. He might loan this young man out to War Plans, but he would retain control. King had told his chief of staff to let him know immediately of Brand's status and to tell Commander Jameson to ensure his safe arrival in D.C. at the earliest possible moment.

Jameson had been on the phone earlier that day with Admiral Willson who had asked again when Brand would be able to come to Washington. Jameson replied that Brand was still in the hospital but expected to be released in a few days. Willson repeated King's impatience with delays and wanted this "whiz kid" under his control immediately. Jameson said he couldn't work miracles but would do his best to comply, thus his questions to Dr. Feldman.

"Okay, Doc, let's say we can go back east in three or four days. I will need to get a plane set up to take us, although that shouldn't be a problem with the priority I've received."

Feldman ruined Jameson's plans by stating most emphatically, "Sir, Mr. Brand cannot fly for at least two weeks, possibly more. The higher altitude would place a burden on his breathing and more importantly on the pressure in his chest, causing severe pain and discomfort. The only way Brand is going anyplace is by train." Jameson started to speak but the doctor, now in control, continued. "Brand will need to be kept comfortable, and that means a sleeping compartment so he can lie down. A trip like this will help him recover as well, and we can keep an eye on him to see how he is doing."

The commander knew he was beaten, so he let it pass. "All right, you're the doctor and by the way, Dr. Feldman, you are coming on this trip as well. You are staying with Brand until he is one hundred percent."

Feldman, who was happy to get out of San Diego, started to say something in protest but was cut off by Jameson.

"Admiral Bridges arranged with Admiral Willson to have you posted TDY and maintain care until Mr. Brand is in top form. Then you will be assigned to Bethesda Naval Hospital and become the assistant to the chief of surgery, which I believe is your true specialty."

"Thank you, sir," Feldman said in total shock and disbelief. "I don't know what to say."

"Oh, Doc, by the way, this new job requires a full lieutenant, and I am glad to inform you as of next Monday you are promoted to the new rank of lieutenant in the Naval Medical Corps, congratulations."

Everyone in the room burst out in cheers at the news because the doctor had won not only the appreciation of the team for his medical talent and strength of character in these past days but also for being a hell of a human being.

"Sergeant Laird, open the door and bring in the rest of the team."

A smiling Laird said, "Aye, aye sir," and opened the door to Gunnery Sergeant Jones and Corporal Pride. As they entered, the gunny turned to the corporal and asked, "Where was that contraband, Corporal?"

"Gunny, I think it is in my tunic, but I do not know if these gentlemen would be aware of its contents." Everyone smiled as the corporal pulled out a bottle of whisky from his jacket and gave it to Jones. Jones then turned and gave it to the commander saying, "Sir, I know that this is against regulations, but I think the good doctor has done great things these past few weeks for the naval service. He deserves to be saluted in the proper manner, which, sir, is not against the regulations."

Commander Jameson smiling and in on the subterfuge having paid for the bottle himself, said, "Thank you, Gunnery Sergeant." He turned to face the doctor saying, "Gunny do you have any glasses or do we have to do this the marine way?"

The gunnery sergeant pulled his other hand from behind his back and produced the correct number of small paper cups. He held them one at a time to the commander who poured out six glasses, one for each of the team except of course for Brand who was too young to drink, plus knowing the doctor would not approve of mixing booze with the drugs the young ensign was taking. Brand knowing the protocol, for he had attended many parties for the faculty where he was too young to partake, picked up his water glass like the rest of the team in a toast to the doctor's promotion.

"Gentlemen," the commander began, "I would like you to raise your glass to Lt. Hiram Feldman, United States Naval Medical Corps. Feldman, congratulations on your promotion. Everyone assembled here salutes you for your skills, professionalism, dedication to duty and above all, friendship." They raised their glasses and said in unison, "Well done, Dr. Feldman."

Each of them drank the deep brown liquid with a few of them gasping as the harsh liquor hit their throats, although the three marine non-coms thought this high-end whisky was a bit weak.

After each man took his turn at shaking hands with the new full lieutenant, Commander Jameson said to the team, "Gentlemen, I guess we need to get some train tickets set up so we can go back to Washington." Everyone smiled at the news. Even Brand, as apprehensive as he was about being stuck in some office for the duration, was happy with the announcement. Anything would be an improvement over being in the hospital.

Jameson smiled, but he also pondered how he would get a Pullman berth in the next few days on a train system that was at overcapacity.

But, then another thought hit him, his orders were from the highest offices in the land, and things could be arranged when you had clout.

9

6 February 1942
Union Train Station
Los Angeles, California

- Naval Coastal Frontiers re-designated Sea Frontiers; Eastern, Gulf, Caribbean, Panama, Hawaiian, Northwest, Western and Philippines.
- United States and Britain established Combined Chiefs of Staff (CCS).

The seven sailors and marines took the train from San Diego to Los Angeles early in the morning and arrived with three hours to kill. Ensign Brand wanted to make a call to a friend in the city, and it was approved by the commander. But, everywhere Brand went, he was accompanied by at least two marines and usually one of the officers. They did not want Brand accosted by the shore patrol or any other individual who wanted to know why this lanky kid was in an officer's uniform. So armed with a dime and two marines, the entourage waited in line by phone booths that were packed with soldiers, sailors and marines. Gunnery Sergeant Jones, scowled at anyone who came near the young ensign which usually made them move to another line.

Finally, a booth emptied. Brand got in and shut the door with the marines standing guard outside. Brand, knowing the number by heart dialed but the phone didn't ring. He dialed again and got the same dead reply. He dialed the operator, asking her to call the number. In the usual gruff manner of overworked operators, she said it was not a working number and probably had been disconnected. He thanked her, retrieved his dime, and walked out of the booth. Jones saw the stern look on Brand's face and asked if he had gotten a busy signal or no answer.

"No, absolutely nothing." Brand continued, "The operator tried calling for me, and she said the number was no longer in service and had been disconnected. Izzy has had this number since I was a student at Cal Tech. We talked last November. I wonder what happened."

When he returned to the coffee shop where the others were waiting, he sat down next to the commander and saw the waitress had brought him another Coca-Cola. He looked at the commander and said, "Thank you, sir, for the Coca-Cola. I seem to be getting hooked on these things."

The newly minted full lieutenant, Dr. Feldman, spoke first. "The reason you like those things is they are full of caffeine, just like coffee. Then you add a big hit of sugar, and you're juiced up like two cups of coffee. Don't drink too many of those things, James, or you will stay up all night."

James nodded his understanding. The commander inquired about his phone call. "Did you get to talk to your friend?"

"No sir. Seems his phone was not working and the operator said it was probably disconnected. I should see if he moved or took on some new work associated with the war. He is a top mathematician, and I'm sure he's in high demand."

The commander nodded at Brand's logical assessment saying, "Well, you are probably right on that. Every top scientist in the country is being rounded up and asked to do their part, especially anyone with heavy math skills. I am certain he will turn up soon. Once we get to Washington, we can put out some feelers to see where he is."

"Great, sir. I will get you his information once we get to Washington." Brand looked to his left and then to his right and moved closer to Jameson. "Sir," he whispered, "my friend's name is Isuro Tomaguchi. Do you think he's in trouble?"

Jameson flinched when he heard the Japanese name but quickly replied, "James, your friend is Japanese?"

Brand nodded his head. "Izzy, actually Dr. Tomaguchi, is a brilliant mathematician and taught me a lot about surviving my years at Cal Tech. He is from Okinawa and dislikes the Japanese a great deal."

Jameson thought about the last comment and wondered if being from Okinawa would help his situation. He had been informed about the Custodial Detention List the FBI used to detain thousands of enemy aliens and wondered if James' friend was caught up in their web.

"James, do not say anything about your friend to anyone else but me. People are paranoid right now about anything that looks or sounds Japanese and your friend, even though he has been in America for many years may be considered a threat." He looked at the face of the young Ensign and saw the sadness expressed in his eyes. "Let me look into this once we are back in Washington. I will see if my friends in Naval Intelligence can help."

James seemed to be all right with the answer and knew all too well about the hate against all things Japanese. "Sir, thank you for your help and I will keep this to myself."

Commander Jameson smiled back and then he turned to see the gunny holding two bottles of Coca-Cola and knew he was coming to the rescue. "Gunny, are those both for you or does the ensign get one?"

The gunny smiled and looking at the commander said, "Sir, both bottles are for the ensign. This stuff is too sweet for me unless you add something to it, but then it would not be good for the ensign."

Both Jameson and Brand laughed at the comment and the young ensign gratefully accepted both bottles.

Three hours later, they boarded their train. Brand had never been in a Pullman car before and was amazed to see the nice size room with upper and lower berths and a private toilet. Very swank, he thought for a kid from Flagstaff. He would be rooming with Dr. Feldman, who always hovered and carried his medical bag wherever he went. The commander and Lieutenant Flannigan were next door. The three marine non-coms were not so lucky but were given separate seats in the car next to the Pullman. Once every few minutes, night and day, one of the marines walked through the car to make sure all was in order. The commander had a word with the porter and chief conductor to explain the situation to make sure no one else asked questions.

The train pulled out at 4:30 P.M. right on schedule and headed east. Around 6:30 P.M., the commander knocked on the door of Brand's cabin, asking if they were ready for dinner. The four officers then went to the dining car for first-class passengers while the marine non-coms used the other dining car, which was still better than normal marine chow. Brand had been on trains since he was young, traveling about freely since he was sixteen, going to meetings up and down the east coast but this was his first trans-continental trip in a private sleeping car.

During dinner, no discussion of navy business was permitted, and nothing was to be said of any scientific concepts or ideas. Jameson didn't want people wondering who these officers were and what they were up to. Most of the conversation was about baseball, the scenery, post-war plans, and finding girlfriends for Feldman and Flannigan. Each of the older officers told Brand they would also find a suitable girl for him, but that would have to wait until he got older, which always riled Brand but in a humorous way.

As they finished their meal, Commander Jameson noticed a navy captain sitting with an army colonel waving for him to come over to their table. Jameson knew he was in for a challenge as to what a commander was doing with junior officers in a first-class dining car or some other sort of senior officer swagger. He told the young officers to proceed to the cabin and turned to meet the captain.

"Good evening, sir, may I be of some assistance to the Captain and the Colonel?" Jameson asked in his most professional manner, showing respect to the senior officers.

The captain replied, "My name is Boswell, and this is Colonel Stone. We were wondering what you were doing with the three young men in this car."

"Beg the Captain's pardon, but they are all traveling with me back to Washington."

"No, Commander," the navy captain said, "I want to know why are those young officers in this car. It is customary that they are in the next car and eat dinner in their respective dining car."

Jameson knew he would use a hammer if needed but started out slowly.

"Sir, the young gentlemen are assigned to cabins in the first-class Pullman and this is where they have been assigned for their meals. The marine lieutenant is in my cabin and the other two are next door."

The colonel now butted in, "Highly unusual that junior officers are being set up this way. Totally out of line with good military conduct. There were several other full colonels and lieutenant colonels who could not get berths on this train with orders to Washington."

The colonel turned to the captain saying, "Captain Boswell, is this the way the navy is running this war? Where are the priorities in the naval service?"

Captain Boswell, like the good colonel had also been drinking but neither were drunk, just getting tipsy. "Colonel, the navy knows its priorities. I will find out what is going on."

Commander Jameson decided to cut the argument short before it got out of hand.

"Sir, if I may show you my orders, I think you will understand the situation better."

"I don't need to look at your orders, Commander. I know when I see things not being done by regulation and this is one of them." The captain was now becoming indignant and pulling rank to impress his army compatriot.

Again, Commander Jameson said with a stern voice, "Sir, I must insist that you review my orders to clarify this situation."

The captain was getting a bit peeved. He noticed Colonel Stone was watching to see how the navy handled a situation like this and said in a perturbed voice, "Let me see these orders, and if they do not satisfy me, I will make sure you are sent somewhere to count spoons for the duration."

The colonel smiled at the threat, thinking to himself he could use that line on some of his people.

The commander handed a brown envelope to the captain who pulled out a single piece of paper and read:

J. EUGENE PORTER

Office of the Commander in Chief, United States Fleet
January 23, 1942
Notice to All Commands: Special Orders

The bearer of this document, Commander Fredrick L. Jameson, USNR, is on an assignment classified top secret. No questions shall be asked of the commander or any individual reporting to him concerning his mission.

All commands are to provide whatever assistance is deemed necessary by the commander in the fulfillment of his mission.

If for any reason, a command is unable to comply with a request made by Commander Jameson or if there are any questions regarding this mission, the command should contact the undersigned immediately providing reasons for not supporting the commander and his team.

All commands are to provide access to all communications as required and transportation requests by the commander are to be handled on a 5A basis.

Admiral E. J. King
Commander in Chief, United States Fleet

Captain Boswell looked at the letter again, saw the signature, then looked up at the commander in a state of semi-shock. He had never seen an order from Admiral King nor did he ever expect to meet him. The commander took the orders from the captain, handed them to Colonel Stone and told the colonel, "Please read this, sir."

The captain was still thinking about what to say to the commander as he looked over to see the colonel turning pale as well. The colonel returned the orders to Commander Jameson who put them back in the envelope and placed it inside his coat pocket.

"Captain, do you have any questions for me?" He looked at the colonel, "Sir, any questions?"

The colonel shook his head no. The captain followed, "No Commander, I have no questions. I apologize for any misunderstanding." The captain now wondered if he would be the one counting spoons somewhere in the Canal Zone for the duration.

U-BOAT SCOURGE

The commander looked at the captain and spoke very softly, "Sir, I did not mean to compromise you or the good colonel," looking quickly at the colonel. "However, our mission is, as you have seen, of an essential nature and I apologize for causing the incident in the first place. I can tell you the young marine lieutenant was wounded in the Philippines and has returned by order of Admiral Hart to report directly to Admiral King on the situation in the Far East. I cannot go any further than that. Rest assured, we will be maintaining a low profile on our passage to Chicago and on to Washington. I have three marine non-coms who are providing additional security. They are prowling the train day and night to ensure the integrity of our mission. That is all I can tell you and I would appreciate your discretion on what I have told you and especially on my orders."

The captain said, "Commander, you have my word, and I am sure the colonel's. There will be absolute silence on what we have seen and what you have told us."

The colonel, still flustered, shook his head in agreement.

"Thank you, Captain, for your understanding. With your permission, I will take your leave."

The commander came to attention in the most formal way, turned, and left the car.

Captain Boswell and Colonel Stone looked at each other. Then the captain spoke, "I don't know about you, but I need another drink, and I don't ever want to run into that commander again."

The colonel slowly replied, "I agree with you, and I think I need two drinks so I can forget seeing those orders.

Jameson walked back to the Pullman car and saw the gunnery sergeant waiting outside his cabin. "Sir, seems you had a discussion with the captain and colonel."

Jameson nodded but before he could say anything Sergeant Jones continued, "I guess there are a lot of nosy people in our navy and army, so we need to maintain a low profile as long as Ensign Brand is in our charge."

The commander smiled, stating the obvious, "Yes, Gunny, there are a lot of nosy and self-important people who are full of themselves. I agree, we are going to have to keep Brand under wraps. I appreciate your keen observations on the current situation within the navy and army. If you will make sure Laird and Pride are on their best behavior, perhaps we can get to Washington without further incidents."

10

8 February 1942
Chicago, Illinois

- Japanese submarine shells Midway Island.
- Japanese naval vessel sunk: Destroyer **Natsushio,** by submarine **S-37,** Makassar Strait, Netherlands East Indies area.

It took two days to get to Chicago. On arrival they had to change trains for the overnight leg to Washington, D.C. Again, the navy had them in first-class Pullmans with the marines in the adjacent car. They had to wait five hours before the train boarded and Jameson did not want to stray too far from the station. There were hundreds of sailors, soldiers, airmen and marines walking about all looking for their next train. There was also a large group of Shore Patrol and Military Police to augment Chicago's finest. Jameson wanted to hide Brand for the next few hours before he could board the train so they looked around to find the restaurant and were lucky enough to find two tables next to each other that would accommodate all seven men. He had been chuckling about this for the past week, ever since San Diego, thinking about how a full commander was leading a ragtag group of sailors and marines about the country to safely deposit one eighteen-year-old boy wonder.

All through dinner and later as they slowly drank their coffee and Coca-Colas to keep the table from being taken, he thought about his situation and began to appreciate this little group of men, especially young Mr. Brand. Jameson had met him only once before when he was much younger, if that was possible, and was taken by his brilliance and his demeanor. Now, he fully realized the other side of Brand who had taken on the sadist petty officer who was beating up recruits, took him down, then survived an even more brutal attack by the brig sergeant who could have killed him. Brand did not discuss the situation further after he provided the facts and an assessment which perfectly coincided with Dr. Feldman's records. Brand was truly an amazing fellow.

Brand started to look around the restaurant and asked a young, but not so pretty waitress for the restrooms. She pointed out the door and to the left. Brand asked permission to use the facilities. Jameson, fearing more challenges from the SPs and MPs, asked Sergeant Jones and Corporal Pride to escort him. Flannigan looked up and said, "I could use the head as well so I'll join this field trip."

Everyone laughed and the four of them walked out of the restaurant in search of relief. Feldman turned to Jameson and asked, "Is it always going to be like this for Brand? Will he always be herded around by a security team?"

Jameson shook his head saying, "I don't know for sure. He is so young and naïve so for right now, I think the answer is yes. He is too valuable to the war effort to have him harmed again. The navy needs him, so we will make sure he arrives in Washington in good shape and without any publicity."

The restroom, or head as the naval service called it, was quite large, which you would expect in a major railway station and reeked of piss and beer, which was also expected. Flannigan told Corporal Pride to stay inside and told the gunny to watch the exit. Each of them, like Flannigan, had a .45-caliber Colt on their belt and took little guff from anyone in the area. Flannigan went to the trough to relieve himself and Brand went in a stall for his business was of a greater nature. After Flannigan had finished, he told the gunny, "I am going over to get myself some smokes at the shop over there," pointing to twenty-five yards away. "Keep an eye on the ensign, Gunny."

The gunny always a man of few words, said, "Aye, Aye, Lieutenant," and walked inside to relieve himself. As the gunny stood at the trough, in came a group of six second lieutenants of the U.S. Army Air Corps, who had finished their advanced flight school and were heading off to their first posting. Each one was highly inebriated and wearing their best slouch hat with the headband removed; most were perched high on the back of their heads. They were quite a sight with most having cigarettes in their mouths and smelling of beer. The gunny, sensing problems zipped up, turned to the stall occupied by the ensign. As he did this, Brand walked out looking for a place to wash his hands.

"Look, fellas," one of the lieutenants pointed, "a real live squid. Hello squid," he said to Brand. Brand smiled and said, "Hello, sir," and walked to the sink.

"Fellas, the squid talks and he seems to be a nice boy. Guess the navy is recruiting from the boy scouts." The Air Corps was still taking only college men with at least two years of college, and many had been in ROTC making them between twenty and twenty-four.

Brand smiled again and started to wash his hands. One of the Air Corps lieutenants walked over to him and slapped him hard on the back yelling, "What kind of boy scout are you?" The slap hit Brand on one of his cracked ribs, and he grunted in pain, turned pale, and began to stumble. The Air Corps lieutenant turned to his buddies and said, "Look the squid grunts like a fish, and he seems to be getting ill. I wonder what happens if you hit a squid, does it make a loud noise or does it just go bang."

The Air Corps lieutenant was just getting ready to swing when a hand grabbed his fist, and yanked it back dropping the fly boy to the floor. Lieutenant Flannigan had been walking slowly to the restroom when Corporal Pride waved his fist in a "come on quick" motion that all marines knew. Flannigan entered, saw the gunny about to take out the flyboy, but jumped in front, preventing the gunny from hitting a superior officer, and stopping the drunken hand from hitting the young ensign.

When the fly boy hit the ground, his comrades stepped toward Flannigan, but right behind the marine lieutenant, the gunny was now pointing his .45 Colt directly at the oncoming aerial heroes, stopping them in their tracks.

The corporal, seeing what was going on, acted on his standing orders and ran to the restaurant for reinforcements. He didn't have to say much more than, "We have a problem. Come quick." The commander, Sergeant Laird, and Feldman followed the corporal, nearly running over a few civilians on the way. As they entered the restroom, they saw an Air Corps lieutenant holding his hand, Brand holding his chest, Flannigan holding up Brand, and the gunny holding a gun on the other lieutenants.

As he entered the room, Corporal Pride yelled, "Attention, senior officer on deck!" The Air Corps lieutenants did not move at the presence of a navy commander, but when Sergeant Laird walked in behind him with an MP captain they slowly stood to attention.

Feldman took immediate charge of Brand and the commander signaled to get him out of there. But first, the good doctor looked at the hand of the offending Air Corps lieutenant and pronounced, "Ligament sprain. It will be okay in about a week, Lieutenant." And then he knelt real close to him and whispered to him so only he could hear, "You were lucky, flyboy. The gunny or the lieutenant would have broken both of your arms and probably your legs, so be very careful."

Feldman then smiled and got up to take charge of Brand. As he started to help Brand move, the MP captain said, "Nobody moves until I find out what is going on in here."

Commander Jameson turned to the captain, but the captain did not come to attention. "Captain, is the Army totally blind to rank?"

The captain, annoyed but saw the equivalent to a lieutenant colonel standing in front of him, came to attention and saluted. Jameson returned his salute and asked the captain to step outside. He motioned for the doctor to help Brand, which he did with the assistance of Sergeant Laird.

The captain started to protest again, but Jameson cut him off. The Air Corps lieutenants were all standing, and the aggressor held his deeply distressed hand. The gunny had returned his sidearm to its holster and the corporal watched everyone else, including three additional MPs who had joined their captain. Funny, Pride thought, when the shit hits the fan, every damn SP and MP shows up to get in a few hits.

"Captain, my name is Jameson, and I will be happy to let this incident slide for the good of inter-service cooperation."

"Sir," the MP captain responded, "no one is permitted to be carrying a sidearm, but my men and a few other men so equipped. This is a violation of the Military District of Chicago, and your men must come with me to make statements. The same goes for the lieutenants in there."

A navy lieutenant walked up with two shore patrolmen. He asked his counterpart in the military police for a report on what was happening. The captain began his report but again was cut off by Jameson.

"Lieutenant, what is your name?"

"Sir, Bennett, Sir, Robert R."

"My name is Jameson and as I have been talking to the good captain, sorry, your name please?"

The army captain was becoming flustered. "Sir, Powell, John D."

"Thank you, Captain Powell, for introducing yourself. As I was saying, Mr. Bennett, this situation, if you would like to call it that, is over. There has been no foul except for a hurt hand on one of the drunken Air Corps lieutenants and the recurrence of an injury caused by a slap on the back of the ensign standing with the good doctor."

"Sir," the captain interjected. "Firearms are not permitted, and a gun was pulled, two officers have received injuries and several army and navy regulations have been broken. I must insist that you and your men accompany me to the station house to make a full report."

The commander now had to use all the command powers he had learned at the academy and in his business career.

"Gentlemen, who are your senior officers?" The commander looked at each one with a searing stare burning into them, they quickly reported.

"Sir," the navy lieutenant said, "my commanding officer is Lieutenant Commander Perkins."

The army captain looked at the commander now bearing down on him saying, "Sir, my commanding officer is Major Stillman."

"Good, now we are getting someplace. And where are these two gentlemen right now?"

The navy lieutenant responded, "Sir, they are both in their offices on the second floor next to the station manager. They work side by side and should be in the office."

"Good, let's go see them. If you would have your men wait here, we will go see them now."

"Sir, they usually are not supposed to be disturbed except in the case of a major situation."

"Well, Captain Powell and Lieutenant Bennett, you are both about to see what a true major situation looks like."

Both officers told their men to keep the area cleared of all other individuals, and no one was to leave the scene.

It took about five minutes to walk through the huge station and climb stairs to the second-floor office of the Shore Patrol and the Military Police Headquarters. When the three officers walked in, there were two non-coms from each service and two very drunk enlisted men sitting in chairs waiting to be charged. When the officers walked in led by the army captain, the sergeant did not get up from his chair but said, "Hello, Captain, how are things on the plat..." Then he saw the man in the back with three broad stripes of a navy commander. The navy rating saw it first and jumped up to full attention, followed by the army sergeant. "Sir," they said in unison. "How can we be of service?"

The army captain tried to say something but was stopped by Commander Jameson, "At ease."

"At least someone in this command understands military courtesy." These comments were meant for the army captain, and they hit like a spear in the heart.

"Where are the commanders of this unit, Petty Officer?" looking at the senior ranking non-com.

"Sir, I will get them for you. They are in their office. Shall I announce you, sir?"

"No need." He walked quickly into the office followed by the navy lieutenant and the army captain. Jameson found the senior officers playing a game of acey-deucy. They looked up to see a very tall navy commander standing in the doorway and jumped out of their chairs in a total disarray. The army major had no tie, no shoes, and smelled of tobacco.

The navy lieutenant commander wasn't in much better shape with no jacket, no shoes, and smelling of beer. The commander in full voice, said, "I take it you two gentlemen are in command of this operation?"

Both officers quickly saluted and the salute was returned with a curt, "At ease, gentlemen. I have your two young deputies with me, and they have a story to tell you that you should hear and then I will tell you what you need to do. Captain, you were first on the scene, so please tell your superiors what is going on."

The captain gave a quick recap of the events, and as he talked of a pulled firearm, the two senior officers began to get very concerned.

"Thank you, Captain. Why don't you and the lieutenant step outside for a minute so I can talk to your commanding officers."

They looked at each other and decided the best thing to do was to comply. As soon as the door closed, the commander asked his question. "Gentlemen, I think it is in the best interest of inter-service cooperation to forget what has occurred. I will not press charges against the Air Corps lieutenant and the other officers with him, but I would recommend that you impress upon them the need to stay sober while wearing the uniform of the armed services." Jameson looked at the navy lieutenant commander and continued. "Are there any questions gentlemen?"

"Sir," Major Stillman said as he regained his composure, "I am afraid any firearm not in the control of a police unit or guard unit of the service is a chargeable offense and we," he looked at his navy counterpart, "cannot overlook this offense. We need to conduct a thorough investigation and then refer this to the Judge Advocate General."

Jameson expected he would not be able to bull his way through this, so he went for a quick kill. "Major, I understand the regulations. The gunnery sergeant was acting as a guard and is authorized to carry a weapon as are the other marines in this command. Furthermore, I would like to show you my orders which should clarify this position."

He pulled out the envelope, handing it to Lieutenant Commander Perkins, who pulled the major over. They looked at the commander who glared at them with a great amount of seriousness. "Gentlemen, if you would like, I will have your petty officer call the number on this card, which is the chief of staff to Admiral King, and he can put you in touch with the admiral. Major, if you need additional clarification, I have been authorized to let any army unit contact General Marshall for validation."

Jameson continued, "Now, I think these orders make it perfectly clear the mission we are on is top secret and requires a high level of security. That is the reason for the armed marines who are authorized to shoot to kill." He wondered if he did have that level of authority. "So, gentlemen, should we take the recommendation I gave you a few moments ago for the good of both services or should we make a phone call."

Both the major and the lieutenant commander looked at one another and again, stared at the name on the orders. Almost in unison they responded, "Sir, I think we must talk to those flyboys to make sure that military protocol is followed at all times, especially in areas populated by civilians." They passed the orders back to the commander and said, "Sir, what else can we do for you and your people."

The commander, still not smiling said, "You can make sure we get on our train which departs in about thirty minutes. Then make sure you forget about the orders you just saw. You can tell your subordinates anything you want but not about this mission. Do you both understand?"

"Yes sir," came the reply. The major asked the two junior officers into the office. They came in and stood at attention.

Major Stillwell in a very authoritative voice said, "You will personally ensure that the commander and his party are escorted to the train and make sure that they board the train. You will both stand by to see if the commander needs any additional assistance until the train leaves. You will have your men escort the young Air Corps officers to the holding area until they are sober. Then you will make sure they get on their trains. Are there any questions?"

"No sir," came the answer and both knew whatever had happened in the office, they were now being ordered to shut up and do as told.

The commander shook the hands of the major and the lieutenant commander and said, "Thank you both for your help and consideration. I think both of these young officers did their job in an exemplary way and should be congratulated on their professionalism."

With that, he took their salutes and walked out with the two younger officers.

U-BOAT SCOURGE

When they had gone, Major Stillwell and Lieutenant Commander Perkins exhaled and looked at each other. The major said, "I still am not too sure what just happened, but I don't want to know any more than what I saw on those orders."

The navy officer sat down and said, "I hope I never see orders like that again, nor do I ever want to see that commander."

Commander Jameson met the others and they were all escorted to the train. As they settled in their cabins, he could see the navy lieutenant and the army captain having one hell of a discussion. It continued as the train pulled out of the station.

As the train picked up speed, the gunny stepped up behind Jameson and said, "Sir, seems that Mr. Brand attracts trouble no matter what. I hope this is just a matter of coincidence, but damn, sir, I am getting worried about him."

The commander turned to Jones saying, "You are correct, Gunny. It appears Mr. Brand is a magnet for trouble and it is up to us to make sure he stays out of it. Once we get to Washington, we will get him up to Bethesda for another medical exam. The doc thinks the hit on the back may have aggravated his cracked ribs. So, once we get picked up at the station, it's off to the hospital where we can stash our man."

The gunny responded, "What's next after that, sir? Do we have a place for him to stay or is he going into BOQ in Washington?"

"Gunny, that is a whole new ball of wax, and I think we had better approach the admiral on this. I think if he is located with a bunch of other young officers, he might get in more trouble which would not be a good idea." The commander again looked out the window before commenting, "I may recommend he stay with me at my house in Bethesda, but whatever is decided someone is going to have to ensure his safety. I don't think our mission here is over, Gunny, but only time will tell."

Gunnery Sergeant Jones remarked, "Sir, I was hoping to get into battle once more or at least serve on a battleship. Don't take this wrong, Commander, but being a babysitter for a smart kid is not my idea of being a marine."

Jameson turned to Jones and replied, "I understand, Gunny, really I do. I don't have a clue what's going to happen next with Mr. Brand or for

85

that matter, what else is going to happen anywhere. We all want to serve our country and if possible, most want to see action. You know better than this," pointing at his top "been there ribbon" denoting the Navy Cross for heroism in action in World War I, "but just like you, our young wannabe hero, Ensign Brand, is being pulled from what he wanted to do. He is now going to play his part to win the war in the best possible manner his education and skills allow. Each of us, including you and me, receive our orders and we hope those orders match the objective in some small or large way of winning this war. That is all we can do and all we can ask for."

The gunny again looked out the window saying, "I know you're telling me the straight story, but I would love to be with my marines doing the things I was trained to do, fighting the enemy."

The commander cut him off saying, "Gunny, you are close to fifty years old." The gunny nodded yes but did not speak. Jameson continued, "I doubt they would send you off to lead a landing party even though you are in apparently good shape. What they would do is have you in a training billet, imparting your knowledge to thousands of recruits who need to learn how to stay alive. That's a very important job, even more important than leading a squad on an assault of a hostile shore. I would love to be given command of a destroyer or even a patrol boat, but the powers that be know my skills and experience are better suited to helping win the war by developing or improving the science of war. But by God, I would love to go to sea again."

Both men stared out the window as the train picked up speed. The gunny finally spoke, "Damn it, Commander, I have not known you very long, but you make good sense. Maybe I won't see combat again, but I can help these young kids coming up learn the skills that will keep them alive. That goes for Mr. Brand as well, but I doubt they will ever let him even leave the country, knowing what he knows."

The commander again turned to Jones, reflecting on the marine's remarks, "Gunny, I think that you and I are going help win the war in a support capacity, but I have a feeling that Mr. Brand will definitely see things in other parts of the world because of his potential. The only danger is making sure he comes out of those travels in one piece. I don't know what is going to happen to him in the near term, but I have a feeling I will be involved in some of his assignments and that is fine with me. It is a blessing to watch him come up with solutions to problems that most of us do not even see. But only time will tell."

The commander and Gunnery Sergeant Jones walked down the small hallway to check in with Dr. Feldman for a report on the ensign and start planning their move to the Naval Hospital in Bethesda, Maryland.

PART 2

Part 2

11

9 February 1942
Bethesda Naval Hospital

- Transport **Lafayette,** (AP-53), former French liner Normandie, burns at New York pier.
- Japanese land at Singapore Island.

Dr. Feldman left the private room of Ensign Brand and waited to speak with Commander Jameson who was on the phone at the nurse's station. Sergeant Laird and Corporal Pride were sitting outside Brand's room as guard and caretaker.

Jameson held up his hand to prevent the doctor from saying anything as Feldman heard one side of the conversation.

"No, Admiral, he will not be able to move out of here for at least two more days. The doctors want him to get some more rest which will allow his ribs to heal. Yes sir, he will be fine and able to begin any projects that may be assigned." The commander stared out of the window at nothing and closed his eyes for just a second. "Yes, Admiral, he can look at some documentation and assessments to get him up to speed on whatever you wish, but it would be best if he did not get involved in any lengthy discussions. He is very strong but, as I said earlier, the doctors here are unanimous that they want him to stay calm and to stay quiet. Yes sir, if you will have the information dispatched to his room, the guards will ensure security. They know who is allowed into his room."

The commander listened intently concerning the materials being sent over and his role in the project. Finally, the conversation, came to an end with the commander saying, "Admiral, if we can have the officer with the dispatches stand by while Brand reviews them, then we can get them back into your safe keeping by this afternoon. The ensign is a very fast reader and has an incredible memory."

Again, Jameson looked out the nearby window while he listened to the orders he was receiving. "Yes sir, I will report back to you once the courier leaves, and I will give you an update on Brand's condition by 1700 hours."

The line went dead without any goodbyes, which was to be expected from the chief of staff to Admiral King. No time for chit chat, or as some people were saying these days, "Don't you know that there's a war going on?" This was getting a bit overdone for Jameson's liking, but it did have more than a kernel of truth.

Jameson asked Dr. Feldman, "How is the ensign?"

Feldman did not answer immediately but asked, "What do they expect at HQ? Brand is doing better than most people under these circumstances, but it is going to take time. And it sounds like they want to put him to work before he gets well."

Jameson smiled knowing Feldman was intensely loyal to the young ensign and was always checking on him like a sheepdog guarding his flock. "Doc, there are a lot of people who are hoping the young ensign can give them a miracle or two and defeat the enemy without firing a shot. Seems that Admiral Turner's report to the chief has made its way to just about every senior department head in the navy. They all have problems they don't know how to solve, or the way they are doing it is too slow for the current situation." The commander looked toward the door where the guards were standing and wondered if he needed even more security for Brand. "Adding to this atmosphere is Admiral King's desire to be as aggressive as possible by taking the war to the enemy. So, what we can do, Doc, is to get Brand healthy but at the same time protect him from every command in the navy who wants a piece of him."

The doctor grimaced a bit saying, "Commander, I know you are doing your best to shield him from these requests, but if we can have just a few more days, Brand will be in much better shape."

Jameson looked around to make sure no one was listening and whispered, "That was the case I was making to Admiral Willson. We must provide some protection for Brand otherwise every Tom, Dick, and Harry will want to control him. I sent a request that Brand be a direct report to Willson and therefore under the umbrella of Admiral King. No one is going to pull anything on King. The admiral said he would take it up with the Boss in the next couple of days and let me know. And, by the way, the admiral agrees that this would be the best thing for the navy and Brand."

The doctor let out a deep breath. "Sir, I know that you are doing your best and if we can get Brand under one leader, he would not be pulled apart by so many competing claims. By the way, what is coming over for Brand to look at?"

"Sorry, Doc, but that's classified. When the courier shows up, no one will be allowed in as Brand reviews the information. I don't even know what is coming over, but I will be asked to sit in as he goes over the documents."

"Well, at least we don't have a gaggle of brass coming over to talk to him. Thank you for keeping it under control." The doctor looked at his watch saying, "I better order up some food and drink for our young ensign so he can do his best and not be disturbed during this review."

The commander smiled and watched as the doctor discussed the ensign's food and made sure there was enough water.

About an hour later, a lieutenant junior grade came down the corridor with a marine guard. Sergeant Laird spied the officer first and gave the gunny the high sign. As the commander had requested, the gunny knocked on the door of Brand's room to signal someone was heading their way. The commander put on his jacket and tightened his tie so he looked the part of an officer and gentleman. Brand, sitting on a chair next to a desk with a typewriter on it, slowly stood and adjusted his robe. The doctor shrugged knowing Brand wanted to be walking around more, so he let his usual "sit down" comment slide.

A knock on the door came, and the gunny opened it saying, "Lieutenant Sullivan from Admiral Willson's office, sir. Please enter lieutenant, you are expected." The gunny stood at attention as the J.G. walked into the room and stood at attention in front of the commander.

"Sir, Lieutenant Junior Grade Sullivan, reporting as ordered by Admiral Willson." The J.G. waited for a reply.

"Sullivan, you must be new on the job. I have not seen you in the admiral's office before."

Jameson looked at the young officer with a marine corporal standing behind him. He noticed the marine was armed with a Colt and Sullivan's battered briefcase was handcuffed to his wrist. "Commander, I began my duties two weeks ago, so yes sir, I am brand new to the job." Sullivan looked around the room and noticed the young man standing by the desk in a regulation navy robe and a lieutenant of the Naval Medical Corps standing next to him. He had been briefed by the admiral personally, which had never occurred before, that he was to bring the briefcase to this room at Bethesda and give it to a Commander Jameson who would be in the company of a young ensign who was a patient in the hospital. He was to give the briefcase to the commander and wait with his escort until the commander returned it. He did not have to ask the admiral how long he was to wait because he was informed the very first day on the job that if an admiral wanted to tell you something, he would. Otherwise, stay with the briefcase until it was returned or other orders were provided.

"Good to have you on board, Mr. Sullivan. I hope we will not keep you sitting around too long. You have no idea what you are carrying in that briefcase, do you, Mr. Sullivan?" The commander noticed the young man in front of him handled himself very well and did not seem too in awe of rank. He looked like a ROTC graduate from an Ivy League school, so he wasn't too impressed by people in high places.

"No sir, I have no knowledge of its contents. I am to deliver it to you, have you sign for it, wait until you are finished with whatever is in the briefcase, then I will take possession of the case, and ask you to sign the return form stating you have returned all materials in the case. Those are my orders, and I hereby request you sign the form the corporal is holding."

Lieutenant Junior Grade Sullivan nodded to the corporal who walked forward to the commander and handed him the forms, which of course had five copies and provided the commander a pen to sign them. Commander Jameson looked at the form, walked over to Brand's desk and sat down to review the pages. He had learned long ago in this man's navy that you never sign anything unless you read it thoroughly. After reading the form, he signed all five copies and returned them to the corporal.

As soon as the formalities were finalized, Sullivan gave the key to the corporal who unlocked the handcuff and handed the briefcase to the commander.

"Sir, is there any place the corporal and I can wait and perhaps get some food while you review the contents?" Sullivan was twisting the wrist where the handcuff was attached and looked happy to be rid of the briefcase.

"Doctor, could you find some place for these gentlemen to get some food and perhaps a few comfortable chairs while we go over these papers?"

"Lieutenant Sullivan, I am most happy to be of service to fellow members of the naval service." He smiled that grin which everyone found so infectious. The corporal and the JG turned and followed the doc out.

The gunny put his head in the door asking, "Commander, shall I secure the room?" Meaning no one was allowed inside while the contents of the briefcase were being reviewed.

"Yes, Gunny, button up the hatch if you would. Admit only members of our team which includes the Doc."

"Aye, aye Commander," the gunny said and closed the door.

Jameson knew no one except Admiral King would get by the gunny and Sergeant Laird while the room was in a secure state. Jameson took the briefcase, entered the combination he had received prior to delivery, and opened the lock. Brand sat down, pulled out a pad of paper and pencils. Several pencils were colored so he could quickly note key facts or issues that concerned him. He had developed his own style of note taking when he was very young and had kept using it throughout his university days. Some of his note taking was in the form of shorthand, but not the secretarial kind. It looked more like some sort of math problem with all sorts of symbols. Only he could unscramble his notes.

"Okay, Mr. Brand, let's see what the admiral sent us." Jameson looked inside the old leather briefcase and found several files with red ribbons, plus several stapled documents that looked to be about forty or fifty pages in length. These did not have the ribbons, but each had Top Secret stamped on every page.

Jameson pulled out the first file titled, *Summary of U-Boat Attacks January-February 1942*. Handing it to the young ensign, he said, "James, I wish you luck with whatever you think you can do about these files. People are dying right off our own coast; I was briefed on this yesterday by Admiral Willson. The navy is under tremendous pressure to stop or slow these attacks, but so far the enemy is slaughtering our ships."

Brand looked to his superior officer and friend. "I will do my best to help. I am not too sure what to do until I find out what the real situation is and what has been occurring on our side to stop it."

Jameson said nothing more but handed James the other reports on ship movements, current air and naval assets with their locations, sighting reports, and intelligence estimates. James began to read.

The first sinking off the east coast of New Jersey was the SS Cyclops on January 11. Two more ships were sunk over the next two days with one sunk off Cape Hatteras. The last reported sinking was on February 6 for a total loss of twenty-five ships totaling 156,000 tons. More importantly, many were tankers moving oil from Gulf Coast ports to New York and beyond to the UK. Ships were sunk as far south as Miami Beach. Fires were spotted almost each night as ships were sunk within twelve miles of the mainland. Hundreds of merchant mariners had died, and more would die unless something was done.

A few planes had been sent up and down the coast with several sightings and supposedly some U-boats had been hit or sunk. No evidence supported the reported sinkings. One of the intelligence assessments stated, and Brand agreed, that novice flyers without any training would find it hard to hit anything, let alone a diving submarine.

The supporting materials detailed what had been done or requested but there appeared to be little accomplished. Brand knew about the large convoys going back and forth to Europe with both American and Allied ships escorting them. Brand scoured the materials and saw nothing being done in the way of coastal convoys. He also saw there was no blackout along the coast, and he read reports from newspapers all the way to Florida of people watching ships burn right off the coast as amusement parks were operating with every light on.

As he reviewed the reports, Brand began to get angry, not at the Germans but at his own countrymen. Several of the intelligence assessments asked for a total coastal blackout to keep the merchant ships from standing out like sore thumbs against the lighted shoreline. But the requests were turned down for commercial interests. No convoys were being set up because they had so few escorts. Senior staffs recommended ships sailing independently would fare better than unescorted convoys. Brand took out one of his red pencils and quickly did several calculations on this probability, finding the assessment totally false. Unescorted or lightly escorted convoys would provide a five-fold improvement in safety and Brand could prove it.

He spent about an hour going through the reports. As he continued to dig he became more concerned about the lack of clarity in leadership and unity of command. The navy did this, the army did that, the Air Corps did what it wanted, which did not include looking for submarines, and the merchant mariners were totally independent of everything. They did not want to take orders from the navy on the coastal routes like they were doing on the Atlantic crossings.

Brand peered at the commander, who was slowly slogging his way through the materials. Jameson could not read and digest the amounts of information as fast as he could so he thought he would summarize it all for his boss.

"Sir, if you would allow me to summarize what you are looking at as well as providing some suggestions that could help the situation immediately, I think we can finish this job."

Jameson, knowing his young protégé was incredibly fast on the uptake, did not take offense at his comment but said, "James, if you have some ideas that could help, that would be great."

"Sir, first there appears to be several issues of political will or lack thereof compounding a bad situation. This would be the blackouts. The senior leadership must get the lights turned out now. Otherwise, there will be even more slaughter. You know the science of backlighting a target as well as anyone, and by not going to full blackout a lot of ships and men will die."

Jameson considered this a hard sell that would require the Chiefs of Staff or perhaps even the president to weigh in on. Civilian control in wartime is one of those sticky issues that weighs heavily in a democracy. Jameson nodded his concurrence and waved James on to his next point

"Sir, this was only a feeler attack. I calculate that based on the intelligence reports and information the Brits have given us on the capabilities of the German submarines, we are dealing with only five or six U-boats. This calculation shows the number of torpedoes that were probably expended, reports by survivors of cannon fire and the range of the Type IX boat we are facing. They have been incredibly successful, and I would think there are more boats on their way. They will probably do this in several waves and start exactly like this attack by beginning up north off Halifax and then work down to Florida. It would not surprise me if they also entered the Gulf Coast and maybe go all the way down into the lower Caribbean where there are lots of fat tankers coming out of Venezuela."

James looked at one of pages of notes and made two more calculations. He looked up at Jameson saying, "I have some suggestions on how we could do some quick coastal convoys in the daylight hours, sneaking the ships into safe harbor at night. It will add three and a half days to their transit, but they will survive. Also, I need to better understand how planes search for submarines. Same goes for attacks by escorts both by depth charge and deck gun. How do they locate targets, how do they perform escort duties, how do they use electronics such as RADAR and ASDIC, etc.? I would like to talk to some of our submariners to get a better understanding of how they operate, which would give me insights on how the Germans run their boats. We could uncover flaws to help us attack the Germans and perhaps use this information to safeguard our own boats."

The conversation went on for another fifteen minutes with the commander providing some additional thoughts on current inter-service relationships plus some ideas on how the escort system in the Atlantic currently worked.

Brand started typing a report even as the commander provided additional background on naval procedures. In less than sixty minutes, Brand had finished a twenty-page report with a two-page executive summary detailing priorities and timelines for accomplishing the recommendations within the limitations shown in the report.

Jameson read the report as Brand continued to do calculations on attack trajectories, air speeds and elevations for best reconnaissance. He had some other thoughts, but needed to do some field work to better understand the current way things were done.

The commander put the report down and then looked at the young man who was using his slide rule. "James, this is splendid. The reasoning is sound, the examples are shocking, and the supporting calculations and explanations make great sense even to a non-scientist, but I think there are some issues concerning people, both military and civilian, that will be hard to overcome." The commander was concerned about the bluntness of the assessment, especially the blackout and the use of convoys. Brand had been quite open about the need to group ships in convoys, and his supporting calculations were exacting and logical. But some of these thoughts were political dynamite. "Do you feel okay about taking on some dragons with this report?"

The young ensign thought for a moment and with a grin on his face replied, "Hell yes, oh sorry, sir, I mean yes, I am ready."

The commander smiled. He liked what he saw in this young man with one of the top brains in the world and said, "Let's finish the report and get young Mr. Sullivan back in here so we can get this thing started."

12

10 February 1942
Office of Admiral Ernest J. King
Washington, D.C.

- Singapore--General Wavell visits Singapore and orders island held and all remaining RAF personnel withdrawn to Netherlands East Indies.
- Japanese land at Makassar, Celebes.
- U.S. detachment arrives to occupy Christmas Island.

Admiral King was always early and since this was a Monday, an even better reason to start early. He did not take Sunday off, nor any day of the year since December 7. There were no weekends or holidays when you are trying to stave off defeat. And defeat was coming from every direction.

In the Atlantic, the U-boats had found a happy hunting ground along the U.S. coastline. Some twenty-five ships had been sunk in less than thirty days. Everyone from Roosevelt on down was asking how this "east coast" Pearl Harbor had happened and what was the navy doing to stop it. It was one thing to clamp down on the news coming out of the Pacific, but when anyone who lived along the beach could see ships on fire off the coast or see the flotsam of sunken ships including bodies of "our" merchant mariners washing up on the beach, there was no possibility of censorship. He knew the Germans were getting verification of sinkings from the press, which was more accurate information than their U-boat captains were sending via radio.

Then there was the continuing bad news coming out of the Pacific. The navy had lost its battle fleet at Pearl, then lost Guam, then Wake, and now the Philippines were in doubt, and the navy could do nothing to relieve them. The remnants of the Asiatic Fleet consisted of one heavy cruiser, one old light cruiser and some ten old four-stacker destroyers that were falling apart. The submarines of the Asiatic Fleet seemed hopeless in defense of the Philippines and the ones based at Pearl had little to show for their efforts.

King scrutinized the stacks of papers on his desk, grabbed his mug of coffee, and began to scan some of the new radio traffic that contained more bad news. A few minutes later his chief of staff, Rear Admiral Willson, entered with more papers.

"Damn it, Willson, more papers. Do you have any good news for me today?"

"Sir, you'll be happy to know I do have something good to show you, and even though some of it might hit you the wrong way, I think you will enjoy it." Willson placed the file on the desk belonging to the head of the navy. "This is the report from the young prodigy Turner was so enthusiastic about. I sent some reports over to Commander Jameson for the young man to look at and within five hours, I had his answer in what I think is one of the best composed and thought out analysis I have seen since I took this job."

King, always knowing he was the smartest and cleverest man in the navy replied, "Well let me see if there is any merit to what you are saying." He picked up the file and began to read.

Within a minute at most, he took out a pad and pencil and started jotting down notes.

Willson stood in front of the desk studying his boss's face, trying to understand if King was mad as hell, which was usually the case, or if he was interested in what he was reading. It didn't take long to find out what the boss was thinking.

"Damn it. It takes a kid to make a fool out of the navy. I don't exactly agree to all that's in this report, Willson, but eighty percent makes perfect sense. I think his conclusions about waves of U-boats hitting us is exactly right and we need to get ready. Where is this young man? I want to meet him now!"

Willson didn't smile, but he was grinning on the inside. He had bet the admiral's senior aide, Captain Reynolds, the boss would agree with the contents of the report and want to meet the ensign. Reynolds now owed him a bottle of bourbon.

"Sir, I told the commander to be available this afternoon to meet with me. Ensign Brand is still at Bethesda but approved for duty. I will get him here as soon as possible." Willson waited for the reply, and it was only a moment.

"Yes, for this afternoon. I have a meeting with Marshall at lunch, then we can meet with the commander and the ensign. By the way, have you met this young man yet?"

Willson replied, "No sir, but I'm sure looking forward to meeting him so I can see what a genius looks like."

"Willson, you already know what a genius looks like so set up the meeting for after my lunch with Marshall."

"Yes sir. I'll get the commander and the ensign arranged on your calendar and let Captain Reynolds know of the change." He came to attention and walked back to his office knowing the genius in question was King himself.

Jameson was told to report to Admiral Willson's office at 1300 hours and to bring Ensign Brand with him. He made sure the young ensign knew who this officer was and ensured that his uniform was ship shape. He also told his protégé to be sure to say, "yes sir, and no sir," and to be on his best behavior. In other words, do not be flippant or overly scientific.

Brand agreed to be a good ensign and follow the lead of the commander.

Jameson had the gunny drive them over to navy headquarters. They arrived fifteen minutes early, but decided to stay in the car for another ten minutes before getting out and going inside. Once inside and through the security checkpoints, the pair arrived at the office of the chief of staff. They were ushered into an adjoining room to await the call to see the admiral. The wait seemed like an eternity but after twenty minutes, the door opened and to their surprise in walked Admiral Willson. Both jumped to their feet and stood at attention. Before Jameson could say a thing, Admiral Willson said, "At ease, Commander, good to see you. So, this must be the amazing Mr. Brand."

James understanding it was okay for him to speak said, "Yes sir, I am Ensign Brand, James E., sir, and I am happy to meet you." Not exactly the appropriate way to introduce himself but the admiral did not mind.

"Gentlemen, would you follow me. We have some other people to meet." Willson's aide opened the other door and followed the admiral down a corridor.

A door with no number or title on it stood guarded by a marine sergeant who quickly came to attention as the admiral came towards him.

"Sergeant, are they still in there?" Willson asked.

"Yes sir, they are waiting for you." The sergeant stood at attention and held the door for the admiral.

Inside the room there were two flag officers drinking coffee with what appeared to be two aides sitting on the other side of the room. When the commander saw who they were, he said to himself in a silent scream, *Oh, shit!*

Willson did not come to attention but announced to the two officers, "Admiral King, General Marshall, I would like you to meet Commander Jameson and Ensign Brand."

Jameson and Brand quickly came to attention and awaited the pleasure of the two top officers in the United States military command.

King was the first to speak, "At ease. Commander, I have heard a lot of good things about you and your work. It is good to finally meet you. And, Ensign Brand, I have been very interested in meeting you to discuss some of your ideas. You have a big fan in Admiral Turner."

King turned to General Marshall saying, "Gentlemen, this is General Marshall, chief of staff of the army and my closest associate in taking the war to the enemy."

Both Jameson and Brand acknowledged the general but said nothing.

Marshall spoke to break the ice, "Admiral King has shared some of your ideas with me, Mr. Brand, and I am impressed by some of your solutions. Tell me, son, how sure are you of your research?"

Wow, thought James, *that was a loaded question.* He looked right at the general and said, "Sir, as in all research, we need to test our theories and be ready to change our thinking as required by these tests. But, sir, most of the calculations I performed are based on the materials provided, and as such, I would say they are accurate to within five or ten percent."

King smiled while looking at Marshall who almost never smiled but he did shake his head in agreement.

King asked, "Mr. Brand, you did some analysis on the U-boat attacks off our coast and concluded that we were dealing with five or six boats. What led you to this conclusion?"

Brand was quick to respond. "Sir, the reports provided had some fairly detailed information given by survivors and other witnesses. I matched this with the number of torpedoes carried in the Type IX which is based on the British admiralty reports and analysis, then calculated the use of torpedoes and deck guns in these attacks. I feel confident no more than six submarines were involved. I think there were only five, but I gave myself a little bit of a slide factor on this one. I also believe the submarines have left the Continental Shelf and are on their way back to France. I would expect another round of attacks with even more boats starting in two to three weeks. I would also surmise we will see the Type VII being used as well, though they do not have the range or staying power to remain in our waters for long."

King looked at him very hard and asked, "What prompted your reasoning?"

"Sir," Brand continued without regard to rank or the situation he was facing, "we are a very easy target right now. If I were the German commander and had received confirmation of the ships sunk in this four-week period, I would flood our coastline with every available U-boat. I would do this until my forces suffered heavy casualties or there were no targets remaining."

Marshall then asked, "Mr. Brand, what can the Air Corps do better to stop these attacks?"

Brand mused about this question for a moment and then replied, "Sir, with all respect, I do not have enough data on what the Air Corps is currently doing to make a valid suggestion. This also goes for naval air support. What I need is to conduct additional research and do field interviews with some of these commands, including obtaining more information on attack strategies, aerial surveillance operations, and current fleet anti-submarine procedures. Otherwise, sir, I would be creating conjectures about the situation."

King did not like these answers but begrudgingly agreed the young man in front of him was no fool and would not jump into something without good information followed by thorough analysis.

King thought for a minute and decided to jump in with both feet. "Mr. Brand, I want you to do a thorough analysis of the current situation. You will have my authority to talk to anyone in the navy to get what you need. Do you understand?"

Brand quickly replied, "Yes sir, when do I get started?"

King looking at Marshall to gain his agreement said, "I think that General Marshall will provide you access to anyone you need to interview as well as army procedures and plans. Is that all right with you, General Marshall?"

Marshall replied, "Yes, Admiral, whatever the young man needs, we will get him. I will let my aide, Colonel Nichols, arrange whatever you require."

"Thank you, sir, I will start immediately," Brand answered.

Commander Jameson interpreted the look from Brand, and said, "Sirs, by your leave, I will provide you with our plan shortly. Thank you for your time and directions."

Both the commander and the ensign came to attention and saluted, this being more of an army protocol than a navy way. The two senior officers returned their salute and the junior officers along with Admiral Willson exited the room.

Following the younger officer's departure, King asked, "Well, General, what do you think?"

Marshall, always taciturn replied, "Impressive for such a young man but based on his background and the enthusiasm for him by the scientific community, it is what I expected."

King thought for a moment and then Marshall added, "Admiral, based upon what Gerow in War Plans and your Admiral Turner have been working on, I would like to have General Eisenhower meet Brand. We are planning our operations for the European theater and need to begin thinking about long range strategy, logistics, and support. Your young man could help stimulate thinking in my strategy group."

King knowing about all of the long-range plans currently being fielded by various planning groups agreed, saying, "Have your man Eisenhower come over when Brand finishes his report on the submarine problem. I believe this young man has enough brain power to share with the army."

Marshall, thinking the same thing, said, "Thank you, Admiral. I know he is your man, but it would be a good thing to have him look at some of the issues we are facing. I promise not to be too needy."

King smiled and knew immediately he had something he could use as a bargaining tool with some of the conflicting army priorities. He would use this wisely but knew the president could overrule him if he got too tight in his resource demands.

13

11 February 1942
Office of Admiral King
Washington, D.C.

- United States troops arrive at Curacao and Aruba, Netherlands West Indies.

Admiral King was reviewing the list of soon to be launched warships, and the officers selected to become their commanding officers when Admiral Willson walked in.

"Sir, I have received the plan from Commander Jameson for expanding their research on the U-boat problem." Willson handed the report to his boss.

King did not reply but quickly looked at the papers. After a minute or two of reading the report, he said to Willson, "Damn, I like how this man writes. He gets to the point without any flourishes or extraneous detail. Did you see this?" King looked at his trusted chief of staff waiting for a reply.

"Yes sir, I did, and I agree with you. We should make Ensign Brand the writing teacher for the officer corps." Willson smiled at his comment, knowing that King almost never smiles, but for an instant, he saw a slight grin.

"Perhaps you are right, Willson. I like the plan, but his insistence on going on plane rides to see exactly what the flyers are doing concerns me." King scanned the papers knowing that Willson would not comment further until he finished his thoughts.

"Authorize the trip and make sure he has top priority. Notify the navy commands and let General Marshall know that Brand wants to go to Langley so he can not only interview the B-25 pilots there but also fly with them. Tell him Brand is only to fly with another airplane in sight and only with the top pilot. I don't want to lose this boy, got it?"

"Yes sir, I will get with the base commander of the Naval Air Station at Banana River in Florida and make sure the ensign gets on the top-rated PBY and that there will always be a pair in the air. I will also contact the commander of the Submarine School at New London to have some of his sub commanders available to be interviewed. I think this is a smart move on Brand's part to see how our people operate and how this may shed some light on the German submarine operations."

King handed the papers back to Willson with his initials scrawled across the top.

"You are right, Willson, finding out how we operate and train may give Brand some good ideas for countering the Germans.

Willson turned to leave, but King stopped him cold.

"I understand we have someone guarding Brand to keep him out of trouble?"

Willson said, "Yes, there is a marine lieutenant and a couple of marine non-coms that sat on him en route from San Diego, and I believe they are still helping him out."

King leaned forward in his chair and told Willson, "Get that lieutenant over here and have him bring his top sergeant. I will not need the commander for this meeting, clear?"

"Yes sir, I will have them over here as soon as I can locate them."

King thought again and said, "Have them here around 1400 hours. I have General Holcomb at that time, and I want to reinforce something with these men in the presence of the commandant."

"Yes sir, anything else?" Willson asked the man swiveling back in his chair, wondering what all this was about.

"No, that should be enough for right now. When is Turner due back from the Pacific?"

Willson quickly replied, "Kelly is due back in a day or two, depending on the west coast weather. The Coronados are pretty stretched, and some of the winds have not been favorable."

King thought for a minute. As a flyer, he knew how the winds could make or break a long flight from Hawaii. "Just let me know when you have a good ETA on him."

"Yes sir," Willson said, and left the commander in chief of the U.S. Fleet staring out of the window.

The two marines were early for their meeting with Admiral Willson and were told they were to meet Admiral King as well. First Lieutenant Flannigan and Gunnery Sergeant Jones were sitting outside the office of their top commander. Jones was getting antsy.

"Gee, Lieutenant, what the hell are we doing here? Did we screw up something and the old man is going to send us to the Canal Zone for the duration?" Jones searched up and down the long hallway before returning his gaze to the young marine lieutenant.

Flannigan felt more exposed than when the bombs fell on him at Cavite, turned to the old sergeant, whom he not only liked but respected, "Gunny, I don't have a clue as to why we are here. I was told not to tell the commander or Mr. Brand we were meeting with Admiral Willson. That is all I know, but I wish to hell I had some idea of why we are here."

Another few minutes went by. Senior officers came and went in the office of the top admiral. The two marines kept jumping to attention every few minutes and early on Jones commented that in all his twenty-eight years of service he had never seen so many admirals and captains in his life.

Finally, a two-star admiral approached them. As the two marines jumped to attention, the admiral said, "At ease, gentlemen, my name is Willson, and I am the chief of staff to Admiral King. He will see you now, please follow me."

Flannigan and Jones followed the rear admiral through the first set of doors into an outer office containing several navy yeomen typing various reports and forms and filing stacks of papers. The next door was guarded by a marine staff sergeant, who snapped to attention and said to the admiral, "Sir, he is waiting for you and these gentlemen." He opened the door, and Willson walked into the room followed by the two marines.

Willson came to attention as did the marines and announced, "Sir, may I present to you, First Lieutenant Flannigan and Gunnery Sergeant Jones."

King looked up, and as the two marines looked a foot over the head of the most senior man in the navy, they noticed a two-star marine general looking out the window who turned and looked at Flannigan and Jones with a gentle smile on his face.

King said, "At ease, gentlemen. May I present your commandant, General Holcomb."

The two marines again went to full attention and looked at the top marine.

Holcomb repeated Admiral King's instructions, "At ease, gentlemen." They went to parade rest and faced the admiral with the commandant standing on his right.

"Sit down you two, you are making me tired," King said with a slight grin as he looked at these two proven warriors. He had examined their records and found out about the Cavite attack and the wounds suffered by Flannigan and how he had been ordered out of the Philippines by Admiral Hart. He also had seen the records for Jones who had won the Navy Cross at the battle of Belleau Woods in France in the First World War. He also noted Jones had served aboard the *Saratoga* when King was its captain.

Both marines sat down with Willson sitting behind them and General Holcomb now sitting to the right of King.

"First, you are here because you have both excellent records and have served the Marine Corps with bravery and honesty. You are to be commended for your recent actions in bringing young Mr. Brand safely back to Washington. Both of you know some, if not most, of the reasons why Mr. Brand is of such great interest to the navy, so I will not belabor the point."

King looked at each of them, seeing they were still ready to jump into action just like he expected his top marines to do. He was proud of the Corps not just as part of the navy, but for the commitment they had made to uphold the history and values of the marines.

"Gentlemen, I asked the commandant to be here while I discuss your current situation. You are not to repeat this conversation with anyone without the express permission of the commandant, Admiral Willson or myself. Is that clear?"

Both marines said in loud and clear voices, "Aye, aye sir."

"Good. Now I want to tell you the bad news. Both of you want to get back into this war, just like I do. However, some of us serve the greater purpose by doing the jobs assigned us by superior authority. My superior is the president of the United States, and as much as I would like to be on the bridge of an aircraft carrier bombing the hell out of the Japs, I am to remain here. You two and the other two marines plus the commander are also serving the greater mission by following the orders of your senior leadership. Do you understand this?"

Again, in near unison, the two marines barked, "Aye, aye sir."

"Flannigan, let's start with you. The Naval Medical Corps wants to assign you to limited duty for the duration which would mean stateside, probably as a training officer or somebody's aide." King could see the dejected look on the face of the young marine.

He continued, "And you, Gunny, I do recall you from the *Saratoga;* you were a corporal about to become a sergeant. You are nearly fifty years old, and the marines need your experience to train the new corps. I know that does not make you happy, but I don't think the commandant would like to see an old war hero getting cut up on a beach somewhere."

King could see Jones was about to speak out of turn, but knew his place and took the lecture to heart.

"So, gentlemen, this gets me to where we are today. You and your fellow marines are going to perform a special mission, one that involves the utmost in secrecy and discretion. Mr. Brand is a one-man task force but one based on science and intellectual curiosity. He may be young, but he has already proven to me that he is a resource that must be protected and nurtured. The commander is the person who is nurturing him in the tasks being assigned. You two are the protectors as are the other marines in your command. Your mission is to protect Brand from any harm. He is not to be put in harm's way and if for some reason he is, he is to be protected with your lives and the lives of all who serve with you. And, please listen carefully, if Brand is compromised and it's possible he may fall into the hands of the enemy, that is not to be allowed. Do you understand what I am saying?"

Both marines looked like they had been hit with a brick. They had never heard an order like this during their careers. They were now being placed in a situation which would cause them to kill one of their own. However, both knew how the Japanese dealt with prisoners. From their experiences in China each had often thought about killing themselves rather than be captured by the Japs.

Before they could answer, General Holcomb said, "Lieutenant Flannigan, Gunny Jones, you both know what is being asked of you. You have both served in China and know how the Japanese handle prisoners. If for any reason, Brand was taken by the Japs, what do you think they would do to him if they had any idea about what he knows? Is there any doubt in your mind about what you would have to do?"

Both marines looked at the commandant. Flannigan said, "Sir, I understand perfectly what you are saying, and I would not want to suffer that fate. If it is required for the good of the nation, I would end Brand's life. Gunny, what do you say?"

Jones looked at Flannigan, then the commandant and lastly at Admiral King. "Sir, I would not want to see young Mr. Brand or anyone for that matter end up in the hands of the Japs. So yes, I would end his life as well. But I would take a bunch of those monkeys with me."

King did not smile for he knew he was asking these men not only to end their own lives, but if necessary, end the life of a comrade. "Thank you, gentlemen. Again, this command is only for your action. I hope you will never be placed in a situation that would require this activity, but it is best that all of us be prepared to face the possibility. I intend to keep Mr. Brand away from any such circumstance, but the necessities of war make for extreme measures."

King looked at both men knowing they would do what was best for the nation. Assured of their understanding, King continued. "The commandant and I have discussed your team, Lieutenant, and have decided to enlarge it. He has selected four men to join you, plus I have asked Admiral Willson to assign a communications expert and a full-time corpsman as well. With these additions, I want to make sure there is around the clock coverage of Brand and to ensure complete security. Gunny, if for any reason these additions do not meet your muster, you are to notify the commandant directly and have them replaced. Do you understand?"

Jones did not flinch one bit and replied, "Sir, if any of these men did not meet the expectations of the lieutenant or myself, I would notify God himself. Sorry, sir."

King finally came to a full smile and remembered Jones from the *Saratoga* saying, "Gunny, you haven't changed from your *Sara* days, and that's good. I don't think the Good Lord needs to be involved, but I think the commandant is very near that level."

Holcomb smiled and looked at King and said, "Admiral, I don't think I am that close to the Almighty, but I appreciate the compliment."

The commandant pulled out an envelope from his tunic pocket and gave it to the Flannigan.

"Here are the people I have assigned to your team. The corpsman is combat trained and used to our way of doing things. The chief petty officer comes highly recommended and has top secret clearance for just about anything."

Flannigan scanned the names and handed the list to the gunny who looked at it and then seeing one name, smiled.

The commandant noticing some sort of recognition on the face of the gunny inquired, "So Gunny, you know one of these men?"

"Yes sir. I served with Sergeant McBride in China, and I think I know at least one of the corporals. This looks like a good list to me, sir." Jones looked up at the commandant with whom he had served on several occasions in the last twenty-eight years.

General Holcomb returned the recognition and the smile saying, "Gunny, let me know if there are any problems. I will replace anyone who does not meet your expectations."

"Thank you, sir. I think this group will be just fine." Jones again smiled and thought to himself, *At least for once I'm getting top people and not cast offs from a brig.* This project was now even more important, and he knew with the best people in charge of the navy, he would continue to get whatever he needed.

King was about to send everyone out of the office but remembered something. "Flannigan, I know you are holed up at Commander Jameson's house in Bethesda. Will it be big enough for these people? I had Naval Intelligence check it out, and they reported it should be able to handle this lot but if it is not, let me know now."

Flannigan immediately replied, "Sir, the commander's house is big enough and will work out fine. The outside wall is secure, and there are only two entrances to the property. The commander evidently purchased the house when he was recalled to duty. His wife is not there because her mother is ill in New York and she is providing care in a nursing home. With a few minor changes, the place will accommodate the entire team and allow Brand to do his work in private."

King looked at the young lieutenant and was impressed by his actions and demeanor. A good academy man and he already had proven his valor in combat. "Lieutenant, as part of the security of the property, there will be a police presence in the area at all times. We have worked this out with the FBI and the local police. They will not be visible, but will keep an eye on the outside of the house. You and your men will have responsibility for the internal security and the security of Brand. Wherever he goes, you will go. He is never to be left alone, understand?" King again stared at the lieutenant and the gunnery sergeant standing in front of him.

In unison the marines barked, "Aye, aye sir."

With that final order, King said, "That is all gentlemen. If you have any problems or a situation that needs my attention, you are to contact Admiral Willson directly. Also, new orders are being processed for you and the entire team which will allow total access to anywhere our flag flies. Dismissed."

The two marines came to attention, performed a perfect about face, and walked out of the office followed by Admiral Willson.

When the door had closed, King looked at General Holcomb and said, "Fine looking marines, Commandant. I hope they are never compromised into even considering my orders on Mr. Brand."

The commandant mused, "If they have to, they will do their duty. I am quite sure they will not let Mr. Brand or us down. They will fight to the end to protect him and any secrets he may have. We need to ensure that we don't send this young man too far into the tiger's lair."

King lamented, "I wish I could get out there and fight this damn tiger on his side of the world, but we are a long way from that now." Dismissing the thought, he continued, "All right, let's go over the makeup of the First Marine Division and see what we are missing besides a few thousand marines."

14

14 February 1942
Bethesda, Maryland

- Submarine **Sargo** delivers ammunition to Polloc Harbor, Mindanao, Philippines, and evacuates certain military personnel.
- Adm. T. C. Hart, USN, is relieved as commander in chief Allied Naval Forces in Southwest Pacific by Vice Adm. C. E. L. Helfrich, Royal Netherlands Navy

Stepping from the shadows, the man holds up his hands to stop the approaching truck and asks the driver for his military ID card. The man carefully eyes the card, then looks in the back of the truck, verifying the identities of the passengers coming to stay at the house he's guarding. He opens the cast iron gate, waves the truck through. After it passes onto the property he closes the gate and disappears back into the shadows. The truck driver is Sgt. James McBride, and he has the rest of the team in the back of the truck. Sitting next to him is a navy chief petty officer named Harry Schmidt. The chief has the hash marks indicating over twenty years in the navy.

The people in the back include Cpl. William "Willie" Dean, Cpl. Clarence "Bud" Williams, Cpl. Harold Dillard and P.O. First Class (Pharmacist Mate) Jonathan Hamlin. The six men had met up that morning and had received their orders from a navy captain who served as aide to Admiral King. Each of them was informed their new assignment was top secret and any discussion outside of the command was grounds for a court-martial and twenty years at Portsmouth. They were duly impressed.

The truck was met at the garage behind the large house by a marine gunnery sergeant. "Okay, cowboys, get out of the truck, grab your gear, and come into the house." The gunny walked back into the house to escape the cold rain that had followed them the past two days. Everyone retrieved their gear, including the rifles and pistols provided before getting on the truck. They also unloaded several large boxes stenciled USMC Rations. No one was sure what this was all about, but food was food. Upon entering the house, the new group was met by Corporal Pride, who pointed them to the largest room most of these men had ever seen in a house.

As they gaped at the fine furnishings, the gunny stepped forward and in a voice only a gunnery sergeant could possess, yelled, "Attention, officer on deck."

Everyone snapped to attention and then they heard a very quiet, "At ease, men. My name is Jameson, and I have the honor of being the head of this operation. I would like to introduce Lieutenant Flannigan who is in command of the security detachment to which you are now assigned. You have met Gunnery Sergeant Jones, and the rest of the team includes, Staff Sergeant Laird and Corporal Pride."

Jameson looked around the room and figured out who was who. It appeared Flannigan and Jones were correct. He was given top men and not hand me downs from some brig. He gave Corporal Pride a prearranged look which made Pride exit the room.

"Gentlemen, I know you have been briefed to some degree on our mission. Let me tell you the mission is to provide security for one man and to ensure the secrecy of any operation involving this one man. Each of you was handpicked for your skills and abilities and how you work under pressure. Security is the watchword for this command. The lieutenant and Gunnery Sergeant Jones will brief you on all aspects of what we expect. If you have any questions at any time about this mission, you may seek me out personally. I would prefer that you did not engage in any scuttlebutt about this assignment even amongst yourselves. Is that understood?"

Everyone said in unison, "Aye, aye sir."

The commander was about to say more, but caught the eye of Corporal Pride entering the room with Ensign Brand following behind. "Gentlemen, may I present to you Ens. James Brand. He will be the focus of all your activities in the coming days. Mr. Brand, would you like to say something?"

Brand had been warned there would be new members of the team. Now he examined each face carefully, then returning his gaze to the first man he saw, the chief petty officer.

"Chief," Brand said, "Welcome to the commander's house. It will be nice to have some new faces around here. Not to say my present company has been anything but wonderful." Brand smiled, and the original team members smiled back. "But it will be good to have some new companions. I do not know what you have been told about me, but to everyone's chagrin I have only one head and I'm not a vampire."

The original team members, including the commander, laughed at his comment, but the newcomers had yet to grasp the ensign's humor. The young ensign evidently had a great relationship with everyone and was very approachable. "Please introduce yourself and tell me a bit about yourself," Brand continued.

He started with the chief and slowly walked around the room shaking the hand of each new man, immediately connecting like he was the kid brother or first cousin they had known since childhood. Each man, in turn, smiled at the young man, so earnest and willing to be friendly. Not at all like any officer that they had ever met, that was sure, thought Sergeant McBride. He would need to sit down and have a good chat with his old shipmate the gunny to understand what was going on at this great house outside of Washington, D.C.

When he had finished, Brand said, "I'm sorry, but I have to go back to my cell and do some more work or the commander will have me put in leg irons again." Again, the smile came out.

The commander shook his head, let out a hearty laugh and said, "James, go back and look up your newest theory, then prove it."

Brand turned to the commander saying, "Yes sir, I'll go back and figure out how we can get five pounds of shit in a one-pound bag. Never a problem for a navy man, sir." With that, he returned to his office.

The commander still smiling turned to the new team members saying, "That, gentleman, is James Brand, an ensign in the United States Navy. He also holds a doctorate degree in physics and advanced degrees in mathematics. I could tell you even more about him but let us leave it at this. You are assigned to make sure that wherever Mr. Brand is sent, no harm comes to him from any source. Do you understand?"

Again, in unison came the reply, "Aye, aye sir."

"Now, I will let Lieutenant Flannigan and the gunny get you settled. Please feel free to ask any questions about the mission." With that final comment, Jameson walked out of the large living area, leaving the team alone.

"Listen up," said Jones. "I have a schedule set up. Sergeant Laird will give you your assignments. He will show you where you will bunk and stow your gear. There is a gun locker on both doors and one upstairs. Laird will show you around, so you know what is where, so to speak. Meals are excellent at this house prepared by our two housekeepers whom you will meet later. As to duty schedules, we will always have two men up and available using standard four-hour watches. When we move out to other locations, we will change up depending on the situation."

Jones looked around and saw serious faces staring back at him. "Any questions for now?"

Chief Petty Officer Schmidt spoke up. "Gunny, where will I set up my equipment? I have a truckload coming with a permanent installation and some portable radios."

The gunny responded, "No problem, Chief. We have a room ready for your installation. Plus, and all of you listen up, we have two storage areas that will be set up for grab and go movements. This equipment will include the chief's radios, the doc's medical bag, and the usual rations and ammo. Laird will show you where everything is located and will get any extra equipment that you don't have now. If there is something special you require, let me know. Any other questions?"

No one answered, and so he said, "Laird show them around. Chief, you are with me."

The new marines and the navy corpsman followed Sergeant Laird and began to tour the house.

As the others left the room, the gunny turned to the chief saying, "Chief, I don't know if we ever served together, but you look familiar."

The chief smiled and said, "I think you and I met on the *Augusta* back in '33 or '34. I was in the radio shack, and if I remember, you were a sergeant guarding the captain."

The gunny smiled, nodding his head up and down, "Yes, I think I remember that. Damn fine ship and some good people on board. The captain was a fine man and that was a happy ship."

The gunny looked around the room to see if anyone had left gear behind and said, "Chief, you and I are going to be bunk mates on this cruise. I think you'll find the accommodations much to your liking with our own bath and lots of space. It looks like we're going to have a good crew on this assignment with only experienced people. No damn rookies to train."

The chief agreed. "Right on, Gunny, glad to have old hands on this mission. Tell me, though, are we going to be moving about a lot? I will be getting several radios including a portable shortwave radio with a bike generator. That sounds serious to me. Do you know where we are going?"

The gunny looked at his new bunkmate and replied, "I haven't a clue as to where we are going or even when. I understand that soon we'll be going to bases on the east coast but that is as far as I've been told. The admiral told us we would be kept back from any front-line activity, but I know young Mr. Brand pretty well now, and he wants to get up close and personal to do his work."

The chief asked, "So what is this work or research he's doing that's so damn important it takes a squad to protect him?"

The gunny smiled and in a low voice responded, "Hell if I know. No one is telling us much of anything and the only person who seems to know what is going on is the commander. He is a scientist as well and one smart cookie. He's very open with us, but when it comes to the ensign, he clams up real fast."

The chief, in the manner of senior non-coms in all the services, replied, "Well, if they expect us to know something, I guess they'll tell us, right, Gunny?"

The gunny smiled at his navy counterpart and began showing the chief their new home.

PART 3

Part 3

15

17 February 1942
Langley Army Air Corps Base, Virginia

- Seabees (1st Construction Battalion) arrive at Bora Bora, Society Islands

The team had been given their orders the day before and left for the Washington National Airport at dawn. They were told to go to the military control desk inside the terminal where they were to be taken to a plane. They did not know a navy R4D, the navy version of the C-47, was waiting for them. The plane was not stripped-down but a recently acquired regular DC-3 passenger plane that was supposed to be sold to Eastern Airlines. The navy had other ideas, and this plane was used to fly senior staff around the country in relative comfort. The pilot was forty-year-old Navy Reserve Lt. Comdr. Walter Shoemaker, who until recently was flying for American Airlines but now was flying VIPs around the country. As he told Commander Jameson, he did the exact same job but now for a lot less money. The co-pilot was young navy Lt. (jg) Arnold Miller who had wanted to fly Wildcats, but was trained on multi-engine aircraft and ended up on the R4D. Again, not what he wanted to do, but he did it well.

As soon as the team was onboard, the plane was first for takeoff. It was a quick hour to Langley. During the flight, the young ensign entered the cockpit. He watched the pilots, but said nothing, observing the instruments instead. He was especially interested in the altitude the plane was flying which was only six thousand feet. He made some notes and after a while went back to his seat. Both the pilot and co-pilot said nothing as they were used to people wanting to see what happened up front.

Only two of the senior non-coms and the chief had flown before. The remaining team members were newbies to the art of flying. It was an exciting experience but somewhat unnerving to people familiar with the sea and land below their feet but not the air above their heads. They were happy to return to solid ground at Langley.

The R4D finished its rollout, and as it slowed onto one of the taxiways, a staff car arrived with a big checkerboard flag and sign with the words "Follow Me" in large letters. It turned onto the adjacent taxiway and the plane duly followed. The car stopped in front of a hanger partially occupied by two B-25 Mitchell bombers. A groundsman waved the plane to a stop and the pilot killed the two engines. As the passengers began collecting their belongings one of them looked out and exclaimed, "Looks like we have a reception committee."

As the airplane door opened, another groundsman rolled up a small ladder. On the tarmac, two staff cars pulled up with two small trucks. The passengers in the first car got out and approached the plane, standing in a reception line like there was an admiral aboard.

Seeing the fanfare, Commander Jameson spoke to the team, "Listen up. Seems we have a reception committee and it appears to be a full bird colonel and some other officers, so look sharp. Flannigan, you are with me followed by Brand. Gunny, get everyone else set up and in line."

The answer from the gunny was immediate. "Aye, aye Commander." Turning to the others in the plane he said, "You heard what the commander said. Look like marines and remember, the Air Corps are our friends." Smiles went up, and everyone readied to depart the plane as instructed.

The commander walked toward the reception committee with Flannigan and Brand a pace behind. Approaching the colonel, he snapped to attention with a smart salute, mimicked by the two officers behind him. The colonel proceeded to give a smart salute back, an uncommon response in the Air Corps.

Jameson, staying at attention, said in a strong voice, "Commander Jameson and Special Research Detachment reporting as directed."

The colonel replied, "Commander, at ease and welcome to Langley. My name is Colonel Waters and these two gentlemen are Lieutenant Colonel Adams and Major Karnes. They are the squadron commander and executive officer of the 312th Bomber Squadron supporting the Eastern Sea Frontier."

Each of the officers acknowledged the other with quick nods. The commander said, "This is First Lieutenant Flannigan and Ensign Brand. The rest of the team consists of a detachment of marines and two naval personnel. Thank you for meeting us. I look forward to working with you and hopefully we will not cause you any problems."

The colonel looked at the commander who was probably five to seven years older and noticed none of them had navy wings, so he was looking at surface navy sailors. But that was not his concern. He decided to go ahead and ask the question that had been burning in his mind for the past forty-eight hours since he received a phone call from Washington.

"Commander, again, welcome to Langley. We are prepared to assist you in any way possible. I received a phone call from General Arnold who told me I was to do whatever you desired and to report to him directly if there was any reason that I could not comply with your request. I have so informed the colonel and the major of this conversation, and we stand by to assist you. If you could help us understand the nature of the mission, perhaps we could be of better assistance. General Arnold told me that you might be able to provide me with some specifics." As he was saying this, he noticed several of the marines had gotten off the plane. About half of them were armed with Thompson submachine guns which he had only seen in the movies, so his interest spiked even more.

The commander noticed the concern as he looked at the contingent of armed marines and quickly helped resolve the colonel's dilemma.

"Colonel, I am sorry to say I can only provide a few details on our mission. The high level of security is part of this mission, and I hope it does not cause you or your men too much concern. Perhaps if we could adjourn to a less public location, I could provide you with some mission details."

The colonel agreed, and he asked the major if his office in the hanger was available. The officers walked over to the small office next to a B-25 which was missing its propellers and had the engine cowlings removed. Three of the armed marines followed the officers. Upon entering the small office, the marine gunnery sergeant asked, "Commander, shall we secure the perimeter?"

"Yes, Gunny, but don't scare any of these young men who are doing their jobs." The gunny smiled and closed the door.

"Colonel, thank you again for assisting us in our mission. I am sure that General Arnold is aware of the reason for this mission and your part in it." The commander looked at the colonel, and he saw a nod, so he continued.

"As you gentlemen are very aware, the Germans are sinking ships off our coast at an alarming rate. You are on the front lines, and your bombers are about the only offensive weapon we have along the entire east coast. There are some old B-18s up in New York, another squadron of B-25s working out of Boston and some navy PBYs ranging up from Florida." Brand was looking at the B-25, noticing the work on the engines. He was paying attention to what Commander Jameson said, but was always observant of his surroundings.

"Admiral Andrews who oversees the Eastern Sea Frontier has some one hundred aircraft and a few sub chasers, Coast Guard cutters and smaller patrol craft to safeguard some twelve hundred miles of coastline. Until we get more planes and ships to support this effort, more ships will be sunk and more men will die." He let this somber information sink in even though they had seen some of the carnage from the air but never one submarine sighting.

"Our mission is to better understand how you are operating and to come up with ways to improve not only your capabilities but those of all the other sea and air units on the coast."

The commander looked at Lieutenant Colonel Adams as he spoke, watching for his reaction. The only response was a somber face staring back at him, but the young Major Karnes wanted to defend his boss.

"Major," Jameson said, "I am not saying anyone in this command is not doing their job. We are looking for ways to kill the enemy and safeguard the ships plying our coast. Is this understood?"

The major looked at Adams first and then at Colonel Waters to see if he was in trouble, then he replied, "Yes, Commander. We are very frustrated doing this job. We all wanted to go and kill some Japs or at least bomb some Germans in France. Doing this job, which we were never trained for and looking at empty seas each day is, well, sir, damn frustrating. Sorry, sir, I did not mean…"

Commander Jameson saw the distress in the young major and knew what he said was more than right. It was an indictment on the entire war effort to date. No training, no resources, not enough people, no strategy, no nothing but lots of paperwork and brass hats who did not have a clue as to what was going on or how to defend against this menace.

Two days before, Jameson had a phone conversation with Admiral Andrews set up by Admiral King. Both admirals had been classmates at Annapolis and "Dolly," his nickname, had bristled when he was told to talk to a mere commander about what was happening in his command. It took only a few minutes for Andrews to realize the commander was the man of science and the academy man which King had assured him was true. This calmed down the admiral who was being second-guessed by everyone from FDR down. The commander's calm assessment of what they were looking at and how they would come up with recommendations based on science, mathematics, and logic instead of politics assured the admiral of the correctness of this mission. He sent top secret messages to all his commands instructing them in no uncertain terms that Commander Jameson and his team were to receive total access and openness.

Jameson sympathized with the young Air Corps major, "Major, I know how you feel. There are lots of men in every branch of the service that want to get at the enemy. You are on the front lines without a lot of support doing a job that few have been trained to do. You are all excellent flyers and you want to kill a U-boat. We do too, and by working with you perhaps we can come up with some new strategies, tactics, and weapons to sink those sons of bitches. We are not here to tell you how to do your job.

We are here to learn about your mission, understand your flight profiles, search patterns, attack plans, and weapons. By analyzing what everyone is doing, perhaps we can build a model of what we call best practices and share these among all navy and Air Corps units. How does that sound?"

The major sought visual support from his superior officers and replied, "Sounds like a good plan, Commander. Again, I am sorry if I stuck my foot in my mouth, sir. We just want to get this war over as soon as possible and if we can do this by killing U-boats, well, sir, that is what we will do."

The commander smiled. "Good, now let me tell you what you can do to help us learn about your mission."

Thirty minutes later Colonel Adams expressed his understanding, "Commander, what you have laid out for us is basically a routine mission except for two planes flying in tandem at differing altitudes. And you want us to take three members of your team along with us in each plane. Is that correct?"

"Yes, Colonel, it is basically a routine mission with two planes in the same search quadrant. As we have shown you on the map, you will fly a shorter mission lasting three and one-half hours, and this will be in the shape of a long rectangle working no more than sixty miles offshore to less than ten miles offshore. I will be in one plane with the gunnery sergeant and one corporal. Lieutenant Flannigan and Ensign Brand will be in the other plane along with Sergeant Laird. We will keep visual contact on one another even though I will fly with you, Colonel, at between eight thousand and ten thousand feet with Lieutenant Flannigan and Mr. Brand in the other plane two thousand feet lower. Our orders are to attack any U-boat sighted using your current attack profile. Are we all in agreement on this?"

The colonel and the major nodded in agreement. "What time do we start?"

Commander Jameson thought for a moment and Brand jumped in saying, "Sir, I would like to begin this mission like any other flight so I guess we should have a flight profile leaving at 0730 hours with a return ETA of 1100 hours. Will that work?"

Jameson waited for an answer from Colonel Adams who did not

think too long on this saying, "Okay by me. Major, is your plane ready to fly tomorrow morning?"

"Colonel Adams, my plane is always set to fly. We will be fueled, armed, and ready to go before the sun rises."

Everyone smiled in agreement. The squadron commander and his executive officer turned to the base commander and asked, "Sir, if you can let flight ops know about our plan for the morning I will alert the ground crew about arming and fueling."

Colonel Waters replied, "No problem, Adams. I will get everything in motion and tell the base operations manager to get meteorology on the phone plus intelligence set for a 0500 briefing."

As the two pilots headed out the door, Colonel Waters spoke, "Commander, would join me for a drink at the officer's club before dinner?"

Commander Jameson quickly replied, "I think that would be a good plan but only one drink, sir. I may need to see clearly in the morning."

Everyone laughed except Ensign Brand who knew that he could only have a Coca-Cola anyway.

16

18 February 1942
260 miles NNE of Langley, Virginia

- United States naval vessels sunk: Destroyer **Truxton** and stores ship **Pollux** by storm, Placentia Bay, Newfoundland.
- War Department orders overseas contract activities throughout the world militarized. All civilian contract activities are to be terminated by 18 August 1942.
- Japanese invade the island of Bali, Netherlands East Indies. This completes the isolation of Java.

The B-25s had been flying about seventy-five minutes. The plane Brand was in flew at an altitude of eighty-two hundred feet. About three thousand feet behind and two thousand feet higher was the B-25 carrying Commander Jameson. The planes were very loud because the exhaust system was within a few feet of where the pilot and co-pilot sat. The wind seemed to whistle in from every angle, making for a chilly ride. At this altitude, the temperature was nearing zero degrees. With a tailwind of thirty knots, the plane was flying at its normal cruising speed of 230 mph. The bombardier sat just ahead and below the cockpit. He was joined in this cramped Plexiglas world by Lieutenant Flannigan. While the bombardier was engaged in checking out his bombsight, Flannigan surveyed the seascape with binoculars.

Brand crouched between the pilot and co-pilot and used the plane's intercom to talk to other members of the crew. He had Sergeant Laird searching through the side window behind the bomb bay doors. The navigator occasionally looked out his window but was more involved with staying on a course within a couple degrees of where he thought he was. None of the Air Corps navigators in this squadron had been trained to work positions over water. So, it was understandable they would be somewhat concerned as to their precise location. Occasionally, the radio operator would contact the other plane to verify they were in sight of each other and to ask for position checks. Brand took note of these activities, wondering why something as simple as binoculars for the entire crew would be an issue or why the navigators who were all officers had little or no overwater navigation training.

After ninety minutes on the same heading, Major Karnes radioed Lieutenant Colonel Adams in the other B-25, announcing he was making a ninety-degree turn to the west for five minutes then he would make another ninety-degree turn to the south for the return leg to Langley. The colonel acknowledged the transmission and prepared to follow the major's lead. After the course change, Brand decided to do some of his tests, which he had not discussed with Karnes or Adams or even with Jameson.

"Major, could you climb to ten thousand feet and notify the colonel to add two thousand feet to his altitude." The major nodded his head and radioed the colonel. Both planes began their climb and within a few minutes leveled out at the new altitude. Brand visually patrolled the sea, pulled out his pad and pen, and made calculations. Brand then asked Major Karnes to inform Adams to drop further behind their aircraft until each could barely make out the other.

Again, the major did as requested thinking nothing of the command. In a few minutes, the top turret gunner announced over the intercom, "Major, I cannot see the Colonel. I think I know where he is which would be at five o'clock and up, but I sure can't see him now."

The major acknowledged this communication. Brand asked Sergeant Laird if he could locate Colonel Adams' plane. Laird reported negative to the request and said he had lost the colonel about a minute before the top turret gunner had.

"Very good, Laird," said Brand. Then he requested the radio operator to contact the colonel for a visual check.

In a few minutes, the radio crackled, "Green two, I have visual on you, and I am on course with you, over."

The major responded, "Green one, thank you for the report. We have lost visual of you and needed to know if you were still present."

Brand now decided to reverse positions. He instructed Major Karnes to have Colonel Adams drop altitude until he was at eight thousand feet, then pull ahead of the major's aircraft. He asked the major to slow to two hundred miles per hour and let the colonel overtake him. As soon as the radio confirmed the instruction, Brand started one of the stopwatches he carried. The major observed Brand's actions but said nothing, knowing he would probably not get an answer.

Ten minutes later, the Bombardier reported a clear sighting of the colonel's plane, saying it stood out well against the open water. Again, Brand was testing the visual sighting of aircraft against the water and color schemes that would or would not help in lessening the plane's visibility. Both bombers were painted in the normal Army Air Corps green used as the camouflage over land but stuck out like a sore thumb over water. A few minutes later, Flannigan was on the intercom asking Brand if he saw the wake of a ship ahead. Brand looked over the co-pilot's head, scanning the sea with his binoculars, and finally saw the telltale faint tracks of a ship that had passed this point some miles ago. The Major got on the intercom saying, "Pilot to bombardier, do you see this wake? What is the heading?"

The bombardier reported back, "Still can't see what the lieutenant is talking about. Which direction?"

Brand reported a heading of 196 degrees. "I can make out a freighter on the horizon now with some smoke. Same heading. Major, please head for that ship at your best speed and pass it at five hundred feet to port please."

The major looked at Brand and smiled. "Finally, some fun. Radio, tell the colonel we are going to do a pass on this ship at the request of Mr. Brand."

Brand quickly interjected, "Radio, this is Brand. Please also ask the colonel to stay at altitude and have Commander Jameson record the event."

As the radio operator sent the message, Brand could feel the plane pick up speed and begin to drop in altitude. Soon he was looking at an indicated air speed of 325 mph, which was fifty miles per hour over the max cruising speed and the plane was still picking up speed. The plane had dropped some three thousand feet in only a few minutes, and the ship was getting much closer. Major Karnes told the co-pilot to get his hands on the yoke in case he needed help pulling up and leveling off. The co-pilot, who had been chewing the same piece of gum since the plane took off, calmly placed his hands on the yoke and watched the major for any indication of an order to pull back hard. The plane was nearly at fifteen hundred feet and still pushing 325 mph when the pilot asked for the co-pilot's help in leveling off. The pilot had reduced engine power, and the plane was no longer buffeting as it had been earlier in the dive.

The crew on the Norwegian tanker was already on edge with submarines reported on the American coast, but they had gone ahead and moved north from Aruba with their cargo of sweet Venezuelan crude knowing it was needed by the Allies. They were to join a convoy in New York heading for England in another week, so if they could make it another two hundred miles, they at least could have some time off in the Big Apple. The ship carried a four-inch cannon on the stern of the ship, and the Norwegian crew was well trained by two years of war on how to use it. They also had four separate 20mm anti-aircraft mounts. These had been used several times defending the ship from the dreaded FW-200 long range bombers that ranged out of France. The anti-aircraft guns were not manned, but the four-inch piece was always manned with a skeleton crew of three who would expect the rest of the gun mount crew of seven to show up on a minute's notice.

U-BOAT SCOURGE

The crew nervously scoured the sea on each side of the big fourteen thousand-ton tanker but did not expect to have an airplane come at them from the stern. With only fifty seconds or so of notice, everyone looked amazed as a big green twin-engine bomber flew by the ship at what they thought was a few hundred feet. The major was right at one thousand feet precisely and about five hundred feet to the starboard side of the tanker. The ship's crew ducked when the plane passed and then recognized the American markings on the plane and all started to cheer and wave their caps. Having air cover, even for a brief period meant that no U-boats would be bothering them for at least a while.

Major Karnes looked at the ship as he buzzed by at nearly three hundred miles per hour and with a smile asked Brand, "Ensign, is that what you wanted me to do?"

Brand looked at the pilot and replied, "Yes sir, exactly. Now if you can turn around and head back to the ship, but this time approach from just off the bow at cruising speed, it would be helpful. Also, Major, you might waggle your wings as you pass to let them know you are one of the good guys. I think I saw some anti-aircraft weapons on board."

"Geez, I didn't see any guns, are you sure?" The major looked at his co-pilot who also shook his head negatively.

Brand said, "Well, Major, at the slower speed and without diving on it, let's see how many they have and where they are located. This could be a useful piece of attack information. Also, would you have your radio operator contact the colonel. Tell him to make a similar pass as if he were going to drop bombs on this ship, but he should not get any closer than fifteen hundred feet from the vessel. I think the ship is Norwegian and these people have a few more years' war experience."

The major informed the radio operator of the request while turning the plane about for the second pass.

Brand then asked, "Sir, can you communicate with the tanker? Do you have their frequencies?"

The major looked sheepishly and said, "I don't have the foggiest idea about that. We can monitor emergency frequencies, but we have no information about who is on what radio channel. That would probably be very helpful."

"Yes, Major, it would be helpful to gain information on where ships are and what they have seen or experienced without clogging emergency frequencies which the enemy is probably monitoring." Brand looked down at his notes, which were getting more detailed by the moment. There were so many small fixes that could improve the situation, but people must get out of their own little world and look at the bigger picture. Not an easy thing to do. Change comes slowly and with much reluctance. Brand tried to remember which of the astronomers back at the Lowell Observatory had explained this concept to him when he was so much younger. Things do not change until there is either a directive to do so or there is so much pain that you must.

Within a few minutes, the B-25 flown by Major Karnes had again passed the tanker at a slower speed and a safer distance. The wagging of the wings had been greeted by the waving of hats from the crew of the slow-moving ship. As the plane started to climb back to a better cruising altitude, he looked back and saw Colonel Adams' B-25 perform its run on the tanker. He noticed the plane was highly visible from their lower altitude and when the bomber had completed its run, it pulled to the right and began its climb. He noticed the major also performed a right-hand turn after his two runs at the tanker as well, and wondered if that was from training or instinct. Either could be important in a real attack on a U-boat.

Brand commented to the pilot, "I guess we should be heading back to the base unless of course, we find a real target."

The major smiled, nodded agreement, and pointed to the co-pilot to take over flying duties, then started to write in his log book about the encounter with the tanker. He wondered how quickly the navy people had seen the ship's wake and knew how to follow it for an attack. Perhaps the young ensign had just shown him how to work up an attack profile for his plane that could kill a U-boat. He would practice this again. He looked at the young ensign with a new appreciation for whatever it was this young man was doing. He hoped to get more ideas from him and knew he would have to get his address so they could keep in touch.

17

19 February 1942
Naval Air Station
Banana River, Florida

- Battle of Badoeng Strait starts at night and continues the next day. Allied naval force (Rear Adm. K.W.F.M. Doorman, Royal Netherlands Navy) of three cruisers and accompanying destroyers attack retiring Japanese Bali occupation force; two Netherlands cruisers and one United States destroyer are damaged. One Japanese destroyer is damaged.
- Japanese bombers raid harbor, airfields and shore installations at Darwin, Australia.
- United States naval vessel sunk: Destroyer **Peary** by dive bomber, Darwin, Australia.

The team had departed Langley at 0700 hours with many feeling slight hangovers. The pilots and crew of the B-25s had been overly generous in both the officers and NCO clubs. The pilot of the R4D observed as the

B-25 pilots got hammered and watched with awe how much the marine lieutenant drank without getting plastered. Commander Jameson, as a senior officer, spent most of his time with the base commander and squadron commander hunched over one drink for most of the evening. With them, was Ensign Brand who drank a few Coca-Colas and seemed to be holding the rapt attention of the senior officers. Apparently, the ensign provided a series of recommendations to the Air Corps officers on ways to improve their U-boat search and attack activities. They seemed to be not only impressed, but took copious notes. The gathering broke up around 2200 hours, and the commander pulled the lieutenant out of the Air Corps pilots' ongoing party.

As the R4D reached its cruising altitude of eight thousand feet for the three-hour flight south, the pilot was visited by the ensign who asked if he could sit in the co-pilot seat. The pilot and co-pilot had no problem letting the young man sit in for a while during the routine flight in near perfect conditions. The morning was warmer than usual with a southerly breeze running no more than twelve knots and none of the fog that often runs in the waters near the Chesapeake Bay.

The pilot began talking to the young ensign about the conversation held last night with the senior Air Corps pilots. "Seems the bomber boys were very interested in your approach to search and destroy missions. How did you come up with some of these ideas?"

Brand thought carefully about what he could and could not discuss before deciding to give a general summary of his recommendations. "Well, Commander, the Air Corps put these people into a situation without any instruction on how to handle it. I demonstrated how to fly at altitudes that would provide good visual observation and limit the enemy's ability to detect the aircraft. Secondly, I wanted to see if pilots could use their superior speed and maneuverability to dive at a submarine plunging below the surface while placing their weapons in such a way to maximize their hits. They need some depth bombs in the worst way, but they could do some damage with their normal high explosive bombs if they hit water when the submarine was no more than twenty-five feet below the surface. Below that depth, a regular bomb will provide concussive force but not enough to do damage to the U-boat. A depth charge dropped in a pattern of four to six weapons with a spacing of 150 feet and set for twenty-five to fifty feet will increase the likelihood of doing sufficient damage, either sinking the submarine or driving it to the surface where a second attack could be coordinated."

Brand gazed straight ahead and asked, "Would it be possible to handle the controls for a while?"

The pilot was still trying to get his head around the information provided by the young ensign, so it took a few seconds to understand the question being asked of him about flying the plane. "Ensign, do you have any stick and rudder time?" He smiled assuming the young man had never been in a plane and certainly didn't know how to fly.

"Sir, I've had a pilot's license for three years. I also have a multi-engine license with over three hundred hours in twin-engine aircraft. Only about thirty hours in a DC-3 but that was about a year ago." Brand again looked at the pilot for approval.

"I guess I underestimated you again, Ensign. If you are ready, let's see what you've got. Your aircraft, Ensign Brand."

Brand took the wheel in his hands, placed his feet on the rudder pedals, and began a series of check-offs that would make any pilot proud. He confirmed the course first, then the altitude, followed by the airspeed, fuel, and manifold pressure. The pilot seeing that the ensign did indeed know how to fly a DC-3 as well as anyone else with the same number of hours, smiled over at Brand and said, "Let me know when you want to be relieved."

Brand smiled, nodded, and continued scanning the skies, the instruments, and the ground below him to ensure he was on course and doing what was professionally required.

At around 1100 hours, the plane touched down at the Naval Air Station at Banana River. The station was established only the year before and had two regular runways, but it had several slipways into the river for the handling of the PBYs and PBMs which were the real attractions at this base. Again, just like at Langley, a staff car with a flag and "Follow Me" sign appeared as the plane slowed. It followed the vehicle to a set of hangers and what appeared to be control towers. One tower was located at the head of a two-story building constructed using only tar paper and wood. The other tower was a few hundred feet further inland and stood next to one of the amphibian ramps. It was connected to one of the new metal Quonset huts that were popping up all over America.

When the plane taxied into its parking place guided by two sailors with small red flags, another set of VIPs appeared from the tar paper building. Two navy captains and a lieutenant commander marched up to the ladder being set at the rear of the R4D and once the door was opened Commander Jameson and Lieutenant Flannigan exited the plane followed by Brand and the gunny.

Jameson walked up, saluted the captains, and introduced himself and the other two officers who returned the salute and then shook hands with one and all.

The navy captain then said, "Welcome to Banana River, gentlemen. We are glad to be of any help to you and your mission. I received not only a phone call this morning from Admiral Andrews but also a teletype from Admiral King wanting to know the minute you arrived and to put you on the phone to Admiral King's chief of staff, Admiral Willson. If you would follow me to my office, we will get you through to Washington."

With that, the entire group walked to the building, containing the captain's office. Once inside, the chief yeoman presented Commander Jameson with three teletypes all marked top secret, then showed them to the base commander's office. Base commander, Captain Ted Young, picked up the phone and ordered a call to the office of Admiral Willson and then hung up as the call was placed and connected.

"Gentlemen, I failed to do proper introductions so while the call is being put through, let me make the rounds. My name is Ted Young, and I am the base commander. This is Capt. Mike Gannon who is the CO of Patrol Wing Eight, and this is Lt. Comdr. George Hamlin who is the CO of Squadron Twenty-Seven consisting of eight PBYs. We are glad to have you with us even though none of us has a clue what you are doing here or what you may ask us to do for you. But, the communications I received said to give you anything you want, as long as you want, so please let us know what we can do to be of assistance."

Just then the phone rang and Captain Young answered. He heard the yeoman tell him the call was through and that the admiral was on the line. The captain gave the phone to Commander Jameson and said, "The admiral is holding for you, Commander."

Jameson took the phone. "Thank you, Captain. I hate to do this, but I need to take the call in private. Is that all right?"

"No problem at all, Commander." The captain and others exited the room.

The commander pointed at Brand to remain. Flannigan left with the others in a scripted move on behalf of Jameson to help with the secrecy and mystery of the mission.

"This is Commander Jameson," he said, knowing an aide or other officer was holding the call for the admiral.

"One moment, Commander, I will put the admiral on," came the reply.

"Jameson, Willson here. Are you in Florida now?"

"Yes sir, we arrived some ten minutes ago and everything is proceeding normally. How can I be of service, sir?" Jameson didn't know what to expect and decided to play it as formally as possible.

"Commander, we have incurred another loss off the coast. It may have been a mine or a torpedo. It occurred on the sixteenth but we just received confirmation. The Brits told us more U-boats were on their way, but I don't have to tell you the boss doesn't trust their intelligence. He does trust young Brand who told him to expect more attacks shortly. What have you found out so far?"

Jameson spent the next ten minutes passing the phone back and forth to Brand as the two men tag-teamed the call. The major points Brand made concerned the lack of training in the Air Corps, the ideas on search and attack protocols, and the need to get heavy depth charges for the army bombers. Also, there was a need to educate them on deployment of the charges to maximize damage to the U-boats.

The commander then fielded several questions concerning the inter-service protocols and the need to tread lightly on the training and deployment issues. Finally, the admiral said, "Commander, you and Mr. Brand go over the navy pilots just as aggressively as you did the army boys. Do not hesitate to criticize any aspect of training, ability, aggressiveness or whatever you find. The boss wants results and is getting a lot of noise from everyone. Understand?"

"Yes sir. We will get the basics done on the ground today and then take to the air tomorrow to see how they approach the job. We will return our findings as soon as we can. By the way, Admiral, Mr. Brand wants to extend this trip by a few more days to better understand how submarines operate. He is requesting we go up to New London and have a talk with a real sub boat commander. Can you make this happen?"

The admiral responded almost instantly, "Commander, finish up in Florida and then let me know when you can get to New London. I'll keep the plane in your care until then. I'll also arrange for a meeting and even a ride in a submarine if Mr. Brand thinks that would help."

The commander knowing the wishes of his protégé replied, "Thank you, sir. That would be most helpful, and as soon as we finish here, I'll contact you for our next trip."

The admiral thanked them both, but before disconnecting asked the commander to round up the base commander and the Patrol Wing commander. He asked Brand to go get the others, and as they came in, Brand closed the door.

"Captain Young, sir, the admiral wants to speak to you."

The captain took the phone and in as strong a voice as he could muster in the situation said, "Sir, this is Captain Young, how can I be of help to the admiral?"

"Young, this is Admiral Willson. You know who I am, is that correct?"

The captain immediately replied, "Yes sir, I know that you are the chief of staff to Admiral King, sir."

"Good. Now that you know who I work for and that I am speaking for Admiral King, do you understand what I am getting at, Captain?"

"Yes sir, I understand." The captain seemed a bit nervous, but this was probably the intent of the interrogation.

"Captain, I want you to inform Captain Gannon of what I am about to tell you and if either you or he have any problems, you are to call me direct. If I am not available, you are to ask to talk to Admiral King. You will be put through immediately, is that understood?"

Again, the captain said, "Aye, aye sir. Totally understood."

"Here is what you are to do and what you need to know." The admiral proceeded to outline the mission and what was at stake to the navy and to the nation. After the minute and a half talk, Admiral Willson asked, "So, Young, do you see any problems or issues that would not allow the commander and his team to fulfill their mission?"

The captain replied, "No sir, everything that can be done will be done and I see no reason the commander and his team will be hindered from completing their mission within the next forty-eight hours."

"Captain, make sure Captain Gannon understands these orders and the pilots who will fly this mission also understand the importance and secrecy of what they are being tasked with. Let me talk to Commander Jameson."

The captain handed the phone back to Jameson and heard a few "yes sirs" and "no sirs" and then heard the commander tell the admiral he would be in contact within the next two days.

The commander hung up the phone and looked at Captain Young and the other two navy flyers. "Captain Young, please inform these officers of the orders you received from the admiral," Jameson said and watched as the captain, almost verbatim, provided the other two officers with the wishes of the navy's senior admiral.

After he had finished, Captain Young asked the other two if there were any questions.

Captain Gannon said he had none but Lieutenant Commander Hamlin began to smile and asked, "When do we fly, sir?"

Everyone smiled, now that the tension was over and waited for the navy commander who had shown up on their base with orders from the top to tell them what was next.

Jameson looked around and then said with a smile, "Gentlemen, I would like to get some lunch and I am quite sure that goes for the other members of the team. Then, let's convene a meeting with the pilots of the two planes who will be helping us in our mission. We'll need to create a flight plan exactly like what you would normally do in a routine operation. We just need to understand the entirety of it all and we will be asking lots of questions about the mission from the time of day of takeoff through all aspects of the flight dynamics, composition and experience of the crew, plus routine maintenance records for each aircraft for the past six months. I am quite sure there will be more requests, but we will try to keep them at a minimum. Any other questions or comments?"

There were none. The base commander led them out of the office towards the base kitchen to get something to eat that hopefully was more than the cold sandwiches that had sustained them on the flight from Langley.

18

20 February 1942
Naval Air Station
Banana River, Florida

- Submarine **Swordfish** evacuates President Quezon and other Philippine officials from Luzon, Philippine Islands.
- Atlantic and Pacific Fleets are directed by Commander in Chief, United States Fleet to establish Amphibious Forces.
- Japanese invade Timor Island in the Netherlands East Indies. Darwin, Australia is abandoned as an Allied naval base.

The ten-man crews of the PBYs were checking their birds out by 5 A.M. Each of the pilots had gone over their checklists three times and talked to the flight engineer about any engine issues. The navigators had spent an hour with the meteorologists looking at all the available weather information so they could construct a mental picture of the winds aloft and how that would affect their search areas. They needed to have a clear understanding of the weather conditions so they could do their calculations for any possible drift caused by the winds and set up their navigation waypoints for dead reckoning and noon sun shots. They had spent the previous evening with Ensign Brand who asked all kinds of questions on navigation, wind speeds at various altitudes, prevailing cloud conditions, and visibility. They were amazed at his level of navigation knowledge as well as his ability to locate stars for night-time sightings. This was far superior to what they had learned in navigator school at Pensacola.

The two planes were scheduled for an eight-hour flight with the outward leg one hundred miles off the coast and an inbound leg of twenty-five to fifty miles off the coastline. The squadron commander Gannon would fly the plane with Brand and the wing commander would fly the number two plane with Commander Jameson. There would be two fewer crewmen on the flight to accommodate Brand and Jameson plus Laird flying with the commander and Flannigan in the plane with Brand.

The PBY was an incredibly sturdy plane with a flight range of twenty-five hundred miles at a cruising speed of one hundred twenty-five miles per hour. This is much slower than the B-25s, but the range was nearly a thousand miles greater. The blue amphibian could carry an additional thousand-pound bomb load more than the B-25s which gave the PBY a total bomb load of four thousand pounds. All of this was carried on hard spots on the wings which were over-engineered to provide immense lift and, if necessary, the plane could slow to sixty miles per hour and without stalling. This ability to loiter at slow speed was essential for the originally envisioned search mission of the plane and had been proven early in the war by the British. It was one of their PBYs that found the German battleship Bismarck which was subsequently sunk by the British navy in June 1941.

Crews were assembled and take off was set for 0700 hours. The planes were in the water and crews went to their respective planes in thirty-foot-long motor launches. Each plane's maintenance crew had already started the engines and gone through all the checks before the flight crew boarded. Maintenance chiefs ran down the list for the pilots and co-pilots on how things were working and verified all fuel, ammunition, and bomb loads. Each plane carried four 450-pound depth charges and four 250-pound general purpose bombs. They did not have enough depth charges to put more on each plane, so the bombs would have to do. Each plane had six .50-caliber machine guns armed and checked. One of the maintenance men had the job of making sure the galley on the big bird was well equipped with coffee, water, sandwiches, fruit, and Coca-Colas for the young ensign.

Brand had never flown in a seaplane before so this would be a new and exciting experience. He was interested in the scientific issues involved in getting a plane to go fast enough to overcome the resistance caused by the sea water. The PBYs and other water-borne aircraft of the navy were called flying boats, and that description was quite accurate. The fuselage of the plane that makes up a normal aircraft like the B-25 they flew out of Langley had a tripod landing gear and the amount of resistance to get the wheels rolling was quite low compared to the tons of sea water that would pile up against the hull of a seaplane. The hull of a seaplane is exactly that, a hull. Just like a regular ship, it's designed to displace water so the plane floats and is angled like the hull of a modern high-speed boat similar to a PT boat. As the plane speeds up, it begins to rise on its hull, just like a speed boat. The wings provide more lift as it goes even faster and more of the hull gets out of the water until the hull is totally airborne and the plane can climb. The opposite happens when it lands. The plane slowly descends so as not to "crash" into the water but slowly touches the water until it is descending to its correct depth, then the plane comes to a slow rest in the water, much like the action when a speedboat slows down and no longer planes on the water's surface.

All of this requires an understanding of the flight physics and the movement of water around the hull. Pilots of seaplanes are a special breed because of their ability to fly and their ability to handle a large, ungainly boat. They need to understand how this ballet between sea and sky works to prevent breaking the plane apart on either takeoff or landing. Many planes had crashed because of human error and today these two pilots were more concerned than usual as they started their taxi to the marked channel serving as their takeoff and landing strip.

Lieutenant Commander Hamlin signaled his co-pilot Lt. (jg) Bob Henson, and looked to his flight engineer to begin revving the engines.

There are no brakes on a seaplane, and they had to begin their movement as soon as the planes got their power up. Both pilot and co-pilot had their hands on the controls, and the flight engineer was calling out speeds as the plane started to go from the wallow of a boat to a slowly lifting plane on the water. With each second the plane felt alive as it bounced very slowly on its way to flight. At around sixty miles per hour, the plane wanted to leave the water for good, but the commander kept it low as it gained more speed and therefore more lift. This was the most dangerous time for any plane, but for a seaplane like the PBY, a loss of power or hitting a wave could easily damage the plane or worse, make it crash head on into the water.

Suddenly, there was no more bouncing. The plane left its water environment and became a true airplane. The engine noise was extreme but nothing as bad as the B-25. The planes two massive engines were high on the wing and more outboard than the army bombers. As the plane reached one thousand feet, the pilot called for a reduction in power and the plane became much quieter. Brand walked back to the huge plexiglas windows on each side of the plane and looked back to see the other plane working its way skyward toward its partner. The key attribute of visibility in the plane was quite evident. Besides the huge window nacelles on the side of the plane, there was a large observatory-like structure in the front of the plane housing a machine gun. Two men could view the world on a 180-degree basis from this location. The pilots also had great window seats to the world. All these features were designed into the plane in 1937. It might be slow, but it was a great observatory in the sky and fulfilled its mission well.

After another twenty minutes, the two planes reached cruising altitude of ten thousand feet with Commander Jameson's plane some half mile off to the right of Brand's plane and behind it by one thousand yards. Over the course of the flight, both planes would trade off positions and altitudes to investigate optimal observation locations. The flight path would take them on a course of thirty degrees north by northeast, then the planes would fly due north for two hours. The planes would then head due west toward the coast at a heading of 195 degrees south by southwest to return. They would be anywhere from one hundred twenty-five miles off the coastline near North Carolina to twelve miles off the coast of Florida. This would permit them the chance to do some small search squares of thirty miles by thirty miles halfway between their maximum search area to the east and their minimum off the coast. The goal was, of course, to look for and attack U-boats, but today's mission was to examine search protocols and experiment with attack profiles with hopefully the real thing but probably a simulated target in the ocean. Both crews had been informed of the mission profile and the guests aboard the two planes were in control.

Three hours passed with the planes jockeying for position to the right or left and then they would swap locations and either gain altitude or drop, depending on the outline for the flight plan Brand had designed. At the three-hour point, Captain Gannon with Commander Jameson as his primary passenger was flying at nine thousand feet and nearly a mile in front of the plane Brand was in. The crew in Brand's plane could still see the captain's PBY just to the right of the nose of their plane. Suddenly, the plane began to drop to the right with an extreme bank.

Before Hamlin could react, the radio operator bounced up to the pilot and shouted, "Sir, Captain Gannon has spotted what looks like a submarine bearing due east from his position and is going down to check it out. He wants you to follow. Shall I signal an affirmative?"

"Damn right, tell him I am on my way." Lieutenant Commander Hamlin now had the controls and ordered full power to the engines. "Crew, man your battle positions. Check all guns and be prepared to drop bombs." The commander looked over at the co-pilot who had pulled out a checklist and was looking intently at the instruments as the plane started to drop at a very fast speed for the big amphibian.

Brand looked out the cockpit window with his binoculars, scanning the seas in the direction indicated by the radio. He had started one of his two stopwatches so he could time the reaction of the crew and the U-boat if that is what it was.

Flannigan was on the plane's intercom saying, "Submarine at two points off starboard and it looks like it is diving."

Everyone on Hamlin's plane looked over to see a submarine on the surface heading in their direction. The plane was now at less than four thousand feet, and the captain's plane was nearing fifteen hundred feet and dropping fast. The submarine had to be a U-boat because no American submarines were operating in this area for fear of being attacked by friendly forces or by the Germans.

The co-pilot shouted, "Looks like it's almost totally underwater already with only a periscope showing. No, it is gone now too, but there is still a wake to follow. Heading straight on the line with the captain."

As the crew looked ahead they saw what remained of the wake where the submarine had been and within a few seconds, the other PBY was over the target area. Two splashes broke the waves. Seconds later, two huge eruptions occurred. Water billowed up, exploding in the air. The captain's PBY was pulling up, and the commander was ready for the attack when Brand asked, "What are your intentions, sir?"

The pilot looked over at the young ensign and almost yelling, "I am going to sink the son of a bitch!"

"Sir, your depth charges are set at fifty feet, and by now the German is down to over a hundred feet and probably turned to either the right or left as he dove which makes an attack a losing proposition. I would recommend we linger over the target at height and see if he comes up again. I think it will take him at least forty-five minutes to an hour to come back to periscope depth to see what's on the surface. He probably can scan the skies as well so if we want a chance to get him, we should get back to at least three thousand feet and circle the area in a five to ten-mile loop. That way if he comes up again, you have a good shot."

Hamlin grimaced knowing Brand was correct. He had been briefed on the Germans' ability to dive quickly when retreating from danger so if he took Brand's advice and waited, he could maybe have a good shot, not a long shot. The commander pulled out of his shallow dive and told the radio operator to get the captain on the inter-airplane radio channel.

A moment later, the radio operator said, "He's on, sir."

"Captain, Brand says we should go up high and loiter to see if this guy will come up again. Your orders, sir." The commander waited a few seconds. "Roger that. How high should we go and what should we do for a formation?" Lieutenant Commander Hamlin looked over at Brand and told him to take his headset to talk directly to the captain.

Brand grabbed the headset and the microphone from Hamlin but stayed right next to him so he could hear both parts of the conversation. "Sir, Brand here. I recommend we go to three thousand feet and fly a long oval with a track of maybe eight to ten miles. Both of us together but spaced by one thousand yards. The German will probably go down to two hundred feet and loiter. They cannot go much faster than six knots submerged, so I calculate if he went either right or left he will not stray more than four miles from where you engaged him. I doubt he would go in a reverse course because he is probably just getting to his station. If we can hang on for at least one hour and stay high, he may come up again. If he does, both planes will need to attack, and he will dive. But this time, if we can drop at sixty-foot intervals and set at twenty-five to fifty feet explosion depth, we may have a chance to at least damage him. Over."

There was a pause of at least a minute from the other plane before Captain Gannon came back on the radio, "Okay, Mr. Brand, let's hang around for an hour, maybe a bit more. I concur in your attack plan. Hamlin, set all weapons for the attack and let's see if he comes back up. I will signal base to alert all shipping of our location and move any vessels out of the area. Over."

Brand gave the headphones and hand-held microphone back to Hamlin and then took out his notepad and started to write again. He did not have time to see the drop by Gannon and the spacing of the depth charges. He would have to rely on Jameson's notes and memory to help in his calculations. He had seen some of the reports from the British admiralty on how they had dropped aerial depth charges and how their effectiveness had improved when using shorter spacing. Also, he had done his calculations before this trip on the need to not waste munitions on badly planned attacks which had a very poor success rate.

The German U-boats could submerge within fifty seconds of seeing an attacking plane, and could dive at two feet per second. The speed of a U-boat under power was still great, and when it switched to batteries it was being propelled by the inertia of the big diesel engines which meant a German Type IX could travel up to one thousand feet during a crash dive to get below periscope depth. The questions to be answered are, where do you drop your weapons, what is the spacing of the drop, and what is the best depth setting for the charges to maximize damage? The British had concluded it was a waste of time and effort to try to conduct an aerial attack when the submarine has submerged and is no longer visible, or has been submerged for more than fifteen seconds.

The other key to successfully prosecuting an attack is to maintain discipline for a great amount of time to get the U-boat to resurface. Holding a U-boat down is the first part in winning this battle because the enemy cannot attack a merchant convoy if it cannot catch them. All submarines were slow under water and had limited battery capacity to sustain any speed over six knots for more than two hours. They could crawl, but they could not find a convoy two to three knots faster than they were.

After a little more than an hour, Captain Gannon came back on the radio. "Hamlin, we are getting near our return time. How are you on fuel?"

Hamlin looked over at the co-pilot and the flight engineer who gave him a hand signal which meant 3.2 hours left of fuel. He reported this information to the captain.

"Let's wait another fifteen minutes, then we must return. The base has no other planes available to take over the search, so if this guy is going to show up for us, he has only a few more minutes left. Over."

Hamlin acknowledged and continued his gaze out of the cockpit window.

The German U-boat commander gave the order to come up to periscope depth to see if the amateurish Americans had left. He had been briefed in La Rochelle fourteen days ago as to the mediocre quality of the American's efforts and total failure to prosecute attacks like the British did. He was glad he didn't have to deal with the British air patrols nor did he relish dealing with the Canadian escorts he had encountered in November as he patrolled near Iceland. His boat was nearly rammed by a Corvette, and he was lucky to come out alive. This was his third war patrol, and he wanted to make up for his poor showing of only one kill on his last cruise. He had read all the messages from people like Hardegen and his successful voyage in U-123 where he had sunk nine ships and had encountered no opposition at all.

He had the boat at periscope depth and asked for the primary periscope to be raised slowly. He was holding on as it went up and barely broke the surface, trailing very little wake. The boat was barely moving forward doing only two knots. The captain quickly spun the periscope around and then ordered it down. "Nothing on the surface. Now let's look at the sky." He had been briefed about planes loitering in the area but staying close to the sea level for a fast attack. He figured if he were a pilot, he would stay under three thousand feet so he could attack quickly. The periscope went up, and he spun it around much slower so he could see the sky situation. He completed two rotations before he ordered it down again. His executive officer looked at him and waited for a command to go up or head back down to a safer depth. After a few more seconds of consideration, the captain ordered, "Surface! All lookouts up and scan the sky. Be ready to dive on my order," as he looked at the exec and then waited for the boat to rise. This was the most dangerous part of the maneuver. He was blind until he could get up top.

Two thousand yards away and three thousand feet high, eagle eye Flannigan thought he saw something. He got on the intercom and informed the pilot, "Commander, I think I just saw something at one o'clock. Maybe a periscope up for just a moment."

Hamlin got back to him immediately saying, "How far out? I am coming back to that course."

Before Flannigan could say anything else, he spied the periscope again. "I can see it now at one o'clock. There it is, barely a whisper behind it. Must be looking at us. Over."

"Got it," Hamlin exclaimed. "Okay people, if it starts to come up we are going in. Radio, notify the captain."

Everyone on the plane looked at the dark blue sea trying to locate what the marine lieutenant had pointed out, but only Brand had a confirmation. "Got it. Yes, it looks like a periscope, and it is looking around. Just saw a flash from the mirror. Okay, Commander, just like we discussed. As soon as we see any more movement come right on the attack course. If we can get it anywhere from fifteen to forty-five degrees off center, that would be great. Just a minute, yes, there it is. It's coming up."

Everyone on the plane looked toward the sub except the pilot and co-pilot who were busy adjusting the plane to the new course and beginning their dive.

"Forward Gunner, get set, if we come close and it's still up, aim for the conning tower and anybody on it. Same goes for the side gunners. As we pass, shoot it up."

The radio operator had been given instructions for this possibility and communicated to the other plane to follow in the dive. The plane was building up speed, and the U-boat was starting to rise out of the depths, slowly at first. Next came the larger periscope housing, then the start of the conning tower and the bow of the boat began to emerge from the sea.

The PBY was less than eight hundred yards away when the first member of the U-boat crew sprang out of the hatch and climbed into their watch locations. The airplane approached from the rear quarter. The submarine's engines were running, masking the noise of the plane's Pratt and Whitney engines throbbing at full speed toward the black hull rising from the sea.

It was at four hundred yards now and less than a thousand feet when one of the German lookouts saw the plane diving on them. He yelled, and the captain who had just got on the deck of the conning tower saw it too. "Crash dive!" He jumped back down the hatch with the other two lookouts as the boat quickly began its descent.

Hamlin yelled, "Open fire, she is going down!'

The forward single .50-caliber machine gun immediately began firing with the young marine helping the forward gunner take aim. The plane got closer and closer, with the other PBY now coming in behind the first one by twelve hundred yards. The submarine was being hit by the slugs of the .50 caliber but not suffering major damage. Brand's note taking and attention were continuous like any good scientist observing a lab experiment. But this was life and death, and he was a witness.

The U-boat was nearly under water as the PBY caught up with it. The first of four depth charges were dropped just as the submarine was covered with the sea, the co-pilot jettisoned the weapon by counting as Brand had instructed to gain the correct spacing. The plane waggled a bit with each drop, but in a few seconds four depth charges were hitting the sea and dropping. The plane pulled up as the other PBY came in for its attack.

First, there was only one explosion, then another and another, but a large bubble burst where the last one had occurred. Was this the kill shot Brand had read about from the admiralty reports?

The second PBY was almost to the target when the submarine's nose came back into view. The boat was being driven up by some magical force. The crew of both planes could not see the damage to the sub's forward diving planes. One was smashed in and up. The other was broken along with a major part of the bow. The boat suffered severe damage, but could surface. It would need repairs to dive again, but with two planes circling above, that was not a possibility.

The second PBY pulled up, and dropped two more depth charges along the hull. They exploded fifty feet below and about seventy-five feet to the right of the U-boat, and the bubble pushed the boat by the stern. The bow dropped into the water, and the boat rolled a bit. The plane carrying Brand turned to attack with bombs as the U-boat regained stability, but it appeared to be dead in the water. Approaching the damaged submarine at cruising speed, the PBY was in line to drop its regular bombs when the submarine's crew appeared on the conning tower with life vests and began jumping into the water.

Captain Gannon yelled into his radio, "Cease firing. Do not fire on the submarine unless fired upon."

Lieutenant Commander Hamlin quickly spoke into his intercom, "Cease firing. Keep an eye on those SOBs, but we are not going to shoot men leaving a ship."

Both planes now circled as more and more crewmen jumped overboard. One, then two small life rafts appeared. Men began to climb on as more crew members could be seen leaving the sub. The U-boat was going down slowly, and was now totally dead in the water. Within four minutes, the boat was no longer visible. Men were clinging to the two small lifeboats, and it appeared several of the Germans were injured.

Captain Gannon looked down at the Germans. He couldn't land and take on the survivors but he could drop one of the plane's lifeboats. He radioed for Hamlin's plane to do the same, then both planes passed close enough to make their drops. Gannon radioed the location to the base asking for a navy or coast guard warship to help in the rescue of the enemy, not just for humane reasons but for intelligence. After a few more slow passes to confirm all the Germans were in the lifeboats, the planes wagged their wings to the German sailors and headed for Banana River. They were now not only veterans of combat but successful warriors who had sunk a German submarine.

All of this was impressive to young Brand, but he was now in research mode reliving the experience for his notes, inspecting his calculations, and thinking of how he could improve upon this result in the future. He had Hamlin get Jameson on the radio and urged him to rescue the Germans for interrogation and validation of his theories. He knew he may get little out of these men, but he might get enough to move his theories into fresh territory.

When the planes landed three hours later, there was quite a reception committee. Captain Young looked on like an expectant parent waiting for his child to come home from his first day of school and the other patrol wing pilots wanted to hear all about the battle. Everyone on the base had heard the news and the captain had already secured the area and made sure no word of the successful attack left the base. He notified Admiral Willson's office immediately, informing him of the request for a warship to pick up the U-boat survivors. He had also sent the same information to Admiral Andrews in New York to alert the entire Eastern Sea Frontier Command about the attack on the U-boat and of the high probability that others were nearby.

Captain Young pulled Commander Jameson and Ensign Brand away from the celebration and gave them a copy of the signal traffic coming from Washington, requesting a great amount of detailed information. One of them confirmed the USS *Jacob Jones* was being dispatched to locate survivors. The ship had been on a search mission south of Cape Hatteras and was approximately thirteen hours from the U-boat's location. Once found and brought on board, the old four stack destroyer was to deliver the prisoners to Charleston Naval Base for interrogation. The communique stressed the utmost secrecy concerning the sinking of the U-boat, and no public disclosure was to be made.

Admiral Willson left instructions for Commander Jameson and Ensign Brand to call him as soon as he landed to discuss the attack and results. Young had seen the request and ushered both Jameson and Brand into his office, and asked his chief yeoman to make the call.

The call went as expected with Willson wanting a complete written report sent by courier as soon as possible. He asked about events surrounding the attack and how it occurred. He was especially interested in the time waiting for the submarine to reappear. Admiral Willson asked, "Brand, what gave you the idea to just wait it out?"

"Admiral, the Brits in their report from late December outlined these steps, and I just expanded on their research. Their experiences and research data are invaluable. We need to dig deeper into their analytics to see what else there is so we don't have to reinvent the wheel, sir."

Jameson grimaced when he heard the comments knowing Admiral King did not like to follow the British lead on anything. Willson also knowing this all too well commented, "Mr. Brand, let me see what other information I can get from our Allies that may make your research easier. Just keep it close to you where this information comes from, is that clear?"

"Yes sir, I understand, and if I may say, I think we have some ideas which will make the Brits better at this game as well."

"Good to know, Brand. Do you still want to talk to our submariners?"

Brand looked over at Jameson who didn't respond. "Yes sir. Based upon the attack we made, I would like to better understand their way of thinking and how they take evasive maneuvers."

"Very well, plan to get up to New London in the next two days. Get me your reports before you go up there. Admiral King is delighted by this sinking. Any information you can share for future operations would be wonderful. And by the way, well done. Now, let me speak to Commander Jameson again." With that last comment, Brand handed the phone to the commander and waited until the call was over.

"Sir," Brand asked, "I would like to be informed if the survivors of the sinking are brought some place so that I may do some questioning. I know they may not be too willing to talk, but my German is good, and perhaps I can get some information from them that a regular interrogator might miss."

"We'll see what we can arrange, James. Are you okay with getting a report for Admiral Willson before we head to New London to meet some American submariners?"

"Yes sir, no problem. I have my notes all organized, and it will only take me a few hours on the typewriter to get it finalized. I would like to see your notes first and see if we agree on what we saw. I am especially interested in bomb spacing, flight speeds, and understanding the original sighting made from your plane. After that, I'll need more time for some of the calculations. I want to help flyers drop their weapons in a more accurate fashion and at depths that will be most effective. I can work up some of that information on the trip north."

"All right then, I'll get the team set to fly out of here tomorrow at noon, if that is sufficient time for you to type your report. I'll arrange for a courier to take it to Admiral Willson. Oh, one other thing, James, the admiral is very happy with what you've accomplished so far and especially for winning over both him and Admiral King. That alone may be worthy of a medal."

Jameson started to laugh as James broke into a smile and realized getting the attention of the navy's top admiral truly was something of an achievement.

19

21 February 1942
Washington, D.C.

- Bataan Peninsula, Philippines: Lull settles over entire front as both sides dig in and prepare for further action. Japanese have completed withdrawal from I Corps area; diversionary forces are employed against II Corps are ordered back to Balanga area.

The plane had left Banana River at 0900 hours and included two additional passengers. A request had been made by Admiral Willson's office for the initial reports on the U-boat sinking be brought to Washington by the pilot and co-pilot of the PBY that sank the submarine. The base commander, Captain Young, received this information around 1800 hours from one of the admiral's aides which required the captain to corral the two men prior to them getting totally blasted in the officer's club.

Every officer on the base who did not have duty had shown up to see the heroes and congratulate them for their success. The captain quickly slowed the festivities when he pulled the young men from the club along with Patrol Wing Commander, Captain Gannon. He also found the scientist Commander Jameson and asked him to join him in the office. Jameson had just finished reviewing the first draft of Brand's report and was watching him work out some theoretical problems with his slide rule when Young came calling. Jameson had no problem leaving Brand alone because he was never alone. Two corporals were sitting outside his door, and if he needed anything, it would be provided by these two marines.

Jameson listened to the captain as he related his call from Admiral Willson's office, which did not please the two young officers. Neither Lieutenant Commander Hamlin or his co-pilot, Lt. (jg) Bob Henson wanted anything to do with going to Washington. They wanted to get back in their plane and find another Nazi sub to sink.

Captain Gannon, knowing these two were going whether they wanted to or not put his foot down and told them, "The party will reconvene on your return. This will be a long war, and you will have many chances to sink another U-boat. The request from Admiral King's chief of staff was not a party invitation. So, you two are forbidden to go back to the club. You will go to your quarters and ensure you have your Class A winter uniforms ready with a change available. You will be prepared to fly out of here at 0800 hours, and you will act like proper navy gentlemen, or you will find yourselves counting socks in New Foundland. Do I make myself clear?"

"Yes sir," came the sullen voices of the two young officers.

"Commander Jameson, will you please ensure these two heroes get off the plane in Washington sober and in proper uniform?" The captain grinned at Jameson, then looked back at his two flyers with a stern countenance.

"Sir, I am quite sure these officers will enjoy the flight and will be in good order when they get off the plane. I understand from the communique that an aide to Admiral Willson will be at the airport with a car and driver so they will not get lost." Jameson remarked with a straight face knowing the two pilots would probably be meeting Admiral King and would be given some sort of medal for their efforts. King needed heroes right now, and almost all the news he had recently received was bad and getting worse. He also surmised the two young officers would be doing several other briefings to other officers at Old Navy and the officer's club would be their not-too-sober home for several days. They deserved their day in the sun, and were certainly going to be the talk of the town for a few days.

The plane arrived at Washington around noon, and as it taxied to the terminal, was met by one of the "follow me" vehicles with the sign and a big checkered flag. The pilot dutifully followed the small truck, and came to a stop outside a hangar at the far end of the regular terminal. Two navy staff cars drove out to the R4D with one of them flying the two-star flag of a rear admiral.

Jameson noticed this as did Flannigan who immediately yelled out to the passengers of the plane, "Look, smart men, there is a two-star flag on the lead car. So, get yourself presentable and straighten your ties. Gunny, you and Laird off first and set up by the door. Commander Jameson and Hamlin, you gentlemen exit first followed by Henson and Brand. I'll bring up the rear with the rest of the detachment. Step to full review positions. Understand?"

"Aye, aye sir," came the reply from the entire plane.

The navy crew chief looked out the window and saw a small stairway coming forward just like this was a regular civilian plane. Two navy ratings pushed it up to the correct position and then jumped up the five steps and banged on the door.

The crew chief opened the door and looked out as several officers were now assembled in front of their cars and only thirty feet from the doorway. He squinted and saw there was more gold braid than he had ever seen before and quickly backed into the plane. He caught Jameson before he could exit and said, "Sir, there are at least three admirals out there, sir, so be careful."

Jameson smiled at the chief and exited the plane followed by the two PBY pilots, Brand, and Flannigan with his marines. A full navy captain marched up to Jameson and received Jameson's salute.

"Commander Jameson, welcome to Langley. Please have your officers follow me."

The captain performed a perfect about face and walked towards the senior officers.

Jameson seeing that the marines were all standing at attention by the plane ordered, "Officers, front, and center."

The officers including Brand and Flannigan marched up behind the commander and moved in unison towards the admirals.

Jameson ordered, "Detail, halt. Attention." The officers saluted and held the salute as is customary until returned by a senior officer.

In front of Jameson and his group stood from right to left, Adm. Ernest J. King, Rear Adm. Adolphus Andrews and Rear Admiral Willson. Andrews was in town from his office in New York City to meet with King about the U-boat attacks up and down the east coast.

King returned the salute and began walking down the line shaking each person's hand. "Jameson, good to see you. Well done, Commander, for you and the team."

"Thank you, sir," Jameson said as King walked to the next man.

"Lieutenant Flannigan, you must have extraordinary eyesight for spotting that sub's periscope from such a height,"

The young marine replied, "Just good training, sir."

King smiled at Flannigan's humble response, because he did not like men who were too proud of momentary achievements. King moved down the line and said, "You must be Lieutenant Commander Gannon and Lieutenant Henson. I wanted to personally shake your hand for doing a great job sinking that German sub."

He extended his hand to each man who in turn shook the hand of the top man in the navy. King admired warriors like these young men, saw the awe in their eyes and said, "You and your crews are doing the job I would love to do. I'm stuck here in Washington with these other old men while you young men win the war. I am very proud of you, and look forward to hearing from you personally about this victory." He smiled at each, then walked to the last man on the line.

"So, Mr. Brand, it seems you are earning your keep. I have read the operations reports, but I know you have some additional information to share. Is that correct?'

Brand, somewhat lost in front of all of the brass, calmly replied,

U-BOAT SCOURGE

"Sir, I have reached several conclusions as to how to prosecute the war against the U-boat. My report on the successful attack carried out by Commander Hamlin and Lieutenant Henson will provide you with some suggestions for current tactics and strategies as well as some new developments which will help in this mission. I have some other research to conduct, but Commander Jameson and I feel confident we can reduce our casualties considerably in the next few months."

King looked at the young ensign and just like last time, approved of what he saw. Brand was not afraid to speak his mind. All his thoughts and ideas were research-based, not just wild-ass guesses.

King replied, "Okay, Mr. Brand. Come back to the office with me and let me see this report. I have Admiral Andrews with me, and he is very anxious to get your ideas into practice. Jameson, you go with Admiral Willson and our two young heroes. Brand is coming with me and Admiral Andrews."

With that last sentence, King grabbed Brand by the arm and walked towards his car. He was quickly introduced to Admiral Andrews and the three of them got in the back seat with Brand in between the two admirals. One of King's aides, a navy captain, got in the front seat with the marine driver. At the gate, two more staff cars were waiting for the admiral's car and both were full of marine guards and other aides.

Willson watched the car carrying his boss and Brand drive off, then waved Jameson over and whispered, "I hope young Brand makes it back to the office with those two. King wants him to help Andrews get the Eastern Sea Frontier Command moving on these recommendations as soon as possible. The president is asking every day what the navy is doing. The sinking of the U-boat really helped, but one sinking does not solve our problem."

Admiral Willson looked over at his aide and asked where the other cars were for transporting the rest of the team to barracks. He wanted to make sure Flannigan was coming with him and the PBY pilots so he told the aide to follow in another car.

Willson got in the car and smiled at the two young navy flyers, whispering to Jameson, "We need to get over to King's office and rescue Brand before he goes off the reservation on something like British intelligence."

Jameson nodded and whispered back, "I instructed James that he was not to say anything about the Brits except in the written reports, but I know he wants to get access to more of their research on their success and failures."

Willson nodded. Turning to the two PBY flyers he asked, "Have either of you gentlemen ever been to Washington before?"

As the small convoy of staff cars drove through the city of Washington, D.C., the questioning of Ensign Brand grew more intense. Admiral Andrews wanted more information about the attack on the submarine, and Admiral King wanted to know more about Brand's ideas on daylight convoys and new weapons to attack the U-boats from the air. King, of course, won the battle for time and Andrews knew his Annapolis classmate was the boss and had the bigger ego, so he interjected his comments carefully. Within ten minutes, the convoy pulled up to Old Navy, as the headquarters of the United States Navy was known, and the marine guard snapped to attention and action. Two aides appeared at the door and opened it, asking the boss if he had time for this or that, and which meetings were being shuffled because of this unscheduled trip to the airport. King brushed all the comments aside. The aides knew better than to push their luck, so they followed behind the entourage until they came to Admiral King's office.

Standing as King appeared was Rear Admiral Turner and an army brigadier general that King had previously met once or twice. The two flag officers stood at attention, and Turner tried to catch King's attention, which he did when he saw Brand coming in behind Admiral Andrews.

"Look what washed up in Washington, but everyone's boy genius."

Brand went to attention at seeing Admiral Turner for the first time since his hospital meeting some weeks before. "Good to see you, sir."

King turned to Turner, "Don't have time for you Turner, I have to ask Mr. Brand more questions before I go to the White House. I will get with you in a few minutes. Good to see you, General. I will be with you both in a few minutes."

"No problem, sir," came the reply from the brigadier general. "I will wait with Admiral Turner."

Brand smiled at the new man with a great grin and followed the admiral into his office.

Another fifteen minutes went by as King fired questions at Brand. He finally wrapped up the impromptu meeting by saying, "Brand, good work on this. I'll look at your full report tonight, and I will be patient for the rest of your observations after you get back from New London. Admiral Andrews will want to be briefed as well so plan to spend some time with him after you finish up with me. What you have done and what you are doing is very important. I like the idea of daylight convoys with our pitiful small number of escorts, even though it will add another day at sea for most ships. I would rather have them late than sunk. Also, your attack plans need to be finalized and sent to all army and navy air units, and your plan to train a few instructors in the tactics is very sound. We need to get people to do their job better and much faster."

King walked around the office for a minute. Brand did not say anything as he was beginning to understand how King operated. Finally, King turned and almost whispered in a conspirator's voice, "Do you think we can get these aerial rockets working so you can, as you say, extend the reach of the aircraft?"

Brand looked at the admiral and replied in a very strong voice, "Sir, the Brits have had some success with small diameter rockets, and the Air Corps has looked at this information as well. What everyone is missing is the correct propellant. Rockets are dumb weapons and go where they are aimed. Getting the correct spin on the rocket as it launches was proven by Dr. Goddard in the '20s. What we need, and I'm sure American chemistry can quickly demonstrate, is a fast burning but powerful solid fuel to propel a rocket armed with a twenty-five-pound warhead, one to two miles before running out of fuel. This is a science problem for our chemists to develop the propellant, and metallurgy to safely allow the firing and flight of the rocket, and lastly, training pilots on how to use it. If we had had some sort of rocket device on the PBY, we would have crippled the U-boat on the first pass." He then looked at his feet for just a moment and collected his thoughts. He continued, "I think this type of weapon would be very useful in ground support for the marines and army troops as well as an effective anti-ship weapon, primarily against merchant shipping and escort vessels."

King looked at Andrews who nodded his head in agreement. "Get me some ideas on paper on how it would work, who could do it and anything else that you think I need to move on this idea."

"Yes sir. I will get this to you as soon as I get back from New London. I think by understanding how our submarine people operate, it will help me get a feel on how the Germans run their boat. Also, if we gain a workable strategy out of this effort, we'll need to come up with a defensive strategy for our people."

King smiled, which was very rare indeed and told Brand, "Mr. Brand, get out of my office before you find a way to replace me with your ideas. Report back to me as soon as you return to Washington."

Brand stood to attention and then executed a proper about face and walked out of the office.

Andrews watched as the young man left, then turned to King, "Ernie, he is everything you told me and more. Where did you find him?"

King looked at his old classmate and replied, "The man in the White House requested I find him at Navy Boot Camp and I did. Dolly, it is a very long story, but at some point, I'll fill you in. I'll send him to you at your headquarters when he finishes his report. But you cannot keep him, all right?"

Andrews looked at his old friend, now commander in chief of the United States Fleet and said, "No problem. If he is this valuable on the U-boat problem, I am sure he has great potential for the future. I think we are in for a long war and we will need strong minds more than strong backs."

King picked up the phone to start the parade of supplicants who wanted his time. Most had problems they wanted him to solve instead of telling him how they had solved the problem. He wished he had a dozen more men like Brand.

When Brand walked out of the office, Admiral Willson was standing with Commander Jameson. They were talking to Admiral Turner and the army brigadier general. Brand walked by but was caught by Admiral Willson.

"Mr. Brand, how did your meeting go with the admiral?"

"Very well, I think, sir. I have more items on my plate than when I went in so I guess things are doing okay." Brand smiled at the admiral who was getting friendlier every time they met. The admiral then turned to the other flag officers and said, "Sorry, Mr. Brand, I did not introduce you to these two officers."

Before Willson could continue, Admiral Turner stopped him by saying, "I'm well acquainted with Mr. Brand. We met in a hospital in San Diego. Isn't that correct, Ensign?"

"Yes sir, and thank you for all you have done for the commander and our team." Brand looked over at Jameson to see if what he said was all right and he saw him nod in approval.

"Ensign Brand, I would like you to meet my counterpart in the War Plans Division of the army. General Eisenhower, this is the young man I have told you about."

The bald but smiling brigadier general moved forward to shake the hand of the young ensign.

"Good to meet you, Ensign. Admiral Turner holds you in high esteem, and I also know for a fact that General Marshall has the same opinion. Hopefully, sometime in the future, I can pry you away from the navy to ask you a few questions on issues common to both the army and the navy." The brigadier again smiled.

Brand could feel the warmth of the man plus a burning curiosity about all things military. "Sir, it would be my pleasure to assist you in any way possible. I have an assignment from Admiral King that will take me a few days to complete, but upon my return, I would enjoy talking to you at your convenience."

Eisenhower, who had been working eighteen-hour days since he arrived in Washington on December 11 did not appear tired but smiled again at the young ensign and handed him a card with his contact information. The card said, "Assistant Chief of Staff–War Plans" and he held the same job Turner held in the navy. He had recently replaced his old friend Major General Gerow in the job and now reported directly to General Marshall. Eisenhower had already met with the Combined Chiefs of Staff of the British and American armed forces plus the president and Prime Minister Churchill. Marshall had been grooming him all along for this job, and he would be promoted to major general in another month and made chief of operations for the army.

Jameson whispered something to Admiral Willson, who in turn told the other flag officers, "Gentlemen, we need to let the commander and ensign get on with their job. They have a plane to catch. Commander, please call me from New London with an update on your progress and your expected return. I believe Admiral King wants more information from Brand soon. Is that not correct, Ensign?"

Brand smiled knowing he was now able to leave the stuffy air of the high command. "Yes sir, we need to get our group together so we can leave."

Just then, one of Admiral King's aides came up to Willson and said something in his ear.

"Understood, Commander, where are they now?"

The commander pointed out of the room to the hallway beyond and said, "Sir, the pilots are out there, and the admiral wants the commander and the ensign present for the presentation."

"Very well, Commander. Go get the pilots, and I will bring the commander and ensign."

Willson turned to face the other two officers and said, "Sorry, but I need to borrow these two again because they are going to watch the two pilots who sank the German submarine get a medal."

Willson ushered in the two latecomers and stood at the back of Admiral King's office as he talked to each of the pilots about their attack and how they accomplished the mission. Both were somewhat shy in their explanation about the attack but then Lieutenant Commander Hamlin said, "Sir, we would have never sunk that submarine, let alone find it, without the help of Ensign Brand and the eyesight of Lieutenant Flannigan. They are the ones who made this attack not only possible but also a success."

King smiled at the commander and replied, "Yes, I know that both fine officers were there and providing you with a plan to make this attack a success but it was you two gentlemen who flew the plane and dropped the bombs." He turned and nodded to an aide who immediately barked, "Attention to orders!"

U-BOAT SCOURGE

Everyone in the room snapped to attention including Admiral Andrews and Willson. The aide, a full captain, then took a piece of paper off the admirals' desk and began to read.

"Commendation for action on the Eastern Sea Frontier, the nineteenth of February 1942.

"On this day, a PBY flown by Lt. Comdr. George F. Hamlin and Lt. (jg) Robert K. Henson successfully located and sank an enemy submarine. The following awards are made to these officers.

"Commander Hamlin awarded the Distinguished Flying Cross."

King took the medal from the desk behind him and pinned it on the commander and shook his hand.

The aide continued, "Lieutenant Junior Grade Henson awarded the Distinguished Flying Cross."

King took the second medal on his desk and pinned it on the young co-pilot and shook his hand as well.

King looked at the aide who backed away from the admiral and then looking at the two flyers said, "I am very proud of you and what you have accomplished. I hope that this is the first of many a German submarine that you and your squadron sink. With your continued leadership, we will win this war. Well done."

King again shook their hands and then made one more last comment. "Gentlemen, I know that it takes more than the pilots to make these missions successful. I am authorizing each member of the plane's crew to receive the Air Medal for their service. I am also doing the same for Captain Young and his crew for their meritorious service in this attack."

This seemed to please the two flyers more than receiving the DFCs. They immediately smiled and caught the glance of the aide standing next to the admiral and realized no further comment was needed. The aide then said, "Thank you, gentlemen, you are dismissed."

Everyone came back to attention as the two young flyers were escorted out of the office.

King looked at Jameson, Brand, and Flannigan and then smiled saying, "Does that make you envious gentlemen?"

The commander did not flinch. "No sir, we were passengers on the plane and did not attack the submarine. They did the work. Thank you for honoring the entire crew of both planes, sir."

"Brand," King looked right at him, "what do you say?"

Brand was quick and right to the point, "Sir, they are the pilots, and we were just cargo trying to figure out what actually occurs in these missions. I was glad we could be of assistance. We were just doing our job." Brand stood silent, then added, "But, sir, I think Lieutenant Flannigan deserves recognition for finding the sub in the first place. If it were not for his amazing eyesight, we would have never seen the U-boat."

Flannigan was not pleased to hear the comment but knew better than to say anything, especially to the admiral.

King, smiling again which was such a rarity that Willson had to struggle to maintain a straight face, looked at Brand and then at Flannigan and said, "Mr. Brand, you are full of surprises and at least you are not afraid to tell me what you think." King thought for a moment and then said, "I was not going to do this now, but each of you is to receive the DFC for this effort. It was you that made this happen. The pilots were just doing what they have been trained to do. But, I want you to know there will be no ceremony for you or any member of your team. You will be awarded the medals, and the sergeants who were on the plane with you will receive the Air Medal. Your records will show this award, and I am going to have Admiral Willson pin it on you. Now, get out of here before I transfer you all to the army."

Willson was almost about to laugh as was Admiral Andrews at this last comment. Willson then said, "Admiral, your meeting at the White House will be starting soon so with your permission, I'll get these men back to their plane so they can continue their mission."

King nodded and Willson escorted the officers out of the admiral's office and into his office where his aide stood by with three medals.

Part 4

20

22 February 1942
New London Submarine Base, Connecticut

- President Roosevelt orders General MacArthur to leave the Philippines.
- United Kingdom--Headquarters of U.S. Bomber Command, USAFBI is established under Gen. Ira C. Eaker.

The office of the commander-submarines, Atlantic Fleet, was in a constant state of flux. The commanding officer was temporary, and he knew he could be replaced at any moment, but still he had a job to do. His name was Capt. E. F. Cutts. He had been the chief of staff to Rear Adm. R. S. Edwards who commanded the fleet submarines and the New London Base, but he had been sent to Washington on January 2 to become the assistant chief of staff to Admiral King. So, until a new man was named, and he knew it would not be him, he held the title and all the problems.

The naval base at New London went back before World War I and was the original location for submarine construction and development in the United States. Up until the expansion of the fleet beginning in early 1940, all submarines were built in the nearby shipyards and all the training was conducted at this location. It had expanded very fast over the past two years, nearly tripling in land area and more than doubling in active duty personnel. He had been doing a near thankless job of juggling priorities and problems for his predecessor, Rear Admiral Edwards but now that he was gone, Cutts owned the entire base and every single complaint or slowdown was his responsibility.

His able assistant came in late yesterday with a signal from Admiral King which got his dander up because he was going to have visitors who would be needing his assistance. From his long navy experience, this usually meant VIPs or Congressmen intent on some demonstration of how submarines work. What was even more troubling was the signal he received early in the morning from the Atlantic Fleet Commander, Admiral Ingersoll, who also encouraged the captain to inform him of any problems in complying with the requests made by this group of visitors. All Cutts knew for sure was the group was led by a Commander Jameson of whom he had no knowledge.

At 0930, his aide announced the special visitors were on their way from the guard shack that sealed the navy base from the outside world. The marine sentry informed the aide that there were two staff cars and a truck carrying some armed marines. The sentry had been told to wave them through as soon as they arrived and alert the captain's office of their arrival. Cutts had been going through dozens of quintuplet forms that required his signature on each copy and these pieces of paper were for important things like transfers of people to mundane things such as requisitions for more forms. Captain Cutts was not looking forward to visitors, but at least it got him out of signing his name. He put on his jacket and made sure he was in proper uniform, then told the aide to send the visitors in as soon as they came into the outer office.

Within ten minutes there was a knock on the door. Captain Cutts spoke up very loudly, "Enter." The aide opened the door and in came a full commandr—*Must be Jameson*, he thought—a marine first lieutenant, a navy ensign who looked like he was sixteen at best and a grizzled marine gunnery sergeant. Both marines had .45 Colt pistols on their belts, and each of these men looked like they knew how to use them. The small group approached the desk, spread out, and came to attention. The commander spoke, "Captain Cutts, my name is Jameson, and this is the rest of the team you were told to expect."

The captain said, "At ease, gentlemen, and welcome to Naval Base New London. How can we be of assistance to you? The information I received from Admiral King's office was sparse to say the least, but I will comply with any request you have."

"Sir," the commander said, "may I introduce the members of the team. This is First Lieutenant Flannigan, in charge of security. Next to him is Ensign Brand and next to him is Gunnery Sergeant Jones. We have several requests involving you and that of some of your submarine commanders. If I could, sir, I would like to give you an overview of what this is all about."

The captain said, "That would be helpful. Please, all of you sit down."

The three officers sat down, but the gunny excused himself by telling the commander, "Sir, I need to get our men situated, so by your leave, I will get them organized."

Jameson smiled. "Sure, Gunny, you already know the story we are going to tell so get the lay of the land and see what else you're going to need."

Captain Cutts quickly added, "Gunny, my chief yeoman's name is Patterson, and he can get you anything you need without a lot of fuss."

"Thank you, sir. Patterson, right?" the gunny looked back at the captain who nodded.

As soon as the gunny left the room, the commander began to speak. "Captain, as you are aware, our orders come directly from Admiral King. That does not mean we are here to disrupt any training or other war-related activities. We will do our job quickly and as quietly as possible. Please note, sir, what we are doing here is top secret and what we divulge to you and possibly other senior officers is strictly confidential and shall not be discussed, reviewed, or in any way communicated without the direct consent of Admiral King. Is that understood sir?"

Jameson looked directly at Captain Cutts who was maybe seven or eight years older. He had been briefed by Admiral Willson as to the nature of the temporary assignment the captain had assumed in early January. The admiral told him Cutts would revert to his previous assignment as chief of staff to the commander of submarines Atlantic Fleet as soon as a new admiral was put in charge.

The captain, having been made aware by two four-star admirals as to the secretive nature of this mission said earnestly, "Commander, I accept the terms that you have stated and what has been previously communicated to me. I will also be happy to inform you of other officers in this command who can be trusted with any information you wish to share. As you know, we pride ourselves on being the 'silent service' and the men in this command and those serving in our navy's submarines continue this tradition."

Commander Jameson said, "Thank you, sir, for being so understanding about this. We are working toward a joint goal which is to protect and defend your boats and submarines and at the same time, we are here today to figure out new tactics to kill U-boats."

The captain's eyes widened when he heard this and was immediately intrigued with this dual mission. He leaned back in this chair. "To kill a submarine, you must understand a submarine, correct?"

"Yes sir, and what we need to understand is how you not only train your crews, but also some of the technical aspects of your boats, the tactics and strategies for both offense and defense. We would like to have an open and honest discussion with some of your boat commanders concerning what they think about when they are attacking or being attacked."

The captain leaned forward in a thoughtful pose. "How do we start?"

Jameson looked at Brand and replied, "Captain, I want Mr. Brand to brief you on what he wants to see, do, and accomplish in the next few days at your base. He is the chief architect of the effort to reduce the attacks by U-boats and then help our submarines improve their defensive capabilities."

He let this comment sink in for a moment as the captain looked rather incredulously at the very young ensign and then Jameson added, "Captain, a few days ago, off the coast of Carolina, a PBY successfully

U-BOAT SCOURGE

attacked and sank a U-boat using some of the tactics developed by Mr. Brand. For the sake of security, this information is not being divulged to the public nor within the navy except for very few individuals. You are now one of these, and it is very important this information is not revealed without the express approval of Admiral King. Is that understood, sir?"

The captain immediately replied, "Yes, of course. I have heard of German subs being sunk by the Brits on convoys, and I guess they have had success with their planes, but I did not know we are killing them off our coast. I have a lot of questions about how this was done. This information could save the lives of our men as well."

The commander added, "Captain, we will be glad to review what we know, although in guarded terms, with you and select submarine commanders. What we want to do is to perform additional tests to strengthen our strategies. Hopefully, this work will help in developing tactics to further advance our ability to nullify the U-boat menace." Jameson looked at Captain Cutts and then at Brand as he continued, "By doing this, we will, of course, learn how this applies to our submarines and with the help of your officers, we can improve the effectiveness of our boats, but even more importantly, save the lives of the men who man them."

The captain was now held in rapt attention for whatever was to come next and waited for the information to flow. Brand stared at the captain and with a deep breath began a thirty-minute monologue on what he had theorized, what had worked in the attack on the U-boat, and what he wanted to learn from the navy submariners.

Brand finished by saying, "Captain, I will be happy to clarify some of my calculations on the performance of the German U-boats and the various methods we might employ to sink them. What I need from you and your officers is not only an understanding of how they are trained to operate a boat, but how they think, and how quickly they can adapt to an attack situation. By understanding these things, perhaps we can build some models for them to evade an attack or reduce the likelihood of them receiving a mortal blow."

The captain had been a serving officer in the submarine service since the early 1920s and knew the risks that those who served on these cramped, wet and always dangerous vessels face. He thought about the sinking of the *Squalus* in 1938 and the use of the new Monson diving bell to rescue some of the crew from the depths of Long Island sound. He knew a lot of the young men who were being trained at this facility would not survive the war. If there was anything that could help improve their odds, he would do whatever it takes. He looked at Brand with a new amount of awe for the human mind and especially the one inhabiting this young man's body.

He asked Jameson, "Commander, tell me when you want to go meet some boat commanders, and I will arrange it immediately. As to getting on a boat and conducting your tests, we have one which is about to go operational shortly. It has been working up, has conducted all its tests, and was commissioned on January 21. It is due to leave for the Pacific in about two weeks. It would be perfect for your mission, plus it would give the crew some real-life situations to master."

The commander looked at Brand who was always eager to begin a new project and said, "Sir, that would work out well. A boat in the last weeks of preparation for deployment should have a high degree of capability established, and the crew should be ready for the real conditions of war. How soon can we meet the captain of this vessel?"

Cutts looked down at a sheet of paper that was always on his desk. It listed the boats that were either about to launch, ready to commission, and those set to finalize their training before actual deployment. His finger went down the page and then looking up at the three officers said, "The boat is SS-213 named *Greenling*. She is a new Gato class boat and her captain is Lt. Comdr. H. C. Burton."

Commander Cramer, chief of staff to Captain Cutts, found Burton and his executive officer, Lieutenant Hayden, on the *Greenling*. Both were sitting on the deck in the forward torpedo room with grease all over their khakis, on their hands and on their faces. They were working with the chief of the boat storing torpedoes, called pigs by the crew, in their racks and were having a tough time making everything fit.

The commander knowing both officers well, looked at the two and chided them, "Mr. Burton, you look like you are working on a scow not a warship. Do you like playing in the grease?"

Burton looked at the visitor and having served with him on several old S-Class boats yelled back, "Look, men, that's a staff officer come to tell working men how to work. Now, what can he add to our discussion with this greasy pig that would make our life easier?"

There were a few chirps of laughter from the enlisted crew which was only found in the submarine service. The notion of rank and power came from respect and experience, not the uniform. Working in extremely close conditions for weeks at a time requires trust not blind obedience to senior rank. The commander laughed retorting as well, "Burton, I have come to save you and your exec from the grease pits. Let the real men who know what they are doing get the job done. You are both required at the captain's office now. Please join me in the nice clean staff car, and if you get any grease on it, it's your funeral."

Burton stood, looked at the commander while rubbing his hands on a dirty rag, and said, "What's up that requires our attention at the captains' office?"

The commander looked at him and said, "Let's say the captain wants to discuss the current war conditions and what your plans are to beat the Japs. How the hell do I know? All I can tell you is there is a group of officers who want to talk to you two and they are in a hell of a hurry, so wipe your hands as you walk and let's get going."

Both officers rubbed their hands on the greasy rags, walked up to the conning tower, got their hats, and exited the sub where the commander was waiting on the dock. Both got to the gangway and turned to the stern of the boat and saluted the flag. Then the captain of the *Greenling* told the officer of the deck to hold the fort until he got back.

Burton and Hayden were ushered into Captain Cutts office by an aide. Coming to attention in front of the captain and a full commander, they received a quick looking over by the superior officers. "Burton, you and your exec look like you have been working in the bilges. The United States provided you a new home and it looks like you have reduced it to a home for grease monkeys." He smiled knowing what it takes to get a new boat ready to go to war. Before the two officers could make amends, the captain said, "At ease, gentlemen. Meet Commander Jameson who is on the staff of Admiral King."

Each of the officers looked at the commander as he put out his hand to shake theirs. Both decided, what the hell and shook the commander's hand which now contained a good amount of grease, diesel oil, and muck. Commander Jameson was not concerned about this at all but said, "Commander Burton, I am glad Captain Cutts saved you from your work with petroleum, but I'm sure you'll soon be able to go back to whatever you were working on."

Everyone smiled and Captain Cutts spoke. "Gentlemen, what the commander says from here on out is to be considered top secret. You are both trained and experienced naval officers, but you are now advised to use caution in discussing anything you hear from the commander or members of his team. Is that understood?"

Both officers quickly agreed. Commander Jameson said, "Gentlemen, the reason we are here today is to use your boat for a few tests. These tests will be of great service to the navy, and you will find them very useful to the success of your future missions. If the captain does not mind, I will now brief the gentlemen on what we require."

The captain agreed and before stepping out of his office said, "Commander, if we can meet at the officer's club at around 1800 hours, perhaps the others can meet Burton and his exec and maybe get a drink. They might all need one by then."

"Good idea." Jameson turned to the two submarine officers and began telling them a story. They listened very intently and occasionally, looked at each other sometimes smiling and sometimes looking frightened at what the commander was saying.

1800 hours came and went and only the captain had shown up at the club. He thought he had been stood up but then a navy lieutenant commander and a lieutenant junior grade, with navy wings on their chests walked in and were directed to the captain's table. As they were introducing themselves, the special team officers walked in with Commander Jameson leading the way. The commander apologized for being late and told Captain Cutts the two submarine officers would be a few more minutes because they needed to get into clean uniforms for the officer's club. *Evidently,* Cutts thought, *the meeting with the secret team people went very long.* Cutts did not think much of this until later when he found out what the mission would entail.

Once the sub's captain and exec arrived, Jameson thanked everyone for changing their schedules and getting the *Greenling* prepared to sail in the morning. The chief of the boat was dragging people back to the sub to get everything ready for the exercise explained to him only a few hours ago. To say he was unhappy at this late request would have been accurate. The commander then outlined the mission for the morning.

"Captain, with your permission, I want to go over the plan for the morning. Everyone will get a copy of the plan as well because of the time constraints and the need to repeat an activity at specific times during the day." He looked around the table and then began again.

"We will leave the dock at 0700 hours and proceed to the training area marked on the chart. The coordinates are also marked, Captain, so that you will know exactly where the *Greenling* is located. Captain Burton estimates it will only take ninety minutes to arrive at the area where we will do the first test dive. We have time for two or three dives and then at 1130 hours our nemesis in the guise of Lieutenant Commander Shoemaker's R4D will make a series of high altitude passes coming from different directions and altitudes. We figure this will take forty-five minutes. He will then circle far away finding the sub from an altitude of his choosing. Upon our sighting his plane, we will crash dive the boat."

Seeing everyone appeared comfortable with the plan, he continued. "After coming back to periscope depth, we will resurface and just like on an operational patrol, the conning tower lookouts will assume their position and search for an intruder. We will not know where he is or from what direction he will be approaching. Shoemaker and the others on the plane will find our sub and it is up to them to attack as best they can. Teams on both the submarine and the plane will time all events and make notations on what works best regarding defense and offense. We will continue this effort until no later than 1400 hours at which time both the R4D and the *Greenling* will return to base. Are there any questions?"

Each person looked at the orders and charts Brand had handed out during the commander's talk and understood their requirements. The only question came from the co-pilot, Lt. (jg) Arnold Miller, "Looks like we'll be good for fuel but if we do a lot of fast climbs, we may have to go back sooner than 1400 hours. If so, should we signal you in some way?"

The submarine captain responded, "Just wag your wings if you have to go and we will signal with a flashing light. Would that work?"

Shoemaker answered, "Sure that works well for us. I don't think we'll have a problem, but it is always a contingency we have to work with."

The commander surveyed the group once more. "Good, if there are no other questions, let's order some food so we can get ready for the morning."

With smiles all around the meals were quickly ordered. The talk now turned to the normal navy conversation, submarines versus airplanes versus anybody in the army.

21

23 February 1942
USS *Greenling*
The Atlantic Ocean near Rhode Island

- Japanese submarine shells oil refinery at Ellwood, California.

The USS *Greenling* had traveled for two hours at its normal cruising speed which was around fifteen knots. It could hit twenty-one knots if pressed but the chief of the boat would have a coronary if they pushed the new engines too much too soon. Since there was no need to be anyplace quickly, the cruising speed would work just fine for the exercises Brand had designed for the sub and the R4D. Brand had placed himself with Commander Burton in the conning tower for the first part of the journey. Once they got on station, Commander Jameson had told him in no uncertain terms he was to wait inside the sub during all the maneuvers. Flannigan would be working the exercise along with Captain Burton and the normal lookouts from the conning tower.

Burton placed four lookouts atop the conning tower. Three were positioned on the racks bolted to the side of the tower and afforded a better view than where the captain and fourth lookout were situated. Each man had a set of high powered binoculars and scanned a hundred-degree area which gave an advantage of overlapping the person next to him. They scanned the sea first then the sky looking up about forty-five degrees from the water. They did this every few moments with deliberate precision allowing them to cover their sea and air assignments every minute. It got boring fast and many times a bird was thought to be a plane or a piece of flotsam became a ship. They would gain more experience over time, but as a new crew, these were the things they had to improve to survive.

The skipper of the boat, a "talker," and another lookout—often a junior officer—were also on the bridge of the conning tower looking forward and to each side. This complemented the three assigned lookouts who were in the watch racks above him. Brand searched the sea with his binoculars then looked to the sky. There were broken clouds a plane could hide in at around eight thousand feet. The winds were moderate at fourteen knots coming from the north. All in all, a good day for a boat ride Brand thought and an even better day to test out his theories.

The young ensign looked at his watch and tapped the skipper's shoulder. When Burton turned to him, Brand said, "Sir, permission to go below. It is about time, and I think we need to get Lieutenant Flannigan up here for the next part of the show."

"Permission granted Mr. Brand. Send up the marine," replied Burton as he continued scanning of the sea.

Brand went down the slippery hatch and found himself below the conning tower in the upper periscope room, which housed the attack periscope. Farther below was the main control room with the diving officer and the plotting desk where attacks were worked up and decisions made for firing torpedoes.

When he got down to the main control room, he spotted Flannigan talking to the XO and told him to go up and take over his place. "Now remember, once someone spots the plane, hit your stopwatch and when you get below with everyone else and the hatch is secured, hit it again. I'll be waiting to get your number to compare with mine. I'll have sergeant Laird work his watch as well, and hopefully, we'll match pretty close."

Flannigan nodded knowing the importance of accuracy on this

test. Before starting up the ladder, he warned Brand, "Take care of yourself down here. Hold on to something as we start to dive. I have been in subs before during my academy days. It's the reason why I'm a marine."

The exec smiled at the young ensign and signaled for him to stand in a specific area so he would not get run over by the crew when they did the crash dive maneuver. Sergeant Laird was also set up in a similar position on the other side. He had been told in no uncertain terms by the chief of the boat not to touch anything. He told Laird earlier, "Bad luck having a woman on board a ship and even more unlucky having a goddamn marine on board. So, you better not touch anything while you are on my boat, understand?"

Laird who was not afraid of anything, especially a navy chief, agreed to be good and not touch anything but was very afraid of being in this metal tube. The idea of going under water scared the hell out of him. The gunny told him he got this assignment because he was the biggest and strongest of the team and he was sure he would take good care of the ensign. Laird wished he was back on the plane right now instead of this damp metal tube.

Brand listened to the orders and information flowing back and forth in the control room. Each order was precisely repeated, and the enlisted men seemed to be handling their jobs with a great amount of expertise. Less than a third of the crew had ever served on a submarine before, and the process to become a useful member of the fleet took a great amount of time and dedication. Any person who did not want to go on the cruise or decided they were no longer capable of dealing with the claustrophobic living conditions, the stress of the deployment, or the general fear of being beneath the waves had only to ask and they would be removed from the boat. The submarine service was very small and one weak or fearful person could sink a submarine.

About ten minutes later, as Brand checked his watch to see if he had miscalculated the timetable for the R4D to arrive on station, a claxon horn went off with the words, "Dive, dive, dive. All hands below. Secure diesels, full power to the electric motors, dive planes full."

What appeared as total chaos was a carefully choreographed ballet of actions, movement, and awareness by the crew and the boat. The throbbing diesel engines died, and a subtle whir of the electric motors began. Tanks were blown, and the boat began to angle down, slowly at first and then very rapidly. The crew from the conning tower dropped through the hatch with Flannigan second after the talker, then followed by the four lookouts and finally the skipper who slid down the ladder like a fireman pulling a rope which held onto the heavy hatch. While he was doing this, a burly chief turned the wheel to set the seal on the hatch so the boat was now watertight. Lights went from red to green on the control boards indicating closed hatches, pumps, ballast tanks, battery conditions and other things Brand did not quite comprehend.

The exec spoke first, "Skipper, we are at sixty feet and dropping. Speed eight knots, bearing 135 degrees."

The skipper looked around to see if all was going as it should and then said, "Take her down to 120 feet and then come to a heading of seventy-five degrees. Hold that course for five minutes then come to periscope depth."

Brand was busy writing numbers down from the other two members of the team plus his own. He asked Flannigan how all of this took place, "What was the plane's heading? What altitude? Speed? Who saw it first?" He wrote the answers to each question and noted his own observations then quickly reviewed them all.

"So how did we do, Mr. Brand?" inquired the skipper.

Brand casually replied, "I would say you and your crew did very well. Let's try it again and see how things go on the next pass."

Up above, the R4D piloted by Lieutenant Commander Shoemaker was heading away from the point of contact and climbing to eight thousand feet. He was cruising at one hundred sixty miles per hour, enjoying the good flying conditions, and relishing being able to play attack plane for once.

Commander Jameson sat between Shoemaker and the co-pilot Arnold Miller. The two pilots were both smiling and enjoying the exercise. The rest of the team was onboard which gave the plane lots of eyes to scan the ocean. Half of them were given binoculars, and the others used their best vision to locate the submarine.

Gunnery Sergeant Jones was the first to sight the sub as they flew at five thousand feet headed due south. The sub was sighted to the east of their heading and just like the U-boat sighting of a few days ago off Carolina, the wake was the first thing visible. At five thousand feet, they had a line of sight of seventy-five nautical miles. The sub was probably only fifteen miles away, but the team picked up the wake first. The gunny, being an old sea marine and having spent considerable time on watch duty back on the *Saratoga*, knew how to scan the seas and not be mesmerized by reflections of light. As soon as he saw the wake he notified the flight deck then scanned from his initial point of reference to where the sub was. It took him only a moment or two to pinpoint the sub and provide a bearing to the pilot.

The pilot, plotted an intercept course with Jameson's help, increased speed to the boat, and began a slow descent. This was part of the initial plan to establish parameters for their research. Evidently, they were discovered during the first exercise when they were some four miles out and at an altitude of twenty-five hundred feet. The sub had dived to safety before the plane could get to the point of interception. Again, as Brand had theorized, this was to be expected. Now the cat and mouse game would begin again with the R4D trying different altitudes, attack profiles, and speeds to get close enough to successfully attack the submarine. That is, of course, if they had weapons to attack a boat.

The game continued for three more hours with a total of four more attacks and passes. Each time the plane got closer, but the sub's crew spotted it far enough out to successfully dive. Finally, around 1400 hours, the submarine stayed on the surface as the plane dropped down for one more mock attack. As the plane passed, the pilot wagged his wings and Flannigan could almost see his team waving out of the windows.

Down below the skipper came on the ship's intercom, "Secure from battle stations. Let's head back to the barn. Well done men. Liberty passes will be available for this weekend to half of the crew on Saturday and the other half on Sunday. Again, thank you for your hard work. That is all."

You could hear whoops and yells of joy from throughout the boat as the crew relished the notion they would get time off from their constant work these past eight weeks.

Brand approached the skipper with his papers in disarray. He looked at the captain of the warship with a great deal of respect and put out his hand saying, "Sir, may I shake your hand. You have a great crew, a great boat, and I would love to serve with you anytime."

Captain Burton shook the ensign's hand, thinking how clever Brand was, and how a compliment from him meant something. "Thank you, Mr. Brand. It was a pleasure to have you on board." He stopped for a moment, then keeping the words formal but also demonstrating their importance to him and his crew continued, "The exercise you created will be very helpful when we get out to the Pacific. I think every one of us has an even better appreciation for what we are facing and I know we are in better condition than before you came aboard." Smiling, he returned to his command post.

22

24 February 1942
Office of the Commander-Submarines
Atlantic Fleet, New London, Connecticut

- Carrier task force (Vice Adm. W. F. Halsey) bombards Wake Island.
- Submarine **Swordfish** evacuates United States High Commissioner F. B. Sayre from Philippine Islands.

Before the *Greenling* had tied up at its dock, Brand put together several ideas based on the information recorded by the three team members. He was especially proud of the way the R4D had been handled and how much he learned from the various mock attacks by the plane on the sub. He had reached several conclusions on ASW attacks both from the air and sea and now had some ideas about how to better protect the crews of U.S. submarines from aerial attacks. Once on shore, he would advise the commander of what he wanted to do with the information.

Throughout the evening, Brand met with Commander Jameson and Lieutenant Flannigan to first compare notes on each attack and what did and did not work. The two senior officers watched as Brand formulated his ideas on a chalkboard so he could express himself in numbers first, then in English so most people would understand. Finally, around 2300 hours, Brand gained agreement from Jameson and Flannigan as to his results and, more importantly, what he planned to do with it. Jameson asked one of the corporals standing outside the door to find Chief Schmidt so he could send a coded message to Admiral Willson.

Schmidt came in looking groggy. Up until a few minutes ago he had been sleeping and serenading his non-com roommates. Now wide awake, he wondered what the commotion was all about. The commander looked at the middle-aged man and regretted they had to wake him.

"Chief, I need to get a long message to Admiral Willson. Can you get this out through the teletype services here at the sub base?"

Upon arriving at the base, Schmidt had checked out the communications and found them more than adequate. "Sir, there will be no problem sending anything out from the base. I have talked to the chief who runs the communications hut and he knows our priority status. Evidently, the base XO alerted them to do whatever we needed, whenever we needed it. How long is the message?"

Jameson handed over the message Brand had typed. It ran three pages with headers and padding. *The kid officer knew security,* Schmidt thought to himself, *and he is one hell of a typist. I would kill for someone to work for me with this quality of work.* As he read through the message, he paused.

Jameson asked, "Questions, Chief?"

"Yes sir, do you want to send this in full code because of the nature of the text? It will take a bit longer to decode on their end, but if they are expecting it, they can tackle it quickly. I think if you were to place a call to whoever is holding the fort tonight in the admiral's office, they could alert Main Navy's communications center that this is coming." Schmidt knowing the contents of the message wanted to ensure full security from any eyes not in the know.

"Chief, that's a good idea. I want this sent in code, even though we are stateside. You never know whose eyes are looking over someone's shoulders. I will make a call. You go send the message." Jameson looked over to Corporal Dillard who had been the door guard along with Sergeant McBride and said, "Dillard, wake up Sergeant Laird and get Dean as well. Then escort the chief to the communications center. Let no one in the room while Schmidt sends the message and waits for confirmation. Got it?"

"Aye, aye sir. I will tell Sergeant McBride to hold the fort until I return. Shouldn't take more than ten minutes, sir."

After the corporal left with Schmidt, the commander picked up a phone and asked to place a priority call. The switchboard was prepared to give the commander top priority for any call he wanted to make. The call was connected in only a couple of minutes, which Jameson thought was good for midnight.

On the other end of the line, a fully awake lieutenant who had drawn night duty quickly picked up the phone, "Admiral Willson's office, Lieutenant Ward speaking."

Jameson spoke quickly, "Lieutenant, this is Commander Jameson. Code Charlie Mike Wilco. Do you understand?"

The lieutenant looked at his special communications list and saw the name and the authentication code and immediately responded, "Sir, I authenticate. How may I be of service to the commander, this evening, no, sorry sir, morning."

Jameson let out a small laugh as it was expected to keep the young communications officer awake in the middle of the night. "Lieutenant, there is a top-secret message being sent to Admiral Willson as we speak. It is coming via teletype from New London. Please ensure a decoded copy is available to the admiral as soon as he arrives in the morning. There is no need to wake him. It requests that once he reviews it, he is to confirm or deny the action requested. This can be sent via telephone to Capt. E. F. Cutts' office at Sub Base New London. The contact information is included in the message. Any questions, Lieutenant?"

The lieutenant wrote everything in a phone log. As he finished, he read back over it to ensure that he had it correctly. He then said, "Sir, I will have the communique flagged as soon as we hang up and ensure that it is hand delivered to this office. If the admiral is not in by the time my shift is up, I will stay to answer any questions that the admiral has. Is there anything else, sir?"

Jameson was aware of the high level of integrity and security in the people serving in communications for Admiral King and did not have to worry about what would happen to the message. "No, that should be all, Lieutenant. Thank you for your dedication to duty, even at midnight." With that, he hung up for he knew the communications lieutenant was already making a call to the secure communications room to expect a message for Admiral Willson. The communications lieutenant knew any message for Willson was actually for Admiral King and it would be unwise for one's career to mess up anything going to the chief.

Jameson looked at Brand and said, "James, get some sleep. We will reconvene at 0600 hours. If I know Admiral Willson, he'll be responding to the message by 0700 hours. We need to get with Captain Cutts to set up the meeting."

Jameson was correct in his estimation of the time that Willson would see the message from New London. He figured Willson would read through it twice, make a few notes, then see Admiral King. King would be in the office early as well. Jameson thought King would approve Brand's plan without hesitation. He was aware of the security concerns of this type of message, but was also concerned for the safety of his warriors. He had a deep bond and respect for the men of the "silent service" and now as the commander in chief of the U.S. Fleet, he was sending these men off to their possible deaths. Any information that could help one of them survive to fight again was well worth it.

Jameson, Flannigan, and Brand were sitting in the officer's mess when a commander, whom they knew as the base training officer, walked in holding a small piece of paper. He made a beeline for their table, and waved the two junior officers down without a word as they were about to stand. "Commander Jameson, my name is Brownlee, and I work for Captain Cutts."

Jameson extended his hand and Brownlee handed him the paper. "The captain wanted you to see this message from Admiral King and asked if you could come see him as soon as you finish with breakfast."

Jameson read the note which was very short and to the point.

U-BOAT SCOURGE

Commander Jameson c/o Captain Cutts
New London Submarine Base
Acknowledge receipt of your message dated February 23.
In total agreement with your plan to brief active duty commanding officers and senior base staff who may be engaged in training of senior submarine officers.
I await your full report. Inform Willson of your ETA to Washington.
King

Brownlee had not met Commander Jameson before now. All he knew was the limited information relayed by Captain Cutts. He had no idea what this man and his team were doing, except for rumors about them taking the *Greenling* out for most of the day and doing some sort of exercise involving a plane. As senior training officer for the base, he was dying to find out what the message from Admiral King was all about. He did not have long to wait.

Jameson passed the message to Flannigan and Brand then addressed Brownlee, "Commander, how many submarines are currently at the base with full crews and designated commanding officers?"

Brownlee thought quickly, glancing at the ceiling as he did a double count of all boats. "Commander, we have four boats in work up, two that have just been commissioned including the *Greenling* and five old S-boats used in training. Each of them has a full complement of officers for training both enlisted crews and officers."

"Commander Brownlee, I am going over to meet with Captain Cutts right now. I do not think there will be a problem in doing a full call of all current submarine skippers for both new and training boats. I would also want to have those officers, like yourself, who are involved in training skippers and executive officers to attend this meeting. If you can alert these people, I will find out if the captain can schedule this for 1100 hours. Will that work, Commander?"

Brownlee looked very excited because he wanted to get his own boat again and head to sea, so if there was activity or information these officers wanted to share, he was all ears. "Sir, I believe all boats are in port or if not, I will make sure none leave until after your meeting. Tell the captain I will phone him with a count as soon as I make my calls."

With that, Brownlee stood and walked out of the mess room. Flannigan observed casually, "Commander, I think Commander Brownlee is primed for some action and would love to get into a boat and sail off into the sunset."

Brand added, "Sir, I hope what we have to offer will be of help to them. If we can assist people with ways to avoid damage, I think we have done a good job."

Jameson replied, "Okay, James, this is your show. Are you ready for it?"

James thought briefly, then slowly exclaimed, "Sir, I will be able to get the information prepared before the meeting, and with your assistance, I think we can make it easy for them to digest. I hope it helps them. The guys on the *Greenling* were swell, and I want them to have the best possible chance at getting back safely."

At 1100 hours a conference room was set up with the required navy coffee mugs, a coffee urn, and two huge blackboards. A pencil and fresh paper tablet for each of the twenty-six participants were placed on the table. Eighteen were for the skippers and executive officers of the operational, or soon to be operational submarines. The rest for the senior staff officers at the base. Each officer was at least a lieutenant commander and all wore the dolphins of a submariner. Each one had been either a skipper of a boat or an executive officer; most had eight years of submarine duty. Captain Cutts ran through his mental checklist of who was supposed to be at the meeting, nodding to Jameson when the last officer came in. Flannigan signaled Sergeant McBride to secure the room.

Captain Cutts began the meeting. "Gentlemen, you have been asked to come to this meeting because you are either a skipper or executive officer of one of the navy's submarines or you train officers to become skippers. Either way, it is the principal job of every ship captain to ensure the safety of the ship in his command and the lives of the crew. It is also a time of war, and the mission of the submarine service is to take the war to the enemy. It is to sink their warships, their merchant marine and to perform other services as required by the high command." He let the words sink in for a moment as he scanned the officers seated around the large table. "Today, we are going to have a presentation that deals with the fundamental first order of being a captain, saving your ship to fight another day. With that, I will turn the meeting over to Commander Jameson who reports to Admiral King."

Jameson stood, looked at the men seated around the table. "Captain Cutts, thank you for the introduction. Gentlemen, what you are about to be told is considered top secret, and any dissemination of this information to individuals without clearance is a court-martial offense. Only submarine commanders and those involved in the training of said officers are allowed access to this information. Are we clear?"

A few "yes sirs" echoed around the room. Some of the officers looked at each other followed by a hard look at the commander who reported to the commander in chief of the U.S. Fleet. They knew whatever this man had to say was important. Most sat up even straighter in their seats and everyone began taking notes.

"Yesterday, these two young officers seated by the wall were passengers on Mr. Burton's fine new submarine the *Greenling* as they were engaged in a series of tests with a Navy R4D. These tests were set up to confirm some theories on anti-submarine warfare." The officers acknowledged the marine lieutenant and young ensign and returned their attention to the commander. Most were now aware of the voyage yesterday of the *Greenling*, but few had gotten any details out of Lieutenant Commander Burton. The comment on anti-submarine warfare got their attention so each in their own way began to listen in earnest as the commander spoke.

"We are at this base because we needed an operational submarine for our tests. As you probably know, the Germans are operating right off our coast. I cannot tell you a great amount of detail about these operations because of ongoing security concerns, but let us just say that the German U-boats are taking a heavy toll on our merchant ships. And more of them are on their way. Each of you needs to be aware of this because you are as much a target as some big fat tanker. We are looking at ways to kill the U-boat before they kill more of our men and sink more of our merchant fleet." He looked around the table for emphasis. Seeing he had a group of people who were now hanging on his every word, he continued.

"Several days ago, a PBY being flown off the coast of Carolina successfully attacked and sank a U-boat. This was accomplished by using some of the theories and attack plans developed by Ensign Brand." Jameson motioned toward the wall. "First Lieutenant Flannigan," again indicating toward the wall, "spotted the sub and helped maintain contact with the boat throughout the attack. I am telling you this in the strictest of confidence. No report has been announced concerning the sinking of the German sub and there will be none for some time. We cannot afford to let the enemy know of our successes or failures. Is that understood?"

Again, a few "yes sirs," rose from the seated submarine officers with a few longer looks at the young ensign and the marine lieutenant. Jameson seeing that he held their attention, plowed on to their greatest fear, attack by planes without warning.

"Again, gentlemen, you are not to let anyone know about this attack or its success until it is announced by Washington. Even then, you will not acknowledge that you had advance information. Now, what did we learn from this attack and what did we do yesterday to enhance our ability to locate and destroy enemy submarines?" He scanned the seated officers and could tell they were now fully engaged in the meeting. "The other question is what do you need to know based upon this knowledge to keep your boat from being located and sunk." Jameson let this harsh reality sink in some more before he announced, "Admiral King personally agreed to the request made by Ensign Brand to share some of his ideas on how to prepare for and defend yourself from aerial attacks. Mr. Brand, the floor is yours."

James walked up to the board and grabbed a piece of chalk. He wasn't going to start writing but rather it gave him something to hold onto as he found his voice to talk to these officers. He looked at Lieutenant Commander Burton who smiled at him and raised his eyes in anticipation. This helped James focus. His mission was to help protect these men and their crews from harm.

"Thank you, Commander. Captain Cutts, thank you for allowing us the time to develop our theories into plans. Hopefully some of these ideas will find their way into your standard methodologies for defense." He turned to the board and wrote out an equation.

$$d^2 = h^2 + 2Rh$$

"This is, as you know, a shortcut calculation to determine how far the horizon is from a point of reference, which, in this case, is a conning tower on a submarine. So, if you are on the conning tower of a Gato class submarine you are perhaps fifteen feet above sea level, thus your line of sight to the horizon is, on a perfect day, perhaps four nautical miles. But what if you were an airplane and you were flying on that same day at five thousand feet. What is your line of sight? The answer would be seventy-five nautical miles. That is a lot of ocean to view, but it is possible to see the wake of a submarine from very far away and it points to your boat heading into danger. This is what happened to the U-boat sunk by that PBY."

He saw that some people had worked up the equation and knew it involved the Pythagorean Theorem to get D and using it to then find a right angle where R is the hypotenuse of the Earth's radius. Most every man in the group was an accomplished navigator and could do a sun shot or a star shot with ease. Going back to high school days to figure out a specific line of sight calculation was easy, but they usually did not think too much about this fact. But now they were interested in the vast difference between a plane up high versus their own small world from the conning tower.

James hit the board again, drawing concentric circles which he described as the danger zones for their subs. Each circle equaled a mile with a total of five circles being represented. In the middle of these circles, he made a big X.

Turning to the officers, he began again. "Each circle is a mile, with a five-mile circle around the boat. Within the center circle, you should be safe from an aerial attack. But you can only visually define a target on the surface at maybe a four-mile distance. A plane even at two thousand feet can scan forty-seven miles. Who has the advantage?" He paused, scanning the room. "The one who sees the other first has the advantage. If you are within this five-mile zone, you are in peril. If you are within the two-mile zone, your odds of being successfully hit increase tenfold. At one mile, if you are still on the surface or just beginning your dive, your chances are very poor indeed. Think about this," he said as he started writing on the second board, "if you are on the surface, as we were in *Greenling* yesterday, you're traveling at eighteen knots equating to 30.88 feet per second. The *Greenling*, like most Gato boats, takes fifty to seventy-five seconds to submerge fully and no longer showing her conning tower and periscope. The wake is gone and the boat is diving at no more than two feet per second. This sounds good, but the plane is traveling at two hundred miles per hour in a dive toward your boat and increasing speed. This equates to 293 feet per second. If the plane is a bomber type or a single-engine dive bomber the speed goes up to three hundred miles per hour or 440 feet per second."

Brand let those facts sink in for a few moments as he put his chalk in each circle denoting five, four, three, two and one. Turning to face the assembled officers he continued, "So, by now, I am sure you have done the math. If you were on the surface and an enemy plane dived toward you from less than one and a half miles away, he would be on top of you with your conning tower out of the water. You would be a sitting duck." He looked around and saw a few men doing the same calculation. "Even at three miles, you would be in peril because he would continue on the path you were steering. You might be down fifty feet or less in the water but that would allow him to drop his eggs at intervals of thirty-five to fifty feet set for twenty-five to fifty feet and you would probably suffer damage. Only if you see him first, at three miles or more do you have a very good chance of no damage. Also, I want you to think about not only getting under quicker, say fifty seconds, but also performing a turn to port or starboard only after you have dropped below the surface. This way, you will have a better chance of being off his dead center drop point of any depth charge or bombs."

Brand continued for another thirty minutes with a few interruptions. He expressed optimism at how the use of the technology he was developing for attacking U-boats could be turned into a positive for the American submariners. He had several more ideas on the use of technology to help these skippers, but was told not to go into possibilities of new defensive tools. He decided to conclude his remarks after the last question on time of day attacks by airplanes.

U-BOAT SCOURGE

"Gentlemen, I have to end our conversation and head back to Washington. But before I leave, I have a final comment. If you can increase the number of lookouts to a minimum of five truly active individuals, you will decrease the amount of space where they need to search. It will improve the likelihood of spotting an intruder by a minimum of twenty percent and by moving their frame of visual reference every five minutes or so, you will keep their eyes fresh. The more eyes searching for the enemy, the better your chance of survival. Practice this on your crash dives and see how much additional time it adds to your dive cycle. I think it will not add more than five seconds, but the extra eyes may see the enemy further out, perhaps before they see you. Thank you for your time. I wish you success."

As he placed his chalk on the tray of the nearest board, he heard something he had not experienced before, the beginnings of applause. Everyone was standing, and a few were even giving him a loud, "Well done."

The embarrassed ensign was saved by Commander Jameson, who was also applauding as well as Captain Cutts, who walked up and shook his hand saying, "Well done, Mr. Brand. You have just given these men sound advice and practical knowledge that will help them succeed in their job and even more important, come home safely."

The assembled officers all walked up, shook his hand, and thanked him for the information and ideas. The last one to approach was Lieutenant Commander Burton, who had stayed back waiting for the rest to leave. Burton put his hand on James' shoulder, taking his hand in a hearty handshake. "Mr. Brand, it was an honor having you on the *Greenling*. I do not know if our paths will cross again, but if that happens, I will buy you the biggest steak dinner available. Thank you for your ideas and for helping me and my crew prepare for the future challenges we are facing. The first Jap ship I sink will be for you." With that, Burton walked out the door before James could say a word.

Jameson overheard the comments as did Flannigan. The commander said, "James, you did a fantastic job. What you showed them was another way to survive. They all appreciated it as did we. But, we need to get back to Washington and finalize your report. I know you had some other ideas that you wanted to share, but you did well not to go into futures."

Captain Cutts overheard these final comments but knew not to ask. Instead, he approached the assembled group, shook hands with each one, and wished them well. "Gentlemen, thank you for sharing your ideas. By the looks of the men, they will be making changes to how they operate and will formalize these ideas into our skipper training. Again, thank you for your efforts."

As they left the room, Brand could see out the window where three of the skippers were standing next to Lieutenant Commander Burton who was using his hands to show how the R4D had been diving on his boat and how he was trying to maneuver it. Brand smiled and walked toward the staff car with Flannigan and Gunny Jones.

Lieutenant Commander Shoemaker had been notified the team would be scheduled to fly out by 1300 hours and the plane was all set to go as soon as they arrived at the airport.

Jameson made a quick phone call to Admiral Willson's office informing him they were leaving New London and would be in Washington in the early evening. Willson was okay with not hearing from Jameson until the next morning but wanted to know when to expect the report from Brand. Jameson was not sure but would let Willson know by morning.

As the plane left the runway, the team members soaked in the wintery countryside of Connecticut; happy they were not driving back to Washington. The only person not looking out of the window was Brand. He was deep into calculations again, constantly scribbling notes on pieces of paper and looking at his slide rule to come up with different ways to express his findings.

Always attentive to the ensign, Jameson sat down next to him. "James, I know you're tired. If you would just shut down for an hour or so, the answers will come."

Brand smiled at his mentor. "Sir, I know you're right, but there are so many things we could be doing to help those submariners. With their current optics and lack of any electronics, they are very susceptible to aircraft attacks. I want to make some recommendations to Admiral King concerning some of the new electronics such as radar that could really help them out."

Jameson was aware of the radar systems now available. He had been privy to some of the early meetings when in late 1940, the British under the leadership of Dr. Tizard brought to America the advances in technology the British were working on or had been using. Radar was the biggest item. Even though the U.S. had been working on it for some years, the British system was far ahead regarding range, quality, and usefulness. The breakthrough they brought was in the form of the resonant cavity magnetron, producing microwave power in the kilowatt range, greatly enhancing the power, range, and usefulness of radar. It was over one hundred times more powerful than anything the Americans had developed. Jameson also knew the lead institution on the development of radar was the Radiation (RAD) Laboratory at MIT.

The staff at MIT was growing daily with many requests coming for land, sea, and aircraft based units. Jameson was aware of the first airborne unit, the ASG which was a British unit now being produced with considerable refinement under the direction of the RAD Lab. The unit became known as the 50kW ASG, known later as "George." Gyro-stabilized, it could detect ships up to fifteen miles away and a submarine periscope at five miles. This was very important because now the planes could find submarines day or night. Jameson was knowledgeable about most of the significant technologies under development or soon to become operational. He knew Brand was aware of most of them, but he did not want to cloud his thinking by considering possible alternatives. Jameson knew the development was difficult and mass producing the equipment, especially the magnetron, would be slow and costly. He also knew that most of the navy brass were skeptical of anything new, especially technologies they could not comprehend.

Jameson left Brand to work away on his ideas, and upon landing, he would have a better chance to talk to him in private about how to present his information for maximum effect.

PART 5

PART B

23

26 February 1942
Bethesda, Maryland

- USS **Langley** (ACV) with 32 Army fighters on board is sunk in route to Java by Japanese planes.

Brand had slept little the past two nights after learning Admiral King would be unavailable until at least February 27. He finished his report two days prior and asked the commander to look through it, requesting suggestions to make it more readable and reasonable. Jameson had told him the first day back that asking for the moon was not possible because of all the other constituencies requesting priorities in people, dollars, manufacturing space, raw materials, and on and on. Every military command wanted to be the top priority in every category. If the navy received priority on steel, the army did not get trucks and tanks. If the army Air Corps wanted more men with college backgrounds to become aviators, the navy would lose valuable talent for their operations, either in the air units or in the fleet. Everyone wanted more fuel and the ongoing attacks along the east coast hampered efforts to get fuel to the cities of New

York, Philadelphia, and Boston, plus the promised shipments to Britain. Everyone wanted everything fast and could not understand why another groups was getting more.

Washington was getting full as well. There were so many jobs opening within the various headquarters of the military, plus all the new war-related commissions and boards, that there was no room for anyone. People were now officially asked to rent out spare bedrooms and public transportation was becoming impossible. There were few cars and with gasoline rationing, car pools were also jammed. Washington, D.C., had gone from a swampy backwater town to a major city in only a year, and with the war now going on across the world, Washington became the focus of all war-related activity in the country.

Because of this unprecedented growth, Dr. Feldman had been happy to stay at the Bethesda home of Commander Jameson. This was highly desired by the commander as well as by Brand who had developed a close friendship with the good doctor. They played chess together and often their medical conversations would bring about ideas that could become useful to the military. Feldman watched over Brand like a mother lion and was very protective of his health, both physical and mental. He was acutely aware of the obsessive nature of geniuses who strive so hard as to hurt themselves. Dr. Feldman enlisted the new corpsman, Pharmacist Mate Hamlin to be vigilant whenever Feldman was not around and to report directly to him of any change in moods, personality, color, or just about anything that would be out of the ordinary. Feldman had also developed a close relationship with Gunnery Sergeant Jones who watched the young ensign like a surrogate father and was also glad the doctor was staying at the house.

After a not so rousing game of chess which the doctor lost in about six moves, he told James that he was going to get a snack and asked if there were something he would like. James looking back at the doctor saying, "Well, I'm not hungry, but would love to get out of prison for a while. It was great going to the bases. Working with the plane and sub crews was a wonderful experience and added a lot to my research. Do you think we can go someplace?"

Feldman anticipated Brand's restlessness and the commander had briefed him on the new wanderlust that Brand was experiencing. He wanted to do and see things that tied to his research. Some were fine with the commander, but he didn't want to risk Brand's talents doing things that were marginally important. The doctor replied, "James, this is going to be a long war; you know that better than most. There are so many things to do, and the country—not just you—has only begun to fight. So far, we have seen very few injuries of war. But from what some of the British doctors tell us, I can wait. I'm sure the powers will have you moving again soon. Until then, get out of this house and go for walks. If you would like, I can take you to the labs at the hospital and show you some of the things we are working on. Would that help?"

James smiled his big toothy grin saying, "That would be great. I would love to see what's going on at that big hospital of yours. Lieutenant Flannigan tells me you're having wild parties with the nurses every night and making all kinds of drinks to keep them frisky."

Feldman laughed. "I wish there were nurses like that, but there are a few you should meet. Quite attractive young ladies of the first order, but they are not frisky."

Feldman walked out of the room and headed for the kitchen to see what was left in the icebox. The housekeeper, Miss Dora Jane, always had good chicken or ham leftovers. The old woman was probably sixty but was very spry and ran the house like an army camp. Her assistant, Missy Rains, looked to be fifty, but was always cleaning the house and helping cook the meals. The food, facilities, and company were much superior to the BOQ at the hospital. He was glad the commander had gone to bat to gain approval for him to stay at the house.

Just as he walked into the kitchen, he saw Lieutenant Flannigan walking out in the other direction. "Flannigan, you got a minute?"

Flannigan turned around. "What can I do for you, Doc?"

Feldman pointed to the kitchen table and sat down. "I'm worried about Brand. He needs to get some exercise on a regular basis and not spend all his time in his room or office. I asked if he wanted to come to the hospital for a tour and that seemed to excite him. Any other ideas?"

Flannigan looked at the doctor and heaved a sigh of relief, "I am glad you see it, too. He seems so consumed in the research that he is not taking regular meals or getting out of the room, let alone the house. I thought about getting the team set up for some PT. Can he handle it yet?"

Feldman thought for a moment. "Sure thing. His arm is doing well, and if you don't kick him in the chest, he should be fine. I would watch him if there is much running involved or if he seems to have a lot of pain in the arm or right shoulder. But I think it would be a good idea. Also, encourage him to do his fighting thing. I saw what he did to that SOB in San Diego, and he should continue to practice that skill." With a devlish grin, he added, "You and your people might even learn something new from him."

Flannigan couldn't help but smile in return. "Doc, I'll get a schedule set up with the gunny starting tomorrow. I'll also ask the commander to join in so there will be no way for Brand to avoid it. I'll make sure Hamlin is watching him always. He seems to be very concerned as well."

"Hamlin is a good man and is up on all of Brand's issues. He will let me know if he sees anything out of place. I will let you know as soon as I set up a tour of the hospital so you can arrange an escort. You should come as well. A dashing marine lieutenant would be welcome by all of those lonely nurses."

Flannigan slowly added, "I will be the judge as to the amount of beauty and variety you have at the hospital. What I have seen of navy nurses does not speak well of the recruiting process."

Feldman laughed, "Well you should come by and see the new crop of ladies. I am sure one or two would meet the muster of the Marine Corps."

24

27 February 1942
Bethesda Naval Hospital

- Battle of Java Sea is fought as an Allied naval force under Rear Admiral Doorman, Royal Netherlands Navy of five cruisers, and 11 destroyers in the Java Sea attacks enemy force covering Java invasion convoy. Two Netherlands cruisers, two British destroyers, one Netherlands destroyer are sunk. One United States cruiser and one British cruiser are damaged.

Feldman had been making his morning rounds since 0630 and with so few patients under his care, he was basically finished by 0800. He had gone off to check with Dr. Baker, the top anesthesiologist at the hospital, to discuss the levels of morphine that should be prescribed to some of his older heart patients after surgery. He was acutely aware of the addictive properties of long duration treatments with morphine, but there was not much else that was effective. He had been talking to some of the younger surgeons about this, and all had agreed when the time came for mass casualties, the overuse of morphine would lead to an epidemic of addiction. Dr. Baker was a leading advocate of alternative treatments, quickly backing off on the amount given even though there was a large amount of discomfort and pain involved. The two had been talking for no more than ten minutes when a nurse walked in and asked if he was expecting anyone. "Would it be a very young-looking ensign and a handsome marine lieutenant, Nurse Warren?"

Nurse Warren enjoyed the sense of humor Dr. Feldman brought to the hospital, and it was nice to see some young doctors these days instead of the old men that had run the hospital for some time. "Yes, Doctor, there are two officers escorted by two marines and a navy corpsman. Shall I show them to your office?"

Dr. Baker shrugged his shoulders at the interruption, knowing that it was a "what if" conversation only and did not involve an active patient.

Feldman acknowledged this saying, "If it is all right with Dr. Baker, I'll talk to them outside and show them around the city streets of our little hospital."

Baker decided to play along. "Dr. Feldman is right. If there is a group of marines around, someone must take them by the hand and lead them to the promised land or the latrine, whichever is closer."

Feldman and Nurse Warren both laughed at the joke by the older doctor. "Okay, Nurse Warren, take me to these wayward souls so that I may provide them counsel."

Nurse Warren, who was a lieutenant junior grade, and a one-year veteran of naval service led Dr. Feldman down the hall to where the ensign and the marine lieutenant were studying the large boards with clinic names, doctor offices, and administration locations listed in alphabetical order with the chief of medicine listed first. Feldman saw them first and had Nurse Warren follow him to the group.

"Nurse Warren," he said loudly, "what you see before you are some of the bravest men in the naval service. May I present to you First Lieutenant Flannigan and his understudy in bravery, Ensign Brand."

Both Brand and Flannigan nodded to the young nurse, and both said something in barely audible tones about nice meeting you or something like that but the nurse could not quite hear them.

Feldman pounced, "Gentlemen, behold a fellow officer of the naval service. I think you can do better than a few mumbles." Gunnery Sergeant Jones was standing behind the ensign and smiled broadly knowing that the good doctor had correctly surmised the two young men were a bit shy around the opposite sex.

"Lieutenant Warren, I apologize for my poor manners. Please accept those of Ensign Brand as well." Flannigan looked at the young nurse with new appreciation and finally came to understand the beauty hidden in the navy's white nurse uniform and the silly cap they all wore. "May I ask how long you have been at Bethesda?"

Nurse Warren smiled broadly at the tall marine officer and paid little notice to the younger officer standing next to him. "Well, Lieutenant, it's nice to know the Marine Corps properly taught its officers to talk to women in such a courteous way. And, Ensign, what do you have to say for yourself?"

Brand became even redder in the face, which was all too frequent when he was embarrassed. He looked at the floor, then at the doctor, and finally after composing himself, he looked at Nurse Warren responding, "Lieutenant, I also wish to apologize for my poor behavior. My dear mother would be ashamed of me for not properly introducing myself to such a lady as yourself. My name is James Edward Brand from Flagstaff, Arizona. And what part of the country can we credit for having given birth to a woman of your grace and beauty?"

The doc and Flannigan both looked at Brand with shock. They didn't expect him to be able to even talk to a woman, let alone a pretty nurse such as Lieutenant Warren.

Before anyone else said anything, Warren spoke. "My, my, Mr. Brand, are all of the men in Arizona so gallant or are you the only one?"

"Well, Lieutenant Warren, or may I call you by your Christian name? Most men from Flagstaff are a hard and crusty lot, spending hours in the saddle chasing cattle around the high mountains. I did have some of those experiences, but preferred spending my time gazing at the stars at the Lowell Observatory."

"Mr. Brand, you are an interesting person. I take it you are talking about the astronomical observatory that discovered Pluto? And by the way, my name is Barbara, and I'm from Ft. Worth, Texas." Nurse Warren presented her hand to Brand so he could shake it like a good Westerner would, then looked again at this tall young man with a greater amount of interest. He was very young looking, but the navy would not make a man an officer until he was at least twenty or so. Barbara was twenty-one and had spent her three years in nursing school in Ft. Worth. As soon as she graduated, she joined the navy to get out of Texas. Nurse Warren had hoped to travel to some place like Hawaii or even further afield but within six months, Pearl Harbor occurred, and she seemed destined to be stuck in Washington for the duration.

Barbara Ann Warren was a skilled operating room nurse with stamina greater than most men and a nearly perfect memory for each procedure and instruments required to operate successfully. Her early training had gone exceedingly fast because of her memory and command of anatomy and physiology, two prerequisites to becoming a top nurse. She had no fear of blood, pain, stress, or the huge egos of doctors. Her oldest brother was a Baylor University College of Medicine graduate and had told her she should become a doctor as well. But the deck was stacked, as they say in Texas, for any girl wanting to go to medical school so she went to nursing school with the hope that one day before she was thirty she could get into a good medical school on the east coast, which was more accepting of women.

Brand looked intently at Barbara and held her hand a long time until she finally pulled it away, but she was now blushing as well. Brand decided to be even more open. "Perhaps one evening, we could meet, and I could show you some of the major star systems. And maybe if we have a clear night, I can point out Pluto to you. That is, of course, if you have some spare time and would want to spend it with a real Arizona cowboy. Perhaps the good doctor could help us, right Dr. Feldman?"

Feldman smiled and quickly replied, "Sure, Brand, I'll see what we can do as long as you stay in town long enough to allow some star gazing. Perhaps we can see if the Naval Observatory could oblige this meeting?"

Brand was almost giddy with the possibility and said, "Wow, Doc, would you do that for us? Do we need permission from Admiral King or something like that?"

At the mention of the admiral's name, Flannigan grabbed Brand's arm to admonish him without saying anything. The relationship with the top admiral in the navy was not to be discussed nor even intimated. Before Brand could say anything, Feldman came to his normal quick rescue.

"I am sure that the good admiral has other things to do, but we could contact the president to arrange some time on the White House lawn." Feldman gave out his biggest grin, and everyone, including Brand, laughed at the witty thought. Barbara noticed the arm movement by Flannigan but didn't give the impression that she had. She had no idea what she had seen, but there seemed to be a lot more to the eye than this first impression. *Who is this young ensign?* she wondered.

Feldman decided to move the little entourage away from the lovely Nurse Warren before any more damage was done. "Gentlemen, I'm sure Nurse Warren has other duties to perform and I promised to show you around our little medical facility. Thank you, Lieutenant, for bringing these people to my location. We will talk again later." With that the good doctor began to move toward the next ward with the marines in tow.

Brand looked once more at Nurse Warren saying, "I hope we meet again real soon and perhaps get a chance to look at those stars." He turned and walked away leaving Barbara wondering more about the tall young ensign that everyone seemed to be protecting.

Dr. Feldman took the group around the major wards and into some of the empty operating theaters to help them understand some of the newer techniques that could save their lives one day. At lunch time, the group went to the cafeteria and ordered a nice plate lunch, but Brand just wanted a ham and cheese sandwich and Coca-Cola. He munched on his food slowly while all the others engaged in lively banter about what they had seen at the massive hospital. Mostly they discussed the large number of nurses on staff and how they wanted to go on sick call as soon as possible. The gunny informed them they would have to be near death to be taken to this hospital and not to try anything so stupid. They all laughed at the serious comment made by Gunnery Sergeant Jones knowing it made him a bit mad, but he was in good spirits. Finally, around 1330 hours, Flannigan announced they had to get back to the house and prepare for the next day. Brand seemed relieved, but still wanted to see

Barbara once more. This was not to be, but he told Dr. Feldman, "Let's have a game of chess this evening. I have a few questions to ask you."

Brand caught up with the group and exited the cafeteria as Feldman watched them leave through the big double doors. Feldman had finished his coffee when two nurses walked up to him asking, "Dr. Feldman, do you mind if we sit and ask you a question?"

Feldman stood replying, "Sure, love to have some company." Feldman now faced the lovely Barbara Warren and her roommate and best friend, Wanda Jackson. Wanda was a lieutenant junior grade like Warren from Shreveport, Louisiana. At twenty-four she had a reputation as a southern lady with a temper and not too quick to become involved with anyone. The rumor was that Wanda had a beau who left her at the altar when she was only nineteen. Because of that she went to nursing school far off in St. Louis, escaping the hometown nastiness and gossip that followed these situations down south.

Warren spoke first, "Dr. Feldman, how do you know Ensign Brand and Lieutenant Flannigan? And why do they have those other marines following them?"

Feldman had been briefed by Commander Jameson on how to handle these type questions, so he was finally going to tell a story about the two, mingling truth with fiction to keep Brand's secret.

"Nurse Warren and Nurse Jackson, I didn't think you were interested in these gentlemen." Feldman looked for the response and saw both getting a bit red, confirming his diagnosis of lust.

Jackson spoke first, "Doc, Barbara told me about these two and I spied them both when you were walking the halls with them. The marine seems to have something wrong with his arm, and he looks like he has some face lacerations as well."

Feldman then went for the truth as it pertained to Flannigan saying, "Wanda, you are very observant in noticing the lieutenant's wounds. What I'm about to say is top secret, and you must not reveal this information to anyone. Is that understood?" Both nodded their heads. Feldman decided to make sure they understood. "I need to hear a yes sir, or no sir, to go any further, understood?"

Both nurses said almost simultaneously, "Yes sir, Dr. Feldman."

"Good, now let me tell you a story about Lieutenant Flannigan. He was wounded in the Philippines at the Cavite Naval Base when it was bombed by the Japanese on December 10. He was attempting to evacuate wounded personnel from the base, going into a burning building on more than four occasions to rescue scores of individuals from certain death. The buildings were not only under attack, but there were secondary explosions when ammunition stored in some of these buildings went off. His wounds were serious enough to have him shipped out of Manila to Java. He was not getting better, and the burns were such that he was evacuated to Australia, then to Hawaii, and finally to San Diego where I met him for the first time. He wants to go back to his men, but it is not to be. He works with Ensign Brand and some other people on special projects."

He looked at the faces of both nurses and saw a level of professional concern and interest, but also one of more worldly compassion on the part of Nurse Jackson.

Barbara then opened up, "Sounds like a real marine hero. He's not married, is he?"

Feldman looked at Barbara and said, "No, I don't think he has had time for marriage or even going on a date for some time." Feldman turned to Wanda, "So, Nurse Jackson, that's what you wanted to know, isn't it? Is Flannigan available and a real hero?"

Wanda nodded her head in agreement and turned a bit redder in the face. Nurse Warren then pushed in, "So what about Ensign Brand? I don't think he has been out of the country because he doesn't look the part. What does he do?"

Feldman now looked hard at the nurses and saw the interest they had in two young men, so he decided to go with the cover story that he and Jameson had concocted. "Ensign Brand is a highly-educated scientist working on special projects for the navy and the army. Yes, Barbara, he is from Arizona, and when he spoke of star gazing, he is quite good at it for he worked with the team that discovered Pluto. He was very young then, and that is all I can discuss with you now." He looked at both, especially Barbara who was letting this bit of information sink in a bit more. Feldman decided to expand further.

"I live in the house that accommodates Ensign Brand and Lieutenant Flannigan along with other individuals. The marine guards are just that, guards. Flannigan oversees security for the location. That is all I can disclose to you concerning these gentlemen and their activities."

Barbara's demeanor turned professional as she spoke, "Dr. Feldman, thank you for telling us about these two officers. Nurse Jackson and I will maintain the secrecy you asked for, and we look forward to meeting these gentlemen again, hopefully in a more casual setting."

Feldman almost chuckled but held his composure. "Nurse Jackson and Nurse Warren, thank you for your understanding. I will do my best to see that you have an opportunity soon to meet these fine young men in, as you said, a more casual setting."

Both nurses stood up and thanked the doctor. They didn't say anything to each other as they walked away, but Feldman knew later in the evening when they were alone, there would be much discussion concerning the two officers. Feldman wondered how he could play cupid and not get into too much trouble. Perhaps a little female company would do Brand a world of good.

25

1 March 1942
Office of Rear Admiral Willson
Chief of Staff to Admiral King

- Battle of Sunda Strait--Allied vessels heading for Sunda Strait are attacked by superior Japanese surface forces. Heavy cruiser USS **Houston** sunk, light cruiser HMAS **Perth** sunk.
- American-British-Dutch-Australian Command dissolved.
- German submarine **U-656** sunk by land-based U.S. naval aircraft south of Newfoundland.

Brand and Jameson stood at the desk of Admiral Willson as he went down a list of problems with their report on anti-submarine warfare. He had spent the previous day working with an edited copy given to him by King which included a fifteen-minute lecture on the impertinence of young men to doubt their seniors. King, furthermore, said to Willson he knew more about anti-submarine warfare on one hair than these two upstarts, especially the boy wonder professor. After he had settled down,

King did make some rather profound statements about the foresight in the report. Even though he hated to admit it, he appreciated the élan of the two officers in challenging current naval strategy. He dismissed the conversation with a thrust of papers into the hands of his trusted chief of staff with the admonition to have more validation on certain points of the ideas outlined in the paper.

Willson had been haranguing both officers about the years of naval history, planning, philosophy and just plain "the navy way," for a good ten minutes before he looked at them. Willson said, "Do you both think Admiral King and the rest of this staff has been sitting on its hands doing nothing about the Nazi subs off our coast? Do you both believe that we are fighting this war using the same tactics we used in the last one? Well, do you?"

Commander Jameson as the senior officer knew it was his place to take whatever blame there was in the findings and suggestions of the report. He replied, "Sir, it was our best intention to provide the admiral with our analysis of what is occurring now, what we can do in the short term to curb our losses and go on the offensive. And lastly, it was our idea to make suggestions where people, ships, and new technologies could be brought to bear on the submarine problem, sir."

Willson looked at his papers and had a sudden urge to smile or laugh or both, but kept a straight face. "Admiral King is very angry at this report. Not for you doing it, nor from the recommendations. He is mad at himself and the entire organization in not bringing forward fresh ideas and suggestions on how to deal with this menace. He is not happy at all being second guessed by a reserve commander and especially a kid professor." Willson stood and walked to the window looking out at the yard of Old Navy. "Jameson, you and Brand have done something no other man has done in my thirty-two years in the navy. You made Admiral King mad; not at you, which is very easily accomplished, but at himself. I have read over the report, and have all the admiral's notes. He wants additional clarification on a few points, and he wants to personally commend you for not only the work you put into this but the way you presented the situation and your recommendations."

Jameson and Brand who were still at parade rest smiled at each other while the admiral gazed out the window. A few minutes earlier they both thought their next duty station would be counting pencils in the Canal Zone.

Willson looked at them saying, "The way you broke up the report with a current situation analysis, including a synopsis of current attack strategies, escorting, aerial reconnaissance, and of course, convoys, was excellent but damning. The next section on immediate actions with estimates of possible results caused the admiral some heartburn, but he acknowledged the medicine was tolerable." Admiral Willson looked down at the report after he noticed a slight grin appearing on the face of Ensign Brand, not wanting to encourage any humor. "The most interesting reaction I had, and I think the admiral had, was in future recommendations which included lessons for our own submarine force."

The admiral finally realized he had these two men standing in front of his desk like plebes reporting for demerit penalties at Annapolis. "Gentlemen, excuse my bad manners, please sit down at the conference table. We need to discuss each of these points so I can get back to the admiral."

Before sitting, Willson opened the door and told one of his aides to have coffee sent in along with some of those powder sugar doughnuts he knew young Brand liked so much. He also requested two of his senior aides, Captain Stone and Commander McFarland, come in to listen and take notes.

Following introductions, Brand downed his second doughnut as Willson began his questions. "Brand, in your report you had several short-term fixes and then you listed additional medium to long-term suggestions. The admiral and I agree with most of the short-term ideas, such as the coastal convoy system, the single ship day port jumping, the repainting of aircraft to make them blend in with the sky and the various attack protocols, as you call them, for aerial surveillance and attack. These can be done with the least amount of cost in time or new equipment and will be implemented shortly. I may need you to work up additional training materials for the air arm, but that will not be too time-consuming."

"Yes sir, we can get that done quickly with the aid of some of your naval air personnel plus the army." Brand added, "Sir, we may want to add some of the attack scenarios to escort vessels as well. The attack profile is similar, and as we get more escorts of any size involved, it will buy us time to drive the U-boats away and eventually destroy them."

Willson was about to say something else, but Brand jumped back in, to the displeasure of the admiral's aides who never interrupted the boss. "One more thing on the attack profile, sir. Would it be possible for me to get a chance to meet and ask some questions of the U-boat crew we sank? I know they will only say things in conjunction with the Geneva Convention, but my line of questioning might give me additional insights on their strategies and defensive measures. My German is excellent, and perhaps my youth will confuse them."

Admiral Willson's aides looked at each other and grinned, knowing this was not in the cards. But Admiral Willson had more confidence in the young professor than they did. "Commander McFarland, get on the horn and find out where those Germans are and make arrangements to get Brand to that location." Willson looked at Brand and knew he could probably learn more in ten minutes with a prisoner than twenty professional interrogators. Willson then asked about the medium and long-term objectives Brand had outlined.

"Sir, I know there are many developments currently in the works that would benefit the anti-submarine program. My report details some of those, such as airplane-based radar, new ship-based radar, and larger depth charges. Also, the aerial depth charges need to be better fused and more aerodynamic to allow for more accurate placement."

Ensign Brand continued his explanation, "One of the other promising things the Brits have worked on is the aerial rocket. My old colleagues at Cal Tech have some brilliant chemists and metallurgists who could create a fin stabilized, non-guided rocket capable of flying some twelve hundred yards with an impact speed of over a thousand miles per hour. These rockets could also be useful in ground support missions as well as attacking small to medium size ships. The key to the anti-submarine rocket is that it uses kinetic energy to do its job. There is no need for an explosive warhead."

Willson had read this in the report, and King had commented on this as well. Willson jumped in with his question. "How does this thing kill a submarine if it has no explosive?"

The admiral's aides had taken notice of his question and were wondering about this themselves.

"Admiral, the rocket is traveling at a speed as fast as any projectile fired from a small cannon, such as a twenty-millimeter rapid fire anti-aircraft cannon. This high speed is the weapon, not the explosive. I have calculated that a twenty-pound solid steel warhead will penetrate up to three inches of hardened steel. One rocket hitting a submarine on the surface would penetrate the outer and inner pressure hulls, taking away its best defensive weapon—the ability to dive beneath the waves."

Brand watched Willson's aides doing calculations on the speed of impact that their math skills could not hope to muster. His "punch" calculation showed the terminal velocity of one rocket hitting a submarine would put a three to four-inch hole through one side of the submarine and then splinter inside the boat causing great damage to equipment and people.

Willson glanced at Brand's report, which showed some of the calculations substantiating the idea., "How soon could this be done?"

Brand knew most of the technology already existed. The only thing to build was a fast burning propellant for the rocket, plus the hardened steel projectile.

"I would say we could have a prototype by mid-summer with tests validating the weapon soon after. Training pilots and crewmen to use it will take longer, but this could be in the hands of the fleet by the end of the year."

Willson made some notes, then asked, "You made some comments on the faster production of ships, escorts and the like. How would you accomplish this?"

Brand jumped on the question with his normal gusto. "Sir, moving American industry to full wartime production is the largest challenge we face in beating the enemy. We need more ships and planes and tanks and all the things that make them run. The old way of doing things will not work." Brand's hands were now gesturing to indicate the size of structures and numbers of units. The more he spoke, the more animated he became. "Mass production of tanks requires moving the auto industry into tank building. This is not that hard to do once the machine tools are set. Building a car or truck on an assembly line is the hard part, and we have the assembly lines. We can expand our production of planes the same way by expanding factories, more out-sourcing of small parts and large assemblies like engines."

Brand picked up a glass of water and took a long sip. He knew he was getting into an area which was already in discussion but he thought his ideas might be of help. "Sorry, sir, if I may continue?" Admiral Willson nodded his head for the young man to continue. He enjoyed Brand's bravado and his seemingly never-ending flow of ideas. "Ships, though are the problem. It takes three to four years to build a battleship or a fleet carrier. My thoughts on this are to go back to school and learn from Henry Ford and mass produce the same items over and over. We cannot make constant modifications of a specific type like I have seen on the submarines at New London. Merchant ships could be built in three months or less. New destroyer escorts could be built in six months or less. We just have to rethink how we do things and experiment using sound engineering and logistical management."

The aides were stunned to hear such thoughts coming from a young ensign. What stunned them was the admiral's response, "I agree. There is much thought being given to these recommendations. The War Production Board is evaluating several of these concepts now, but you have some excellent ideas and plans specific to the navy. I think I will need your help on these later. One last thing or maybe two, tell me about the escort carrier and homing torpedo."

"Sir, the escort carrier concept the Brits have used was aimed at fighting off German aircraft, and now they want to expand this to convoy anti-submarine duties. They have lost some of their small carriers, which were converted merchant vessels, to both aerial attacks and submarine attacks. The recommendations show a need for the anti-submarine variant working initially with convoys and then with hunter-killer groups as more escorts become available. Additional escort carriers can support ground attacks, build small ship formations and movement of short-legged fighters and bombers to resupply the fleet carriers. These ships can be built from the ten to twelve thousand-ton hulls of tanker types and completed in months instead of the years it takes to build one of the new fleet carriers."

The admiral completed his notes then signaled for the next topic—homing torpedoes.

Brand continued his analysis. "The acoustic or homing torpedo is an idea that has floated around for some time. The key is our ability to provide power for the sonar detector and the ability of the torpedo to follow these location beams to the submarine. I feel that with our increasing technology capability, this type weapon could be made viable in a year and implemented in eighteen months."

Willson looked at the young man and at his notes. How could someone so young come up with so many ideas, some of which were now on the drawing board, but also others that were only suggestions? It was exciting for him to watch the young genius at work and his calmness in expressing his views in front of senior officials. He also knew one of the ideas on the development list was moving steadily toward completion, the variable proximity fuse for anti-aircraft usage. But the ensign's ideas were even better than the team who were working on it.

"Mr. Brand, tell me about the proximity fuse."

"Well, Admiral, I know the researchers at the National Defense Research Committee have been working on this and the original British design has been improved a great deal. Using commercial hearing aid tubes, modified by Western Electric and others, these designs should handle the enormous stress of being shot from a cannon and then use constructive and destructive interference to activate the explosion. Basically, think of a Doppler shift from the oscillator frequency by the relative motion of the fuse and the target. By getting this into production and with additional refinements, we can improve the lethality of each shot by five to ten times. This will save countless lives and when one thinks of the shells expended to hit one airplane flying at three hundred miles per hour, well, the cost savings are enormous in both dollars and the logistics to transport them to the war zone."

Willson was familiar with the work being done but had not thought of it in this way. By introducing a better way to down an enemy plane faster and at lower cost in terms of ammunition, it would be a great advancement and save lives and ships. He had seen reports about the amount of ammunition expended at Pearl Harbor with only a dozen Jap planes shot down. Not a good showing for the navy.

"Brand, get connected on this project and see what you can do to move it along. This would be most helpful to the fleet, and if we can get this sooner, we will be much better off."

Willson checked the report and told his aides, "Captain Stone, I want you and your team to look at current fleet build projections and give me an updated report, so I can review it. Then give it to Brand to see what else he can do with it. Commander McFarland, get with the science office for an update on the radar program and the proximity fuse. Admiral King wants us to be more involved in making these projects top priority."

Both the captain and the commander said in unison, "Yes sir. Will that be all, for now, sir?"

"Yes, gentlemen, give me your notes on what you heard and think concerning this briefing. And, keep it short too. I would like your ideas, not a novel, understood?"

Both men stood and replied, "Yes sir," then both left the office with confused looks on their faces. They had heard about this young man and the scientist commander, but did not know of their involvement with the admiral, nor had they known of some of the things being discussed. They understood they had a lot to learn and to be careful around the commander and the ensign because they had a major "in" with the big boss.

After the two aides left, Willson turned to Commander Jameson, "Both of those men are top flight staff officers and want to get back to sea duty. I think by learning a bit more while in these roles, they will become better fleet commanders, but they need to think beyond their old way of doing things. Too many officers in our fleet have been around too long, probably me as well. Admiral King is doing all he can to find the best and brightest to lead the navy."

Willson paused to scan his notes and thought more about what he had just said. He looked back at the two scientists and continued. "Some men are cut out for command at sea, he tells me, while others are good at staff work. He's afraid there are not enough of both and with the growth of the navy to thousands of ships and millions of men, we are going to have to place a premium on leadership and smart thinking. But this is not our topic for today, just keep this to yourselves as you see people moved around at an alarming pace. Some are going to fail but hopefully not so bad as to lose ships and people, but this is a war. Loss is something we must deal with."

Jameson and Brand listened to the admiral who was staring into space as he spoke. His job was to do the bidding for his boss, and as King's role grew, Willson would be the enforcer. He did not look forward to that part of the job. Willson had the authority to interpret the musings of Admiral King, and put them into orders meaning life or death. It could enhance or kill a career, and possibly win a victory or lose a battle.

Jameson for one knew from his Annapolis education the mantle of authority is a tricky thing and some men are not cut out for command at higher levels. He did not envy Willson or King. They would pay the price just like any officer in the fleet or any marine or sailor who had to face the enemy. Hopefully, he thought, that the work he was engaged in with Brand would help win the war sooner and with fewer casualties, both physical and emotional.

Willson refocused and asked, "Well, gentlemen, you seem to have been made members of the inner circle or as I put it, the King's trust. Are you ready to do some more work for the chief?"

Both Jameson and Brand offered a hearty, "Yes sir." They wondered how Admiral Willson would look when this war was over, if he survives.

"Good to have you on board. The first order of business will be to get you connected with the surviving German sub crew. It will be interesting to see if you can glean anything from the Germans that would be helpful in your work. Remember, Jameson, keep a tight leash on Mr. Brand and keep him safe."

"Yes sir, I will make sure Brand keeps a good distance from the Nazis and hopefully we can learn something of use to our people. Thank you, sir, for making this possible."

Willson set the report aside and offered a final comment, "One more thing. It seems you are invited to dinner with Admiral King. This invitation includes Lieutenant Flannigan as well. A car will be sent for the three of you at 1700 hours. Be on your best behavior, Brand, and look the part of a naval officer. Jameson, make sure Flannigan is squared away and wearing all his decorations. Same goes for you two as well. I want to see the DFC on both of you. Got it?"

"Aye, aye sir." Jameson looked at Brand and shrugged. "Admiral, may I inquire as to where we are going for dinner?"

Willson, knowing the entire story of the dinner, smiled. "No, Jameson, I can't help you out on this. I have been sworn to secrecy on lots of things around here, and this is one of them. Just be ready and be on time. Have one of your cars with the gunny and one of the other marines follow you. They will be taken care of separately for dinner. It is a wonderful place for sure, but I'm never too sure about the day's special." Again, he grinned.

Both Jameson and Brand had puzzled expressions on their faces, and both wondered what all the mystery was about. They would learn in a few hours' time what a special dinner looked like.

Jameson and Brand arrived back at the Bethesda house around 1300 hours. They had remained at the admiral's office meeting with various aides who offered their time and services with various reports and activities of the team. The German sub crew was locked up in Charleston, South Carolina, and efforts were being made for a meeting with some of the prisoners. Brand wanted a cross section of officers and enlisted men, especially any surviving junior officers and engine room crew. Brand was working up a set of questions and opening gambits to hopefully trick some of the crew in offering up information they might be unaware they were divulging.

Jameson had called the Bethesda house earlier to alert Flannigan about dinner. He wasn't happy being told he would be having dinner with Admiral King, but orders were orders and he would comply. His best uniform needed pressing, and all his devices, ribbons, and other uniform adornments needed to be attached in the correct order. He and Gunny Jones were making sure all looked good, including the Sam Brown belt still a proscribed part of a marine officer's uniform. One of the corporals was busy polishing his shoes and the brass buttons to ensure the lieutenant looked his best. They were all proud to serve with Flannigan. Every man in the unit found his story compelling, plus he was very approachable, which was a rare thing in an officer.

Jameson and Brand also got cleaned up. Both shaved again to make sure they met navy regulations. Their uniforms were being pressed by the chief who knew a good officer was always well groomed, and since this assignment beat most of his previous duty stations, he didn't want anyone thinking his commanding officer was out of uniform.

Jameson asked Gunnery Sergeant Jones who should accompany him in the staff car that would follow the officers. The gunny thought hard about it, knowing Admiral King always liked to see new people as well as old hands, he picked Sergeant McBride to go along. They made sure the car was as clean as possible and had it washed before the appointed time. The gunny and McBride were all decked out in their best uniforms with service ribbons and awards correctly attached.

On schedule, Brand, Jameson, and Flannigan waited in the house for their ride to show up, while Gunny and Sergeant McBride stood outside by their staff car ready to follow the admiral's car. Five minutes past the designated time, a navy staff car appeared. It was the usual Ford, a late 1941 model in navy blue driven by a navy petty officer. Next to him was a lieutenant with the gold ropes of an admiral's aide flowing off this right shoulder. The petty officer and the lieutenant saluted Commander Jameson, and the petty officer held the back door.

"Commander Jameson, my name is Bitner, Alex J. I will be your escort to the dinner. Admiral King and the rest of the party will be there when we arrive. If you will please get in the car, I will inform your sergeant as to where we are going so he can follow us." The lieutenant moved over to the gunny who came to attention along with Sergeant McBride.

"Gunny, this card has the address of the location where we are meeting Admiral King. You will follow us and stay right behind as we enter the compound. You will be directed where to park once we are inside. Any questions?"

"No sir. We will be right behind you," answered the gunnery sergeant as he read the address of their destination.

Once they entered the car, Sergeant McBride asked, "Where are we going, Gunny? What's all the mystery about?"

"Just shut up and drive." Gunny read the card again, watching the car in front of them carrying the three officers in the back seat. "When we get to where we are going, don't say a goddamn thing unless you are spoken to. Understand?"

"Gee, Gunny, I just wanted to know where we are going. I don't know many places in D.C., and I don't want to get lost."

"Just drive, McBride, just drive." The gunny looked again at the card and said out loud to no one in particular, "I'll be a son of a bitch." He was very proud of the men riding ahead of him and very proud to be a marine.

As the car approached the main gate of the presidential mansion, all three men in the back seat stared in amazement. The admiral's aide asked them to have their military identification cards ready. A marine with a submachine gun and a uniformed police officer waved them through. They drove up to the main portico where they were again eyed by a marine guard and a secret service agent. They entered the building and were told to wait in the main hallway. All three voiced their excitement and utter astonishment at being in the house of the commander in chief. Finally, a secret service agent and a White House butler led them to the president's side office where he hosted his cocktail hour for various guests. When they entered, they did not see the president, but did see four men in suits, three were familiar to Brand.

The first, whom Brand did not know, was Dr. Vannevar Bush, chairman of the National Defense Research Committee. He was also president of the Carnegie Institute and had developed a close relationship with the president through his contacts with Harry Hopkins, who served as FDR's closest advisor and lived at the White House. The other three were Dr. Frank Jewett, president of the National Academy of Science and Bell Laboratories; Dr. James Conant, president of Harvard

University; and Dr. Karl T. Compton, president of the Massachusetts Institute of Technology. Each had met young Brand at various stages of his career.

Conant was the first to notice Brand. "James, you look like a real sailor. I am so happy to see you again. I am pleased that the president managed to find you out there in San Diego and bring you back to Washington."

Before Brand could say anything, the others came over and shook hands with Brand and introduced Dr. Bush. "Vannevar, this is the young man we told you about several months ago. Meet Dr. James Brand. James, this is Dr. Bush."

"It is an honor to meet you, Dr. Bush. I have read many of your articles and papers. It's super to have this opportunity to finally meet."

Bush greeted the tall ensign, who held a Ph.D. in Physics. "It is my honor to meet a young scientist who is helping to win the war in uniform. I have heard about your report to Admiral King. He is very impressed with your work so far on the submarine issues."

Brand was taken aback by the comment because of the secrecy of his work for the admiral but quickly realized Bush was the lead man for science in the war effort and knew much more than most people about what was going on in the war.

Bush, being a good host turned to the other officers, introducing himself first to Jameson then to Flannigan. The others followed, but one was always nearby Brand to keep him company.

A few minutes of small talk ensued until a door on the other side of the room opened. A very thin man entered the room followed by a man in a wheelchair pushed by a White House butler. The thin man was the sickly Harry Hopkins and the person in the wheelchair was the president of the United States, Franklin D. Roosevelt.

The officers jumped to attention and the scientists stood straighter even though they had been acquaintances of the president for some time. President Roosevelt in his usual manner had a long cigarette holder perched in his teeth like a bird of prey and quickly took it out saying, "At ease, gentlemen, this is a social setting not a parade ground. That goes for you, too, Vannevar."

Each of the science leaders chuckled at the little jokes FDR was famous for and he had the butler push him to the table where he made his cocktails. He wheeled himself around looking at the three newcomers and smiling. "Well, this must be the famous Dr. Brand or shall I call you Ensign Brand?"

"Sir, you may call me anything you wish, Mr. President."

"Yes, that is my prerogative, so I will call you James. Is that all right with you, James?"

"I would be honored sir, thank you." Brand blushed a bit as FDR motioned for him to come closer to shake his hand.

"Vannevar, see what a well-trained scientist is capable of? Good manners and a very nice looking suit."

The science leaders laughed at the joke as did the other two officers. FDR shook Brand's hand, then looking over at the other two officers said, "You must be Commander Jameson, and you must be my marine hero, Lieutenant Flannigan."

Both officers went back to attention and replied, "Yes sir, reporting as ordered."

FDR looked at Brand said, "Will you tell these two fine examples of Annapolis training they are not on duty now and to come over and shake my hand?"

Brand did as asked, and the two officers came up to the president who offered his hand in a grip known to be close to a vise when he wanted to exert extreme pressure to someone. He made some quick comments to both men but especially to Flannigan.

"Lieutenant, you know that my son Elliott is a marine as well and is now serving with Lt. Col. Evans Carlson. He is quite proud to be serving alongside marines such as yourself."

Flannigan quickly replied, "Sir, I did hear that your son Captain Roosevelt is serving, but I did not know that he is with Colonel Carlson. I served with him briefly in China. He is a very strong leader. I am sure your son will learn a lot from the colonel."

Roosevelt smiled, knowing more about Carlson than most in the Marine Corps, but did not comment further about his son. "I received a report about you from Admiral Hart back in January, and he was quite impressed by your heroics in the Philippines. I have ordered him back to the states because of the deteriorating situation in the Java campaign, so perhaps you will see him again soon."

"That would be good, sir. I would like to see the admiral again whenever possible." As he backed away from the president, Flannigan wondered why Hart would be coming home from the campaign in the Java Sea. He had heard only scant reports on the issues facing what was known as the ABDA force. This force was commanded by General Wavell of the British army with Hart as the sea commander of the joint American, British, Dutch and Australian forces. From his own brief experience in Java, where he was sent following his departure from the Philippines, he knew there was no common operational plan, code, signals, or much regarding leadership. Unity of command was essential to any operation and with four countries involved, sharing various responsibilities and with the constant strife of competing interests, things were bound to go from bad to worse. He would make some inquiries as soon as possible to find out what was really going on. The president was famous for showing great charm and optimism in the face of almost all adversity and this was probably the case as well.

The president began his ritual of making cocktails for his guests. The White House butler provided the glasses and the ice, but kept a good distance from the wheelchair-bound president who loved his nightly ritual of making drinks for his guests. Most of the cocktails were weak, and his Manhattans were famous for their poor quality. For a wealthy man, the president of the United States did not spend a lot of money on quality booze. He made drinks for each of the men, but offered Brand a Coca-Cola.

The president did not talk shop during his cocktail hour and spent time asking Bush and Conant questions about some of their research programs. Brand heard about ongoing developments at MIT's Radiation Lab, which was doing incredible work on increasing the power of the magnetron the British had provided back in 1940 and how they were working up new shipboard models and, like Brand had requested, new airborne models for the PBYs. Brand asked some technical questions of Conant but was quickly shut down by Bush who knew the details bored

FDR. So, they talked about adding people and how the Harvard campus was changing with fewer men and lots of new women students plus workers. FDR was very proud of his Harvard background and hoped any new development would not detract from Harvard Square. Bush assured him he would not see any difference in the main parts of the campus, but outside areas were now being acquired for some of their research.

This light banter continued for another fifteen minutes as the men slowly sipped their drinks to make sure they did not finish before the president. As Brand thought about the pace of the conversation and the topics, another door opened and in walked Admiral King and an army major general. The officers immediately snapped to attention as the big boss of the navy walked in with a perpetual scowl on his face.

FDR immediately turned in his wheelchair to face the admiral and the general who came to attention in front of the president. "Admiral, you don't have to come in here and be at attention every time you show up. You may scare our scientists."

Admiral King went to a more leisured posture and nodded his head in the direction of Jameson, Flannigan, and Brand. "Sir, I am sorry for being late. More war communique that will need to be reviewed with you came in an hour ago. General Watson is making sure these are posted in the map room." Watson was Edwin Watson, who served as FDR's senior military aide and appointment secretary. His nickname was Pa, and was close to the president and very protective of his time. Nothing moved or happened at the White House without his approval.

"Ernie, I guess you and Pa and I need to talk about this after dinner if that is all right with you?"

"Certainly, Mr. President, I'm happy to be of assistance in any manner I can." King looked at Brand and gave what for him was a smile, but it was difficult to detect. His ability to be in a bad mood all the time did give way from time to time, especially to James Brand.

"Well, since the admiral has some issues to discuss, why don't we go in for dinner, and then I can find out what is going on that needs my attention." The president looked over his right shoulder to the butler, who immediately began to wheel him towards the dining room. Everyone followed Roosevelt and found their places set with name tags. Interestingly, Bush and Brand were sitting at each side of the president who presided over the long table at one end and Admiral King sat at the other. General Watson sat next to Admiral King with Commander Jameson at his side. The butlers then began to serve a rather bland meal consisting of pot roast, one of FDR's favorites, and green beans. The days of high cuisine in the White House were a generation away.

The president was in a jovial mood, acting the part of the "all is okay" leader of the Allied Powers and engaged people scattered around the table in small talk. Brand fell under his powers early on when asked about his work at the Lowell Observatory. He also commented about Brand losing his father as a young boy which was similar to FDR's loss of his father. Brand was touched by this knowledge and thanked the president for his understanding and concern. The president then began a conversation with Lieutenant Flannigan about his time in the Philippines and Java. He was especially interested in the bombing attack at Cavite where Flannigan had been wounded. He pressed for details about the height of the Japanese bombers and the lack of anti-aircraft weapons that could hit the high-flying planes. Flannigan held nothing back and was concerned the commander in chief would not be happy about his commentary.

FDR was more than interested in his discussion of the attack. As Flannigan answered more and more questions from the president, he noticed other conversations had ceased and everyone's eyes were on him. This unnerved the young marine, and he tried to stop discussing the topic, but the president asked one more question.

"Lieutenant, I want to thank you for your candor. I know Admiral King feels the same way. We cannot win this war without firsthand information from people who are doing the fighting. We need to know what works, what does not work, and what we should be doing to win this war." As the president finished this last remark, everyone became silent. His voice went up in inflection just like one of his addresses to the nation. He was not being overly theatrical, but for once was being emotional about the reality of the war. "Tell me, Lieutenant, what went wrong in the Philippines and in Java from your viewpoint? Do not worry about what you say, for I have heard lots of viewpoints from the great to the small, but I have not heard from someone who was there."

Flannigan could see the president staring at him with his fork and knife down on his plate and knew he had to give President Roosevelt his best reply. He thought for a minute and took a sip of water. Thinking this would be the end of his career, he began, "Mr. President, I'm not sure of what happened when or who was in charge or not in charge, but it appears to this marine that coordination of command was lacking and is lacking to this day. In Manila, I heard the navy was making certain plans without benefit of what the army was doing and vice versa. The Air Corps wanted to be more aggressive, but failed to have enough spare parts or trained pilots for the role. The lack of communication between commands is a major problem, as well as the use of old equipment such as the three-inch anti-aircraft guns which could not get near the Jap bombers."

Flannigan stopped as he noticed Roosevelt's frown deepening but the president waved him on. "Sir, when we lost Clark field on day one, we lost the ability to fight back. Air power is needed at every step of the battle going forward, and close communication between commands is essential. In Java, before I left at the end of December, no one on our side was sure of who was in control. We were blind and could not talk to anyone. Our patrol planes got out and fought as hard as possible, but there was no strike capability. The poor PBY pilots who tried to attack were chewed up in their slow planes, and it was usually a one-way mission for them. The old navy four-stack destroyers were in need of constant repair, and they had almost no anti-aircraft protection to boot. The radar systems Mr. Brand has been pushing for would have been of enormous help in knowing the enemy was on his way. But you cannot stop an attack when you have no weapons to fight with."

Flannigan again reached for his water glass as FDR looked right at him with a steel-eyed glare that would have killed a lesser man, motioning for the lieutenant to continue.

"Sir, I don't have much else to say, but the one thing I learned from the time I spent under attack by the Japanese is they are well trained, disciplined, supplied with the most modern weapons, and are very organized in their attack plans. I fear we have underestimated them, even though I had spent some time in China watching them at war with the

Chinese. I thought the Chinese were just not putting up a good fight, but I now think the Chinese are hard fighters who are poorly led and poorly supplied. We can lick the Japs, sir, but it will take a lot of coordination at the top and training at the bottom to do it. I am sorry, sir, if I have said anything to upset you, I didn't..."

"Lieutenant," FDR said holding up his hand, "you did nothing to offend me. I asked for your assessment and your candid comments, and you did exactly what I wanted. I think these gentlemen understand the gravity of the issues we are facing, but when a young man who has been under attack, fought back, and was wounded, tells you the truth as he sees it, all we can do is to commend you for your actions then and for your words today. Thank you, Lieutenant. I agree with everything you said, and I know Admiral King understands the issues you brought up. Isn't that right, Admiral?"

King looked at the president but directed his comments to Flannigan, "Lieutenant, what you shared with us tonight is exactly the kind of report I want to hear from every commander. I also want them to come to me with solutions to these problems and how we can never make the same mistake again. In war, there are many variables, some of which these distinguished men of science are helping us on, but it is up to you in the field to drive change and make the hard decisions that will win this war."

President Roosevelt gave King a quick nod of approval and looked back at Flannigan. "Lieutenant, I think some people may have short changed you in some of your recent experiences. I received a communique from Admiral Hart who informed me of your actions before and during your time in the Philippines. He was especially interested in your well-being after you left Java and the treatment you received at Pearl and San Diego. It seems you have several admirers in high places and now you have one more in me." The president looked at General Watson who stood and moved to the president's side.

"First Lt. Robert J. Flannigan, attention to orders." The general barked next to the president.

Flannigan jumped up and looked at the army general.

Pa Watson read from a piece of paper, "First Lt. Robert J. Flannigan, while serving with the Asiatic Fleet, Department of the Philippines, demonstrated tremendous courage, leadership, and initiative on December 10, 1941. While under attack by enemy forces, Lieutenant Flannigan rescued over twenty-three men who were in burning buildings and under constant bombings by enemy aircraft. He went into various naval buildings to find severely wounded men and bring them to safety. He also volunteered to remove vital naval equipment from these same buildings while they were on fire and under constant threat of explosion. He then supervised firefighting and secured weapons which were mounted on trucks to fight off the attacking planes. He was wounded several times and severely burned. He refused evacuation until he fell unconscious from his wounds. Therefore, the commendation of the Navy Cross is authorized this first day of March 1942."

Watson pulled out a small box and handed it to the president.

"Lieutenant Flannigan, I think this award tells you and everyone else that you did a great job in the Philippines. You are an inspiration to all of us. Well done. Now, if you would lean down to my level, I will pin this on you."

Flannigan leaned down to the president who artfully pinned the second highest medal bestowed by the navy on the young marine. As he finished, FDR said, "Flannigan, I expect you not to take too many risks from now on, but I don't think you will pay heed to my request."

Flannigan stood upright and shook the president's hand. It was then he saw that all of the people around the table were standing as Admiral King started clapping his hands saying, "Hurrah! *Semper Fidelis*, Flannigan."

Flannigan, more than a bit embarrassed by all this attention, moved to sit down when FDR waved him back. "Marines are all hard heads you know. I will tell you when I am finished with you." The president smiled again and looking at Admiral King who was in lock-step with the president's plans, said, "It seems to me, Admiral, that as commander in chief of the United States military and naval forces, I can promote anyone I wish. Is that correct, Admiral?"

King did not smile, but he was beaming inside because he liked to see men get recognition for honorable and brave service to the navy. "Sir, you have the authority to promote, fire and probably shoot anyone you want to, sir." The last comment got a laugh from everyone including the president.

"Shooting sounds like a good idea sometimes, Admiral, but I like promoting people more. So, Lieutenant Flannigan, you are now a captain in the United States Marine Corps, and I think Admiral King agrees wholeheartedly with me on this." King nodded. FDR then made another announcement. "Seems that Captain Flannigan needs some help in the promotion department, so Admiral King and I discussed the other members of the team seated with us this day. Commander Jameson, you are now Captain Jameson and your mission will be expanded by Admiral King shortly. You may regret this day for you are about to get more troubles than you ever expected." Another round of applause sounded, and King shook the hand of the new navy captain.

"Finally, there is a very young ensign who ran off and joined the navy to fight the enemies of his country. It took the intercession of one of the world's great scientists to find you and get you doing things that will really help the war effort, so it is also appropriate that you now become the youngest lieutenant junior grade in the U.S. Navy."

Everyone started to clap as FDR motioned for Brand to come over to stand next to him to receive the applause from his scientific colleagues as well as his navy comrades. The president shook his hand once more and whispered, "I have more plans for you, young man, and I look forward to your candid assessments in the future."

When the commotion subsided, the president motioned to General Watson and announced to the assembled group, "I have some things that I need to be made aware of, so I will give Admiral King my ear for a few minutes. Brand, stay around if you can so I can talk to you some more." He looked over at Bush and added, "Vannevar, set up a time to bring young Brand up to date on some of the developments you and your colleagues are working on and what progress you are making."

Vannevar replied, "More than happy to and I think his input will be helpful regarding our priorities."

FDR waved back as he was pushed into his study followed by Admiral King, Harry Hopkins, and General Watson. The assembled men, officers, and scientists all stood at attention while the commander in chief was wheeled away. As soon as the door closed, Bush asked Brand, Jameson, and Flannigan to sit down at the table followed by Dr. Conant and Dr. Compton who both had opened briefcases and pulled out binders marked "Top Secret" in at least three places, all in red.

Bush began to give an update on the radar programs, followed by the proximity fuse and radar guided gunnery, including synchronizing the radar to the proximity fuse. They also discussed the proposal Brand had provided on the 3.5-inch aerial rocket for anti-submarine attacks. They liked his work, especially improving propellants that would be helpful to other munitions projects. The group also discussed the need for faster-calculating machines and Bush discussed his work with Conant on getting a "computational computer" program going. Brand agreed in principle to the concept whereby machines could somehow be programmed to run lengthy mathematical calculations and somehow maintain records of these for future use. Currently, hundreds of mainly female mathematicians were being recruited to work in Boston building gunnery tables, using mostly mechanical calculating machines and pencils. This slowed down the process and as Brand stated to Conant, "The more people you add, you only get an incremental improvement because of the sheer force of will. We need a new and better way to do complex mathematics and to be able to quickly adapt this to our scientific challenges."

Conant briefed the group on the work currently underway at Harvard and MIT using the hundreds of new people being hired to create the math tables for use by the army and the navy. He agreed the initial design for any machine that could do it faster and provide some sort of recall would be of immense help. Bush also brought up some of the aeronautical issues since he was the president of the National Advisory Committee for Aeronautics of which he was extremely proud. Bush asked about Brand's knowledge of airfoil designs specifically about wind drag and coefficients used to address stall and high-speed flight. Brand gave a brief overview of his knowledge which was extensive and Bush looked at his colleagues with a nod of agreement and satisfaction.

Conant smiled saying, "Brand has a better understanding of drag, stall, and high-speed shudder than most of the people who hold doctorates in Aeronautics. Only later did I find out he had a pilot's license and had flown more hours than most of our military pilots." He then asked Brand if he would like to look at some of the newest research in aircraft design. Brand said he would be very happy to see what was being developed.

Jameson finally spoke after what seemed to be only a few minutes but forty minutes had already passed. "Gentlemen, please remember that Ensign, sorry, Lieutenant Brand has lots of commitments and as he stated in his report, setting priorities will be the father of success in the war. So please, let's get some clarity around what is most important and I will run it past Admiral King for approval."

Bush immediately backtracked knowing his enthusiasm in having some very bright and fresh young eyes looking at projects could be immensely important but also knew Brand was first and foremost a naval officer and reported to Admiral King.

"Jameson, I am sorry for my overt enthusiasm involving young Brand. I understand the chain of command and know we can ask but don't always receive approval for every project or the use of every individual. I will make a concerted effort to work through you first to get the admiral's permission."

At that moment, the door of the study opened and General Watson appeared. "Lieutenant Brand, the president will see you now." He held the door as Brand walked through alone. Jameson and Flannigan knew if they were to meet with the president, they would have been called by name.

Brand found Admiral King sitting next to the president's desk, both smoking cigarettes. Brand did not like smoking and would never take it up, if he could hold out from the constant pressure from his friends, superiors, and now the president, to start the habit.

Watson pulled a chair around to sit next to the president, while he motioned Brand to sit next to Admiral King. Presidential advisor, Harry Hopkins leaned on the president's desk looking like a man in need of a new suit.

"James, I wanted to have a private chat with you and Admiral King about your future. We had talked a bit about it before you came in. Both

Harry and Pa gave us some other perspectives we had not breached. Here is what we have decided to do with you. First, you will continue to report to Captain Jameson who will be appointed senior science aide to the admiral. You will both work through Admiral Willson, but you report to Admiral King. Do you understand what I am saying, son?"

Brand looked at the president and Admiral King replying, "Sir, I guess what you mean is that on paper I report to Captain Jameson then to Admiral Willson, but unofficially I report to Admiral King. Is that correct, sir?"

FDR smiled and said, "Damn, Ernie, this kid is smarter than his years. He will make a great politician someday or even an admiral."

King smiled at the joke but did not like references to his high office and duty to the navy and the country by being lumped in with politicians. Vice Chief of Naval Operations Vice Adm. F. J. Horne would be his point man with all the bureaus, commissions, and the Congress. He detested having to testify and attend the rubber chicken dinners for which Washington was famous. King had requested Admiral Horne be named to this new role as soon as it was announced he would be replacing Admiral Stark as chief of naval operations. Stark would be named commander of Naval Forces, Europe, and begin operations in London in support of the U.S. offensives against Germany.

"James, you have it correct. On paper, you report to Jameson and then to Admiral Willson and then to Admiral King. You need to connect the dots further, young man. You also report to me, through Admiral King. Your job is to continue what you have been doing. Looking at what is possible, examining options not yet on the table, looking for new ways to use science, engineering, mathematics, whatever, to win the war. You will make your normal reports to Jameson who will move them up the chain of command." FDR took a long drag on his cigarette and continued. "If for whatever reason you see something that needs to be given top priority or needs new leadership, or perhaps a project will fail where success is possible but misguided, you are to get in contact directly with Admiral King and to me. Admiral King and General Watson will work up a protocol on how this is to be accomplished without upsetting anyone else or anyone else even knowing. You are going to be our eyes and ears. You are not out to ruin a man's career, but if someone is blundering his command or could be detrimental to the war effort, it is your duty to let us know. You may be wrong in your assessment, but we have a feeling you will probably be right. This could mean weeks or months of lost time and more importantly lost lives."

King took over for the president, "Mr. Brand, I am ordering you to do something most officers would not want to do. You are to report on conduct, decision making, leadership, and all other aspects of operations that concern the prosecution of the war effort. You will be allowed free reign to go anywhere and look at anything. The cover for this will be Jameson, who will be given similar instructions but not to the extent we are giving you. As a junior officer, most senior men will not even notice your existence. That is what I am hoping for. You are a staff officer, a non-academy man and a scientist. This is a perfect cover for what needs to be accomplished. You have proven to the president and to me that you can handle just about anything in regard to the mission and with your intellect and scientific methodology, you will be very helpful in focusing on what needs to be done and when we should do it. Do you understand the mission?"

Brand glanced at the president who was peering over his glasses, looking just as serious as the admiral, as they awaited an answer. "Admiral, I believe I understand the mission and the issues you want me to examine. I understand there are a lot of variables in building the war effort and some men are often the reason for slow progress. I will do my best to inform you whenever I see something that needs addressing. When do I start?"

FDR smiled at Admiral King. "Ernie, our young lion is ready, and he should also be made aware his initial report, which contained many of the items we wanted information on, has been acted upon. Most of the things in the report on the U-boat attacks we were aware of. You made a better case than everyone else and were not afraid of telling us the truth as you saw it, but also how to start solving the problem. I wish I had more people like you in senior positions."

Admiral King looked at his watch, and the president picked up the hint. "Pa, go get the new captains and bring them in here."

General Watson returned in a few moments followed by the two newly promoted officers. They came to attention upon entering the room, just like two good academy graduates should. As they stood at attention, they saw Admiral King sitting on a chair next to Brand engaged in a whispering conversation that neither could hear and saw the president leaning in to hear what was being said. FDR looked up and saw the two navy officers standing at attention at the doorway and exclaimed, "How many times do I have to tell you that this is not a parade ground, Captain Jameson? Come in and take a seat."

Pa Watson had moved two more chairs into a semi-circle in front of the president's desk. As they sat down, they saw King patting the back of young Brand and giving him a weak smile, which is more than almost anyone in the navy received.

FDR looked at the two new arrivals and began his little speech. "Captain Jameson and Captain Flannigan, again congratulations on your promotions. Each of you will have additional responsibilities, and I am sure Admiral Willson will be briefing you both on what these are. I wanted to tell you a bit more, so you understand the orders you will receive. Is that all right with you both?"

Jameson and Flannigan answered in unison, "Yes sir, Mr. President." They knew that was all they should say until asked something else.

"Good, here is the story on what you are going to be asked to do for the country. Get that meaning gentlemen, the country. Not Admiral King or your president. Not the navy or the army. It is the country you serve first, and you should always use that as your rudder in all future endeavors. First, Captain Jameson, you are going to be appointed as Senior Science Aide to Admiral King. You will report directly to Admiral Willson, and he will provide you specific orders. Captain Flannigan, you will continue to serve as the security officer for the Science Advisory Team led by Captain Jameson. You will be entrusted with a significant amount of secret information, and you will ensure it is secure at all times. You and your team will provide a security screen for Lieutenant Brand. He is not to be placed in any harmful situation unless it is of the utmost importance. Both of you will receive additional written orders that you will divulge to the team so they have a set of cover stories for those who might get nosy. Your communications chief will be provided additional security information that will be known only to Admiral Willson. Understood?"

Again, in unison, "Yes sir, Mr. President."

"You and your team may be sent any place in the world with very little notice. You should be careful in granting leaves, including medical leaves. If someone leaves the team and cannot catch up with a movement, they will be dropped, and a replacement found. Captain Flannigan, you will make sure each member of the team is above reproach and can maintain secrecy. Anyone who violates this policy will be court-martialed, and charges could include treason. Again, any questions?"

"No sir, we understand," Jameson spoke and Flannigan nodded his understanding.

King added, "Jameson, you will perform duties as my science aide but many times people will wonder where you are. Whoever makes persistent requests should be reported to Admiral Willson. Same goes for you Captain Flannigan."

Both agreed but wondered to themselves what the hell was going on. King added more to the story. "The president and I have a lot of faith in you, as well as Mr. Brand. You are to pay close attention to whatever Lieutenant Brand is doing and support his actions. From time to time, he will be in contact with Admiral Willson or myself, and you will not question what he is reporting or doing. Understood?"

"Yes sir, we understand completely."

FDR now turned on his famous charm. "I hate to get serious men, but these are not normal times. I want to assure you that you are supporting the war effort in a unique and very substantial way. Your efforts along with Lieutenant Brand will help us win the war. Just keep an eye on what he is doing but unless he offers, do not ask."

He looked at General Watson and said, "Pa, I think we need to go down to the map room before it gets too much later." Watson moved toward the president to take hold of the wheelchair handles. As he did, everyone stood at attention.

"James, it was grand meeting you and remember what I said. Don't let Bush and his people get too much of your skin in their game. You work for Admiral King and me first." With this last comment, he was wheeled out saying, "Good night gentlemen and get some sleep. I need every man in the navy awake and at the helm."

King turned to Jameson saying, "Captain, report to Admiral Willson at 0800. I will have him make some time available on my schedule so we can review some of the actions the president wants you and your team involved in within the next few weeks."

"Yes sir, Admiral. I will be at Admiral Willson's office at 0800. Anything else, sir?"

King turned as he was leaving the room, "Get some sleep, and that goes for you, Brand. That is an order."

Jameson watched King's back as he walked away and turned to Flannigan. "Damn, this was a strange night. James, can you provide us some details on what is going on?"

Brand looked at his mentor and immediate boss and at Flannigan, his bodyguard and friend. "Sir, I can tell you a few things about what went on, but not everything. I need to run this through my brain before we can talk about it. Is that all right?"

Jameson smiled and replied, "Sure thing, James, we can discuss it tomorrow."

"Now, all we have to do is get out of this fort and get back to the house. That's what the president ordered, and I think that's a good idea for all of us," remarked Captain Flannigan.

While the young navy officers were escorted by a secret service agent out of the White House and into their waiting car, President Roosevelt had General Watson take him to the Map Room on the first floor. At one time, it was a billiards room with a table and a supply of cues mounted on the wall. Eleanor detested pool, billiards, snooker, etc., and had the room turned into a small meeting room until Winston Churchill had shown up in late December 1941. The first request he made of the president was a place to put his war maps so he could track the progress of his armies and fleets, as well as the Nazis and the Japanese. Winston had shown Roosevelt all the map details and how they were updated several times a day. It was important for Churchill to see locations of convoys to Russia as well as the ones to Britain. Now with the disasters unfolding in the Far East, he was looking globally at all his assets and threats.

Roosevelt ordered a map room of his own and the old billiard room was renovated to meet the need. Several officers and enlisted men manned the room twenty-four hours a day, updating the maps to show movement or position of not only American forces but also Allied forces and the location of enemy dispositions and intentions. FDR found having access to the maps provided him a better overview of the situation and how Allied forces could be better utilized to meet enemy threats. Upon entering the room which was guarded by a marine sentry, all activity stopped, and all personnel snapped to attention.

"At ease, carry on," barked General Watson as he wheeled the president close to the map of the Pacific theater of operations.

"Any news, Commander?" Roosevelt asked a navy commander who had the evening watch.

"Sir, we have had a few developments from the Philippines, plus a communication from the ADBA command."

Watson went over to the commander's desk and was handed the communiques in question. He read the ones on the beleaguered garrison of Bataan and knew they were barely holding on and running low on supplies from food to ammunition to medicine, everything but Japs. He looked up at FDR and shook his head which was his way of letting the president know there were no changes occurring on the far away battlefield on the other side of the world. He looked at the other message from ABDA command. This one made his face curl into a scowl. He walked over to the president who was staring intently at the map of the Philippines. When General Watson neared, he held out his hand for what was certain to be worse news.

The message dated February 28 detailed the complete rout and destruction of the combined ABDA fleet under the command of Dutch Admiral Doorman at what would become known as the Battle of the Java Sea. Two Dutch cruisers were sunk as were three destroyers, one from Britain and two from Holland. The report continued with damage reports on the British cruiser *Exeter*, the hero of the Battle of the

River Platte, and the Grey Ghost of the Java Coast, the USS *Houston*. Both ships along with a few destroyers and the Australian light cruiser HMAS *Perth* were trying to exit the Java Sea from two different directions. The American destroyer *Pope* was providing cover to the *Exeter* which was moving very slowly and had little in the way of defensive firepower remaining. The *Houston* was previously damaged from a bombing attack a few weeks previous and only had two operational turrets.

"Anything else on the *Houston*?" asked Roosevelt.

Watson went back to the commander's desk and received no more information, only conjecture that the American and Australian cruisers were trying to head west to escape through the Sunda Strait. Watson came back to the president and shook his head no.

President Roosevelt continued to inspect the map. First, he looked at the Philippines then down to the southwest and Java and the Java Sea. He pushed himself closer to the map and studied the area with the Bali Strait on the east end and the Sunda Strait on the west end. The more appropriate passes through all the islands were even more east of Bali such as the passage around Lombok or Timor. All these islands were now in the hands of the Japanese. Only the Dutch garrison on Java still existed. The entire Indonesian Archipelago along with almost all the Philippines were now occupied by the Japanese. They had made landings along the New Guinea coast and taken the Australian territory of Rabaul. They were moving further south and further west. The president wondered, *Was the next target Australia?* Ten days prior, the Japanese fleet had conducted a raid on Darwin which was the stepping off point for supplies to both the Philippines and Java. Several merchant ships carrying vital supplies were sunk as was the destroyer USS *Peary*. Almost all allied combat aircraft and support facilities were destroyed making this location no longer tenable for a major base of operations.

As FDR contemplated further, he looked toward the Australian west coast. There was only the city of Perth, a thousand miles further south than Darwin, offering any hope of refuge for the remnants of the Allied fleet. The Japanese were picking off ships one by one as they tried to escape south to Australia or east to India. Supplies were being sent to the bottom of the sea along with experienced sailors, troops, and air crews. Efforts to help defend Java had failed, and the joint command under General Wavell was no longer in existence, with no hope of further reinforcement or retreat. Roosevelt looked at his friend Pa Watson and commented, "I always loved the *Houston* best. She was my ship. Do you remember our first cruise on her back in 1934? Going down to the Caribbean and fishing plus seeing all of those local people in bright colored clothes while everyone else up North was in heavy wools and somber as a funeral."

"Yes, Mr. President, I do recall the first cruise, and the following year we did another cruise on her. A very fine ship indeed and a great crew. They really did love you, sir."

Grasping his cigarette holder, the president stated resolutely, "If she is gone, she probably took a bunch of Japs with her. No matter what, there will be another *Houston*. Make my wishes known to Admiral King."

Watson could see the anger in the face the president's face. He loved his navy more than just about anything except his stamp collection. It was personal to him and if his most favorite ship was no longer, he intended to get another one built fast.

"Yes, Mr. President, I will let the admiral know." Watson waited while FDR stared at the map once more in the location of where the *Houston* might be. His gaze traveled north to the island of Japan, searching for ways to strike back. One of his plans was nearing fruition, but he needed to hit harder than one mission. He wanted more answers. Perhaps the young Mr. Brand could be one of his more successful tools in accomplishing that objective.

He motioned to General Watson that he was ready to leave. To Watson this meant the president was not only tired but exhausted and needed his rest. This was one job Watson took very seriously and he tried as much as possible to shield FDR from too many requests on his time, and as he thought, the president's mind. As the faithful aide wheeled the president out, Map Room personnel continued reading reports, plotting locations, striking ships or entire islands, and making notations on men, ships, planes, supplies, etc. This was total war, and even though the U.S. was late to the game, the engine of victory was starting to warm up.

Part 6

PART C

26

3 March 1942
Charleston Naval Yard, Detention Center
Charleston, South Carolina

- United States naval vessels sunk:
  - Submarine **Perch** damaged by depth charges and surface gunfire, scuttled by the crew in the Java Sea.
  - Gunboat **Asheville,** by naval gunfire, south of Java.

The day after dinner at the White House, Admiral Willson's aide called Captain Jameson telling him a plane would be made available to take the team to Charleston, South Carolina, to interrogate the U-boat crew. Jameson informed Flannigan first and told him to pick four marines to accompany the officers plus Chief Petty Officer Schmidt who may be needed with communications. The gunny picked himself and Sgt. James McBride, Cpl. Timothy Pride and Cpl. Clarence "Bud" Williams. These four would be all the security the team would need at a naval installation. Staff Sergeant Laird and the rest of the marines would stay at the Bethesda house until the team returned.

The R4D was the same as last time with Lieutenant Commander Shoemaker in command along with Lieutenant Junior Grade Miller flying the right seat. They were glad to see the "Science Team" again and were amazed at the new ranks the three officers were now showing on their jackets. Shoemaker was glad to see Jameson get the eagles on his shoulder boards and the four stripes looked very impressive. He could see by the ribbons on Captain Flannigan's chest that he was finally rewarded for his meritorious service in the Philippines. He would love to know more, but his job was to fly the team south and await their return. "Not bad duty," he told Miller, "because this is a lovely time to visit Charleston."

The base had been alerted by Admiral Willson personally, and the base commander, a navy captain, was waiting for them at the air station. The team loaded into cars and a truck carried the marines and their equipment, including a large portable radio, which seemed to many a bit of overkill, but this was the navy. The base commander, Capt. Steve Ewing, knew they were at the station to meet the U-boat crew. Other than that, he knew nothing. He inquired as to the duration of the visit, but Captain Jameson informed him they were unsure of their plans until they began interviewing the German crew.

A lieutenant commander who worked for Naval Intelligence was disgruntled about this group of people coming down to interrogate the POWs. His name was Robert Hartung. He had already sent a protest up his chain of command that was answered by a phone call from the assistant head of Naval Intelligence telling him to shut up and follow orders or he would be working on a minesweeper as the junior officer. The assistant head of Naval Intelligence did inform him the navy captain reported directly to Admiral King and served as his senior aide on science. This got Hartung thinking about the line of questions these people might be asking the U-boat crew. Not that this would be of much use because he and two other intelligence officers had gotten zero out of these men. The three officers who were rescued said nothing except the required name, rank, and serial number. The senior surviving officer was the executive officer and had informed the Americans the captain had been killed in the attack by navy planes. The intelligence team had not been able to garner any more information.

Lieutenant Commander Hartung waited in the outer office as the three visiting officers, two navy and one marine met with the base commander. The meeting did not take long, but Hartung found it odd the base commander's office, which was usually quite informal, had become a hotbed of traditional navy behavior. Every enlisted man was in proper uniform and no slovenly behaviors were evident. Also, the office was immaculate with no piles of papers or things out of place. He guessed that anyone who was a direct report to the commander in chief of the navy would report anything non-regulation to his boss, and the captain's boss was at the top of the food chain. Hartung smiled because he thought the entire base was a joke and poorly run. A graduate of Vanderbilt, he had enrolled in ROTC in the mid-thirties to impress the girls with his uniform and help him in his future career at his father's law firm. He had stayed in the reserve after graduation and enjoyed the benefits of association with other well-connected reservists, not only in the south, but Harvard and Yale grads who helped steer business to his father's firm.

Hartung had spoken German from his early days because his grandmother on his father's side was from Switzerland. He found languages easy because of this and became quite proficient at French and Spanish. Again, these skills helped him in his business career and in the navy. His language abilities and then law school helped him get into Naval Intelligence in late 1940, and when the war began, he was sent to Charleston for what reason he did not know. He had attempted to pull strings to go to Washington, which again would enhance his post-war career, but he was stuck in this small city far away from the political action of the capital.

Finally, the door opened, and the marine gunnery sergeant standing outside the doorway shouted, "Attention on deck." Everyone jumped to attention followed by a smiling Captain Jameson saying, "At ease, gentlemen, carry on with whatever you were doing. And thanks, yeoman, for the great coffee." He smiled at the senior enlisted man who served as the base commander's chief of the bullpen. Jameson came up to the lieutenant commander, introduced by Captain Ewing. The officers all shook hands and Hartung led them off to where the POWs were housed.

"Commander, I want to compliment you on the information you sent us before our coming down. I think you have a good feel for these men and your report provided us with some useful insight into their various roles and functions on the submarine. Do you have anything new to tell us before we meet them?" Jameson asked the young lieutenant commander, knowing his background from the personnel files he had reviewed prior to flying south.

"No sir, I don't think there is anything else. My report was complete on each interrogation performed as were the notes from the other two interrogators sent down from Washington to talk to them. I doubt if there is much else these men will tell you sir besides the normal name, rank, and serial number obligation under the Geneva Convention."

The captain smiled at Commander Ewing, replying, "You are probably correct and we may not get anything out of them, but you understand that I have been sent down here anyway and I will do the best I can."

Jameson glanced over and caught Brand smiling weakly, then not at all. Brand stood to the right side of the captain, taking the stance of an aide. They had spent several hours over the past two days formulating a plan to gain information from the U-boat sailors by other means than normal interrogations. Brand's plan was inspiring or so thought Flannigan, and with a little luck, it might work. Having Hartung around would make the task even easier because the good lieutenant commander wouldn't have a clue what was occurring in front of him.

When they got to the stockade holding the captured German sailors, the newest and youngest lieutenant junior grade in the navy handed Hartung a list of who they wanted to interview and in what order. Hartung took the list and thinking nothing of it, gave it to the marine second lieutenant who oversaw the prisoners. He passed it on to a sergeant who went off to get the first interviewee. Jameson, Flannigan, Brand, and Hartung entered a small office building next to the enclosed holding area where the POWs were quartered. These were temporary buildings constructed of wood, tar paper, and few bricks. They were exactly like those used by the U.S. Armed Forces for holding their own soldiers, sailors, and marines.

Nothing better, nothing worse was the order of the day for all POWs. All prisoners would get the same rations and health care afforded to any person of the same rank in the U.S. military. Officers had their own building and were housed based on rank as to the space allotted to them, which equaled the space allocated to an American officer. The order had gone out by General Marshall and Admiral King that all Prisoners of War were to be handled strictly by the rules of the Geneva Convention and those who violate these directives would be severely punished.

Inside the small building next to the barbed wire enclosed stockade, the officers sat down at a small table while the gunny and Corporal Williams occupied the hallway. They were armed with regulation .45 Colt Automatics and .45-caliber Thompson submachine guns. The marine guards at the prison were very envious of the Thompsons because all they had were standard 1903 Springfield rifles. When the first prisoner was brought in, Captain Jameson was the first man to stand followed by Captain Flannigan, Lieutenant Commander Ewing, and then slowly, Mr. Brand. As he stood, he dropped a file on the floor which contained three photographs of American S-Class submarines, plus a photo of a German Focke-Wulf 200 Condor long-range bomber. Brand fumbled as he picked the file up, leaving the photos for the last thing to put back in the file.

Jameson jumped all over Brand nearly yelling, "Lieutenant, which navy do you serve in, the Italian navy? Pick that up and sit down." Looking over at the now totally befuddled Hartung, "I am sorry commander, the lieutenant is brand new and has a steep learning curve, which I hope will end soon."

The German petty officer, who worked in the control room, saw the mess of papers on the floor and noticed the unusual looking submarine along with the more familiar Condor and then he heard the navy captain yelling at the very young officer. He could speak a few words of English and had learned more in the past few weeks as a prisoner and understood the captain was very angry at the poor showing of the junior officer. This was just like the German navy. He felt sorry for the young officer as he picked things up off the floor and tried to reorganize them. He thought this interview would be quite interesting and he would learn more than the stupid Americans.

The German petty officer second class (*obermaat*) sat down in front of the three officers. He knew the American interrogator, Hartung, from several encounters. He knew the American was very self-important and not a regular line officer. He was in intelligence, and his German was not too bad. Swiss-German by the sound of it, but the petty officer was from a village near Munich, so he had no problem understanding the commander. He sat ramrod straight and did not smile nor make any attempt at eye contact. He waited to be asked the same questions again and but this time in the presence of an American naval captain. He wondered what was going on, but it did not concern him. He had been told several times by the executive officer of his boat the Americans were just like the British in their persistence of trying to gain information from the elite submariners. He thought to himself, just like the last time but now with a much more impressive officer. This would be interesting in a very perverse way. But, as a POW he knew they would grow tired of talking to him and the other survivors.

The captain spoke directly to the petty officer. "My name is Captain Jameson, and I have a few questions to ask you. I know you will invoke the Geneva Convention, but I will ask them anyway. What is your name?"

Lieutenant Commander Hartung translated the introduction and question into German.

The petty officer spoke in very short and precise German, "Sir, my name is Gert Schiller, I am an *obermatt* in the Kriegsmarine. That is all I have to say."

"Very well, Herr Schiller," came the voice of Hartung also in German. "What was your role on the submarine?"

"Sir, I cannot reveal the nature of my function on the U-boat. I can only give you my name and rank. That is all you will receive from me."

Hartung interpreted to Jameson who spoke German as well as Hartung, but did not reveal this fact to Hartung or the base commander. The captain wanted to go into the meeting just like a regular line officer without the benefit of knowing German.

As soon as Hartung repeated the sailor's statement, he added, "Sir, this is the story from every one of them. I have gotten nowhere with these men, and since they are an elite group of people, I doubt we will make any progress today."

Jameson looked at Hartung and in his best-downtrodden expression replied, "You are correct of course commander, but as you know, we were sent down to talk to these people and report back our findings. So, we will repeat this process with the others on the list and see if we get anywhere. I understand the next man is in the room across the hall, is that correct?

"Yes sir, he should be there now. Shall we go?"

Jameson looked at Brand who was still looking through the files and gave him a disgusted look. "Lieutenant, why don't you stay here and entertain the petty officer with your high school German until they come and get him. Let's move, Commander."

Brand stood up as did the German until the captain left with Hartung. The gunny stood by the door looking very menacing to the petty officer. He had heard stories the U.S. Marines only enlisted gangsters and murderers, so he was a bit concerned. He looked over at the bumbling young lieutenant and the young man smiled at him.

Brand, stammering a bit, began to speak in German. "I am sorry for being a poor German speaker. Don't worry about the big sergeant by the wall. He will not harm you. Would you like some coffee or something while we wait?"

Petty Officer Schiller eased back in the chair, and for a moment looked at the marine sergeant glaring back at him. He clutched a submachine gun and seemed to want to use it. Schiller returned his attention to the boy lieutenant and decided he would take him up on the offer. "Herr Lieutenant, I would like some coffee, that would be very nice of you."

Brand smiled, knowing that he had broken the ice with Schiller. "Sergeant, would you please go get some coffee for the petty officer. Bring some sugar and milk too if you can find them."

The sergeant glared at the German but quickly said, "Aye, aye sir. Do you want some coffee, too?"

Brand decided to change up on the agreed strategy he had advised the gunny about, "No, bring me a Coca-Cola if possible and maybe some cigarettes."

The gunny opened the door and instructed the marine guard on the other side of the door to do the lieutenant's bidding. The gunny returned to his station next to the door and continued staring at the German, this time seeming to be even angrier, if that was possible. The German got chills thinking about the large marine staring at him, so he went back to watching the young lieutenant arranging his file. Brand stopped and pulled out the photo of the four-engine Condor, which had a very long range, and caused the British convoys a lot of problems, not only in bombing them but locating them and vectoring in U-boats for the kill.

Brand placed the photo next to the file followed by photos of the control room of an American S-class submarine. These were the oldest boats in use by the U.S. Navy, some dating back to the end of World War I. They were serving in the Pacific even though their living conditions were horrible in the tropics. The newer fleet boats like the Gato class were much larger with air conditioning, which was very valuable not only for the quality of life of the crews but for lowering humidity in the boat and reducing electrical problems caused by the dampness inherent to submarines. The German subs did not have air conditioning and the crews who ventured to the southern Atlantic and beyond suffered in the heat of the tropics.

A knock at the door alerted the gunny who opened it to a marine private from the stockade command carrying a large mug of coffee, sugar bowl and a pot of cream on a steel plate, which also included two bottles of Coca-Cola. The private put the plate on the table, and also pulled out a pack of Chesterfield cigarettes and a pack of matches. The lieutenant thanked the private who exited under the continuous stare of the gunny.

Brand spoke his broken German to the petty officer, "Well, seems they brought everything I asked for and even an extra bottle of Coca-Cola. Have you ever had one of these before?"

The petty officer looked at the bottle and said, "No, I have heard of it, but I have never had one before."

"How do you like your coffee, Obermaat Schiller?"

Schiller looked at the container of milk and the big bowl of sugar and replied to Brand, "Sir, I would like both the sugar and the cream."

Brand passed Schiller a spoon. "Here, make it up the way you like. I like a little sugar in mine because my mother always had it that way, and so I guess I do, too. The older men kid me, saying I should learn to drink it black and thick. But what I say is that if you have the right ingredients, you should have it anyway you want. Right?"

"Yes, Lieutenant, I would agree with you on that. Sugar is very rare in Germany, and I would love to have all of this in the bowl to share with my family back in Bavaria. But, I guess that is not possible."

Brand opened the bottle and took a big drink. "Boy, do I love these things. A doctor friend told me one of these drinks has as much caffeine in it as two cups of coffee. Have you heard that about coffee, the caffeine I mean?"

Schiller was stirring in his second heaping spoon of sugar as he heard the young lieutenant talk about caffeine. "No, Lieutenant, I have not heard about this thing called caffeine, but the men in the U-boat fleet all talk about how the coffee will keep you awake better than anything else." He took a sip and let out an audible, "Wow," then took another sip. He looked at Brand saying, "Thank you, Lieutenant, for the kindness. This is very good coffee, much better than what we get on the boats or in France."

Brand avoided making eye contact, but felt the first tremor of information passing to him. It did not take a genius to figure out that this crew was based in France in either Lorient, St. Nazaire, or La Rochelle. That the German opened up for just a minute to say anything of use was important. Brand decided to play along and see where all of this went.

"Well, sugar and good coffee are all from the Caribbean and further south. I do think we grow a lot of sugar in the swamplands of Louisiana and maybe Florida, but I just don't know. I was never a farmer. I grew up in the mountains of Arizona. Do you know anything about Arizona, Herr Obermaat?"

Schiller shook his head no.

"Well, Herr Obermaat, Arizona is where all of the cowboys come from. You know, the wild west, Indians, gunfights. You know, don't you?"

Schiller lit up immediately saying, "Yes, the cowboys and Indians.

All the movies I saw before they were no longer allowed into Germany. Men on horses and Indians shooting guns or bows and arrows. Yes, this I know. You grew up there?"

Brand moved in closer, "Yes, Schiller, I grew up in the mountains of Arizona. I shot mainly deer and a few bears but never Indians. They were my good friends and showed me a lot of ways to live in the wilderness. Great people from that part of America. You should tour the country after the war is over." Brand left it there to see what the petty officer would say or do. It did not take long.

"Lieutenant, in Arizona, are there many farms like in Germany?"

"Herr Obermaat, yes there are many farms, but we call them ranches. We do raise some big crops in the southern part of the state, but it is very much a desert there. Have you ever seen a desert before?"

Schiller took the bait and said, "Yes, I have been in North Africa briefly, but I did not like the heat. I grew up in the mountains of Bavaria. My family raised milk cows and we grew some grain. That is why I joined the navy to see the world, but what I have seen makes me want to go home to the mountains."

Brand shook his head in agreement saying, "I feel the same way, I plan to go back to my home in Arizona and maybe become a doctor or dentist. I like being on the land but," he showed his right hand that had bulging knuckles from the days of hay baling and cleaning out stables, "I would like to have less strenuous work."

Schiller smiled and looked at his hands as well and said, "I agree with you. I loved working with the cows, but milking them each morning and evening became more demanding and left me with little time to do much else. I learned to work on some farm equipment, and that got me into the navy as a machinist."

Brand was connecting more dots but did not want to rush the conversation. He picked up one of the photos of the S-class submarines and showed it to Schiller. "This is one of our submarines. It is not very good like yours but then it takes a good mechanic to make anything work well."

Schiller looked at the submarine and saw many similarities, but the conning tower on the American boat seemed way out of proportion to the size of the boat. Foolish on the part of the Americans to have such a large tower on such a small boat. He felt his Type IX was the best even though it had a very slow dive rate. As he handed the photo back to the American, he saw another photo of the inside of the conning tower and what appeared to be the American control center. Brand noticed this and handed it to the German. "Sure, no big secret on this one either. I guess all submarines look alike anyway. I have never been on one of these boats, and I don't intend to. Too small and dangerous."

The German was now intently studying the photograph and could make out some of the instruments that appeared to be just like his submarine. He saw the big diving levers like those on his submarine. He looked over at Brand who was not paying attention to him but was busy drinking the last drop of Coca-Cola.

Brand looked back at Schiller after he knew the petty officer had been staring at him and quickly said, "Oh sorry, Schiller, I was thinking about the mountains and not about the war. So, your boat looks like this one, I guess?"

"Yes, it does, but I think my boat was much larger in the control room than this boat. It looks very small like one of our training boats when I first went into the service after I had finished my engine room training."

Interesting, Brand thought, *he had not divulged this earlier nor was it on his record. Perhaps he was in the control room when the boat was attacked and could get out faster than the others in the black gang who may have perished. Might as well push some more and see where this leads.*

"Herr Schiller, tell me, when the war ends do you want to go back to the farm or with your new mechanical skills want to stay in the navy or maybe get a land-based job working with diesel or electric motors?"

Schiller was finishing his last sips of coffee and sat back to contemplate the young man's question. "I think I will stay on land. If you know a diesel and all the pumps and gears of a submarine, you can work on anything on land. Perhaps, I will get a job on the railroad working on big trains. I think I would like that."

Brand opened the pack of cigarettes and handed it to Schiller saying, "If you smoke, go ahead and light up. The big marine will not care. I don't smoke so take it with you if you want."

Schiller who was getting a small ration of cigarettes, immediately opened the pack and pulled out one of the American cigarettes and lit it. He knew American tobacco made all the difference compared to the horrible things the German navy gave him, which was still far superior to anything handed out to the army.

Brand looked at the file again and this time pulled out a photograph of an American PBY to see what the petty officer would say. "Tell me, Herr Schiller, have you seen one of these planes before?"

Schiller saw the plane and asked, "Did you know one of those planes sank my boat and killed our captain and many men?"

Brand feigned ignorance, "No, I am sorry to have shown you this. I was just wondering if this plane is like your big four-engine planes?"

Schiller almost clammed up for good but smiled back at the baffled teenager in the officer uniform. "Herr Lieutenant, the German plane is vastly superior to your slow flying boat. Your plane got lucky, that is all. Our people simply did not see it soon enough to dive so the attack by your planes was successful. I cannot say anything more."

Brand again showed artificial grief over the photo, apologizing, "Herr Schiller, I am very sorry to show you this photograph. It must bring back painful memories of the loss to you and your crew. I apologize for my inconsiderate behavior." Brand spoke in a halting way to demonstrate he had a poor command of the German language and an even worse command of the various tense forms. Brand quickly pulled all the photos back into the file and then again told the German, "I am very sorry, and I hope you will not think of me poorly for this, how you say, mistake."

Schiller felt the young American was truly contrite, something a German officer would never do. "No, Lieutenant, your plane was able to get low enough on the sky to sneak up on us. It was a well-performed attack. We use the same skills when sneaking up on your ships. I guess it is war and war alone that makes us enemies."

Brand considered that last remark and decided to ask more questions that would be useful to the Allied side. He had opened a dialogue with the petty officer, and any information he gleaned could help in slowing or stopping the U-boat menace.

At last, on a pre-arranged schedule, a marine guard came in to retrieve Petty Officer Schiller who thanked Brand for the time, coffee, and especially the cigarettes. He had no idea how helpful he had been by being so open to the young lieutenant.

Over the course of the next two days, Brand interviewed ten other enlisted men from the U-boat and spent fifteen to twenty minutes with each one. Some were quite closed in their answers, but others, like Schiller, were more forthcoming. Some of the information he developed from these conversations was a good estimate of the range of the Type IX, diving ability and even through some mathematical gaming, an idea of the maximum crush depth. He also learned about the problems the Type IX sometimes had in maintaining trim, plus battery problems were causing distress in the more common Type VII boats. He was able to discern information about past voyages of the sunken U-boat, plus information about previous boats, commanders, training locations and current basing in France.

His biggest discovery was about the supply submarines being dispatched to the Central and South Atlantic. These expanded versions of the Type IX had enough extra torpedoes to resupply up to five boats, as well as additional fuel and food to maintain a boat in U.S. waters for an additional four weeks. This was bad news and had to be corroborated with the British and forwarded to Admiral King.

Hartung was totally unaware of the ruse he was involved in. He figured Brand was an inept aide to a reluctant and bored reserve captain who didn't have a clue what he was doing. Jameson made sure the deception was complete by verbally abusing both Flannigan and Brand at dinner on the first night. He had told Brand that he would be transferred as soon as he could arrange it and make sure he never held a security clearance. Brand and Flannigan were equally negative to others about the reserve captain and his disliking non-academy officers and ROTC graduates. The plan the three of them had hatched back in Washington worked its magic, and they decided to play it until the end. But, Jameson decided he wanted a go at the executive officer of the U-boat, and that would require a different approach.

27

5 March 1942
Charleston Navy Yard

- Dutch continue a losing battle for Java. Batavia is reported evacuated.
- Burma--Lt. Gen. Sir Harold Alexander arrives at Rangoon to take command of the Burma Army.

After two days of interviews that went seemingly nowhere, Lieutenant Commander Hartung was amazed that Captain Jameson wanted to talk to the executive officer, Kapitanleutanant (Lieutenant) Erich Milner who had been very disagreeable from the start of his incarceration. When Milner came into the room, he saw there were three other officers in the room with Hartung. Being a good German naval officer, he jumped to attention and saluted the U.S. Navy captain. His salute was returned by the captain who introduced himself in halting German as Fredrick Jameson. He also introduced an American marine captain named Flannigan and lastly, he introduced Lieutenant Junior Grade Brand. He was told to sit down and did so with a severe glower on his face.

Before Hartung said a word, Milner began to speak in German

aimed directly at the captain. "Sir, I would like to protest your interviews with the members of my crew. You have talked to many of my enlisted men and provided them with cigarettes to bribe them into talking and this is a violation of the Geneva Treaty."

Hartung spoke first to the German officer, "Duly noted, Herr Milner. I shall be happy to forward it to higher authorities."

Milner again spoke this time looking at Hartung, thinking the other Americans were not very literate in German. "Commander Hartung, I want to know what is the purpose of this meeting. You know I will not provide you any details on the operation of my ship or its crew. If you want me to repeat my name and rank, so be it."

The captain now looked at Milner and said in much better German surprising both he and Hartung, "My dear Kapitanleutanant Milner, it is not our intention to ask you for any information that would violate your oath as an officer of the Kriegsmarine nor violate the Geneva Convention. We would hope that in a different situation, you would afford us the same courtesy, do you understand?

Milner was taken back by the quality of the captain's German and his attitude and replied, "Thank you for being so understanding, Captain. I would not want to be impertinent, but you have to understand my situation and that of my crew."

"Certainly, Herr Milner, or may I call you Erich?"

"It seems improper, but if you wish to call me Erich, that would be all right. You are the senior officer and can do as you wish."

"Thank you, Erich, I appreciate your allowing me to call you by your first name. It is so much easier. Now, I am not here to ask you a lot of questions that you will not answer. Rather, I am here to brief you on the war."

Milner looked at the captain very strangely, and so did Hartung who became very uncomfortable with the situation assuming this reserve captain was incompetent at best and was about to divulge classified information.

"Mr. Brand, would you like to give Erich some updates on the war?" Jameson looked at Brand who opened a file and pulled out some papers and photographs.

Now, in flawless German that totally surprised Hartung, Brand began with an introduction. "Herr Milner, the captain requested I bring you up to date on the war between our two countries. You are probably able to listen to some radio broadcasts in your quarters, and there are many in your crew who probably speak some English, so much of this will come as no surprise." Brand now began a synopsis of the war effort in the European theater as well as the Russian theater. This took about five minutes, and when he finished, Brand asked if there was need for clarification. Milner shook his head no, even though he would like to hear more about the German successes on the Eastern Front where he had several relatives fighting the Bolsheviks. He knew the failure to seize Moscow in December ended in retreat and the number of casualties was enormous on the German side, which concerned him more than anything else. Brand saw this and decided to ask Milner a question.

"Kapitanleutanant Milner, do you have relatives on the Eastern Front?" Brand kept his eyes on the papers so he would seem unconcerned about his answer.

"Yes, there are several members of my extended family in the army fighting these Russian pigs." His comment was laced with hate and at the same time, Brand thought, there was a serious amount of concern on his part for the family members engaged in the fighting.

"So, I guess it is better to be fighting us on the sea than in the coldness of Russia," Brand said as he shuffled through more papers.

"Yes, it is much better and cleaner at sea than in the cold of Europe, but I don't seem to understand why you care about this." Milner glanced at the captain then back at the young lieutenant.

"Good question, Herr Milner. We must care about everything in war, don't you agree?"

"Yes, I guess it involves us all in some way or another." Milner's voice lost its edge.

Brand decided to take another shift in the conversation. He held up a photograph of a U-boat and handed it to Milner. "Is this your boat, Herr Milner?"

Milner had never seen the photograph before and held it very closely so he could make out its hull. His boat did not have a number on it, but it did have a crest of a large pelican that was his captain's favorite bird. He had always said a pelican was very awkward looking, but when it swooped into the sea, it always caught something tasty, just like his submarine. Milner did not say anything but continued looking at the photograph.

Brand gave him another picture, this time of the same boat but with splashes all around it from explosions. "Tell me, Herr Milner, were you up top when the attack began or were you in the control room?" The lieutenant stared at Milner while he waited for an answer.

Milner studied the new photograph. When he lifted his chin, his expression had turned stern and his voice was weaker. "Where did you get these pictures, what else do you have on the attack?" Milner looked back down at the photograph as Brand pulled out several more to show him.

Hartung was now taken back even more. The young lieutenant was now shredding the confidence of a German submarine officer and getting him to open up as if he was a young school girl.

"Here, Herr Milner, is the second bomb which hit your boat. You can see the boat rocked to port and the stern rising. Were you down below?"

"Yes," Milner said staring at the photos of his boat as it was being hammered from above by the two planes. His voice dropped to whispers as he squinted at the picture to see who was on top in the conning tower.

Brand did not let him contemplate too long. "This is the most interesting photograph, Herr Milner. It shows the crew jumping off the submarine, and in the near distance, you can see the plane that had made the last attack. Your men are getting clear, and there are at least two of your small rafts in the water. Out of a crew of fifty-four, I am sorry that nine men did not get out of the boat. I understand your captain was killed in the second pass by the plane. He was on the conning tower, is that correct?"

Milner looked at the tragedy unfolding in the photographs. He had relived those dreadful minutes for the past weeks while in captivity. He had nightmares as he looked down into the boat seeing that several men were trying to scamper up the ladders to safety but were being sucked under by the rising water. He remembered the body of the captain as it floated in the "tub," the top part of the conning tower where the crew stood for watches and nighttime attacks. He thought of the wounded men who were being pulled into the little boats and the miracle of the float planes dropping several large life rafts into the sea and waited for the men to be pulled into the safety of the boats.

Brand drew out the last photograph which showed one of the planes dropping its life raft near the sinking U-boat and marking the location of the boat with dye packets.

Scanning the last photograph, Milner commented, "These planes killed my submarine, and many of my fellow crewmen, and then they saved the survivors. I know we would not have done the same for the crew of the plane if we shot it down, so I guess I owe the crew of those planes for our lives."

Jameson now saw his opening and said in his now flawless German, "Herr Milner, you may thank Lieutenant Brand for that act of chivalry to sailors lost at sea. He was in one of the navy bombers along with Captain Flannigan. I was in the other plane, and we are all glad that you and most of your crew survived. War is hell, so said one of our generals during our Civil War, but it does not mean our humanity should succumb to the vilest parts of the human condition."

Milner now stared at the captain and the other two officers with great concern and clouded emotion. He knew for him the war was over. He would survive. He had been serving on submarines since 1938, and he was slotted to get a new Type VII when this cruise ended. He was thrilled at the possibility of command but also apprehensive about his ability to be ruthless to the enemy and at the same time uphold his Catholic beliefs.

Brand detected the conflicting emotions going through the German's head. He decided to go on the gentle side for now. "Herr Milner, I do not take any great satisfaction in sinking your boat. Nor do I or the rest of our crew feel good about you losing members of your crew. We are not as war weary as other nations. We believe in fair play, openness, and the freedom to have different opinions even in times of war. I doubt that any of us could leave your crew to die on the open sea. I have seen the damage done by your submarines to our ships and seamen, and many have not been as fortunate. We intend on waging a total war, but we will do it with humanity, and we will end it with a clear conscience."

Milner looked at the young lieutenant with new respect. He had heard the platitudes the Americans bragged about. The German media had blasted these as being soft and immoral. Yet, here he was with three officers who gave him more information about what happened to his ship than he knew himself. He also found out what had saved him and how it came to pass. He felt even more conflicted and stared once more at the photograph of the planes dropping life rafts. He saw the navy captain looking at him as an older brother would look at his younger brother after a losing day at a track meet.

Brand noticed the expression and began to walk Milner back to his first experiences in the Kriegsmarine and his training as an officer. Within an hour, unbeknownst to Milner, he had provided the U.S. Navy with significant intelligence that seemed innocuous to him, even months later after he had been moved to a new POW camp in Hearne, Texas.

When the interview was finished and the German U-boat officer was returned to the prisoner compound, Captain Jameson looked over at Brand saying, "Damn fine job, James. I did not think this would have the effect that it did. Did you get what you were looking for?"

"Yes sir. I think I have enough pieces of information that can be spliced together to make a very accurate picture of their intentions, capabilities, and personnel challenges. The crew will be the key to breaking the sub menace, and if we can undermine them in any way, we can get a leg up on their offensive plans."

"Captain, may I ask a question?" Hartung spoke hesitantly not knowing what he had witnessed nor able to make a clean assessment of what all this meant.

"Commander, I guess you are wondering why we made you the odd man out in this project?"

Hartung nodded yes and began to speak, but Jameson continued. "Commander, you were left in the dark on purpose. You had conducted your interrogations like others who were trained to deal with enemy combatants. Your legal training gives you an edge in normal interroga-

U-BOAT SCOURGE

tions and briefings in peacetime. It does little to help in times of war. We came here because of our need to uncover more information about the sinking of the U-boat, and yes, all three of us were on the two planes that made the attack."

Jameson looked over to see James shuffling his papers and looking at the photos of the U-boat. He turned again to face the commander. "It was Lieutenant Brand's strategy and tactics that won the battle with the sub and he wanted to come full circle to learn even more about the crew and the specifics of the attack. Rarely in warfare, do you get to interview the man you were trying to kill only a few weeks previously. It is very important that we learn everything we can about the enemy, not only his equipment and tactics but the men themselves. What makes them tick and what makes them fight until death."

Hartung looked at Brand now seated at the desk furiously writing notes and Flannigan putting away the submarine photographs. He opened his mouth to speak, but again, Jameson stopped him cold.

"Commander, I am now ordering you to forget everything you saw or heard in this room. Any divulgence of the information you heard or witnessed here will result in a court-martial. This series of interviews did not happen. I have seen to it that there is no paper record of any of these meetings and there is now no record that we were ever on this base. The base commander was so notified under the same order you are receiving now. We will be leaving shortly for our base of operations. No additional questions or inquiries as to this mission will be tolerated. Do you understand, Mr. Hartung?"

In his entire life, Hartung had never been spoken to like this captain had just spoken to him. He could see the navy captain had a large amount of disdain for him and it was now evident in his manner. He was unsure of the violent nature of this man or the marines who accompanied him. He suddenly felt the need to use the head, but had the mental prescience to say, "Yes sir, Captain. I will comply with your orders."

"Good for you, Mr. Hartung. If I even suspect you will mention the names of the officers' present to anyone, I will make sure you are sent to the most remote naval facility on this planet to sit out the war playing with yourself because you will be the only one at that base. You are not much of an officer are you, Mr. Hartung? You decided to stay in the navy to help your business and legal career. You don't want to see any action in this war, and God help us if you did. You would not last one day with real men in a real war. You are lucky I'm in a kind mood right now, otherwise I would have you transferred somewhere very cold."

Flannigan gave a nod of his head which Jameson interpreted as everything was cleared and they could leave. Brand had stopped writing in his strange shorthand and was also standing. The gunny instinctively opened the door, and the two junior officers walked out.

Before walking through the door, Jameson said, "Hartung, let me never find out you said anything to anyone at this or any other facility in the world about what you saw or heard. That includes your family, your girlfriends and your pet dog. You will be watched so behave." With the final admonition, the captain left with an impish smile on his face knowing that Lieutenant Commander Hartung would never whisper a word to anyone even on his deathbed.

Part 7

28

8 March 1942
Bethesda, Maryland

- Japanese forces invade Lae and Salamaua, New Guinea.
- Japanese occupy Rangoon, Burma.

Shoemaker was a good pilot and was ready for the team. They were in the air within thirty minutes. The base commander did whatever he could to ensure this group from headquarters was gone and out of sight as quickly as possible. Air traffic control had been notified, and they were number one for takeoff. As soon as the plane leveled off at six thousand feet, Brand started to compile his notes, and everyone else just looked out the window, except for Jameson and Flannigan who were having a private conversation. What they were saying to one another was anyone's guess, but the gunny knew it was none of his business, so he decided to snooze a bit on the flight back to Washington.

The flight went as planned and the plane arrived late in the evening. By the time they got to the house in Bethesda, or as the marines called it, the mansion, everyone was ready to hit the hay. Even Brand looked bushed. He gladly said goodnight to Captain Jameson and Captain Flannigan, went into his room, and turned off the light. Everyone knew he would start banging on his typewriter within a few hours, so it was a good time to get some sleep.

Two days passed while Brand wrote his report with the aid of Captain Jameson. They also spent some time at Old Navy digging into intelligence reports on U-boat sightings and attacks. They were also looking at the classified reports the British continued to send to Admiral King, although he didn't take their advice seriously. Brand and Jameson knew differently and were preparing a report based on American-supplied information and their own work with the POWs. Jameson thought the crux of Brand's arguments would stand on their own merits, but he wanted as much additional corroboration as possible.

Flannigan wasn't involved in these activities and stayed at the house talking to his men and reading some of the reports Jameson passed on that he would otherwise never see. Chief Schmidt provided sanitized copies of reports he picked up on the radio and chatter from other top secret cleared radio operators. Jameson had warned him of sharing too much, but he knew Flannigan was no security risk. This evening was a bad one for Flannigan. He had a chance to see a classified report on the probable sinking of the USS *Houston* and the HMAS *Perth* off the coast of Java. He knew some of the navy officers on board and many of the marines who manned the open-deck guns, forming the marine detail on the cruiser. There was no confirmation from the navy, but the Japanese had claimed to have sunk the Galloping Ghost of the Java Coast many times. Flannigan knew things were getting worse for the men left on Bataan and elsewhere in the Philippines, but he had hoped remnants of the old Asiatic Fleet would somehow make it out like he did.

He was sitting at the table in the kitchen looking at a piece of warm bread that the assistant housekeeper and cook, Missy Rains, had given him after pulling it out of the oven. The smell was something that drove most of the marines crazy. The gunny always commented fresh baked bread was better than anything else in the world including a woman, but he was known for stretching the truth.

Dr. Feldman had just come in from the Naval Hospital after another uneventful day of taking care of senior officers and malingering sailors. He found Flannigan sitting at the table scrutinizing a report that could only be top secret from all the red ink stamped on top. He walked over to the newly minted captain and saw him distraught over whatever he was reading. "Hey, Robert, what are you doing home? No training problems to attend to today?"

Flannigan looked up and saw the smiling face of Dr. Feldman. "No, just hanging out looking at more sad news."

Feldman almost sat down beside the marine but then thought differently. "Hold that chair for me, I'll be right back."

Flannigan said nothing as the doctor walked back to his room, the one he now shared with Flannigan. He had moved out of Brand's room to give the young genius more space for chalkboards and files. He rummaged around in a small chest of drawers that contained his uniforms and some non-regulation clothing for going out on the town and found what the navy considered contraband.

Returning to the kitchen, the good doctor went to one of the cupboards and retrieved two glasses. He sat down next to his friend, still engrossed in his reading. Feldman placed both glasses in front of him, pulled out a bottle of first-rate scotch and poured two inches into each glass.

Flannigan finally acknowledged his friend. "So, Doctor, do I look so bad that the physician of the house has to prescribe some sort of medicinal brandy to improve my health?"

Feldman pushed one of the glasses to Flannigan and picked up his own saying, "Well, my young captain of marines, it is sometimes important for members of the naval medical community to spend quality time with the downtrodden, the insane and the feeble. Which I have been told means members of the United States Marine Corps." Feldman picked up his glass and looking right at his close friend said, "*Semper Fidelis,* Captain Bob."

Flannigan could not turn down the toast to the corps, but he did have ideas on how the naval medical service could be improved with better breeding habits.

"*Semper fi,* Lieutenant Feldman, *semper fi.*" Both men downed the contents of their glasses and placed them firmly on the table.

"Doc, seems the naval medical service has access to a much better quality whisky than we poor members of the Corps. Where did you find this stuff?"

Feldman looked at the last drops in the glass and then turned to Flannigan replying, "My dear Bob or should I call you Captain Bob? It seems that as a resident physician I picked up a few pointers on the finer aspects of American whisky. I also have a refined palate for scotch whisky as well as the Canadian variety. My family is always searching for a good value and when you have an uncle in the booze business in New York, what would you expect me to serve my brave comrades in arms?"

Flannigan eyed the bottle and mouthed, "More."

"Why sure, Captain Bob, let us drink to the team or Admiral King or to whatever you choose." Feldman poured two more fingers of scotch into each glass and waited for a toast from the marine captain that he had grown to admire and love like a brother.

Flannigan picked up his glass and in a strong voice said, "To Capt. Albert Rooks and the gallant men of the USS *Houston*. May God be kind to you and ease your passing into Heaven." Flannigan threw back the dark liquid and placed the glass on the table.

Dr. Feldman did likewise quietly setting his glass next to the marine captain, sensing his friend must have received some information concerning the ship and its crew. He decided to go ahead and see what kind of non-alcoholic therapy he could administer. "Bob, it sounds as if you have received some bad news on the *Houston*, can you tell me what you found out?"

Flannigan turned toward his friend and physician, picking up some of the classified papers. "You're not a spy so you can look at these as well. Just remember, you didn't see a thing nor do you know anything, got it?"

"Sure thing, Bob, but what's going on?" Feldman took the onion skin copies called "flimsies" by radio operators who would have to make five or six copies of each message using the "flimsies" and carbon paper. Feldman knew you needed lots of paper to win a war and the U.S. Navy was very good at paper.

Feldman started reading the reports which went back three weeks. Seems there was a confusing naval battle in the Java Sea involving the

Houston and several U.S. destroyers along with two Dutch light cruisers and a couple of Dutch destroyers plus the HMS *Exeter*, the HMAS *Perth* and a few British destroyers. The battle was a mess of misdirection and leadership with the Dutch Admiral Doorman in charge instead of the American Admiral Glassford. Glassford had replaced Admiral Hart earlier in February but because of the nature of the multi-nation forces involved, the Dutch Admiral was in command. Evidently, the two Dutch cruisers were sunk along with one of their destroyers plus a British destroyer. The *Exeter* was badly damaged and steamed away with two of the American destroyers. They were not heard from again.

The next report mentioned the *Houston* and *Perth* heading back to someplace called Surabaya. Then under constant aerial attack, both ships left the harbor trying to escape the Java Sea by heading through the Sunda Strait, the water passage between the islands of Sumatra and Java. Nothing was heard from either ship again nor was there word from a Dutch destroyer that tried to negotiate the same passage.

Feldman put down the report and saw the grief of not knowing written on Flannigan's face. The greatest fear of war is not knowing what happened to people or places or ships you have known. You often place guilt on yourself for not being there, or not being adequate or strong enough to help in their hour of need. Feldman had seen this expressed on the faces of parents and siblings of people involved in disasters, which left survivors searching for answers to prayers that never came. He decided on a dual strategy, booze and talk, so he poured another round. This time both he and Flannigan slowly sipped the brown colored liquid and each man stared deep into the bottom of their glass.

Feldman waited a few moments, studying the face of someone he had come to know and respect over the last few months. He could see the scar tissue around his left eye where he had been hit with fragments of shrapnel. He looked at Flannigan's left hand holding some of the papers. Scar tissue was visible from burns that Feldman knew went all the way up the shoulder. Were these burns from fuel oil or perhaps just flames licking at the buildings when he tried to rescue people trapped inside? He wondered about the other injuries on his leg and back from shrapnel penetrating deep inside. Feldman wondered if he would have the courage to go back into a burning building with exploding munitions or oil drums popping off like the Fourth of July. He had seen the commendation the president had bestowed, which made Flannigan a decorated hero. The doctor remembered what Flannigan had told him, "A decorated hero did something someone else saw. It must be a brave thing because few would do it. An undecorated hero is what everyone does, but no one sees it or reports it, or it doesn't matter because you're dead."

Feldman decided to dig this time. He had not done so when they first met, and he had taken care of his hand and arm. The good doctor had commented on the quality of the surgery and the lack of scar tissue from the shrapnel wounds and told the young marine the burns would look better with time. But he never found the time to talk about the how and why of his injuries or the mental process he went through to recover. His clinical mind needed an answer to those questions while his friendship slowed down his zeal to uncover the details.

Feldman finally went for answers. "Bob, I didn't know you served on the *Houston*. When was this? Before the war began?"

Flannigan stared at the whisky in the bottom of the glass and took a sip. "No, I never served on her, but I had spent some time with two of her marine officers while I was in China. That was early in '41. The *Houston* would come and go during the hottest months in Manila and spend that time in Shanghai. Not much cooler, but less humidity, and you could buy a lot more for your money in China than in Manila. I was getting set to leave the Fourth Regiment in early August for a rotation back to the States. I took the mail boat to Manila and reported to the captain of the Port when I got there in mid-September. Suddenly, I was whisked away to the office of Admiral Hart who told me I would not be going back to the States for a while. He wanted a marine officer on his staff to run courier messages to the other commands, and he especially wanted a man with recent China experience. So, that's how I got to be in the Philippines instead of some nice duty Stateside."

"So, tell me about the Japanese attack and what happened at Cavite." Feldman poured more whisky into Flannigan's glass to keep the conversation flowing.

Flannigan looked at the refilled glass and did a short glass salute to the good doctor and took a small sip followed by an audible sound of pleasure.

"Doc, for the rest of October I ran around Asia being a courier, which usually meant waiting for someone to reply to a message, then hightailing it back to Manila. As the story goes, I would wait and then wait around some more. In late October, I did get to fly to Guam to deliver a package of orders to the naval commander of the island and after a week, flew back on the China Clipper. Now that's the way to fly. Beats the hell out of a PBY."

Flannigan took another hit of the booze and was feeling less pain, or so the doctor thought. "Then in November things got hot. Hart decided to get the marines out of China. It took him most of October to get permission, and I went up with the evacuation transport. I got back at the end of November and expected to go to work for Colonel Howard of the Fourth Regiment. Hart, however, had other plans. He wanted me to be his marine aide and head courier. He knew I had spent time with the Japs and knew how they thought. Two years in China makes you go oriental they say, and good old Tommy Hart wanted people with experience, not new kids. So, it was on December 8 over there, not the seventh that we were alerted of the attack on Pearl Harbor. Admiral Hart immediately set in motion the war plans he had and notified MacArthur of the attack and his plans. Mac A, as we called him, had not heard the news and his aides were not convinced we should be doing anything. To say the least, the navy and the army in the Philippines did not get along. Hart wanted to control all sea patrols from the air, and Mac A didn't want to go along with it. But eight hours later, after the Japs caught our planes on the ground, it became a moot point."

Feldman did not push anymore but waited as Flannigan took another sip and stared out into space. He could almost feel his marine friend being thrown back into the lurch of the war in Asia. He just sat and waited until it was time for Flannigan to speak again.

"Well, anyway, we had no air cover, and the admiral had wisely dispersed the fleet, or whatever you call two cruisers and a dozen old destroyers, the week before. He had received a war warning and took it seriously. Evidently, others didn't and we're paying the price for their negligence. But the story continues, Doc. Any more of that high-quality booze?"

Feldman smiled and poured another shot into the glass Captain Bob was holding. He took a sip and then continued. "Where was I? Oh yea, Cavite. The admiral sent me over to the base to see if we had been moving the spares and ammo to someplace safe. I was there when the Japs came over. It was around noon as I recall. Our anti-aircraft guns, or as I called them rock throwers, could not shoot high enough to hit the sons of bitches." He looked at the glass and seemed to be studying the movement of the liquid. He took another sip and continued his story.

"They flew over in nice V-shaped formations and dropped their bombs like they were from the post office. Perfect hits on some of the ships in dock and they blew the hell out of the buildings. I think we lost five hundred men. Just torn apart into big pieces and little pieces and blood everywhere. The poor Filipinos were massacred, and everyone fought the fires. I was an officer and tried to direct the firefighters, but there was no water pressure. The mains were out, the trucks were destroyed, nothing worked. I ran into some of the buildings to get the men out, and hopefully, some of the stores. You know you cannot fight a war, Doc, without stores. Stuff like food and torpedoes and ammo and parts and bullets and guns. Stuff we needed more of and it was all gone to hell."

Flannigan appeared drained as he relived the fire and bombs and explosions at the base. In his mind's eye, he could see the carnage of the dead and the dying, and was mostly helpless in doing anything for most of the attack victims.

"Well, finally the Japs left us alone. Things burned for hours I guess, maybe days. I was already at the hospital and in a bad way, or is that what all doctors say, Doc?"

Feldman didn't comment, just smiled and sipped his drink.

"Two days later I had a visitor. It was the commander of the Naval District, Admiral Rockwell. He told me Hart was ordering me to Java with orders to report to Captain Parnell, who would oversee forces in the Dutch East Indies until he could get there. He wanted me to take some papers and await further orders. This was December 11. The next day, the doctors wrapped me up again and took me to the USS *Whippoorwill*, a little minesweeper from World War I, heading south in company with the old Yangtze river boats *Asheville* and *Tulsa*. I think the *Lark*, another minesweeper, would come with us."

Flannigan took another sip as his eyes misted over a bit. "The little flotilla of barely seaworthy boats left on the night of the twelfth. Our first stop was a few days out in Balikpapan, Borneo. We fueled and met up with some of our destroyers. From there we slipped slowly down the coast to Java arriving on December 22. The captain of the *Whippoorwill*, Lt. Comdr. Charles Ferriter, ordered me off his ship with a wink of the eye and into a Dutch hospital. There I was greeted by Captain Parnell who told me I would be leaving on a PBY in two days for Darwin on the north coast of Australia. I was in too bad a shape to help anyone he said, and Admiral Hart had some handwritten reports I was to carry all the way to Hawaii to give to whoever was in command of the fleet. I was in a good deal of pain. The doctors said the shrapnel wounds were healing well, but the burns would take time. The bastards were right about that for sure." He took another sip and asked, "Am I boring you with this saga, Doc?"

Feldman sipped his whisky. "No, please continue, I want to know how you got home."

Another sip and Flannigan returned to his story. "I got on a PBY Christmas evening and flew to Darwin. It was a long plane ride in a slow plane, but we made it. Upon arriving in Darwin, I was put on a train that took three days to get anywhere. I think it was Adelaide or something like that. I was met by an Australian officer who helped me get to the airport where I boarded a very nice DC-3 for Sydney. Then I got on a Boeing Clipper and flew via Fiji, Samoa, and Johnson Island to Honolulu. I think I arrived on the second or third of January. I could be wrong, but didn't care. The bastards took me to the hospital where I was not the only burn patient. There were many men still there from the December 7 attack and I felt guilty for being in pretty good shape. They held me for four days, and after a stop at the office of the new admiral in charge of the Pacific Fleet, or what remained of it, I flew to San Diego where we eventually met."

Doc Feldman looked over at his friend, noticing the whisky had made a significant impact. He was somewhat inebriated or in the non-medical terminology, drunk. Feldman didn't think they had consumed that much until he realized only a quarter of the bottle remained. He knew he was getting tipsy, but he didn't realize Flannigan was down for the count. His speech was getting more slurred, and he seemed to have a tough time fixing his eyes on any one object. The doctor conferred with himself and decided his patient and the attending physician, needed to retire for the evening. Feldman turned toward the living room and came face to face with Gunny Jones.

"Doc, it seems that the captain needs assistance getting to his quarters. May I be of assistance, sir?" The big sergeant looked kindly at the doctor who needed assistance as well.

The doctor declared in his best voice, "Why, Gunny, how opportune for you to be waiting for my call for help. Yes, I think the good captain is now set for some sleep so if you would assist me in getting him to his room, we will have accomplished a great deal this evening."

Feldman realized, even in his condition, the gunny had been listening to the kitchen conversation. Not in a malevolent way but in a comradely manner, taking care of his own like a good marine gunnery sergeant would do in all cases.

Feldman and the gunny gently pulled the wavering captain to his feet and slowly steered him to his room. The captain said nothing on this short journey until they were inside the room. "Gunny Jones, are you responsible for my current predicament?" he asked in a semi-intelligent manner.

"Captain, a marine sergeant always looks out for all the men assigned to his care. The doctor and I are helping you find your quarters." The gunny smiled at Feldman who was about to laugh but thought it best if he kept it straight. Flannigan smiled as the doctor pulled off his shoes and the gunny held him up so the doc could unbutton his shirt and trousers. Finally, they had him down to his skivvies, and tucked him into his bed like a troublesome four-year-old that had run out of steam.

The two men walked out of the room as Feldman remarked, "Gunny, you are a good man and a great marine. It's good having you around to take care of the men in this unit, especially the captain. I fear there are still some demons lurking in his mind and it may take a long time to remove them."

Jones glanced back at the door and replied in a near whisper, "Doc, you are a good friend to the captain and to the men. What you did tonight was the proper medication to help Mr. Flannigan come to grips with his experiences. War is a strange thing and sometimes things stay with you for many years. I know that I still have dreams and recall the names of the men who didn't make it out of the Woods in France."

Feldman knew the gunny's record in the marines and how he had won the Navy Cross at Belleau Woods in France during the Great War. If any man in the unit knew the challenges Flannigan faced, it would be a veteran of the terrible war to end all wars. The doctor looked over at the gunny and said, "Thank you again for the help and the vote of confidence. Keep an eye on him because I need to get some sleep, too. You marines are going to destroy my whisky collection and my brain."

The gunny laughed and wished the doctor good night and pleasant dreams, something that came very hard to those who had endured the pain and suffering of battle.

29

9 March 1942
Office of Admiral King
Washington, D.C.

- Java surrenders to the Japanese.
- Philippines--General MacArthur reports that General Yamashita has replaced General Homma as CinC of enemy forces in the Philippines.

Brand had finished his report on the seventh and after a review by Captain Jameson, it was sent to Admiral Willson who reviewed it before giving it to King. They had been called early in the morning to come to King's office at 1100 hours to answer questions from the admiral and his staff.

As scheduled, Brand and Jameson were waiting in Admiral Willson's office talking to one of his aides when a marine orderly came in to take them down the hall to a conference room. Brand and Jameson both thought they were going to have a briefing with the admiral's staff and get shot at by everyone who objected to some of the recommendations or observations contained in the report. They were surprised to learn this was not the case.

When they entered the room and came to attention, they saw Admiral King, Admiral Turner, Admiral Willson, and two British officers, both of flag rank. King didn't speak but Willson did. "Come in Captain, Lieutenant, we have some people who would like to meet you."

The two officers approached the big dark conference table that could seat at least twenty people. When they came near, King stood and introduced the two British officers, "Admiral Sir Charles Little, Field Marshal Sir John Dill, may I present to you, Captain Jameson and Lieutenant Brand."

Dill jumped up first and shook the officers' hands saying, "Jameson, good to meet you. And you are the young scientist, James, I think it is?"

Brand immediately responded, "Yes sir, James Brand, sir." He was getting somewhat tongue-tied meeting a field marshal who had no equivalent in the American military. Also, he was an English Lord, and that was something very special.

Admiral Little went through similar introductions, but was more reserved than Dill who enjoyed the American culture and Americans in general.

Admiral King told everyone to be seated. Brand took a seat next to Admiral Willson who served as his protector when dealing with higher ranks.

With a bit of hesitation and scanning the report in front of him, King began, "The field marshal and admiral are our principal liaisons with the British Combined Chiefs of Staff and serve as the eyes and ears of His Majesty's government. We are working with our British Allies to design the strategy and build the tools to win this war. Having them in our headquarters is very important to the war effort. We have American's serving in London in a similar capacity. That is one of the reasons I have asked you two to come today and meet these gentlemen. The other reason is your research and recommendations for defeating the German submarines. Your analysis is thorough and at the same time, challenges much of our thinking. Our Allies have the same issues and challenges, but they have been involved in some of these things far longer than we have."

King hated to admit it because he didn't trust the "Allies," especially the Brits. But he knew his boss, the president, had set in motion the Joint Chiefs program and the combined strategy included him. He wanted a quick answer to as many complex questions as possible, but he knew it was not in the cards. So, he had to get along with his "Allies" as best he could, but with as much American planning, ingenuity, and fighting as possible.

Dill spoke up, "Gentlemen, Admiral King was most kind to let us review your report, and I am very pleased with your efforts. Lieutenant Brand, you were generous to mention the work of our British scientists, engineers, and countless sailors who have worked on many of these problems for two years or more, but you have taken some of these ideas much further. I think that taking the best from both of our efforts and sharing the successes achieved will help end this war in a much shorter time frame."

Admiral Little added his comments, "Gentlemen, as the field marshal stated, you have given us credit where it is due, and you have taken the research forward beyond what we have accomplished. You do this in a very scientific and, if I can be so bold, a non-parochial manner. This bodes well for future shared opportunities. You are both a credit to your navy and to the ideals set forth by your president."

Brand didn't know what to think about the high praise but was about to speak when he was saved by Admiral Willson, who sensed some duress in young Brand.

"Mr. Brand, what Admiral Little and Field Marshal Dill want to express to you and Captain Jameson is that your work has opened up our collective eyes to some new opportunities in dealing with the German submarines. It is critical to the war effort that we understand their operations first and then eradicate them from the Atlantic. We cannot win this war by building planes and tanks here without being able to deliver them to where they are needed."

King joined in with the real reason for the meeting. "Captain, I want you and Brand to go to London and meet with some of their people, your counterparts, and see what else we can work on in collaboration with one another to fight the Germans. I want you to be briefed by

Admiral Turner on the navy war plans, and General Marshall wants you to meet with General Eisenhower to understand the army's current vision of the war effort. Then Admiral Willson will arrange for your travel to England. Admiral Little and Field Marshal Dill will arrange for high-level meetings with their planners and members of their scientific development teams. Your goal is to come up with plans that are practical, fast, and like your other work has shown, prioritized to maximize the investment in time, money and people. Are there any questions?"

Jameson responded, "No sir. We will meet with Admiral Willson to arrange meetings stateside and prepare to move the team to England."

"Very good, Captain. Willson, take them out of here so I can continue my discussion with the field marshal and Admiral Little. Turner, you stay here."

Willson stood and came to attention as did Jameson and Brand. Outside Willson smiled and commented, "Well, your work is getting you in deeper and deeper. I hope you see daylight before the war ends otherwise you will look like some mole in a garden and now it will be an English garden."

He led them to his office and told his chief of staff to set up meetings with Admiral Turner as soon as his schedule would allow and to do likewise with Major General Eisenhower. Willson told his capable assistant that General Marshall had informed Eisenhower to expect the meeting and to brief the two navy officers. Both Jameson and Brand were somewhat dumbstruck by the turn of events. It was the furthest thing on their minds to assume they would go off to England for clandestine meetings with their British counterparts.

Willson told them travel to Britain would be via the ocean on a warship or on a plane being ferried over to Britain. He was unsure which one but would let them know shortly. In either eventuality, the trip would happen in a few days. They were expected to spend a few weeks in the UK and return home. Things were brewing in the war effort, and King wanted his science team available for his own use and not that of the Royal Navy. He also informed them that they would meet the two American officers leading the American effort in England. The army commander was Maj. Gen. James E. Chaney, who held the title

Commanding General, U.S. Forces in the British Islands and Vice Adm. Robert L. Ghormley, who had been sent to England in 1940 as special observer for President Roosevelt and now headed up the naval build up in support of the British.

Willson told them the entire trip was top secret and only the senior American and British officers had knowledge of their mission. The goal was to develop a better understanding of the current capabilities of the Royal Navy and Coastal Command. They were also to examine the ability of the British to expand their operational capabilities in support of the surge of American men and material. Willson also said King wanted a candid assessment of the American personnel currently in Britain, which they took to mean, were these people up to the job and could they handle the strain. Jameson was concerned about this last piece of business, because as a navy captain, he was in no way capable of determining if current personnel were fit to handle tasks which were changing daily. This became more concerning when they met with General Eisenhower the next day.

The team spent much of the remainder of the day at Old Navy receiving additional reports from members of Admiral Willson's staff. It was nearly 1900 hours before they reached the Bethesda home of Captain Jameson. Flannigan had already informed the gunny about troop movement which would occur in a few days' time. The security team was checking out their gear, which they now knew would include winter weather uniforms, but they were not sure where they would be heading. As the gunny explained earlier in the day, "If the captain wants us to know where we are going, he will tell us when he is damn well ready. Questions?" There were none.

Brand was having a conversation with Dr. Feldman, who was upset about not being asked to go wherever the team was heading, but he held his concerns for now. The two men were discussing their last chess game, which had lasted six moves, making the doc a happy man.

He had lost the match, of course, but not in the usual five moves. As the two were discussing improvements in the doctor's strategy, Captain Jameson walked in.

"James, I hate to interrupt your conversation with the doctor, but I need to have a quick word with you."

Feldman quickly stood up saying, "James, I will get back to you later tonight or tomorrow."

Jameson stopped him, saying, "Doc, maybe it would be best if you stayed. It might be good for you to help James process some information."

"Sure, Captain, I'd be happy to listen and help."

The doctor sat down and Jameson sat next to James. He pulled out some papers from a file he was holding. The file was marked SECRET and had the insignia of the Naval Intelligence Service on it as well.

"James, I wanted to tell you about what I have found out about your friend Iggy."

Feldman had been told a little about the illusive Japanese professor who had been a force in helping James establish his academic career. The Doc had not heard anything about him since James had told him about his mentor during his hospital stay in San Diego. He knew the man was a Japanese American but that was all he knew.

Jameson pulled out the first piece of paper and handed it to James. "Your friend Professor Isuro Tomaguchi has been on the FBI watch list since early in 1940."

The list was established in late 1939 to investigate certain leaders in the Japanese-American community. Key religious leaders, political figures and educators were placed on the list and in the case of war, they were to be detained. The official name for this was the Custodial Detention List. Nisei Japanese, those born in the United States, and all foreign-born Japanese were considered suspect. Those who had higher visibility in the community were placed on the list. Within a few days of December 7, 1941, several thousand individuals were "detained" until they could be deemed either patriotic or a security risk.

James read the paper and looked at the captain. "Sir, Iggy is a loyal American and he really dislikes the Japanese. He is from Okinawa, which was annexed by Japan in 1879. They have their own language and culture. It's more Chinese than Japanese."

"James, I didn't know about how Okinawa is different until I talked to some of the people in Naval Intelligence. But it does not matter. Iggy's father came to Hawaii as a laborer on a Japanese work permit and even though Iggy was born here, there is a lot of bad feelings about anything Japanese." He pulled out another piece of paper and gave it to James.

James began reading, looking up several times at the captain. His face was full of concern for his friend but finally he showed a smile. Before he could talk, Jameson spoke.

"Seems the FBI sent him to Angel Island where many of the other Japanese were being housed. Some were foreign nationals living in California while others were from Hawaii and for some reason, they were sent there as well. He was interviewed by a team of agents after they had received numerous calls from professors and leading educators across the country." He pointed to some of the names on a separate sheet and James could quickly see the names of Enrico Fermi and James Conant as well as most of the faculty at Cal Tech.

Jameson handed another piece of paper to James to examine and continued his speech. He was doing this more for the doctor than for James, who could speed read anything faster than a normal human could speak.

"Your good friend Iggy, was asked to join a special unit of Military Intelligence in Monterrey, California. He is now teaching Japanese at the Military Intelligence Language School and is officially a sergeant in the army. It appears there are fewer than one hundred officers in the entire American military who can speak Japanese. We will need hundreds more each year and your friend Iggy is one of the first Nisei doing this."

James looked at the papers and then he turned to the captain handing them back to him for return to Naval Intelligence. "Sir, thanks for finding him. It angers me to think someone would treat Iggy as an enemy of this country. If it was not for him, I would not have survived my years at Cal Tech."

He looked at the doctor who was analyzing the conversation in a way only a Jewish doctor would understand. He thought to himself about a young man encountering racial prejudice for the first time and how his scientific mind could not comprehend the stupidity of it. This would be a good first lesson on how the world really works.

"James, I have an address for the professor if you would like to write him." He handed him a note card with the information and then quickly admonished the young genius. "Do not inform him of your status, your duties or where you are located. Keep it general and as time goes by, perhaps you can tell him more. And, James, this is an order. Do not deviate from these guidelines. Understand?"

James looked at the paper with the contact details and he understood the message the captain was giving him. He quickly replied, "Yes sir. I understand what is at stake so I will keep any correspondence very general. Do you want to review anything I write?"

Dr. Feldman jumped in to defuse the situation. "James, why don't you give me any letters you are going to send out and I will act as the censor. As a physician and a gentleman, I am sure I can fulfill this duty. Is that all right with you, Captain?"

Jameson saw what the doctor was trying to accomplish and quickly agreed. He then picked up the file and said good night to both the doctor and the genius. He hoped he was not opening a can of worms by passing on the whereabouts of Professor Tomaguchi. With a thousand other details needing his attention before the meeting with General Eisenhower, he let this one slide for now, but he regretted not requesting to take the good doctor along on this trip. Perhaps the next time, he would ask the admiral for permission for Dr. Feldman to accompany the team.

30

10 March 1942
Office of Maj. Gen. Dwight Eisenhower
Washington, D.C.

- Aircraft from carriers Lexington and Yorktown bomb Japanese shipping at Salamaua and Lae, New Guinea.
- Japanese invade Finschhafen, New Guinea.

Brand remembered the smiling bald general officer he had met a few weeks earlier in the office of Admiral Willson. He also recalled Willson telling him that General Marshall had great faith in Eisenhower and he thought the Chief of Staff had even greater plans in store for him soon. But for right now, Marshall needed a strong man who could concentrate on the things that would win the war, without getting sidetracked by requests from all over the command structure, including Marshall. This ability to determine a sound, long-term plan consistent with present and foreseen capabilities made this newly minted major general essential to Marshall. King also saw in him a leader who could get things done and not get overly caught up in emotion or political maneuvering. This was a rare gift in Washington and would help cement Eisenhower's place in history.

The smiling major general was waiting for Jameson and Brand but did not anticipate the appearance of Captain Flannigan. These kinds of additions were common to Ike, as he told his friends and senior leaders to call him, so it did not bother him to have the tall marine added to the meeting.

Eisenhower escorted them to a nearby conference room where Brig. Gen. Walter Bedell Smith was introduced to the team. Smith was serving as secretary to the Combined Chiefs of Staff (Britain and the U.S.) and had intimate knowledge of not only the war plans being developed by Eisenhower but had broad knowledge of what the British military planners were thinking and doing.

Jameson, Brand, and Flannigan were very impressed by their hosts and their knowledge without letting the newcomers feel left out of the loop. Eisenhower, especially, was quite good at making everyone feel at ease. His smile encouraged the team to be as straight forward as possible. Brand listened to the orientation of current war thinking from the army point of view plus his interpretation of what the Air Corps was doing. Moving hundreds of thousands of men, thousands of planes and tens of thousands of vehicles of all types was a daunting task.

Eisenhower explained this movement to the British Isles as Operation Bolero, which was to become one of the largest undertakings ever tried by modern man. Brand thought about this from the standpoint of the number of munitions, materials, and rations it takes to support one combat person per day in the field and his head began to hurt as he extrapolated this to over a million men. The oil required alone was a staggering number and pointed to the need to make the convoy system work with minimal losses to the U-boats.

Smith added to the team's understanding of the losses sustained by Britain since the beginning of the war which totaled over a thousand ships. At this rate, Britain would not have a merchant navy nor would she have any crews to man any new ships the Americans could build. He put it rather emphatically, "If we cannot stop the U-boat, there will be no invasion of France and no victory." Britain was making headway he informed them, but they were having manpower issues, hardware issues, and intelligence gaps. The Germans were ramping up production of their submarines and the hardened sub bases in France and Norway meant their boats could stay in the sea lanes longer and kill more ships. The Allied air forces were working on ways to attack these "sub pens" with more sustained attacks and bigger bombs, but that would take time.

Brand waited for Eisenhower to finish his briefing. When Ike asked if there were any questions, all eyes turned to Brand, whose reputation was familiar to these men. "General Eisenhower, you stated the Allies need to concentrate exclusively on operations necessary to defeat the enemy. You also called for disciplined strategies that focus on what is practical and does not divide our forces into smaller components. Sir, how does all this fit with the war in the Pacific and what are the priorities?"

Smith observed Eisenhower who smiled and said, "Lieutenant Brand, your reputation of getting to the point is well proven, and that question is at the crux of our strategy. The Allies have determined that Germany is the biggest risk and must be defeated first. We can hold our lines and make progress in the Pacific, but if Germany knocks out Russia or takes England, then all bets are off. The Germans have the industrial capabilities, not Japan. They have a huge internal base to move troops and supplies around totally within areas they control. The Japanese control a lot of territory but most of it is water. Their plan to control a ring of islands around their home islands is fraught with danger for them and presents major opportunities for us. We can attack Japan at will, and they must defend every place, every time. The Germans, on the other hand, can rapidly move men and machines from one side of Europe to the other with their typical Germanic efficiency. Until we can degrade their transportation and communications system from the air, we are going to have a tough time dealing with the Germans."

Ike looked over at Flannigan, recalling the marine had escaped from the Philippines and these comments in this meeting were not being made public. Roosevelt had promised all sorts of aid to MacArthur, but it would not happen. The capabilities to relieve the garrison on Bataan simply did not exist. Eisenhower had reported as much to Marshall in January saying the Philippines could not be saved but their heroic stand would help in the long term. "Captain Flannigan, I realize you were in the Philippines, were wounded there, and sent out by Admiral Hart. I also know that you are a realist and know what I am saying is true but unwelcome. I wish we could do more to help your comrades, but there is no way we can find the forces, the ships, or the planes to make a difference. You saw what happened with our piecemeal efforts with the ABDA command and the failure of shipping troops and planes to Java. Neither the men nor the machines were ready to deal with the Japanese. They have had years of bitter war experience, and we have none. Defeating the Japanese will take time, and I assure you, we will get our revenge."

Flannigan looked at Eisenhower and without emotion replied, "Thank you, General. I know you have strong feelings for the Philippines from your days serving with General MacArthur. I realize we were not prepared for the attacks, nor were we mentally prepared for the Japanese. We all thought, even those of us who saw them operate in China, that we could easily defeat them, but our vision was obscured by our lack of knowledge of the enemy. Thank you, sir, for what you tried to do and for your leadership."

Eisenhower had to look at his friend Smith to avoid showing any emotion in the face of comments coming from a man who had been there and had been wounded. This man had seen combat, but for all of Eisenhower's years in uniform, he had never heard a gun fired in anger.

"Captain, thank you for your kindness. I promise your comrades will be avenged in time. But first, we must come to grips with war on a scale never seen before in the history of the world. Distance will be a deciding factor in winning or losing this war. The logistics alone dwarf anything ever attempted. Mr. Brand, I understand from Admiral Turner you had some ideas on shipping materials to the war front which he is turning into operational plans."

Brand nodded his head in agreement to what Eisenhower stated and wondered what else Admiral Turner had revealed to the smiling general.

"What I want you and the rest of your team to investigate is when we get men, tanks, planes and the whole host of supplies to England or wherever we must fight, that we can be assured of matching these items to the job at hand. If we ship a combat division to England, are the British able to handle them? Where do they stay, train, eat, unload, play? God only knows how long some of these men will be in place before we are able to launch an attack somewhere in Europe."

Eisenhower picked up his Camel cigarette and took a long draw. Then as if the general had seen a vision, he continued, "Think about this; if we are to attack someplace in France to help the Russians and we must do it even though we are not ready, what do we have to do first, second, third, etc. What is our plan and even more important, what are the contingencies?"

Brand peered at the now serious general and decided to speak his mind on a subject for which he had no military education or experience. But he did have the raw brain power to visualize the size and scope of the situation. "Sir, it would appear if we had to attack by the end of this year, it would be a short hit and run to draw the Germans away from the Russians. We would have to have an incursion that would pull at least one hundred thousand troops from the Eastern Front. It would have to be aimed at capturing a port for supply and one that could be reinforced as a strongpoint which the Germans would have to attack like at the Battle of Verdun."

The young genius stared at the ceiling and the two army generals waited for his next comment. Brand, did not smile but closed his eyes and then opened them as if he had seen more answers to his questions. "General, it would require a large portion of Allied air forces being prepared for great losses, because it would necessitate mauling the Luftwaffe to the extent that they would have to pull forces from the East as well. An attack like this would require two divisions with at least three in reserve."

Brand looked at Jameson who smiled back, encouraging him to continue his analysis. "I would imagine that it would pull German troops from all of France, the Low Countries, and even Norway. The fear that Hitler must have is a two-front war, and from his experience in the last war, he realizes the problem of holding on one front and attacking another. This would probably work in giving the Russians time to rebuild, but I would estimate a fifty percent attrition rate for our people and supplies. Could we hold a city like Cherbourg or perhaps La Rochelle? I doubt we could hold out for long. But if we were afraid that we would lose a Russian multi-million-man army to the enemy, then it is a loss we must incur."

Smith wondered if the young scientist had seen the war scenarios played out by the Joint Chiefs of Staff for the past month. The young scientist with no military training had just outlined Operation Sledgehammer, which was a last-ditch effort to intervene on behalf of the Russians to keep them in the war.

Eisenhower looked at Jameson and said, "Captain, your young protégé just figured out one of our war plans in five minutes which took a team of over 140 officers on both sides of the Atlantic thirty days to build and not as well." Ike offered his commendation. "Mr. Brand, that was well thought out, well stated, and as I have heard before about you, offered without any apology or hesitation. We need that kind of thinking in all our efforts around here. If I thought for a minute I could get you away from Admiral King or the president, I would have you on my staff immediately."

Brand blushed at the kind comment.

Eisenhower added, "But you have a mission as well, and it ties to both General Smith's and mine. We want you and your team to look at what is real. Things that exist now or could be quickly organized. What is possible and what appears to be impossible. Who is thinking like you and who is sitting on their hands. Do not worry about the individual. I need to know. That goes for General Marshall and I am sure for Admiral King. If people are the problem or systems are an issue, please let us know. Do not hold back. If you hold back on your assessment Mr. Brand, it will mean the lives of countless Allied soldiers, sailors, and airmen. It is time to step into the batter's box, Mr. Brand, and swing."

Brand smiled at the baseball analogy having been told about Eisenhower being an excellent baseball player and how he enjoyed the team atmosphere of the game. There were specialists on a ball team and many generalists. You had to hit, throw, run, and know the rules of the game. A team affair was needed in this war as well, and Brand sensed the concept of unified control was what was needed to make the war go well. Plans were great, but not everything could be planned.

The rest of the meeting went quickly with Jameson receiving a briefing book put together by Eisenhower's staff, which included key personnel for the army and the army Air Corps as well as the locations of currently deployed American assets in Northern Ireland, Scotland, and England. The book also contained an analysis of the current Lend Lease supplies sent since the first of January and the items being pre-positioned for the arrival of American forces, especially air units, and support troops. One section profiled the British leadership the team might encounter, up to and including Prime Minister Winston Churchill. These materials were placed in a weighted bag that could be jettisoned in case of a plane crash or fear of capture. Jameson and Flannigan had been given more instructions in case of any downing of the plane or sinking of their ship. Those details were kept from Brand.

The meeting broke up with lots of handshaking and God speed comments. When the team had left, Smith looked at Eisenhower who had lit another cigarette, saying, "Ike, that is one smart kid. Are there more like him anywhere?"

Ike puffed a few times, gazed at the glowing embers of the cigarette, and casually replied, "No, Beetle, I doubt if there is one more like him in the entire country. General Marshall told me about him a month or so ago, along with the most amazing story about how the president found out about him. Do you want to hear it?"

Smith nodded his head.

Eisenhower took another puff. "Beetle, have you ever heard of Albert Einstein?"

Coming Soon
from author

J. Eugene Porter

The Naval Odyssey of Professor James Brand:
Mission to Britain

and the

Brad Bayle Mystery Series:
The Container Affair

Made in the USA
Coppell, TX
06 October 2025